The Truth of Her Heart

Highlander Heroes, Volume 5

Rebecca Ruger

Published by Rebecca Ruger, 2020.

This is a work of fiction. Names, character, places, and incidents are either a product of the author's imagination or are used fictitiously, and any resemblance to actual persons, living or dead, events, or locales is entirely coincidental. Some creative license may have been taken with exact dates and locations to better serve the plot and pacing of the novel.

ISBN: 9798590550548

The Truth of Her Heart

Written by Rebecca Ruger

Cover Design by Kim Killion @ The Killion Group

Disclaimer: The material in this book is for mature audiences only and may contain graphic content. It is intended only for those aged 18 and older.

Chapter One

January 1307
The Northern Highlands

BODIES WERE EVERYWHERE—ON the ground, in the middle of the road, some near the trees at the edge of the village. All on their stomachs. They'd been running for their lives. A woman's cold corpse was closest, a gaping slice slashed across the top of her back. Hatchet, or ax maybe. She was dead many days now, yet the deep burrow of scratches dug into the mud near her face suggested she'd not died quickly. Her chin was dipped into the mud, her sightless eyes facing the body of a child not more than ten feet away.

If she hadn't died immediately, she would have been witness to the three men and one woman who had been strung up from the peak of the tithe barn. Like fish on a line, they swung from one shared rope, their bodies clumped together, turning around each other as the main line still swayed.

Iain McEwen stood with his hands on his hips, mentally counting, stopping when he'd passed twenty-seven bodies. It was all of them, the entire tiny village gone. Slaughtered. And for what? His lip curled. He turned and squinted into the sun and then away; sheep and cows dotted the meadow and the hill outside the line of thatched homes; hens darted here and there, loosed and wandering, one plucking at the fabric of the sleeve of a dead man further down the lane; draft horses and carts, one laden yet with hay and feed, remained where they'd been left. Nothing had been stolen. The motive then was simply violence, bloodlust, murder. And not an English arrow in sight, embedded into any of the bodies to say that the culprits had come from the south. No, these were crimes committed against innocent Scots by their very own countrymen.

Same as the last.

Craig was near, crouched on his haunches, using his finger to make a circle in the drying mud. He pivoted on his heels, met his laird's gaze, and tapped his finger now at the ring he'd drawn.

Iain strode to him, peered down at the impression inside the circle. Craig moved his finger over the marking, showing the pattern. A horseshoe.

The print was distinct, having seven holes around the shoe. Horseshoes were not terribly common, but generally the farrier created them with three nail holes on each branch of the horseshoe, but usually not with any directly in the middle of the arch, or the toe, of the shoe. These prints, all similar, showed a pattern of seven nail holes, with three on each side and one directly in the center. This was rare enough that it was easy to suppose the perpetrators of a similar attack at Wick last month were the same bastards that had made war on this sleepy little village.

"Alpin," he said, his hatred for that otherwise unnamed devil evident in the seething of his tone.

Craig nodded.

"Round 'em up, lads," Iain called out then to his men. "We bury the dead."

This would now be the third time they will have done so. The massacre at Wick had not been the first crime committed around Caithness by the band led by a man known only as Alpin. But his crimes, and the brutality of them, were escalating, and Iain was losing his patience and any desire to hold to the promise he'd made to Robert Bruce that he would deliver the infidel to the Scottish courts. Iain McEwen's bloodlust for the devil Alpin screamed for highland justice, in their own land, and by their own hand.

With great care, he lifted the body of the dead child up in his arms, clenching his teeth so hard he felt the motion in his neck and jaw.

THE WIND SLASHED AT her cheeks and eyes as she rose from her haunches at the beach. She squinted out at the sea and sky and considered the direction of the winds; it was never a good sign when they shifted, even if only modestly. Pivoting, she put her back to the churning water and walked toward the dark frowning rocks which flanked the beach. She hefted her haul of shells and stones further up her arm, onto her shoulder. They clacked in response, shifting and moving inside the woven basket. She shouldn't have traversed so far but had been lured as always by the possibility of *just a few more further ahead*—stones along the river and shells down here at the shore—which had her now several hours into today's hunt. 'Twas an easy hike to make, as the river had no turns from its rise near the keep until its fall into the sea.

She'd have remained, gathered more of the precious bounty, if only to have stayed away from the keep longer. But the wind had indeed shifted, and though she'd dressed with particular care for the cold, it seeped still through her many layers that she thought only a brisk return walk would heat her again. She'd cut the fingers off the heavy woolen gloves a long time ago, that her fingers were now red and stinging from the cold. She curled those cold fingers into the front of her cloak, drawing it tighter against her chin, holding the hood in place, and kept her head low even as the wind was now at her back, marching along as the clouds above turned grayer and meaner.

She followed the river, keeping to the west side of it even at those points where it was thin and shallow enough to cross. To do so would put her instantly onto Mackay land, as the river was all that separated the centuries-old enemies of the Sutherlands. She was not a Sutherland, but a guest of a minor Sutherland family, as she had been for several months while a betrothal agreement was worked out between her father and the great Earl of Sutherland, William de Moravia, on behalf of his nephew, Kenneth Sutherland. While she was in no hurry to have the terms defined and agreed upon, she knew that the matter would have been handled with more haste if either the earl or her betrothed were not gone so long or so often from home.

All her anxiety over her impending wedding and the bridegroom himself, whom she'd yet to meet, might have only been kept at bay these last many weeks by the beach and the sea and the river. She'd found ease and escape here and would be sad to be so far away from the shore when she did marry and traveled with her husband to his holding further inland.

She made no stops now on her return trip, would not allow herself to be enticed by any shiny and colorful stone, that the walk now took less than half the time. When the manor came into view, just as she passed a grove of tall, windbreaking pines, Margaret Bryce turned right and followed a path whose grass she believed she herself had worn toward the home of Adam Gordon, a minor landholder and his Sutherland born wife, Elizabeth de Moravia. They had graciously served as hosts to Maggie and her father, and rather as intermediaries between the earl and Kenneth and John Bryce.

To Maggie's dismay, she knew the time was drawing near that she would soon meet her expected future husband. She'd heard tales of Kenneth Sutherland, none of them good, had tried to not be distracted or made distraught by them. Even now, she thought of the weather and what tomorrow might bring up onto the beach, and not at all of her betrothed, when she could help it. She passed through the gate of a wall that seemed to have little purpose—being neither too high nor too thick to prevent an attack—and paused at the well. Here, she plopped the basket onto the ground and rolled her shoulder for several seconds to relieve the ache, noticing just now that the wind was much calmer here, away from the sea. Reaching for the bucket, she startled when she heard her name called. For the briefest of moments, she closed her eyes. And then, with a deep breath, she turned and faced her father. The tone he'd used to bark out her name suggested he was, once again, annoyed with her. Possibly, as indicated by his impatient growling, he'd been looking for her or waiting on her for quite some time.

"Where the hell've you been?"

Maggie resisted the urge to shrink into herself. John Bryce's enormous, hulking presence sometimes had that effect on her. She was tall for a woman, she'd always thought, but her father still towered over her, boasting possibly three times the weight of her. The hair at the top of his head was long gone, but he compensated for this by allowing the rest of it to grow long and wild, the once dark auburn liberally tinted with gray now. The long beard he wore was grayer still, and thick, though it managed to appear straggly as it was habitually unkempt. Her eyes were begotten from her father, she'd been told often enough, wide-spaced and bright green; she hoped hers did not shrivel into her skull as she grew older, as her father's had, seeming to be overtaken by an increasing brow and forehead that pushed down until it appeared always that he squinted.

"Down to the—"

"Get on in here, you squirrely girl!" He cut her off. "Your own betrothed has arrived, and with the earl no less. And you're nowhere to be found! Go on now, use the back door, and hie up to your chambers and make—do what you can to be presentable."

He grabbed her by the arm, his blunt tipped fingers cutting painfully into her skin, and herded her around to the back of the keep. She was forced to stride very quickly and still, with her father's long legs moving so swiftly in his anger, she was turned almost sideways by his hand yanking at her.

At the kitchen door, which she likely would have used as her entrance anyway, he thrust her inside, releasing her arm that she dashed through the warm and smoky room to the slim back stairs, which she climbed past the second floor and family apartments and onto the third floor to find her own lent chambers.

Inside, she wasted no time but stripped off her cloak and gloves and the topmost kirtle, the extra one she'd donned earlier for added warmth. She tossed all these things haphazardly onto the thin straw mattress and checked to be sure the remaining kirtle, her least favorite blue one, was presentable. She struggled only briefly to remove her wimple quickly, shaking it out and perusing it swiftly to be sure it was clean still and then wrapped the cloth once more around her head, covering all her hair.

Somewhere in the back of her mind, she understood that she should take more time to make sure she presented herself in the best possible form to the man who was likely to be her husband. But then her father's ire and impatience suggested she had no time to fuss over herself, and too, there was a large part of her that hoped the man, Kenneth Sutherland, was unimpressed—or better still, completely offended—by her slapdash efforts that he might suppose he had no interest in marrying her.

Less than ten minutes after her father had discovered her in the courtyard, she presented herself in the hall of the keep.

The first thing she noticed upon entering was that a man, who was not the very affable Adam Gordon, under whose roof she dwelled, sat in the lord's chair upon the dais. Maggie assumed this must be the earl then, and instantly assumed that he must be a *lord of lords*, one who preferred that no one forget who he was. It was probable that his very short stature, among the giants of her father and Adam Gordon and several men-at-arms nearby, forced him to adopt a clearly assertive personality to establish his own importance, as if only a child standing on a stool in the midst of so many adults that he might be noticed.

Adam's wife, Elizabeth, was in attendance and swept up the slight train of her burgundy gown to rush to Maggie's side at her entrance. Nearly twice Maggie's age, she was very plain with pale eyes and thin brown hair and a rather unfortunate chin, which protruded as a rounded red-tinted sphere beneath her lips. But she more than made up for her lack of beauty with her generous and pleasing personality. She stopped before Maggie and put her hands on Maggie's arms, giving her an encouraging smile, or trying to, as it really didn't show in her gaze, essentially emerging as nothing more than a grimace.

"Come to meet your betrothed, dear Maggie." She traced her hands down Maggie's arms, squeezing and holding one hand to pull her forward.

"But first," her father called as she neared the men around the dais, all of whom were standing and posing around the man in the chair, "meet the Earl of Sutherland, at whose mercy we've arranged your happy future."

Maggie had never heard such bombastic congeniality from her father.

Moving forward, leaving Elizabeth behind, Maggie set her gaze upon the earl, dressed as finely as everyone around him was not. She thought his coat, a long flowing thing that spilled to the floor as he sat, might be made of silk, red and vibrant, the brightest thing in this dim hall. He was older than her father, and not unpleasant looking, but then neatness and cleanliness were often very attractive.

He watched her approach with one lifted thin brow of gray, over eyes the color of some of her favorite brown river stones. Maggie bowed deeply, but truly had no idea if this should take her all the way to her knee at the floor, and so it did not. Lifting her face again, she held the man's gaze levelly, as she'd been governed often over the years that honesty and integrity were found in a steady gaze. She knew also not to speak until first she'd been spoken to.

The earl, whose kind gaze had Maggie wondering if she might refresh her first, unflattering opinion that he acted the short man among his taller colleagues, gave justification to her preliminary judgment and forced several more into her head when he said, "Margaret Bryce, I wonder you do not tip right over, those breasts being so heavy upon the front of you."

Maggie blinked at him, incapable of thought or speech.

All the silence and somberness of the room in which she'd entered vanished as every man burst out with laughter, guffawing at the earl's crass words. Startled by his vulgar speech, and that these should be the first words he spoke to her, Maggie turned her head, saw her father chuckling along with the other men.

"Top heavy, she is!" Called out one man.

"That's why you put her underneath ye!" Said another, and more laughter followed.

Adam and Elizabeth, standing apart but side by side, looked decidedly uncomfortable, their expressions tight.

"I'll turn her over, like a dog, and not be slapped by those things."

Maggie swung around and favored the man who'd uttered these words with a gasping frown. This, then, must be Kenneth Sutherland, if he were imagining he might be doing *anything* with her. Saints alive, but how dreadful! Not him, he was not unhandsome—tall and lean with pretty brown eyes to match his uncle's—but because he was actually standing in this hall, meeting his affianced for the first time, and making motions with his hands and hips to suit his loutish words.

Honest to God, she was stunned speechless. But only momentarily. Before she thought better of it, she clamped her fists onto her hips and said, "That is how you greet me? And before we've been introduced? Like a rutting stag?"

"Aye, and feisty!" Called out one of the men-at-arms.

"You'll have to knock the obedience into her, I'm thinking," said the earl, his tone laced with both humor and a warning to Maggie, if she read it correctly.

Kenneth Sutherland's face lost all good humor as he stepped closer to her. Maggie stiffened and forced herself to not step backward. She was accosted by a nasty scent, which sprang from her future husband, and curiously was rather incongruous with his tidy breeches and tunic.

"And that'll be the last time you take any tone with me," he said in a silky, deceptively calm voice. And then, with a smile that moved only his lips, and barely at that, he said, "I am Kenneth and you are Margaret and now, wench," he said with great purpose, "we have been introduced."

Frightened now, as his eyes were neither warm nor friendly upon closer scrutiny but promised retribution it seemed, Maggie swallowed and nodded, thinking silence would benefit her greatly at this moment. She kept his gaze though, not inclined to sink or wilt before him, and was frightened by what she saw in this man's eyes, this man who would be her husband. The liquid brown of his eyes had hardened, showing a startling coldness that hinted at callousness and something darker. To Maggie's horror, she understood immediately that this man was not a good person.

"Aye, and that's enough of that," called out the earl. "You'll be scaring her off and running."

Maggie turned and met her father's eye. He, too, stared at her with some rebuke in his gaze, the darkness telling her to be mindful of her tongue. Some bit of sorrow colored her own gaze, that her own father should give her away to a man such as this.

And what did he get? He gained the protection of the Sutherland, she must assume, but traded his daughter and possibly several hundred acres of his not inconsequential land holding. John Bryce was a large landholder, but not a great lord, with neither a title nor an army, which essentially made him naught but a vulnerable farmer.

"Go on, then," said the earl, waving a careless hand in Maggie's direction. "We've contracts to settle, and your bridegroom has rutting, as you say, to consider."

Maggie ignored the answering guffaws, and allowed Elizabeth once again to take her hand, this time pulling her away from the hall. They spoke not at all, but ascended the main stairs, onto the second floor's narrow corridor and the next set of steps that led to the third floor. Elizabeth delivered Maggie to her chambers and only then spun her around to advise, her voice laced with sympathy, "It won't be that bad. It won't be awful. Maybe for the first few years, and then you'll have children and he'll leave you alone." Her brows lifted, she forced as smile. "And then you'll have your own keep to manage and children to raise and it will be fine."

Maggie stared at her, her mouth falling open. *It won't be awful.* Dear Lord! So much to look forward to!

Elizabeth was lucky, in that her husband was kind and not at all coarse or violent. She smiled at her friend, expressing some appreciation for her attempt to cheer her, as if that were possible now.

"Thank you, Elizabeth. For everything."

"Very well, and now I'll get to the kitchens and make sure we don't embarrass ourselves in front of the earl with some less than fabulous supper."

Maggie nodded, her tight smile still in place, and closed the door behind her. With one hand on the door latch and the other flat against the cool wood of the door, Maggie leaned her forehead against the door and sighed. Closing her eyes, she resisted the urge to weep.

It might only be awful for the first few years, Elizabeth had suggested hopefully.

Forlornly, she turned and leaned her back against the door, staring straight ahead, seeing nothing, and wished her mother were alive still. She'd not have allowed this. She'd have immediately put a stop to the very idea. And she'd have given Kenneth Sutherland a mouthful—without cowing in the face of his dreadful threat—and would have had that boorish man begging forgiveness for his uncouth behavior.

Twenty minutes later, in which time Maggie had done little more than flop onto the bed and lament her sorry fate, her father barged into the chambers. She jumped from the bed, hoping to God he might say that the Sutherlands were severely displeased with her and had begged off. She thought she could bear her father's immediate displeasure over that more than she could stand to be married to that man belowstairs.

No, that was not the case, she sadly learned right quickly.

"Maggie, I'm tempted to beat some sense into you," he growled out, no preamble given. "You're goddamn lucky the man still wants to wed with you, and that the earl will let him."

"Lucky?" She scoffed. "Father, I would not consider myself fortunate to be married to that man."

"Aye, you're just like your mam, curse her wretched soul."

Maggie gasped.

"But you'll no have love and all its frills, lass," he said harshly. "The world ain't made like that, and you weren't born as such who could make it so."

In an exceptional move, Maggie grasped at her father, clinging to his forearm. "Please father, I'll marry anyone, any other Sutherland if that's the name you need me to wed, but not that man. I beg you—"

"Think you'll get a better deal?" He jerked his arm, his lips thinned.

"Hah!" She derided, removing her hand from him. "The deal is yours and not meant for me. I'm naught but the chattel, sold for rutting and—"

"And what did you want? You're a woman, rutting and birthing are what you're made for, that's what's expected of you!"

That's *all* that's expected of you, she thought he meant.

"I won't do it," she said, with a rare burst of defiance. Crossing her arms over her chest, she stalked away from her father and toward the window. "I won't have anything to do with—"

Her words were yanked away, as was her person, spun about by her father's meaty paw, turned around just as his other hand swung out and cracked her smartly across her face.

Only his hand on her arm kept her on her feet, though she stumbled with the force of the blow, throwing out her hand as the ground came close. But she was jerked straight, her face brought close to his.

"You'll do it, goddamn you!" He hissed at her. "You'll do it with a bloody smile on your face! And I'll hear no more about it!"

It wasn't the first time her father had hit her, but it had been a very long time since she had felt the back of his hand. There was no point in leveling any accusatory glare upon him; he'd proven immune to that justified impertinence when she'd tried exactly that many years ago, when she was so much smaller, so much younger.

He towered over her, red-faced and seething while they squared off.

Shaking herself free of his arm, she allowed only anger—and sadly, a bit of hatred—to color the glower she did fix upon him. And then she turned her back on him.

I don't deserve this, she thought with no small amount of self-pity. Staring blindly out the small slit of a window, she heard him leave, closing the door with a sharp thud.

Chapter Two

THREE DAYS LATER, MAGGIE once again found herself with the long strap of the basket slung over her shoulder and on her way to the river and the sea. She'd barely spoken any words to her father since he'd struck her. Sadly, she could not honestly say that she'd even been rewarded with his indifference to her silence, as he paid her so little attention that she wasn't sure that he'd realized she wasn't speaking to him.

She was more than an hour into her walk, idling carelessly, finding more cold and hard stones in the river bed. She had no use for them of course, nor the shells she'd collect from the shore when she reached it, but the hunt brought her peace and the textures and colors of the rocks and shells brought her joy. She'd already unloaded several baskets into Elizabeth's kitchen garden. The plot would see no activity until spring, and mayhap the addition to the soil would keep weeds at bay. She had no idea if that might be true, but she'd boldly suggested as much to Elizabeth.

Three nights ago, Adam and Elizabeth had hosted a dinner for the Earl of Sutherland, with Maggie and Kenneth toasted as newly betrothed. At the time, she'd been particularly peeved, the imprint of her father's hand still stinging and the introduction to Kenneth Sutherland still miserably fresh in her mind. She'd forced herself to smile, had listened to more tasteless chatter, had even bowed her head meekly when the Earl of Sutherland had made mention of the rising red stamp on her cheek, cautioning her, "Likely to be more of that, if you dinna learn to mind yourself and your tongue."

Her soon-to-be husband had, for the most part, ignored her presence, choosing instead to band with his brothers-in-arms, making raucous noises and telling wild tales of bloody battles that seemed to have no place at the supper table.

However, she could now objectively look back and say the meal had not been horrible, not completely. Perhaps her own certain distress that day had only made it seem so at the time.

Bending down presently, she reached for and scooped up a smooth stone that was banded with lines of pink and gray. Another caught her eye, this one dotted with flecks of silver that sparkled under the midday sun. She added both to her basket and continued on, intent on dwelling no more on her unfortunate circumstance. She must embrace Elizabeth's prediction, that one day she would be happy, with bairns to love and a home to oversee.

At one point along her trek, well before she'd reached the sea, Maggie turned back and considered the distance between her and the keep. She'd come to an open area along the river, where no trees crowded the banks, and the keep, sitting not quite majestically atop a small berm, was clearly visible. 'Twas a pretty view, to see the keep nestled among rolling hills and clusters of the regal pines.

The sky then caught her attention. A surging line of thick gray clouds would soon overtake the clear blue above. It was a curious sight, as the line between blue and gray nearly cut the sky in half. She watched the far clouds moving for a few moments, wondering how much time she had before the sun was shuttered behind those patches of gray.

She resumed her walk, reaching one of several small sections of the river that were thin and shallow. It was funny that all these weeks she'd been walking this route, that area across the water had seemed to her to be a dangerous place, home to the unpredictable Mackays and their kin, surely a violent and treacherous place. Today, she gazed rather longingly across the river.

She'd not ever be found by any Sutherland if she dared to cross onto Mackay land. Never have to wed Kenneth Sutherland.

The notion came unbidden, and innocently enough.

She did not let it go, as she should have.

She glanced down at the ground beneath her feet. She pushed one foot forward, the toe of her thick leather boot peeking out from the hem of her gown. She moved the other foot as well, stepped onto a rock that was not wholly submerged in the water, and then another, further across the river. She had to skip to the next one and the one after that.

And then she was on the other side, looking back onto Sutherland land from her precarious position on Mackay soil. Biting her lip, she stood very still for many minutes, trying to decide if fear might send her back, or if fear might propel her further.

For several seconds while the enormity of what she dared crashed into her, she only backed away from the water until finally, she turned and ran, away from the open area of the river bank, deeper into Mackay territory. At first, her thinking wasn't particularly defined or conscious, but she did eventually acknowledge to herself that she was actually, and now purposefully, moving away from the Gordon keep and the Sutherlands, and the bleak future designed for her. Her mouth formed a small *o* at the very idea. Her mind began to whir.

When snow began to fall, she pulled her hood up and over her wimple and clutched her hands in the folds of her cloak, stepping around short scrub brush and over the cold, hard ground.

She walked for quite some time, the continued snowfall naught but a gloomy backdrop to her heart-pounding boldness. But where might she go? She couldn't return to her own home; her father eventually would as well, and there would be hell to pay for her dereliction. She had no other family, none that remained, none that she knew. And just as the winds began to howl and snow punched her in the face with stinging barbs that she was forced to tuck her head down nearly into her chest, Maggie remembered the abbey at which she and her father and their small group had begged respite for one night while traveling north to the Gordon keep so many weeks ago.

Oh, but it had been lovely. Not the formidable Abbess Joan Alnwick, who had quite terrified Maggie with her stern demeanor and unwelcoming tone, who had only given refuge to their party after her father declared that he was about the business of the Earl of Sutherland.

The quiet and the peacefulness of the abbey had intrigued her. Often throughout the night, she'd been lulled to serenity by the faraway sounds of chants and prayers and hymns, the hypnotic noise seeming to thrum through and live in the cool gray walls. She'd felt that any novice or nun she'd come upon during their brief stay must surely walk on air, their gait so tranquil and smooth, seeming to float along the quiet, candlelit corridors. And when they'd joined the ladies of the house in the refectory for a light repast before their departure, Maggie had been delighted with the smiles and giggles exuding from one particular table of girls about her age, and many younger. They'd seemed so happy. Never mind that they were garbed in dreadful and uniform gray dullness, nor that they must rise several times during the night for prayers and matins. Never mind that the entirety of their vocation, for the rest of their lives, would require naught but labors and prayers, and prayers and labors. Never mind that the Abbess Joan was indeed a dour character, likely to shrivel a girl with merely one glare from her shrewd brown eyes, Maggie had thought, even at their brief interaction.

There was joy and peace and a sense of comradery and well-being there, Maggie had thought rather wistfully at the time. Surprised at her own daring, she decided right then and there that she would indeed find shelter now, and when the snows cleared and the sun shone, she would better be able to determine her direction and head south.

To her new life.

"YOU'D NO' HAVE TUPPED her," said Daimh, addressing his brother.

"I could have," returned Donal, "if we'd no' taken to the road, being on our way."

"She'd no' have any part of it." Daimh said, shaking his head.

It was only those closest to the brothers who could tell the twins apart. Born of a litter, they were sometimes teased, Donal being the runt then, but still large and broad—*as pretty as ye are tall,* their sweet mam often mused. And it was no lie. The twins were possessed of thick and glossy brown hair, hazel eyes to tease and tempt, and pleasing grins which they put to good use in their never-ending quest to win over any fair-haired wench, lady, or—as their captain had once quipped—"any female, be it animal or no, so long as she contained within the requisite parts".

"She would have," insisted Donal, "And I'd have made sure she liked it. I'd no' do it half-arsed like you, brother. And no' like Hew," he said, inclining his head toward the lad riding nearest them, knowing the very earnest young man listened intently, "who does no' do it at all."

"Are you blushing, Hew?" Asked Daimh. "Still have no idea what the tupping's all about?"

"Aye," laughed Donal, "but he'll get it when he finally *gets* it."

"Aye, and won't you shut up now?" Begged their captain, Duncan McEwen from behind. "You're turning the mead in my belly sour."

Daimh chuckled. "Och, that's the picture we put in your head, Duncan—young Hew with his trews around his ankles, a squinty-eyed wench before him, and him wondering where to put the little Hew."

The twins laughed uproariously at this, while Duncan said, "Aye, and that's the right of it, but bloody bollocks, do you two ever talk about anything else?"

Donal and Daimh exchanged grins. Donal wondered with a shrug, "What else is there?"

Duncan rolled his eyes. "There's only several wars going on at once, there is."

"Plenty of war indeed. And here we are, roving 'bout the crags and beinns, naught but scouts while Pembroke rides roughshod over the Bruce down at Methven."

Duncan turned a scathing eye to Archibald Fraser. "Get over it already, Archie. Methven was months ago. 'Tis done," he reminded the wretched man, not for the first time. "We've been charged by the Bruce himself—the king personally and specifically tasked the lad with ridding the north of that scourge, the one they call Alpin." Duncan's voice was tight, grounding out the words, perturbed that he so often needed to have this conversation with the man. "You want another massacre like that one at Wick? Like the one we saw no' ten days ago in Helmsdale? Think those bastards who did that should go unpunished?"

Archie, being of an age with Duncan, which was twice the age of any other man in this unit, made a noise that was unmistakably disapproving, but said no more. He scratched at his thick, more-gray-than-brown beard and turned his black eyes onto the trail again. Duncan supposed there might be some truth to what the twins often presumed, that Archie would be only half as miserable if he plowed the wenches twice as much. As if any would let him. He stood about as much chance as the infamously shy Hew, Archie's hindrance being his God-awful mug, only made uglier by his perpetually menacing scowl.

The lad who'd been tasked by the Bruce to rid Caithness of the thieving, heartless Alpin was Iain McEwen, nephew to the great Donald Mackay, holding lands for the Mackay chief in southern Caithness, currently riding point as they finally made their way back home, if only for a wee bit.

Duncan and Archie had been swinging claymores for years when the lad took his first breath. Ten years ago, Duncan would have said Iain McEwen, his brother's son, boasted as many assets as he had weaknesses, being proud and strong but impetuous and impatient, fierce and decisive in battle but then not always compassionate with the people under his care. He was hot-headed and irrational at times, but then cool under pressure and there was none you'd choose before him to have your back, if need be. Duncan liked to think he'd played some part in toning down the lad's flaws, as he'd matured and settled into the role of laird to hundreds of people. He could safely say the lad's virtues far outweighed his faults these days, even as shades of the former reckless boy reared its head now and again. Sadly, Duncan understood that seven months as a prisoner of the English was what had changed him most, had tamed all the wildness and recklessness.

Just now, Iain stopped, several lengths ahead of the rest of their party. The other men—the twins and Hew, and Archie and Craig, that one as quiet and simple as his namesake rock—reined in as well. Duncan rode forward, until the nose of his destrier stood side by side with the lad's.

They sat atop their mounts, on the crag that overlooked the River Oykel, and stared out over a view they'd been treated to a hundred times before.

But Iain McEwen saw not the vista; not the swell and curve of a line of Scots pines, dusted still with a coating of the wet snow that had come a fortnight ago; not the river itself, which meandered lazily, forming its own valley between the hard rock of earth; nor even the familiar cairn below, the ancient rock formation, taller than any man and shaped so peculiarly like a bee's hive that Duncan would never believe it wasn't man-made.

Iain stared at the sky. Above their heads hovered thin hazy clouds whose only occupation seemed to be denying the sun. But north and beyond, and headed toward them with apparent ferociousness, black and white rolling clouds, forming a straight line to distinguish their storminess from the unexceptional clouds above.

"We'll no' outrun it," Duncan commented. That expanse of sky that was so ominous seemed to stretch into forever. Further ahead, far across the glen below, Duncan could well discern the falling snow, which seemed naught but a wall of white, though still several hours ahead of them, he assumed.

"Nae. We can make use of the bothies up at Reay."

Duncan cursed quietly. He hated those old huts, tucked into the hills. They were often used in summer months by shepherds and their families while their livestock grazed the common land, but they were desolate and eerie in the winter. Having once found the decaying bodies of some poor stranded travelers in one of them a few winters back, he'd done whatever was necessary to avoid them since. He glanced again at the coming storm. *Bluidy hell.*

Iain clicked his tongue and moved his mount forward, throwing a grin back at Duncan, his blue eyes dancing with delight at his uncle's disquiet.

Aye, there'd be mountains of fun at his expense this night, Duncan surmised, suddenly disgruntled.

They moved with more speed than they had throughout the morning, and a good thing, too. The storm, when it came, thrust snow at them from every direction. The temperature dropped and the snow grew beneath the hooves of their mighty destriers. If not for the fact that they knew the region as well as the back of their hands, they'd likely have no idea in which direction to travel, since they could not even see the backs of their hands if held at arm's length.

’Twas mostly Craig who led them. Simple the big oaf might be, though a bloody executioner with a double edged sword in hand, but aye, he knew every rock and tree and hill of the border of Caithness. Duncan squinted up ahead at Craig; the lad didn’t know enough to bend his face away from the pelting snow, but trudged on mindlessly, while they’d formed a tight line—stem to stern, his seafaring da’ would have said.

Only a short-lived reprieve from the wind and blinding snow showed Duncan that they neared the bottom of the Isauld hills. The silver birch here were particularly plentiful, he recalled. He’d just tucked his face down into his neck, needing only to see the butt of Iain’s horse ahead of him to keep pace up the side of the hill, when he heard the short jip-jip call they regularly used to signify halt. Duncan tugged on the reins and waited.

“Blood in the snow,” Iain said, maneuvering his mount around Craig and then Duncan.

Duncan peered down and around him, noticing what Iain had, little droplets of blood, fresh, and dotting alongside a set of tracks. Turning in the saddle, Duncan followed the tracks, unwilling to move his horse lest they disrupt more of the footprints. The spots of bright red blood were very small and stark against the snow, indicative of a wound, but possibly not a grave one.

The snow here was not more than ankle deep, he discerned from the impression.

“Fresh,” he said to Iain. These hills wouldn’t have retained much of the snow from a fortnight ago, as the ground being presumably warmer than the winter air would have warmed and melted it by now. The winds and current snow had done their best to obliterate them, swiping sideways across each track, but they were still clear, and Duncan guessed, not more than an hour old.

"Small. Child, mayhap," Iain guessed. He pulled his long sword from its sheath at his hip and instructed Craig, "Lead on."

Each man, likewise, withdrew his blade, eyes scanning the entire area. Truth be told, they saw only white, or occasionally a tree or brush as they passed close. A person or many could be standing ten feet away, inside the swirling snow, and they'd not know it. If they were to be attacked, they'd not see it coming until it was possibly too late.

They encountered no one, but found that the tracks, which they followed just to the left, continued up to the old huts, just as they did. There were three such huts on this side of the hill. The original builders had made fine use of the hard rock and occasional level spots to serve as at least one wall of the aged dwellings. The outer walls had been built with whatever was at hand, twigs and brush and clay, forming thick walls that would serve them well through the storm. The first one they came upon was the largest and tallest, and they dismounted, swords still drawn and poised, while Donal and Daimh gathered all the leads and dragged the horses within. There was no door, of course, naught but an opening, and they could only hope the daft animals were at least smart enough to stay inside.

Archie and Iain followed the blood trail and footsteps, which circumvented this first hut, as if the owner of the footprints had not noticed the closest shelter.

The next hut was the deepest, being more of a cave, a depression in the rock serving as three sides and a roof of the shelter, with only one wall of wattle and daub supplying the barrier against the weather. At one time, it would have been Duncan's favorite one, as it was deep enough to allow for a fire if the winds were agreeable, without smoking out the whole of the interior, but that was before they'd stumbled upon those corpses. They'd been a mother and child, he'd known—he'd never be convinced otherwise—the image of those embracing little figures, decayed beyond stench even, haunting him since.

And damn if that wasn't exactly where these prints led.

The opening to this shelter thankfully faced the opposite direction from which the winds came. Craig and Archie posed like sentinels just outside, while Iain ducked and entered, Duncan fast on his heels. Pitch black was all that greeted them, not any wild animal or frightened and injured child. There was no noise within, save for the occasional drip of some water somewhere deeper inside.

Iain and Duncan stood, swords raised to strike blows if need be, while they waited for the brothers, who would bear the packs and supplies from the horses.

"Light a torch," Duncan said when he heard the sounds of the twins entering. "Or a char cloth, at least." Aside from the bare and occasional glint of his own blade, he could see very little.

It was another full minute while the brothers rooted through the worn leather bags to find the necessary implements—flint and stone and cloth—before a bright light burst into the cave before settling down to a smaller golden glow.

They were shown instantly the uneven rock of the inner cave, gray and black and glistening with patches of ice. Iain stepped forward. Duncan noticed the remnants of an old fire, possibly their own from years past, and kicked out a thick piece of wood back toward the twins. In another minute, the char cloth had been set to the stick and another flame glowed.

Donal moved around Duncan, providing light for Iain in the lead.

Iain stopped, not more than ten feet in front of Duncan, having just come to the part of the cave where the ceiling was higher and the need to hunch over was not required, when Duncan noticed the prone form on the ground before them.

"Och, no' another one," he groused, determined to proceed no further. He hadn't any intention of inviting more hauntings. He squatted where he was, let the lad and the boys pursue the pitiful, doomed creature. He'd have no part of it. "Only begging nightmares, you get any closer," he warned them.

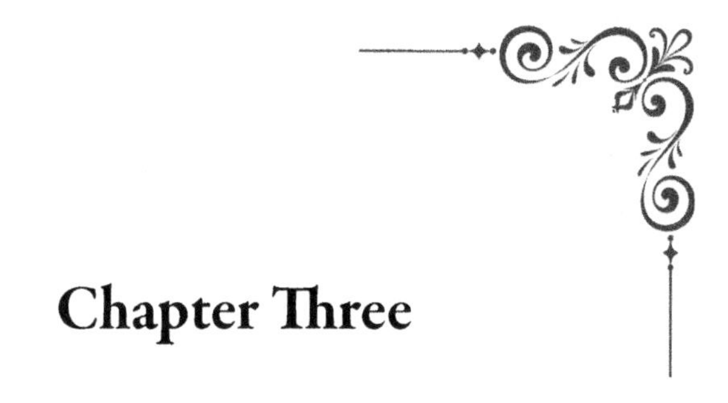

Chapter Three

IAIN THREW A GLANCE back at his uncle. Amazing, he thought, the man didn't blink an eye when cleaving a man in half upon the battlefield but was disturbed to near hysterics by a frozen corpse.

And yet that blood had been fresh.

Moving closer still, Iain saw that the person was curled nearly into a ball, legs drawn in and head tucked down. It lay on its side, facing away from them. He approached slowly and prodded its back with the tip of its sword. The blade met with cushioned softness, suggesting many layers.

It didn't move.

"Ho there," he called and nudged again.

Nothing. Likely dead, he supposed, sheathing his sword and stepping closer. They would have to move it out, to the third hut further up the hill, as Duncan would have fits if he were forced to take shelter with a corpse.

And then it moaned.

Iain startled, nearly jumped back himself.

"Jesus bluidy Christ," he heard his uncle blaspheme behind him.

'Twas a decidedly weak and feeble moan. Not dead, but very near, it sounded.

Circling the body, he approached it from the front, guided by the light as Donal followed him. He pulled out his short blade and went down on his haunches within a foot of the moaning body, prepared for a surprise attack, though truly expecting none.

He tugged and pulled at the thick woolen cloak, trying to find where it might open. He pushed his hand into the folds and met with cold, but not frozen flesh. A hand. Iain circled his fingers around the smaller, colder ones and withdrew a hand from the shelter of the cloak. The hand was covered with part of a glove, as the fingers were protected by the non-descript brown wool only to the second knuckle, leaving the tips bare.

The body made another noise, less a groan, more of sound of acknowledgment of their presence.

"Aye now, we mean no harm."

The hand fell limp as he released it to further open the cloak. His fingers moved the stiff, icy fabric of the hood aside, revealing a cotton gauze wimple of nearly white and a smooth forehead, and then closed eyes, two milky crescents fanned by a thick fringe of dark lashes, and lower still to produce a nose, slim and straight, and finally lips, wide and full, though presently quite blue.

Iain stared, rather transfixed, realizing this was no hearty but wounded shepherd, nor a child who well might have perished in the storm. This was a woman, and a bonny one at that.

And then she opened her eyes and rather amazingly, fastened two gloriously green orbs with unexpected clarity upon Iain. The eyes were large and round and glassy, too large for her tiny face, too...perfect to be real.

"*Jesu*," he breathed, believing he'd found a fae creature, come from some fairy realm, tiny and blue veined and deathly pale, save for those bright eyes.

The men had gathered, drew closer, Donal lowering the torch, which pointed out a smattering of freckles across her cheeks and over the bridge of her nose. The light also showed a bruise across her cheek, several days old perhaps, shades of red and purple, extending to under her eye. This was not fresh and not the source of the blood.

"It's a lass," mused Craig as her eyelids drifted closed again.

"Aye, canna get nothing by him," noted Donal, with some humorous disdain.

"Bound to die, I'd say," observed Archie, seeming put out for the possible inconvenience this might cause him.

"The whole bottom half of her is soaked through," young Hew said, frowning and placing his hands about the cloak, not familiarly but objectively. "Up to her hips, nearly."

Iain shifted on his haunches to consider Duncan, still hovering near the entrance. "Aye, come on now, 'tis no corpse. Dare we make a fire?"

Daimh bent low and placed his entire hand over one side of her face, his paw huge and colored with life compared to her pallor. "Bonny, she is."

"If you favor the look of death," Donal said with a grimace.

Duncan had ambled closer, peered over the shoulders of the men on their knees. "Get the wet stuff off, might be helpful. Fire should no' be a nuisance. 'Tis large enough within, air flow should move the smoke outside." He moved his hands in a motion that swept low to the ground with an inward direction and circled round higher, heading back toward the entrance. "Cold air moves in low; warm air—and smoke—should move out from above." He shrugged then. "Or we build two fires, use only the embers deep inside."

"Let's start with one, further inside," Iain decided and nodded to the twins. "Any kindling in with the horses?"

Daimh lifted his shoulders and let them drop. "Dinna see any." He pulled the axe from his belt, inside the heavy fur cloak. "But we'll get the fire bits."

"From where comes the blood?" Hew asked of Iain, when only the two of them remained hunched over the lass.

Duncan was investigating the interior of the cave; Archie had sat his rump on a boulder, which sat closer to the entrance; and Craig was tracing his fingers over something on the jagged wall of the cave, lifting the torch Donal had left with him to better identify whatever it was that had drawn his silent interest.

"Bring the torch," Iain said with some impatience to Craig.

Returning his attention to the near comatose woman, he rolled her onto her back and pulled the cloak wide open. He and Hew examined the front of her, saw no tears or blood on the thick woolen kirtle. Something about the bulk of the kirtle caused Iain to squint down at her. He pulled the wimple out from where it was tucked into the neckline and began to unfasten the buttons down the front of the gown. If Hew thought this odd, he said nothing, but worked at removing the lass's boots.

It had not gone unnoticed by Iain that while the lass was very small and slender, she seemed to be possessed of a very ample bosom. When he'd pulled the wimple away, he'd been greeted by mounds of creamy white flesh, spilling over the neckline of the gown. Under the brown kirtle, Iain discovered another thick woolen gown, this one of blue, and wondered about the intentions of a lass, who'd purposefully donned many layers of clothing, lost in a snow storm. He left off, leaving the blue kirtle intact, finding no injury that was bleeding.

"Toes are wet," Hew commented, lifting a slim foot to show only that she wore a cream colored linen hose.

Iain nodded at Hew, and considered the fine linen, suggesting she was a woman of some means. "Take them off." He recalled a Mackay soldier, once lost to a storm, years ago. He'd somehow made his way back to Caithness, half-dead on the back of a cart. Most of his fingers and toes had frozen and were black as tar as those extremities had died off. His father had ordered the man's fingers and toes be hacked off, to save the arms and legs. Iain had always thought it had been fortunate that the man had died before the directive had been carried out.

Iain joined Hew near her feet and removed the other boot, noticing that Hew had gone completely still, having set the lass's leg onto the ground again. Iain stared at him.

"I canna...undress her."

Rolling his eyes, Iain yanked off the boot and reached his hand up, over her ankle and calf, expecting to find her garters before the knee. He did not. Frowning, he moved his hand higher, over her slim leg, finding the garters circled around the middle of her thigh. He ignored the offense he gave, touching the girl so intimately, ignored too the smooth softness of her skin beyond the hose while he employed some practicality to untie the garters and yank the hose down and off her leg and foot.

Her naked foot was slim and pale, light in his hand, while her toes were bright red and noticeably swollen. Immediately, he cupped his hands around her toes, holding them tight for a moment before chafing his hands and fingers back and forth over them. He nodded to her other leg and instructed Hew, "Get that one warm."

Hew gulped down a strangled bit of discomfort and did as his laird had, reached up under the lass's skirts to find the garters. His boyish face, all pinkened cheeks and nary a sign of any whiskers, scrunched up with his distress. He grimaced and closed his eyes and fumbled under her skirts.

"Bloody hell, Hew," Iain growled, "get the hose off."

The lad nodded awkwardly and sent his hand further up her leg, pulling a face the whole time until several long moments later, he had successfully removed her garter and hose as well. He watched Iain's hands for a moment before imitating the same maneuvers, chafing her toes and feet to warm them.

Donal and Daimh returned then and Duncan directed them about the location of the fire, having found several pieces of slate that he'd stacked to be used for warming hands and feet as needed.

"First time young Hew touches a lass," Donal called out cheerfully, "and here she is, numb and near to death. Aye, but that's a bollock's luck, aye, Hew?"

"The only way he'll ever be allowed to get near one, I'm thinking," Daimh chimed in, causing more than one person to wonder if either of the twins ever knew an emotion that was not sprightly. But then, they were rarely chastised for their good humors, nor Archie for his bad ones. They'd seen too much, too much bloody war and grisly deaths and senseless violence; they were all allowed their own methods to get on with life as if they hadn't.

Ignoring Daimh's quip, as he normally did, Hew wondered to Iain, "But where's the blood coming from?"

"I dinna ken. But we can no' undress *all* of her."

"Her finger," Duncan commented, coming to stand beside the lass while Iain and Hew remained near her feet. Duncan squatted and pointed to the hand Iain had not touched, almost completely covered by the cloak he'd flung open.

Duncan lifted the hand, showed it clamped tight around a small, well-crafted but inexpensive knife. Blood rivulets ran over her fingers and covered much of her glove. Most of the blood was dried or frozen, being tiny hard bits stuck to the wool of the glove. "Clamped so tight, she cut herself," Duncan surmised. "Hand so cold, she dinna feel it." Carefully, he unfolded her fingers, away from the knife, and set the implement aside and then removed the glove from her hand. Iain tossed him the lass's hose which he'd discarded, and Duncan cut away a dry strip from the top. He wrapped the wound with some expertise, the strip circling between her thumb and forefinger several times before he secured it around her wrist. Next he frowned at and then peeked inside the woven basket that had been at the lass's side.

He held up a smooth river rock for the inspection of Iain and Hew. It was about the size of Duncan's palm. "The basket is half-filled with them."

"Nice ring for the fire," Iain commented absently, giving no thought to what purpose the rocks might serve to the lass, nor why she'd not abandoned them when the storm mayhap chased her away from the river and up the hill.

Removing his fur cloak, Iain laid it on the ground next to her, and he and Hew wrestled the woolen gray cloak away from her. Iain lifted her by the shoulders while Hew tugged the cloak away. Once her arms were free, Iain stood and lifted all of her, abandoning the cloak to the ground. She was small in his arms and shivered violently against him. He'd meant to set her down on his fur, but held her close for several moments instead, absorbing her tremors, some instinct telling him to hold her close to his own body heat.

He stood like that for several long moments, clutching the lass to his chest, her bare feet dangling over his arm that Hew continued to chafe and warm them.

"Coming down hard, getting deep out there," Archie noted, turning his face away from the opening, glowering when he saw what Iain and Hew were about. "Aye now, you do naught but waste your own heat. Lass'll be dead by morning."

"She will no'," Hew insisted with a peculiar sense of resolve. "Already, her lips are no' so blue."

"Aye," Iain agreed, tipping his gaze down at her, her wimpled head drooped lifelessly against his shoulder. His eyes rested easily on the delicate features. Everything about her was soft; the line of her cheek, the fullness of her lips, the weight and curves of her body, even her pale feet were soft, not angular and bony as her slimness might suggest.

After a few more minutes, the twins had the fire blazing nicely and Duncan stood nearby, faithfully watching the path of the smoke to be assured it would indeed abandon the cave and not be contained within by the baying winds outside. Iain set the lass down on the fur he'd laid out. Hew hovered still, arranging several more furs over her until she appeared no more than a plump wolf in repose.

With naught else to do, the men gathered round the flames, warming themselves. They doffed their own boots and lined them up around the fire, Iain noting with some interest that Duncan had indeed ringed the firepit with the lass's curious collection of stones. Leaning against these, facing inward toward the heat and flames, Duncan had lined the entire ring with decent sized, flat pieces of slate. When they were heated, they would be utilized as drying frames for their hose and boots and gloves, as needed. Hew had already folded and stacked neatly the lass's hose and gloves upon one of the slate rocks.

They knew better than to drink melted snow without warming it, but their leather flasks made this a slow process, having to keep the flasks far enough away from the flames to cause no damage to the leather, which would shrink and crack, but close enough to draw in the heat.

There would be no food, but not for want of trying. Their trek earlier to outrace the storm had been made with at least one eye toward their surroundings, looking for any potential prey, but they'd had no luck snaring even one pitiful hare or squirrel.

The afternoon dwindled away. The evening came and so did more winds and more snow, that they began to understand they would travel no more this day.

The lass barely moved. Her shivering had stopped, and Hew often checked in on her, lifting the fur and wrapping his youthful fingers around her narrow wrist, which advised him that she was warmer and yet maintained a pulse.

Donal teased the attentive and dedicated Hew, "Aye, and you'll be a fine mother one day, lad."

It wasn't at all akin to a summer evening, making camp under the stars, where the moderate weather lent itself to late nights of jovial stories around the dancing flames. On this night, in this cold and well before midnight, they each found their own fur pallets and drifted off. Likely each man hoped and dreamed of better weather on the morrow. Save for the twins, who possibly dreamt of their last or their next service of Venus, for Iain was genuinely persuaded they thought of little else.

Late into the evening, Hew had declared the lass's hose dry and warm and there was more good-natured mocking from Donal and Daimh and even Archie as Hew insisted the lass would be warmer if these were returned to her feet.

"Go on, then," dared Archie.

"Aye, now give him time, Arch," chided Donal, "he's trying to figure out which end is up."

As he was never one whose actions—or lack thereof—were dictated by the regular tormenting of the twins, or any other McEwen or Mackay, Hew ignored them all and did what he knew to be right. He returned the lass's hose to her feet, though not without some stuttering of his hands and a full redness to his cheeks, as Donal and Daimh kept up a steady stream of raunchy encouragement.

When he was done, Duncan shooed Hew aside, away from the lass, asserting age and ascendancy to claim the even ground there, forcing Hew to take up the unlevel and lumpier ground further around the fire.

Iain found his ease next to the lass, lying on his left to face her, while Duncan then flanked her backside as she had shifted once again to her side, curling her legs up into her chest.

He stared at her for quite a while, wondering at her tale. Only the white of her wimple and her closed eyes and nose were available to his scrutiny, but he was no farther advanced in his understanding for his grand perusal, and eventually he, too, found slumber.

MAGGIE BLINKED SEVERAL times until she was able to keep her eyes open.

She recognized immediately a severe ache about her temples and understood she was lying down. She breathed in a deep gasp, but then clamped her lips tight, afraid to make any sound.

A man was lying next to her.

He was sleeping, or at least his eyes were closed.

Dark and short cropped hair; stubbly growth over his cheeks and jaw; broad shoulders, standing twice as high as hers as he was on his side. Maggie shook her head back and forth, pinching her lips to keep from crying out. She had no idea who this man might be, or why she was lying next to him.

With a swiftly growing panic, she moved only her eyes around, afraid any sound or movement might wake the man. Her alarm only increased, as did her breathing, forcing her to push out a frantic breath. She did not recognize her surroundings, seeing only rock all around her, which moved with dancing shadows, suggesting some fire nearby. Some of the swaying lights glistened on the wall, where dripping water had saturated much of the rock.

Her anxious gaze returned to the man. He was huge beside her, lying on his side, facing her, one arm folded and cushioned under his head. He was so close she could feel his very even breathing against her cheeks. She could contain her breathing no more again, felt she would burst with her efforts to do so noiselessly, and let out a whimper with a surge of breath through her mouth.

He didn't move. Maggie began to pant.

But where was she? And who was this man?

Closing her eyes, she listened to sounds around her, easily understanding the slight crackle and hiss of the fire and an occasional drip and plop of water, and then, what sounded very much like heavy snoring. Opening her eyes, she stared at the man before her. He was not snoring.

Sheer black fright swept through her, her heart pounding in her chest. She wanted very much to sit up and discover more of her circumstance but was rendered motionless by her fear. Her gaze remained fixed on the man in front of her, watching for any movement. Nearly paralyzed, she closed her eyes again and courted calmness, willing herself to be brave, wondering what she should do, or could do.

Of course, she must get away.

Opening her eyes again showed the man still sleeping. Commanding more courage than she was sure she possessed, she pushed her hand against the ground and lifted her head. She glanced around to see several more men, just like this one, sleeping upon the hard ground, draped and huddled in furs, tucked close together. One was at her back, pressed close, his rump nearly touching hers.

Her eyes lit on the wall at one end of this room, the one that was not made of rock. She stared, transfixed, until she realized what it was, the mouth and opening of the cave. A cave, yes! She'd stumbled upon this cave, she recalled. These men must have done the same, sought refuge within as she had. This offered her only slight ease, barely at all, surveying the bodies of all these men surrounding her.

Rolling her lips inward, she knew she must leave. This appeared a very dangerous circumstance. Pushing herself further up from the ground showed a fur beneath her, and another, falling off her shoulder, and being dragged away from the closest man, as she appeared to be sharing it with him. She glanced down at herself and noted her missing cloak, and that the buttons of her topmost kirtle were undone. *Oh, dear Lord!* She touched her hand to her head, finding her wimple still intact, though askew.

Her cloak was not seen, but she could use the fur if she dared to rise and flee. She kept her eyes on the man before her as she shifted her legs under her, intent on rising to her feet. Maggie gasped and pushed her foot out. She had no boots. Her foot showed only her hose, covering her foot, but not much more, bunched around her ankle as if—*oh, my God*!

Chapter Four

"IT'S NO' SO BAD AS it seems."

Her gasp now was vocal. She jerked her face toward the man.

His eyes were open.

The pain in her chest just then, of shock and dread, gave some endorsement to the oft-heard expression, *died of fright.* Maggie was sure she was about to expire on the spot.

His hand touched hers, wrapped firmly around her wrist.

Maggie swallowed hard and breathed rapidly through her nose.

Very calmly, his voice low, he explained to her, "We happened upon you in the cave, seeking relief from the storm, same as you. We only did what was needed to get you warm, nothing more."

She could only stare at him, at his piercing but calm dark eyes. She thought that he made some attempt to appear non-threatening, keeping his features relaxed. No frown marred his forehead; no menace colored his expression; no dastardly light shone in his gaze.

She nodded, letting him know she understood even as she was quite sure she did not.

"But I must—"

"Aye, you'll no' be going anywhere until the storm quits its raging." Even his interruption was calm, even-toned. "None of us will."

She couldn't seem to control her breathing, seemed capable of naught but those short raspy breaths.

In the same level and mild tone, he said, "Lie down now. We mean no harm. We're no' in the habit of fixing up a person only to bring harm to them." He stared steadily at her. "Lie down. Ask what questions you might, if it'll make you feel better. You're in no danger."

Her voice quaking, she asked, "But have you—am I a hostage?"

He smiled. Maggie drew in a sharp breath. The smile was neither insincere nor ominous. It was...simply beautiful. Full-mouthed, crinkly-eyed, and meant to reassure, which it inexplicably did.

"You are no' a hostage. I promise you'll come to no harm in our company."

"What time is it?"

Another smile greeted her query, this one slightly lopsided. "That will be your most pressing concern?"

Maggie expelled a nervous laugh of her own. "I only wondered how long I—we've—been here."

"We came in after midday and guessed you hadn't arrived much sooner than that. Well after midnight now. The storm hasn't let up much, no' enough to venture out yet."

She liked his voice, a nighttime whisper voice, one that might tell secrets in the dark. It was deep and smooth, and whether intentional or not, it did imbue her with a certain sense of calm.

He pulled his hand away from her wrist. Maggie glanced down, having forgotten that he'd held her still. She watched the large hand move away from her, removing the last hint of any threat, she imagined. Lifting her own hand, she considered the linen wrapped around it, took note of the part of it between her thumb and forefinger that was coated with blood.

"You had a knife in your hand," the man said. "Must have cut yourself."

She recalled this, withdrawing the knife from the belt at her hip. Something had scared her, some noise that had seemed to her to be not of land or wind or critter, that she felt at least less defenseless for having the weapon in her hand. Whatever the noise had been, it had chased her out of the trees and further into Mackay land, she recalled thinking. But it had been auspicious as well, for when the noise had quieted, when her fright had waned, she'd found herself at the bottom of the hill on which sat this cave. She hadn't noticed the cave at first, had thought only to reach the higher ground and attempt to get her bearings, or any indication of direction. The trek up the hill had been treacherous and lengthy that when she did spy the curious outer wall of the cave, she'd happily changed course, and had given up on reaching the summit, or defining her position, to seek shelter and warmth instead.

"It's there, beside you still," he offered, "if that might settle your nerves."

Maggie glanced around her, saw the bloodied knife on the ground near where her head had lain. She did not reach for it. She didn't know if she were in danger presently, yet she was quite sure her tiny blade would be but a nuisance to a man such as this, twice her size perhaps and with that gaze that said he missed not much.

It was impossible to steady her erratic pulse, but she did lay down. A lean bough of logic insisted that if these men had any nefarious intent, they likely would have undertaken any wickedness while she'd slept, while she'd been nearly comatose with the cold. And too, he'd likely not have suggested she was free to arm herself with her own knife if his plans were dreadful.

"You had a curious basket with you, filled with stones."

"From the river," was all she said, so much whirring through her mind. She was still, staring into his eyes, trying to make sense of this situation, and of this man. "I like the feel of the smooth stones," she expounded further, after a quiet moment in which she decided his eyes might be blue, not exactly black as they nearly appeared in the dim but glowing light. "I like the colors and the lines and the patterns." She didn't know why she told him this, didn't know what prompted her to add, "They make me happy."

He made a face, one of discomfort, his mouth moving a bit before he admitted, "We may have used a few to contain the fire." He lifted a thick brow, seeming to wait her reaction, and then went on, more regret oozing into his tone, "Mayhap more than a few."

Maggie knew just then that she was safe. No person, intent on or guilty of nefarious deeds, would show such contrition for having made such excellent use of her silly stones.

Her lips curved a bit as she tucked her hands under her head. "A small price, I should imagine, for the aid you've given me."

"But what were you about in the storm, lass? Would you no rather collect your stones in fair weather?"

"Naturally, if this region saw any such thing," she said, keeping her voice as quiet as his. She shrugged, which may have not translated well from her position. "Cold doesn't bother me—not the normal cold. The sky was clear when I left the keep."

"Aye, which begs the question, from which keep? Only so many near Reay."

Maggie chewed her lip, recalling that she'd trespassed onto Mackay land, not recollecting in her attempt to find shelter that she had somehow moved herself back onto Sutherland land.

"The home of Adam Gordon," she said weakly, hoping to God this man was not one of those extreme Mackays, who might make sport with any Sutherland—which she essentially was, or was bound to be—merely as a means to harass his enemy. She knew such men existed. Even in her rather unspectacular home near Torish, more than a day's ride away, she'd heard the tales of the feud, and all the brutal crimes committed in its name. When he said nothing, she asked quietly, "Are you a Mackay?" She needed to know if she should allow her panic to soar again.

He nodded, his expression shuttered. And then he said, his tone as level as it had been, "McEwen, actually. But a Mackay by blood. And that's it? You were out collecting stones and became lost in the storm?"

Besieged by inspiration, or more aptly, by desperation, she recalled her plans to flee and passed it on to him. "Are you familiar with St. Edmund Abbey? Yes, well, I am bound for the good convent there. The blessed Abbess Joan expects me anon, as I am meant to take my vows," she said, unaware how her voice quickened with her lies.

The man considered this, his brow lowering fractionally. His gaze moved to her lips and then back to her eyes before he asked, with seeming disbelief, "You want to become a nun, cloistered away for the rest of your life?"

Maggie was quick to assure him—or convince him—with more lies, "I have burned with a zeal since my earliest childhood to be converted. In fact, my poor dear mam grew tired of my constant pleas of, *Mother, please make me a nun*. It is my dream that God may not leave unrewarded so fervent a desire to enter religion."

Possibly, she'd overstated it. His frown deepened, but when he said naught to gainsay her fiction, Maggie pressed on with her tale, "So it was, I'd bid goodbye to my dear friends, the Gordons, and was off to St. Edmund Abbey when the storm caught me by surprise."

"They did no' provide you a cart, nor least of all an old nag to see you safely there?"

"Oh, but of course, they tried," she lied, devising, "but I could not accept such a gift. Not even as a loan, as I feared the responsibility of a thing that was not my own."

"Is that so? So, you planned to go by foot, walk for three days or more over hill and mountain and crag?"

Maggie nodded, wondering at the exact depth of his skepticism. "But I'd done as much already. I walk hours every day." She might have added more but opted to arrive at the purpose of her fraudulence. "Might you and...your friends be able to direct me proper toward St. Edmund Abbey when the snows clear?"

He hesitated, considering her, his gaze sharp and assessing, even as she eagerly wished that it was not. "We might, at that," was all he said.

"Oh, thank you, sir. You have my gratitude," she said, and thought to add, "and the Lord's blessing, I'm sure."

"Aye, I'm sure."

IAIN WASN'T SURE WHY the lass lied to him, but he recognized truth telling—and its counterpart—when he heard it. *Nae, this one was no' bound for any convent.* The good Lord hadn't made those lips for mumbling prayers or chanting choruses.

He'd let it go for now. Likely, the lass's falseness was a product of her fright. He'd witnessed that very thing, through slitted eyes when first she'd woken. Iain had waited, hadn't wanted to startle her further, or upend her anxiety into some full-scale horror. And she'd calmed quickly enough, though her eyes had remained huge and round in her face. He'd appreciated her relative calm, having some brief fear of his own, that she'd have started wailing or screaming or taking up with any such tantrum. She'd not even given him grief for making loose and free with her stones.

And yet, she lied to him.

Iain moved his hand and indicated the bruise on her cheek, near her eye. She went completely still, until he asked, "Who gave you that?" She moved then, lifted her bandaged hand to cover the discoloration on her face for a moment, her gaze leaving his, as it had before when she'd lied.

"I fell," she said, and tried to smile, turning the questions around onto him. "But what were you and these men doing out in a storm?"

"Same as you," he answered, "going from one place to the next. It did rise quickly, the storm. Aye?"

Her green eyes found his. "I don't ever remember a wind like that. Blew the snow sideways, straight across, that I marveled that anything landed on the ground. It's the first time I've ever been trapped in a storm."

"I'd no' want to alarm you—what's done is done—but you're lucky we happened upon you. You'd no' have survived had we no'."

"Then I owe you and your companions my life. How shall I repay you?"

With a kiss, was the immediate answer that sounded in his brain. Iain scowled, refusing to give attention to so ignoble a response, no matter that it had come so swiftly and with such pleasing possibilities. "Aye, we'll make you take charge of the horses," he said, withholding his grin, "feeding, grooming, shoeing."

A thin auburn brow arched upward. "Shoeing them? Oh, sir, I know nothing about that."

"No worries," he said. "But you'll need to be housed with them as well. Makes it easier to keep them well tended."

"Oh." She nodded, chewing the inside of her cheek, while those delicate brows lowered into a frown. Her green eyes found his again, scrutinized his expression, perhaps noted the laughter in his gaze. "You are teasing me?"

"Aye."

"Oh." And she smiled at him and he thought he might want to tease her often. The lass was bonny enough, but when she smiled she was radiant, those tempting lips open and curved, showing neat white teeth and just one dimple, indenting her left cheek with no small amount of charm. The smile grew, danced into her eyes, as she suggested, "You should have played that out more, should have told me I'd be required to walk behind your marching men, using my clever basket to clean up anything your horses dropped along the way. That would have really caused some hysteria."

His shoulders shook and his grin flashed briefly. "But would you have done it?"

She lifted and dropped her shoulders. "I would have no choice," she returned gamely, "though to do so would be to equate the value of my life, which you have so generously saved, with that of horse dung. Aye, I might need to rethink the extent of my gratitude."

He didn't think he was easily captivated, but he knew he was just now.

"Is the good abbess expecting you, that a delay will cause her some worry?" He wondered.

"It might," she said, putting her gaze onto his neck, avoiding his once again as she perhaps told another untruth. Quickly, she brushed this aside. "Of course, there's naught to be done about it. I'll arrive when I arrive."

"Aye, and dinna you seem so calm,' he commented, "trapped in a cave with a band of hard-bitten Mackays, wind and snow howling all about, and you so near to death today. Yet, you give nary a cry of distress and shed no' a single tear for your troubles."

In a very small voice, she admitted, "I'm terrified, if you must know." And because her green eyes were fastened on his, he guessed she might be truth-telling just now. "I am hoping that the safety of which you've assured me will be a matter of reality."

"Hoping? Should no' a nun be praying?" He was fairly certain he'd caught her off-guard, challenging her piety, but she recovered quickly enough.

"The words of hope become prayer," she said evenly, needing only seconds to concoct this drivel. "God loves that we remember Him to ask for help, and with the indulgent smile of a father, He responds benevolently."

She was clever, he'd give her that.

And he was still convinced she was lying.

"Aye, and close your eyes now, lass," he said then. "'Tis a long, cold night and no' a warmer day on the morrow, and no' to be without its share of troubles, getting out of here and on our way."

"I don't think I can sleep anymore," she said as Iain adjusted the fur over the both of them, bringing it back up around her shoulders.

"But you will no' be minding if I do?" He asked, showing another short grin. He could not, he believed, continue to talk to her, and have those lips so close and have her eyes fixed so beautifully upon him, and...*Jesu, she could no' take the vows*. She'd have the priests all sinning, or no less than dreaming on it.

Iain slept, as did the lass, despite her concern that she might not. And when next he woke, he thought that morning had not yet come, but that it was nigh. Sometime during the night, the lass had drawn near to him. Or he to her, that her face was nearly pressed into his chest, her arms and hands curled up between them. He took note of all parts of his body and thought the tops of her tiny feet might have sought out warmth and were now bent against his shins. He hadn't moved at all from his side, nor had the lass, facing him still, but he found that his hand was settled over the fur that covered them, resting on what he imagined was the curve of her hip.

He needed to get back to Berriedale, to the village beyond, and visit Fiona. One good release between that one's milky thighs and he'd not be lying here thinking that almost-but-not-quite holding the fibbing though tremendously bonny stranger in his arms was about as near to pleasant as he'd known in a long, long time.

Glancing down showed him only the top of her wimple covered head and Iain cast his glance off toward the cave opening. 'Twas dark yet, the blackness gone with the departing night, chased by the morning gray. He listened but heard no howling wind and decided the storm must have moved on and away or withered to nothing.

"Seems we might get about early."

Iain shifted his gaze, over that of the lass, and found Duncan awake as well. The old man was on his back, his head tilted toward Iain, his gaze beyond, to the mouth of the cave.

"Aye, and home before dark tomorrow, God willing."

"What's to be done with the lass?" Duncan wondered, settling his eye onto her fur clad form between them, employing naught but a whisper.

"I'm no' sure. She asked for some direction, but it seems a perilous thing, to send a lass off on her own." He knew she wasn't awake, that she couldn't hear them speaking about her as if she were not immediately between them. The hand he'd kept on her hip detected no movement at all, no stiffening of her body to indicate she'd woken and now eavesdropped on their conversation.

"Aye," Duncan agreed. "Lass got a name?"

Iain shrugged. "I dinna ask."

Duncan's bushy gray brows scrunched down over his dark eyes. "You were chatty enough though, talked for quite some time. Dinna occur to you to wonder 'bout her name?"

"Her lies cast but a dim light on the trifling matter of her name."

"Her lies?"

"Aye," said Iain, "the lass'd have me believe she was on her way to a convent when struck the storm."

Duncan scowled with his own disbelief. "Going to tuck that face away in a convent?"

"She says aye."

Duncan nodded briefly and voiced his ideas for the day ahead. "We'll see how the snows have fallen. If they stayed up here in the hills, we'll make good time once we get down. If the entire area is blanketed, will be a slow go."

"But go we will."

"Aye, we'll get back home and dinna we ache for it? But we can no' rest for too long, no' until he's rooted out and destroyed."

Iain concurred. "That bit we heard up at Brim's Ness bears pondering."

"Credible, I'd say," Duncan said. "The man's no' a phantom. And an army of fifty—if those be his numbers—canna go unnoticed and undetected in Caithness for two goddamn winters. Makes sense, then, that he's a Sutherland, finding refuge across the river when he's no' about the industry of those vicious and ungodly attacks."

Iain realized the lass was awake now. Under his hand, he felt her go rigid, though he couldn't know for certain if it had been Duncan's gravelly voice, rising with his frustration over their inability to find the ghostlike Alpin, or the mention of the name Sutherland that had roused her and braced her. He recalled that last night she'd asked if he were a Mackay.

More of the linen wimple covering her head appeared as she lifted her face above the fur. She pushed away from his chest with motions jolting enough to suggest she was embarrassed to have been so close. Some mumbled sound, which he thought might have been an apology, went with her as she moved away from him, sliding her hip out from under his hand. It occurred to him then to wonder at his own actions, that he had kept his hand on her person, with such unfounded familiarity. He shrugged internally, thinking the lass hadn't given any indication in their short conversation that she was the type to grouse overloud about such a thing, being that it was fairly harmless, even if she likewise questioned it.

"There you be, lass," said his captain as she rolled onto her back. Her face swiveled toward him. "I'd be Duncan, captain to the lad's army." He inclined his head in Iain's direction. "That'll be Iain McEwen, Laird of Berriedale, kin to Donald Mackay, defender of Scotland's freedom, so on and so forth."

"Oh," said the lass, turning back and raising a brow at Iain at this exaggerated announcement of his identity. Facing Duncan again, she said simply, "I am Maggie. Margaret Bryce, actually. Pleased to meet you, sir. And many thanks for your kindness to a stranger."

"Aye, we could no let you freeze to death," said Duncan with a charming grin, one he likely hadn't used in years, Iain was sure. "The lad says you're destined for a nunnery?" he asked, his tone intimating his incredulity.

This did not go undetected by the lass. "Have you and your laird something against a woman taking lifetime vows, her heart pledged to the Lord?" Her tone was light while she addressed Duncan. "Your laird gave off a likewise dubious aura that you have me wondering that I should be questioning my life choices."

"Aye, and dinna let us contradict you, lass. The thing is, you're a mite too bonny for the cloth, I'd have guessed."

"Sir," she returned, a hint of laughter heard, "are you suggesting I might not satisfy the Lord—"

"I'd no' suggest any such thing, lass," said Duncan quickly, "but there's plenty of earthly men might like to take you to bride, be sore at the Lord for taking up the bonny ones."

"Good heavens, Sir Duncan," the lass said, still the suggestion of humor in her tone, "I hope I don't get turned away at the gate—either at the abbey or in front of St. Peter—because as you say, I'm bonny."

Duncan laughed, rather loudly, that Iain detected movement around him, as others woke. "Och now, lass. It's just Duncan. We're the informal kind, no sirs hereabouts. But aye, I'm sure the good Lord welcomes all to His army. But just so you ken, there'll be plenty of lads crying while your dear God rejoices."

So there it was, Iain thought, and just like that. Duncan, who had barely noticed any female in all the years Iain had known him as a man, was right smitten with the lass who likely only pretended she'd been called to take up with vows to serve God.

As the morning would come soon, and as so many of them seemed to be wakeful now, Iain sat up and rolled his shoulders, moving the kinks and aches and pains away from his neck. He stood and Duncan did likewise, stretching and groaning as he normally did.

Iain faced the lass, hands on his hips. Maggie was her name. Seemed to fit, he thought. Maggie of the green eyes and beguiling smile.

She wasn't looking at him, but at Hew, who had made his bed just beyond where Duncan had. Hew had pushed the furs off him, was putting his boots back onto his feet.

"That's Hew," Iain said to her. "You've him to thank for your dry hose and warm feet."

"My name is Maggie," she said brightly, "and I do thank you. All of you," she finished, turning her gaze around to each man 'round the fire.

Duncan went around, pointed to each man. "There's Donal and Daimh—you can see their mam thought they were so pretty there should be two of them. And Archie, his heart's as ugly as his mug. And that's Craig, to whom you need only speak slowly and use simple words."

She grinned at all this while each man stared at her, none of them offended by their introductions, nothing they hadn't heard before.

Iain watched Hew, who had turned his gaze to her now that she wasn't staring directly at him. The lad would not be able to cope with that, being the recipient of such singular attention from one so bonny. Hew was completely still, his arms slung over his bent knees, his fingers idle near his calves where he'd let them stay after donning his boots. He just watched her, seemed pleased to be able to do so, stared at her with some kind of wonder, as if she truly were some fae creature. The boy was mesmerized, Iain could easily see. Duncan had noticed this as well, Iain saw, and they exchanged grins.

Iain and Duncan walked over to the opening of the cave to survey the results of the storm. They'd not been able to see much last night of its progression, and even now, this gray morning predawn light would show them little, perhaps.

The man made outer wall had been crafted and placed in such a way that the opening was situated at the left side of the wall. The wall then faced completely north, but the opening, at the corner, was further along the ledge of the cave and faced the west. Only the jutting side of the hill, further outside the opening, had kept the winds from blowing directly into the cave.

They moved along the ledge, until they were completely outside the cave, putting themselves immediately into knee high snow drifts.

"*Jesu*," Duncan breathed.

All that they could see was white—the ground, the trees, the sky. Though the wind no more seethed with any wickedness, it continued to snow, that the vista painted before them was no more than an endless blank canvas of white.

"Like as no, we ride off the hill, we ride away from the worst of it," Duncan supposed.

Iain wasn't so sure. "I'll take Donal with me, ride on down ahead, see how it looks from below." He gave a call to the older twin and within minutes they'd left the relative warmth and safety of the cave.

Chapter Five

MAGGIE WATCHED THE laird, Iain McEwen, wrap himself up in the very fur under which they'd slept and step outside with one of the handsome twins.

The older man, Duncan, must have sensed a question in her gaze while he stood across the fire from her. "Naught to fuss over, lass. They're only aimed at the bottom of the hill, to see what might be noted about the complete effects of this weather."

She nodded and accepted a flask from the lad, Hew.

"'Tis only water," he said to her when she sniffed at the small round opening. She drank only a bit, having some concern that she already had to relieve herself and any more liquid in her system would only make that dilemma worse.

"Aye, now, and stop gawking at the lass as much, Hew," instructed Duncan. "Any of you. The fair Maggie is bound to be a bride of our good Lord, and no' meant for such depravity as you're likely imagining with her."

The man named Craig looked up at Duncan and then to Maggie, and then back to Duncan, clearly having no idea of what his captain spoke. Daimh tossed a rock into the fire, pretending a great distress that Maggie was quite sure was feigned. The man Archie moved his tongue around his teeth inside his mouth, as if he worked to remove some bit of lodged food, which seemed unlikely as it was possible they hadn't eaten in as long as she had not. He stared at her while he did so, and Maggie had the impression she was meant to be cowed by his hard stare while he pretended to take her measure. She was not intimidated by him, but in fact decided fairly quickly that he only liked people to be afraid of him, but that he wasn't actually very mean.

She returned the flask to Hew with a smile of appreciation, finding the youngest man's clear blue eyes fixed upon her yet again, or still, despite Duncan's notice. Sitting upon her rump, she drew her knees up, nearly to her chest, wrapping her arms around them. It wasn't very ladylike, though she did make sure the many layers of her numerous skirts covered all of her limbs, and even her stocking-ed toes. She'd abandoned the fur blanket when she'd originally sat up this morn, and would have drawn it up and around her now but that the man, Iain, had taken it with him. The fire had been stoked and blazed attractively, but it was still very cold in this cave.

"Where were you coming from and going to when you were caught in the storm?" She asked Hew.

"Going home," said Hew with a smile, as if he'd delivered greater news than this. "Been gone for months now, all over Caithness and further south."

"Chasing the devil named Alpin," Duncan added, lifting a brow to Maggie. "Ever hear of such a name? Or the mayhem he's been charged with?"

Maggie shook her head, the name not being at all familiar to her. "Is he a bandit or—?"

"That and more, aye," Hew supplied. "Thieving and raping and murdering all over the place."

"Oh, my."

"Been carrying on for two years," said Archie.

Next to him, Duncan nodded thoughtfully, his gaze transfixed by the fire. "More devil than man," he said. Very quietly, he told this tale: "Took twelve churchmen from the monastery up at Wick and nailed horseshoes to their feet. Made them sing and dance for the entertainment of his men. This went on for more than a day, so say some. Gelded a few, hung them all in the end. Burned the priory and the fields to the ground. Dinna even bother to justify this abhorrence with any robbing of the place. Took nothing, seemed he only wanted the amusement."

"Aye, a sick bastard, he is," Archie said, his hands on his hips, staring likewise blindly into the fire.

Maggie was overcome with the senseless brutality of the tale and knew from the somberness that invaded these men now, that they had witnessed some part of this, mayhap had come upon the wreckage of this Alpin's horrid violence. How awful. She gave some brief thought to how fortunate she was, or had been, in her short life. She had ofttimes bemoaned the lack of true love from her sire and the dreariness of her little life in Torish, and even now, the fate that had been extended to her, marriage to Kenneth Sutherland; but she had never known a horror such as those poor souls did, had not ever been the victim of any true violence or injustice. She ought to remind herself more often of her own blessed circumstance.

"There was more brutality," Hew said. "Small village near Helmsdale, entirely wiped out. Came across them days later, bodies scattered everywhere—men, women, children. The slices in their throats were the least of the harm done to them."

"But he must be stopped," Maggie said.

"Aye, lass," agreed Duncan. "And that's what we're about."

The laird and the twin named Donal returned shortly, looking like two snow monsters, the white precipitation clinging to almost every part of them, hair and fur, and breeches and boots. They both shook off much of this near the door, removing their furs and flapping them about to rid them of the moisture and the cold. They stomped their feet and ruffled their hands through their hair, until most of the snow had been removed and they once again looked human.

The laird shook his head in answer to the probing glances thrown his way. He walked around the fire, saying, "We'll go nowhere today. Maybe no' for several days. Deep as a horse's belly even at the bottom of the hill. And heavy." He moved around the circle of the fire, behind the people sitting so close. When he stood behind Maggie, he flicked the fur once more, away from her and behind him, and then settled the whole thing over her shoulders. "No sign of clearing," he said, as if he hadn't just done the most kindhearted and remarkable thing, remarkable in that it was so casual an action, as if he regularly offered his cloak to cold women in need. "Sky looks the same in every direction."

"Winds have died down," Donal added, plopping down next to his brother, "but that'll no work in our favor."

Duncan nodded, understanding immediately. "Storm could hover for days, just over our heads."

"Aye," said Iain, "and we'll need to plan for just that. Need to hunt and heat more water, get the horses fed."

"I'll get to the hunting," said Archie, spitting into the fire. "I'll go batty if I've to stay too long in this small space." He looked around the group. "Come on then, Craig. I'll no want to be aggrieved by the yapping of either of them." He inclined his head to the twins. "And if we're lost, I imagine you're the one to get me back."

Craig nodded, possibly understanding only that he was expected to leave the cave with Archie, and stood and dressed as the old man did, bundling up for the cold and the hunt.

There was some discussion between Duncan and Archie about whether they would actually be fishing or hunting, supposing if they could find a loch named Calder, and it wasn't frozen, they might stand a greater chance of catching fish than trying to find any critter—or better, something larger—that wasn't hunkered down in its own den or lair, same as the hunters were.

Iain sat down, taking the blank spot next to Maggie. He inclined his head to her but said nothing directly, holding out his hands closer to the fire, chafing away the cold. Maggie noticed just now his plaid, which she hadn't before as he'd mostly been covered by a fur. The thick woolen fabric was draped over one shoulder, the pleats and folds not so neat as a laird might normally wear them. The McEwen plaid was colored with earthen green and brown threads, altogether rather subtle and subdued in tone. The Sutherland tartan was of bold colors, green and blue and red; Maggie had seen it often, had always been struck by how vibrant the Sutherland colors were against the drab gray lives of Sutherland's lesser folk.

The laird caught her staring at his shoulder, his head turned to the right to consider her.

"I feel rather useless, just sitting here," she admitted. "Isn't there something that I might do to be helpful?"

Duncan answered before his laird did. "Aye, now, you just sit there being bonny, lass. That's all we'll ask of you."

While Maggie favored the captain with a smile for his politeness, Iain McEwen shrugged and said, "None of us will be doing much. And there's no' so much to do now but wait." And then, with a tilt of his head and the barest hint of a grin, he added, "Aye, but you might be praying on us, lass, you being more devout than any of us regular heathens."

Something about his tone and the quirk of his lips suggested that he mocked her, but Maggie could not be sure, and so only replied with a nod.

The morning stretched on, with the twins taking care of most of the conversation as they huddled around the fire. It was not hard to like those two; handsomeness aside, they showed no concern over their circumstance, proved extremely capable of entertaining themselves—and others by way of the close proximity—with their talk and their play. At one point, they both lay on their bellies, facing each other, their arms presented forward, their hands intertwined, while it seemed the goal was to send the back of the other man's hand to the ground. Daimh proved victorious, and then ignored his brother's demand of another try. After a while though, even the twins seemed to run out of energy and settle down.

The day would be long, with naught to do but sit and wait. When she could stand it no more, towards late morning, Maggie leaned toward the McEwen laird and quietly asked of him where or how she might take care of her personal needs.

"Aye," he said, nodding and standing. "Sorry, lass, I should have thought of this earlier." He stretched out his hand, into which Maggie put her own.

She nearly gasped, the warmth of his fingers shocking her as he pulled her to her feet. She'd kept her fingerless gloves on, but her hands were still very cold, and his were absolutely not, that she did not at all resist when he squeezed her fingers and did not immediately release them.

"We're no' used to having female company, lass," he explained.

Standing next to him now, his full size was revealed to her. He easily stood a head taller than her, and so much power was revealed in the breadth of his chest and shoulders. She thought he might be twice as wide as her and very little of this could be attributed to his clothing or gear, as he was garbed now in only his tunic and plaid. She was made almost breathless by his physical presence, by the aura of sheer strength that emanated from him.

He glanced around the cave, causing Maggie some concern now, hoping he didn't think she was going to relieve herself amidst these close quarters.

Duncan must have heard Maggie's request, that he advised, "Might want to hie up to the next hut there, lad."

"Aye," agreed the laird. Iain McEwen lifted the fur again, the one he'd covered her with earlier, that she'd allowed to slide off her shoulders when she'd risen. "Wrap up, lass. I'll have to carry you or you'll be drenched in snow to your belly."

Oh, my. How awkward, she thought, embarrassed now for her need and for the nuisance it would cause him.

"I should wrap in my cloak, if it's still available. And you make use of the fur, as it is your own." She had some idea that being held in his arms, while awkward, would shield her from the cold.

Hew jumped up and scurried over to a boulder that rather sat in the middle of the cave, collecting what must be her cloak from atop it. He presented this to her, favoring her with a now familiar expression, both eager and intense.

"Thank you, Hew." She shook out the cape and turned it around her shoulders, flipping the hood up over her wimple and latching the frog closures near her neck.

The laird had moved away, strode over to the doorway. Maggie met him there. He'd been staring outside, but turned when she approached, giving her a grin. "All bundled up."

Clenching her fingers, she wondered how he might carry her, having some idea of climbing onto his back as she'd once seen a woman do. The woman, she recalled, had jumped quickly out of the way of a fast moving horse and cart, twisting her ankle in the process; when her husband had come to collect her, she'd been truly unable to put any weight on her foot so that the man had turned his back to his wife, crouching down so that the woman could wrap her arms around his neck; the man had straightened and carried his wife home that way.

Her deliberations proved unnecessary, as the McEwen laird simply bent and scooped her up, one strong arm around her back, the other under her knees. Maggie gasped as he gathered her firmly against his chest and waded out into the snow. She squinted hard against the obscene brightness of the day, tucking her face against him, having not expected the light to hurt her head. Instinctively, she latched onto him, her fingers curled into the fur wrapped around him.

Their progress was slow and plodding. Despite the man's great size, he had to lift his leg up out of the depths of the snow with each step, tilting them left then right, again and again, as they trudged further up the side of the hill. Thankfully, at this elevation the hill was not so steep as it had proved at lower sections, but it was still a very slow progression. His steps were measured and careful, but the snow was deep enough that he lost his balance at one point, tipping precariously toward the ground. Maggie shrieked and grabbed on tighter, pinching her fingers around his neck, hoisting herself up against him when she thought they were going down.

She felt his chuckle under her fingers and against her side and at his face as they were nearly cheek to cheek now. "I'll no' let you fall, Maggie Bryce."

And he did not. He recovered smoothly and carried on, though Maggie still clung fiercely to him, as she'd rather not be dropped or accidentally thrown into the cold and deep snow. Almost in the very next moment, her worry over this was overshadowed by her increasing awareness of their proximity. Maggie was suddenly conscious of the warmth and strength of his flesh under her fingers at his neck, became very aware of how solid and hard he was against her soft curves. Against her ribs, which were pressed firmly to one side of his chest, she felt every movement in the motion of his muscles, rippling heatedly against her. Cold and ice and snow seemed to be lost then, as Maggie could fathom no other sensation but that of his strong body moving. She might have relaxed then, at the sense of strength and security his steadiness offered, but that she was overcome by some other emotion, as yet unnamed, though she knew well it was some reaction to the feel of him.

"You've gone as stiff as a dead steed, lass. Relax."

She tried, she really did, but could not. She could not now pretend she wasn't aware, that she suffered no reaction at all—whatever it was—to being in his arms. But she did turn her face away from his cheek, looking forward, hoping their destination wasn't too much further.

"You've got freckles on your forehead and chin, too," he said with some wonder, telling her that he was watching her and not his footfalls.

This brought her gaze back to him. "They're everywhere," she said, before she thought better of it. Once said, she rather cringed inside, wondering that her statement sounded so intimate.

He lifted a brow at her, one side of his mouth quirking upward.

Perhaps when the ground was not covered by snow that reached to this man's thigh, the trek from the cave to the next hill bothy might only take a minute, or two if made without a purposeful gait; just now, in these conditions, it took almost five minutes, Maggie feeling more and more like a nuisance to this man for the inconvenience.

The third hut sat much like the first, in which the horses had been stashed, with three man-made walls closing in on the rock of the hill as its fourth wall. This one actually had a door, but the winds must have blown it open and the drifting snow then kept it that way, that the snow was blown into the first ten or so feet of the hut. Iain McEwen stepped further inside than the wind-blown snow and finally set Maggie down.

She grimaced at him, sorry for the trouble she'd caused. He wasn't panting from his exertion, but he was clearly breathing harder than when they'd started out.

"I'll step back outside lass. Call when you're ready."

She groaned inwardly with more embarrassment. She wished there was some way to keep her personal business, well, personal. But with nothing else to be done about it, and with her need pressing, Maggie did the best she could in the deepest corner of the shelter. She gave up a length of her innermost linen undergarment, tearing off a good section of the hem and using that as needed, having a bit of a giggle at the thought of the kirtle being hacked away up to her waist if they were trapped out here for too many days.

When she was done, she stepped carefully toward the front of the hut, keeping to the left side wall, where the snow there had not risen higher than her ankle. She called out to the McEwen laird and he appeared a moment later, looking again much as he had earlier, covered in snow almost head to toe. He stood in the light of the door, that she could well see that his hair was a very dark brown, not black as she imagined previously. It was cropped close but unruly, curling at its own discretion, one lock dangling with some charm over his forehead.

She realized he was chewing just as he strode toward her, lifting his hand to show a cluster of bright red-orange berries. With the brilliant white of the snowy day shining into where she stood, Maggie recognized the beady little rowan berries. They were sour, and now likely frozen solid, but she hadn't chewed on anything in more than a day and happily plucked some from the tiny branch he offered, plopping one then another into her mouth.

Immediately, crunching down through the indeed frozen solid berry, she pulled a face at exactly how sour it was.

Iain McEwen chuckled and advised, "Keep chewing, lass. It gets better." He lifted his cupped hand to his mouth, tossing in a few more berries.

He was right. While it didn't get sweeter, the initial sourness definitely lessened with more chewing. While they snacked, he dragged his foot sideways along the ground, clearing a path in the snow to the doorway. Maggie followed his progress and stopped when he did at the opening, still under the canopy of the hut and able to see the entire north side of the hill. They stood there, side by side, watching the snow fall, quiet just now as was everything around them.

He plucked three or four more berries from the vine and dropped them into her hand.

"I suppose it would be lovely, if this were in fact a house—with all the blessed amenities—and not a hovel on the side of a hill," she commented.

"Very peaceful," he said.

"That seems like something a laird or soldier," she turned and waved a hand, vaguely indicating his warrior's breastplate and the mighty sword at his hip, "might often find lacking—peace."

"That is so, lass. Canna recall the last time there was peace," he said with a bit of a shrug. "No' in a decade or more, to my thinking."

"I'm sorry for that. Would that all people knew peace."

She stared again at the white blanketed scenery, disturbed only by this man's footprints, and felt him tip his head toward her. "Will you pray for me, sister?"

Maggie turned her face and squinted up at him. He really was very large, standing so close. "Sir, you seem to find great humor in the fact that I will pledge myself to our Lord."

"'Tis no' humor, lass," he said, even as he spoke through a grin, "but a general lack of belief."

"What does that mean?" She frowned, nearly ready to slap her hands onto her hips at whatever he was having fun with.

"It means, lass—or sister, or Maggie Bryce—that I dinna believe for one minute that you are meant to be a woman of the cloth, or that you were on your way to any convent, near or far."

Her frown deepened with his words. "What are you saying?"

And now he laughed outright, and truly, did he have to be so handsome when he did so, marking his cheeks with long and deep brackets on either side of his mouth, brightening the blue of his eyes to near beauty? "Aye, lass, I said what I said—you're lying to me. I'm no' sure why. I dinna blame you. A lone female, lost in a storm, overtaken—so to speak—by a band of weary soldiers. Was a good play, to go that route, inject the safety of the Lord between yourself and any nefarious designs we Mackays might have on you."

"But I—"

"Aye, it's fine, lass. I dinna hold it against you." He held up his hands, palms facing her, while the smile still played about his lips.

Maggie clamped her lips together. Why, the impertinence! Never mind that he was right, that she lied to him, but to call her on it! And really, it was only partly a lie; she wouldn't have been allowed to enter the convent, her father having greater plans for her, but it had been—just before the storm had come—her most recent intention. With a lift of her chin, she said with some snap, "Think what you will. I may not be the most pious person, but my plan suits me greatly and it *is* what I shall do."

He shrugged. "As you will, sister."

"You don't believe me still?" She rather needed him to since she'd asked him for escort to the convent. "But you've said you would take me to St. Edmund's." She did now plant her fisted hands onto her hips.

It was the McEwen laird's turn to frown. "Lass, I said I'd show you the direction. I'll no' be driving my men one hundred miles in the opposite direction, when we're so close to home."

Of course, she could not force him. And they had already done so much for her. She nodded, trying not to show too much upset. When the idea had formed in her head yesterday afternoon, she'd had no plan for an escort, had thought she might negotiate the countryside alone to reach the abbey; she would be then, when they parted ways after the storm, in the same circumstance as yesterday, only with three feet of snow to trudge through. Maggie bit her bottom lip and glanced down, flexing her cold fingers now in front of her. She lifted her gaze again to him, found him watching her intently, his smile gone.

"Is it really a hundred miles?"

His broad shoulders lifted and fell again. "Sixty? Eighty? One hundred? 'Tis all the same in this clime, aye, lass?"

Maggie's own shoulders slumped with dejection. "Aye, I suppose." She guessed she might just hold out longer inside the cave, maybe even after the McEwen Mackays had gone, wait until the countryside offered a kinder earth to negotiate. Absently, she plucked another berry from the nearly bare cluster he still held. She chewed thoughtfully, considering any other option until she felt his eyes still upon her. Straightening her shoulders, she tried to smile for his benefit. Of course, this man shouldn't be concerned with any stranger's ruined plans. 'Twas neither his concern nor his business. And it would be even less so if he discovered that she was actually set to marry a Sutherland.

"Aye now, dinna fuss," he said as some consolation. "We'll figure out how to get you to your nunnery."

The laughter had returned to his voice, she thought, but shone not in his eyes just now when she met them again. Though the berries had left no mark or stain, she swiped her hands together and asked, "Shall we return? I think I might manage the trek myself, since you've so kindly made such a nice path." She stepped forward, considering the slogged through snow disgruntledly. It was not actually a very clear path, only deep snow with deep impressions of each of his steps.

She gathered her skirts at the front of her, thinking she might hold them aloft, out of the snow when she was again scooped up into the arms of the McEwen laird. A startled, "Oomph," escaped with her surprise.

"It's still too deep, lass," was all he said, holding her high up against his chest.

Maggie shifted, meaning to bring her arms up around his neck but he stopped suddenly, just outside the hut and turned right, toward the hill.

"Pluck some berries, lass," he said, tipping his head toward the smoothed bark tree growing on the side of the hill, "for the lads."

Maggie glanced up, and did as instructed, using both hands to snap off several berry clusters, wrestling with a few stubborn ones. There were not so many left and the clusters she could reach no longer contained the usual generous number of berries, likely having been feasted on by birds and critters since last fall. But she collected several, laying them against her folded belly, until the laird said that was plenty and conveyed them back to the cave. While he walked, Maggie organized the clusters so that she held them efficiently by the broken part of each thin branch, all in one hand.

Chapter Six

IAIN SET HER DOWN GENTLY once returned to the much warmer cave. Maggie brushed off what little snow the hem of her cloak had accumulated and presented their bounty to the men while Iain McEwen again went about removing all the snow from his person.

Maggie walked around, doling out near equal shares to each man, saving two extra shares for Archie and Craig who were not yet returned. She took her spot next to Duncan and the laird sat on her other side in the next moment. Stretching her hands out to the low burning blaze, she glanced around. They were all so quiet, munching on the gift of the berries, most gazes occupied by the mesmerizing lure of the fire—save for Hew, who was watching her from the other side of Duncan. Reflexively, Maggie smiled at him. He nodded and smiled back with some stiffness before removing his gaze from her.

And while she by no means considered herself an extrovert, rarely having found herself in larger gatherings, she thought the air about them was both dull and depressed. Perhaps they were accustomed to it, the silence; perhaps it was only awkward to her because she was the outsider, was unused to keeping company with all men. But was it normal that they only sat and stared and made no conversation? Not even the twins, who had seemed to her so jovial and garrulous earlier, made any attempt at chatter. The one she thought was Daimh—she hadn't truly determined any significant difference in them; if they changed seats, she would not know—had fallen back on his pallet, one knee bent, the other leg thrown over it, his foot swinging.

Another minute went by. Maggie listened. Yet even the fire made no noise.

Turning toward Hew, she found his gaze upon her once again. She liked the lad, guessed him about an age with her, and thought there were possibly many a lass at home who were charmed by his easy good looks, pitch black hair and intense blue eyes, his face as of yet unbothered by so much facial hair. Mayhap with persons he was more familiar with, he would behave with less...intensity.

"Have you a big family, Hew," she wondered, "awaiting your return?"

He shook his head before he spoke. "Only me and my mam, lass," he said, moving forward on his pallet, so that less of Duncan blocked his view. "Da' was gone at Stirling Bridge and my brother at Falkirk."

"I am sorry to hear that," she said genuinely. "Thankfully, you still have your mam."

"Aye," said Daimh, from his prone position, "but ever'one's had Hew's mam."

Donal guffawed at this and Duncan shook his head, though he said nothing. Maggie watched Hew's telling cheeks pinken once again.

Maggie frowned and turned toward the laird at her other side. He shook his head as well, giving her a look which she interpreted to mean, *leave it, it's just what they do.*

Her brow furrowed more. That was unacceptable to her. But then it wasn't her place, certainly, to take these men to task over their behavior. However, she could remove the attention from the lad, so that they were given no opportunity to tease him.

"And what about you, Duncan? Wife? Bairns?"

"Nae, lass," he said, his fingers entwined, hands dangling over his bent knees. "Just me. Had a wife, way back when. Aye, but she's long gone."

"I'm sorry," she said, afraid to ask anyone else of their familial situation, lest she uncover more sad stories.

"I'm no'," Duncan said, keeping his gaze on the small flames. "Aye, she were a shrew, truth be told. Ran off with some farmer, went down to Glasgow. I dinna care enough to chase her. *Jesu*, bring back all that nagging and caterwauling?" He harrumphed. "No' for me."

Maggie couldn't decide if his tale or Hew's was the more sorrowful one.

"But what about you, lass?" Duncan thought to ask.

Maggie shrugged. "Same as most, I'm sure, lost some person to war. My father is alive but my brother fell at some place called Roslin" —several of them nodded, Donal made a critical noise, all of them apparently acquainted with the battle— "which left only me and my sister, and she married years ago, went down to Perth and perished with her babe in the birthing." She found Donal's sympathetic gaze on her. Seeking to improve the somber mood, she said with some lightness to the twin, "But you two are the only children of your parents, I'm guessing."

He lifted a brow at her. "Aye, but how can you ken this?"

Daimh sat up, frowning quizzically at her.

"You both have an air about you—sometimes very charming—that says you've not ever been denied too much," she said, and added, mischievously, "from your mam and mayhap not any woman." While Maggie had always had what some called an unnatural ability to read people, this guess was easy—these brothers were entirely too lighthearted, all things considered, to have been anything other than spoiled bairns.

Duncan barked out a laugh beside her. "She's pegged you proper, lads."

Daimh squinted at her. "What else do you think you might ken about us?"

Maggie considered them and recalled their play and conversation earlier. "You are the firstborn," she guessed—correctly, it seemed, when Duncan chuckled again beside her. "And you," she said to Donal, "are the more intelligent one."

"Canna argue with that," said Donal.

To both of them, she speculated, "Everything is a competition between you, but neither of you think you are better than the other."

The twins glanced at each other, Daimh shrugging while Donal nodded with consideration.

"Might be," said Daimh.

There was some noise then just outside the cave. In amazing synchrony, every man around her leapt to their feet and drew their swords, only relaxing when Archie and Craig appeared at the entrance. Neither of the two hunters seemed aggrieved by the poor reception, Archie lifting his hand to show a line of strung fish, his scowl evidently a perpetual thing, not removed with the advent of his success. Those two spent some time near the entrance, not advancing to the group and the fire until they'd removed what snow they could.

Iain McEwen did not retake his seat, but met the two men, receiving the fish from Archie while Craig showed his laird a bundle of twigs and sticks in his meaty, ungloved paw. The three men hovered near the front, possibly making some preparations to the fish.

"Aye, do me now," begged Hew, getting back to Maggie's seeming ability to read a person as he sat back down.

"Och, you'd like that, would you no', lad?" Teased Daimh, pretending to misunderstand Hew's request.

"Enow! Quit with your prattle," Duncan chided, finally with some conviction.

"What might you ken about me?" Hew persisted.

Maggie likewise ignored Daimh and pivoted on her bottom to face Hew, giving him the same calculating look she'd given the twins. "Hmm, I'll state the obvious, of course, that you are the most sincere in the group," she turned her gaze around, over the others, "no offense, good sirs." She faced Hew again. "You aren't afraid of things that you should be but show fear over those that you should not." The lowering of his brows, while he considered this, suggested she might be on to something. "Altogether, you are the extreme in almost any group in which you find yourself—the most sincere, the most intelligent, the most respectful, the most loyal perhaps–and yet you doubt yourself the most." And then she smiled at him. "But of course, you should not."

He nodded at her and Maggie sipped from the shared flask, which had lain at her feet. She hoped that Duncan or the laird didn't ask for an intuitive reading, as she was quite sure she didn't know what to make of either of them. The captain was solid and dependable, she guessed, a calm and reasonable presence when needed, but with some ability to fly off the handle when his hackles were raised or his patience at an end. The laird…? She could only know, as of yet, that he was considerate of others, very easy to look upon, and that his eyes could delve deep into her soul, so probing and intense were some of his stares. And that he believed her a liar.

She felt Hew's continued scrutiny as she lowered the flask. She smiled at him, not at all unnerved by his constant attention. She felt only that he wished to talk but didn't have any ideas about what he might say.

"Do all of you have specific jobs inside the army, Hew?"

"Aye," he said, pushing his body forward. He went nowhere, simply expressed his readiness to talk, perhaps thankful for the question. "Of course, we've all the single goal of Scotland's freedom, but I, myself, am normally tasked with the logistics of any move."

She was sorry she didn't know what this meant, but then pleased to ask, thus giving him further reason to speak, as it seemed to be his want. "I'm not familiar with that. What does that involve?"

"Well, whenever we plan for a large movement, like the one that took us off on the last campaign, there is much to organize. The chief will plan the route and the captain will put out the call to arms, but all the little things—which turn out to be quite significant—need to be readied." He ticked off on his fingers the different examples. "Horses need to be provided, if we've called more than soldiers; food stuffs need to be prepared, stored and transported; wagons of replacements of arms and boots and shields and a myriad of other things need to be collected, and drivers hired; and log books kept, tracking each item and person included on the campaign."

The more he spoke, the easier it became for him. Maggie was very pleased by this.

"You are likely perfect for that job," she supposed, "as I imagine this requires great attention to detail and a very deliberate sense of order and efficiency, at which you likely excel."

"Aye, it does," he responded with some bit of awe, that she'd deduced as much about the position, and him. "Of course, this now, what we're about, is different, as we broke off at the end of the campaign," he explained. "We've had to address our needs day by day."

Archie came to the fire then, looking older and wearier than before he'd left. Maggie stretched around the fire to hand a branch of berries to him. He seemed surprised at the offering, or that the gesture had come from her. But he took the fruit, giving a curt nod of thanks.

The laird and Craig joined them after another few minutes, Craig carrying a tray of sorts, which he'd obviously woven together from those twigs he'd clenched in his hand moments ago. It was flat and not completely solid, resembling the wattle fence Maggie sometimes wove for her kitchen gardens at home. The fish, eleven small cod unless she was mistaken, were laid out haphazardly to fit across the top of the tray. Maggie was surprised when only a few rocks were rearranged to hold the tray of fish, being only a few inches above the highest flame, seeming precariously close.

"But won't the woven sticks catch fire?" Maggie asked.

"Aye, they'll burn," said Iain. "But they're wet and by the time they burn through, the fish will be cooked."

Archie said, through a mouthful of the rowan berries, "The lad made some traps, set them under the ice in the loch. Might be easier tomorrow, just go down and collect what's caught, if any."

Maggie remembered the last cluster of berries and passed them around to Craig.

"How's it look out there, further away?" Duncan wanted to know.

"Snow is everywhere," Craig said simply, having taken his seat between Hew and Daimh, accepting the fruit from Daimh without any question as to its origin.

Archie rolled his eyes at this vague description, and further explained, "It's no' an easy go, even half mile away from this hill. The horses dinna like it so deep and heavy, had to prod them along constantly. We'll go nowhere anytime soon."

"Have any of you ever been stranded like this?" Maggie wondered. "For any length of time?"

"Winter of '03, just before Roslin as a matter of fact," Duncan said, inclining his head past Iain to Archie. "You recall that storm? Nestled us in with the Cameron army for nigh on a week. Out in the heather, no' a cave or hill or tree around, trying to get down to Comyn and Fraser—nearly missed the battle."

"Could've done without that one," Archie said.

The twins, perhaps enlivened by the prospect of a meal, maintained a steady stream of conversation once again. At one point, Daimh very casually said to Archie, "You'd heard about the poor simpleton down there in Dunbeath, aye?" At Archie's blank look, Daimh went on, "The one delivering the babe? Och, but she was in some pain and the ordeal was getting on too long that the midwife, with candle in hand, made to inspect her secret area, to see if the bairn was coming at all. The poor creature says to the midwife, *Aye, look on the other side also as my husband sometimes takes that road as well.*"

Equal amounts of groans and laughter followed this, while Maggie lowered her head to hide her own smile at this bawdy yarn, delivered so sincerely that she'd expected a true story coming.

Without missing a beat, Donal said, "Aye, and wasn't she the mam to the little boy who'd wanted to ken if the father he'd never met might have some disfigurement as well that had given the boy the lump on his back. The mam wondered, *Why would you think that?* and the boy says to her, *I just have a hunch.*"

This absurdity was greeted by decidedly more moans than chuckles. Maggie clapped her hand over her mouth, caught by surprise again at such silliness from these warriors. She caught the laird's eye, her own crinkled with laughter over her hand.

He rolled his eyes and told her, "You are fresh ears to their old jokes, lass. Hunker down, they've got more to share."

"Good heavens, but I hope they improve," she said, keeping her grin while she lowered her hand. "Those are awful."

"You can do better?" Donal challenged, his grin as handsome as the rest of him.

Gamely, Maggie said, "I think I can."

"Let's have it, lass," enthused Daimh.

Hoping they didn't require too many examples, as she had so few to share, she said after a moment of thought, "Well, one day I came upon a group of lads having some competition," she began, hardly able to refrain from smiling while she told the tale. "They were using bows and arrows, trying to shoot an apple off some poor lad's head, if you can believe it. So the first lad takes his turn and slices the apple perfectly in two, each part falling down either side of the boy's head. The shooter thumps his chest proudly and declares, *I'm William!* so that all will know of his triumph. The lads all cheer. The next archer takes a shot and he, too, slices another apple right down the middle. He exclaims with his success, *I'm Robert!* Another boy takes his turn, but his aim is not so good," she said with a grimace, "and he shouts out, *I'm sorry*!"

Maggie held her grimace, while no one made a sound.

And then they all burst out laughing and groaning at the same time, led by Duncan's loud chortle.

"Aye, lass," cried out the captain, "You fit right in, you do!"

"Just as dreadful as ours!" Daimh said, slapping his knee.

Maggie turned to Iain McEwen, who was staring at her with something akin to horror, his mouth agape. Playfully, she leaned over and nudged her shoulder against the laird. "Aye now, it wasn't so terrible."

He smiled finally, shaking his head at her. The crinkling of his eyes was now familiar to her. She decided she liked it very much.

"Aye, it was a wee bit worse, lass. You're making the lads look like regular mummers."

IAIN MCEWEN WATCHED her tease a grinning Hew that if he thought he could do better, he was welcome to try. Her laughter was decidedly infectious, but Iain didn't know quite what to make of this lass.

She had no fear, or none that wasn't—or hadn't been—swiftly tamped down. She amused herself with these men as if she'd known them forever. She was capable of putting out silly anecdotes and pretty blushes and inexplicable lies, while possessed of an enviable temperament and apparently an inherent ability to rather glide along with whatever life threw at her.

She was...remarkable.

Sometime later, after they'd eaten, when naught but bones remained of their tiny feast, he watched her use a sparse amount of water from the flask that Hew had been sharing with her to clean her fingers. Her hands were small and blue veined, but efficient in all their movements. She'd removed those silly gloves some time ago, mayhap before she'd taken the pieces of fish into her hands.

He tried to remove his gaze, thought others made some effort not to stare as well here and there. Save for Hew, who unaccountably suffered no qualms about openly ogling her, though honest to God, Iain would swear the lass was either immune to it or oblivious. Maybe only polite, he considered, intent on stirring no fuss over the lad's regular gawking. In his peripheral then, he saw her lift her hands to her wimple. He gave this not much thought, assuming the fabric must get bothersome after a while, rather expecting that she only meant to scratch her scalp a bit or adjust the many layers and folds of the piece.

She did neither, only surprised more than him by completely removing the fabric from her head, revealing a tremendous mass of shiny hair, the shade somewhere between red and blonde. With one tug at the lone ribbon that held it, the entire length of it unfolded around her.

"I said to the lad that we ought...." Archie was saying to Duncan, but his voice slowed and then completely stopped.

Not a person moved. Even Maggie Bryce had gone still. Her gaze darted from one to the next at their sudden quiet, every eye set upon her. Her fingers, run through her hair with the intent of pushing it all back from her forehead, stopped in mid-motion. Her gaze finally landed on Iain.

He gave up any pretense that he hadn't been watching her.

Her mouth fell open. And then clamped shut. Only her eyes moved for a moment, from his left to his right, before she said in a small voice, "I'm sorry...I shouldn't have—I didn't think anyone would mind—"

Several of them spoke at once.

"Och, go on, lass."

"Aye, you get comfortable."

"No bother to me."

"That's a powerful wealth of hair, lass."

This last came from Archie, whose tone possibly hinted at some concern for the weight and upkeep of it. He hadn't misspoken, the mass of it fell in thick waves over her shoulders and tumbled carelessly down her back, the ends of it nearly touching the ground between Iain and her.

Nervously, she fussed with the wimple, her freckled cheeks glowing pink by the light of the fire. Thinking she intended to return the wimple to her head, Iain placed his hand over the fabric and her hand, stilling her. She lifted her green eyes to his again, her worry sincere.

"It's fine, lass. More comfortable, aye?"

"You only startled the lads," Duncan chimed in. "Haven't seen anything that bonny since the last time Archie smiled at us."

She laughed, still nervous, and sent Duncan a winning smile. Her hands stilled though, and she quipped, with a recovery that was quickly becoming endearing to Iain, "I don't suppose any of you would have a comb?"

"You'll get your gawking, lass, but no' a comb," Duncan said cheerily.

"But how do you comb your own hair?" She wondered.

"With our hands, lass," said Duncan.

"Sometimes with Hew's hands," Donal added. "Much softer than my own."

This spawned more laughter, and conversation resumed, even as so many pairs of eyes kept on Maggie Bryce and her magnificent bounty of hair. While she listened to the talk around her, she very slowly and with bare motions braided the length of her hair, evidently wanting to draw no more attention to herself. A few minutes later, she stood, appearing at first to only need to stretch her legs, walking around the circle of men, and then pacing a bit at the deepest part of the cave. She returned and addressed all of them, "Whom might I trouble this time to escort me to the bothy further up the hill?"

Hew leaned forward eagerly, which had Iain wondering if the lad, though proficient with a long blade, had the strength to carry her such a distance, and through the deep snow. But before Hew, or even Iain could claim the job, Daimh, who sat directly in front of where the lass stood, jumped up and offered himself.

The lass smiled kindly at the twin and arranged her hood once again over her head as she and Daimh made their way to the entrance. The lad said something to her, Iain could not hear what, and she turned and grinned at him, returning some words that had Daimh chuckling in appreciation. Iain's brows lowered over watchful eyes, and then more so when Daimh playfully made a generous bow to her and she answered this with a not-unimpressive curtsy before they laughed yet more and Daimh lifted her into his arms.

Chewing the inside of his cheek, Iain kept his gaze on the opening while Archie and Duncan engaged in some heated debate over what Robert Bruce's best chance at success might be in the near future. Duncan thought diplomacy was his only hope at this point, winning over the Scottish earls first, the church second, and the people after that; Archie scoffed at Duncan's idea, saying that more battles, fought to take back from England what was rightfully theirs, was the only course of action that would keep the crown upon his head, and make him a true king.

Iain lent only half an ear to this discussion. When it seemed more than enough time had passed for Daimh and the lass to have gone and returned, Iain rose and strode to the doorway. The earlier brightness had given way to a distressing gray, the sky and clouds heavier with still more snow, it seemed. He stepped out of the cave, further along the ledge, and glanced up toward the third hut. The pair was nowhere to be seen, must still be within that next bothy.

Returning to the circle around the fire, Iain found Archie's gaze settled upon him, his lieutenant's brow lifted with a vague question, which Iain ignored. It was another ten minutes before Daimh and the lass returned. They all but bounded into the cave, as if Daimh had tripped in his last few steps. Maggie Bryce had her hands locked around the twin's neck, much as she'd held onto Iain earlier, and the two of them were laughing again, seeming even cozier than they had when they'd left the cave. Even when Daimh set her down, they remained there at the entrance, standing face to face, sharing a quiet conversation.

"Daimh," Iain called out, "since you're already wet and cold, might well hie down to check the horses, bring back more kindling as well."

Iain would have termed the look Daimh threw to him as disgruntled, but the lad did as he was bade and left the cave again. Thus, Maggie Bryce took her place once more between Iain and Duncan, laying the hood of her cloak down around her slim shoulders.

"It's not even true nightfall," she commented, "and I'm exhausted."

"Aye, the less you do, the less you can do," Duncan said sagely.

"Just sitting here, getting weaker," added Archie. "Too little food and no' enough motion, and it'll only get worse, you ken."

"But then we probably cannot do too much," she supposed, "and sap what little energy we do have?"

"Aye, that's the right of it, lass," Duncan agreed.

She turned to Iain and said in a near whisper, "Is there any chance that we might go to sleep and not wake up, just freeze to death while we slumber?"

The abnormal gloom of her query rather surprised him. But he answered truthfully, "The longer we are stuck, the greater becomes that possibility. But aye, we'll force our way out and down well before it comes to that. You'll no' freeze to death, Maggie Bryce."

This seemed to mollify her. "Very good."

Sometime later, whatever wind blew outside the cave must have shifted direction, that the smoke from the fire did not escape but clouded the whole of the interior, that they had no choice but to extinguish the small blaze.

It was dusk now, not truly late enough to find their beds if these had been normal circumstances, but they were rather forced to do so to maintain warmth.

"Tighten up, lads," Duncan instructed, and each man shifted his pallet, shrinking the circle so that it resembled more of a horseshoe, as all their bodies were closer together.

"We'll rest now," Iain said to Maggie.

Duncan had already laid down, on his side with his back to Maggie. Iain waited, watched her assess their closer circumstance and choose to lay on her side facing him. He did likewise, arranging his fur over the both of them. Only their very close proximity allowed him to see her. Indeed, they were close enough, all of them, that he felt Archie's rump at his back and the lass's drawn up knees at the front of his thighs.

"It's close quarters, to be sure," he said, by way of apology for this situation, "but we'll be warmer for it." He felt rather than saw her nod.

Some did sleep immediately. He could hear Craig snoring, hear Donal's normal nasal whine of slumber, and not much else. The lass slept, too, her hands held tightly at her chest between them.

Chapter Seven

THE NEXT DAY PASSED much as had the one before, with the seven of them seated around the fire most of the time. Some came and went, Donal and Hew taking turns seeing to the horses, scrounging up what feed they could; Archie and Craig tramped down to the loch, returned an hour later with the bad news that the trap had snared no fish, and Archie's additional efforts brought only four small cod to the table, so to speak; Duncan disappeared for a while and did not return until Maggie had begun to worry about him, his arms filled with more chopped wood and kindling, his small axe then reunited with his belt; Iain McEwen left as well, giving notice that he would ride down off the hill once more and gauge the possibility of travel.

Donal and Daimh played some game that served as entertainment for many. They sat facing each other, legs crossed, holding strict eye contact. Donal's hands were raised, palms up, and Daimh set his hands onto them, palms down. While not looking away, Donal would try to swipe his hands out from under his brother's and slap the top of them. Of course, it was frivolous, and then more so when it escalated into a wrestling match, after Donal moved his hand and slapped his brother's face instead.

They tried a fire again, but to no avail. The cave swelled with smoke and it was quickly extinguished. Another was built closer to the opening and kept alive only so long as necessary to cook the fish. Maggie initially declined her portion, sorry that she added an extra person to feed in their ranks. Both the laird and Hew scoffed at this.

"It's no' one for each, and then we're short a few," Hew said. "Divided equally, seven people, seven parts." He nodded to accent this.

By early evening, having barely moved all day save for one span of time in which she purposefully rose and walked around the circle, again and again, to move the blood in her body, Maggie felt more sluggish than ever. She'd changed positions so many times today, she didn't know of another that might give her some relief from the hard ground, and so lay on her back, hoping sleep might come soon.

No sooner had she done this than Laird McEwen had come to tower over her.

"One more time up to the next bothy, lass," he said, "before you fall asleep."

"Likely by now, I can manage on my own." Surely, the now thrice-taken path must be worn down that she could traverse it herself.

"Aye, like as no'," he agreed. "But it's getting on dark now. C'mon."

Maggie sat up as he reached for her hand and pulled her to her feet. In the next minute, they had tightened up their outerwear and then Iain McEwen, Laird of Berriedale, kin to Donald Mackay, defender of Scotland's freedom, once more conveyed Maggie Bryce out of the cave and up the hill and into what she was now referring to inwardly as her own private piddle hut.

She was deposited onto her feet in the bothy and Iain made himself scarce while she took care of business, returning at her call as he had yesterday, with rowan berries in hand. Maggie chewed slowly, savoring the sour berries while they stood just inside the opening and stared out over the landscape. Looking either left or right showed much the same, snow covered hills and glens and hundreds of pine trees, beautifully painted with the brush of God and snow, and now the gray evening.

"Will we be able to get out tomorrow?" She wondered.

"Mayhap," he said. "Sun may have shrunk some of this today."

"Daimh said he'd never seen so much snow, save for when he was out on Skye," she mused.

"Aye, unusual."

A few seconds passed, while they ate and stared out, away from the bothy, before he said more.

"You got on well with Daimh, it seemed."

Maggie jerked her gaze back to him. Did she detect some hesitation in his tone? She considered his query, offered with purposeful indifference, it seemed.

"You must be very proud to call these men your own," she said. "They are, each and every one of them, very fine gentlemen."

"Dinna think they've been called that too often," he said, sending a wry grin her way. He tossed the branch, now devoid of fruit, out into the snow.

She finished off her own berries, assuming they would return now. But Iain McEwen crossed his arms over his chest and leaned against the edge of the doorway, contemplating her. She lifted a brow to him, but he said nothing, just pinned her with his piercing eyes.

When it continued, she gave him a nervous grin. "If it is your intent to cause menace with that scowl, I must tell you it's come a bit late."

His eyes narrowed while one brow lifted.

"It's just that you've been—as have all of your men—very kind to me, very solicitous. So I'm not sure what this scowl is for now, but—"

"I'm only trying to figure you out, lass."

She said nothing to this but swallowed hard.

"You still carry the bruise and I know well the mark of someone who's been struck. You're off and running in a storm, bereft of the proper fear you should possess, and would have me believe you're destined for the convent. It's no' making sense, lass."

Boldly, Maggie responded with, "I suppose you'll have to ask yourself how essential are the answers to what only you suggest should be questioned." She gave further thought to his words—*bereft of proper fear*. 'Twas true, she considered herself quite safe right now. Well she might be deeply entrenched with six soldiers of a warring clan, and on the run from her own father and betrothed, but she had known little fear after her initial waking next to this man.

He inclined his dark head, his lips pursed until he said, with more threat than she'd perceived from him as of yet, "But if what you hide will be a danger to my men, then I say to you, lass: aye, it is verra essential."

This gave her pause, as she hadn't given much thought to any possible danger these McEwens might know simply because they'd happened upon her. To him, she allowed, "The...mark on my cheek will see no danger brought to you. And I *am* committed to making my way to St. Edmund's—by myself if needs must.

That is truth." She convinced herself she told no lie, forcing away any remorse for the niggling shame that she wasn't being *entirely* honest with him. But as of two days ago, this was truth. Likewise, she convinced herself that the possibility of him learning the actual truth was so remote as to be non-existent; the storm would end, the snow would melt, and they would part company. She saw no reason to reveal to him that she was unhappily betrothed to a Sutherland, assuming it had no bearing on their present circumstance.

He nodded now, content—if not with her answers, then at least with his own patience. Maggie released her breath and removed her gaze from him.

"Aye, but there's one more thing, lass," he said, pushing away from the doorway.

Maggie turned back to him. He moved at the same time, surprising her as he stood so close already and then more so when he lifted his hand and gently took hold of her cloak, wrapped his fingers around the edge, just under the closure near her neck. Her eyes widened as he pulled her near, at the same time taking one more step toward her. Some bit of panic caught her breath, sent her own hand to cover his and yank at it. How dastardly, to have lulled her so expertly, all of them, and then present this peril to her, whatever his objective now. And here, she'd thought him so gallant and beautiful.

"It's no' to be helped, lass," he murmured low. "I'll be needing to kiss you."

His eyes were dark now, heated as he drew closer still, not entirely frightening, even as he lowered his head and very softly touched his lips to hers.

Maggie went completely still, squeezing her eyes tightly shut, clamping her lips together.

It took her a moment more to understand she was not being assaulted and was not a victim of this man's evil ambition. His words finally registered.

Good heavens, but she was being kissed!

IAIN PULLED BACK, STARING down at her. It was almost humorous, how tight and fierce her grimace was just now. Almost. He didn't think he'd ever received quite this reaction to his kiss.

He shifted, drawing her near, while her fingers pinched with greater panic over the back of his hand. He paused, not meaning to frighten her. "Just a kiss," he coaxed, purposefully sliding his closed mouth along hers, left to right, and back again. Some sound emerged from her. He convinced himself it was half-wonder. He opened his mouth and covered her cold, berry red lips with his. She remained still and rigid before him, but not for long, as her nervousness forced her to breathe through her mouth, this done with a burst of breath and a strangled whimper.

"I'll no' take more than a kiss," he promised against her mouth, his voice naught but a whisper, and then suckled upon her ridiculously tempting bottom lip. He wet her top lip with his tongue while she panted against him but otherwise did not move. "This will be much more enjoyable if you kiss me back, Maggie Bryce," he promised, his voice as light and encouraging as he could make it just now.

This would see her startled out of her shock, would likely have her pushing violently away from him, he thought with some regret when the words were said. She might now rail at him and perhaps swipe an indignant hand across his face. Instead, little Maggie Bryce, who vowed she would give herself to God and not any man, opened her eyes and said to him, "I don't know how."

He smiled inside, maybe outwardly as well. And it was fairly triumphant, he imagined, as this was more than he could have hoped for. Slowly, he tugged her even closer and slanted his head to her. He decided it was not fear, but curiosity that showed in her glorious eyes just now. "Aye, but I'm happy to show you, lass." His lips met hers again, warm and wet now. Her fingers still clenched around his hand, but her short nails no longer indented his skin. He sent his tongue once again, tracing it along the soft fullness of her lips while he fought with himself, aching to crush her against him though he knew he must proceed slowly, without any fantastic menace. He pressed on, covering her mouth fully again, and sliding his tongue within. He caught her reacting shiver and pushed on, tracing his tongue around, inside her sour berry sweetness.

In the next moment he felt her tongue meet his. So tentatively, so briefly, he slowed himself at once, moving his own tongue only near her lips until he felt hers touch his again, giving consent. Iain was invigorated and thrust his tongue with larger intensity, caressing and tasting and exploring. Aye, and the lass who claimed with such passion that she wanted only to serve God responded beautifully, eager and hungry and willing to learn. Iain could not say if mere seconds or many long minutes had passed, lost as he was in everything that was Maggie Bryce.

But his name was called. The sound penetrated all else. It was Duncan's voice, booming up the side of the hill, though his captain was still a distance away, likely at the cave yet, wondering what delayed them no doubt.

Iain lifted his head and stared down at her, wonderfully breathless. He laughed or smiled, he did not know, but it opened her eyes. The green of her eyes was bright, he thought her cheeks might be pink now in the twilight, her lips a perfect shade of very-kissed red. They stood there, breathing heavily onto each other, silently marveling at their kiss. Her gaze darted here and there, from his left eye to his right, and then to his lips.

Duncan called again, pulling them further into reality.

Iain puffed out a huge breath and turned his face toward the sound. "Aye! Coming!" He called back. When he faced Maggie Bryce of the tantalizing kiss, he found only the top of her head, as she'd lowered her gaze between them. Her fingers clung still to his, where his own held yet at her cloak. Slowly, he unfurled his fingers, the slight movement sending hers away from his.

With her face still hidden from him, that all he saw was the tip of her hood and only a small section of her shiny hair, she said, "Did you do that—kiss me—because you wanted to show me how ungodly I truly am?"

He shook his head immediately, a smile of wonder tugging at him, even as he was sorry for the sadness that tinted her voice. "Nae, lass. I kissed you because I wanted to feel your lips against mine. Have you no' ever wanted to kiss a man before?"

She shook her head slowly back and forth and put more distance between them.

He felt no guilt, felt nothing but...her. He'd had to kiss her, that was all. He'd make no other justification, but that he'd had no choice. But how did he explain to her the why of it? Iain almost floundered, considering the extent of his reason.

Nae, something was not right with his own answer. He kissed a woman when he wanted to bed down with her, that was all. There was never...another reason.

Until now? Had he even given thought to bedding the lovely Maggie Bryce? He didn't think he had. He'd watched her often, continuously it might appear, for two days now, had been enchanted and beguiled and mayhap several other things. Yet he didn't think he'd had any particular thought about anything beyond a kiss. And truth be told, it had only been just now, when they'd walked up to the third hut, when he'd held her so close, when her eyes had shown so remarkably green, when her freckles were so inescapable, dotting so adorably across her cheeks and nose and all the rest of her face, that he had his first distinct thought that he must kiss her. That he must know if she were as bonny as she appeared, if she would taste as sweet, and feel as soft....

Jesu, he might well be Hew, with reflections such as these, as if he were untried and unprepared for a new and brilliant kiss. As if he'd not bedded his own fair share of wenches in his life.

"Are you regretting now...that you kissed me?" She asked, raising those green eyes and freckles—the culprits, he was convinced, or at least one of the reasons he'd needed to kiss her.

Regretting that he'd kissed her? That he'd been assured that all that he'd imagined was true, that her kiss was as captivating as she? Nae, he regretted nothing, save his own unexpected response, whatever the whole of it was.

I don't know how. Ah, the lass's first kiss. And now this, this anxious gaze, the near trembling of her lips that he must assume had little to do with the cold, as heat still fired every nerve in his body. Iain moved his head side to side. If nothing else, the lass must not ever think that.

Iain let a smile show, ignoring Duncan's third call, keeping his gaze steady on her. He let the smile display some reverence and adoration, for this near stranger who could kiss a man senseless on her first try and then wonder that he might not have liked it. He stepped forward again, intent on showing her exactly how much he enjoyed their kiss.

But she shocked him by wondering, "Am I in danger now?"

This wrought a fantastic and swift frown from Iain and stopped him in his tracks, until he understood the exact reasoning behind such a sad question. Of course, it made sense. She—this entire situation—made her extremely vulnerable. The kiss would not have settled fears but raised them. It wasn't unreasonable, the question, but it sat unwell with him, nonetheless.

He was eager to discourage her from allowing that line of thinking to expand. "I'm no' in the habit of forcing a woman. 'Twas only a kiss." And now it was ruined by her suspicion and this last, the lie he'd just told her. Ruined, indeed, that she was not as affected by the kiss that her mind was able to be seized by other concerns.

Grounding out a mumbled curse, he said, "I shouldn't have kissed you." But the sparse apology tasted bitter. In fact, he thought what he meant was, *I am sorry you did not like the kiss because I enjoyed it tremendously.* "Let's get back before Duncan begins to have fits." He hated that he couldn't entirely conceal the rancor from his voice.

Maggie rushed forward and tugged at his sleeve as he turned toward the opening.

"I'm sorry," she said quickly. "I—I wasn't accusing you of anything. I only thought—"

"Dinna apologize." He pulled his arm away from her grasp. "Let's forget the whole—just forget it happened at all."

She was still and small at his side. "I...I don't know if I can do that."

Internally, he rolled his eyes, now sincerely sorry that he had kissed her. Sighing, he turned and confronted her. "I've said you'd come to no harm. You needn't have any worry that I will—"

"Kiss me again?" She ventured. "Have I removed that possibility?" A wince appeared, in both her words and on her face.

Iain stared at her for a moment, trying to make sense of her, of what had just happened. He couldn't, or didn't want to assume anything further, that he required clarification. "What is it, then?"

With a fortifying breath, she rushed out, "I've offended you with my fears—which are unfounded as you've been very kind to me. It's just that you caught me so completely unprepared and...truth be told, the...kiss rather muddled my mind." She lifted her hand and jerked her gaze from his lips to his eyes to clarify quickly, "But not in a bad way, just...it was unexpected. Still, I did not...." She let this trail off, her voice shrinking into nothingness.

Possibly his hard scowl scared her off. And damn if she didn't appear suddenly so forlorn.

"You did not...?" He prodded, his tone even.

She swallowed. "I did not dislike it."

He barked out a bitter laugh. "A resounding bit of praise." And then, at her crestfallen expression, a million curses sounded in his head. "Are you about to cry?"

She shook her head, pinching her lips. "No."

The head-shaking was near frantic. Iain wished himself an ocean away. "Can we return? And seriously, pretend this never happened? I can assure you now, with certainty, this will never happen again."

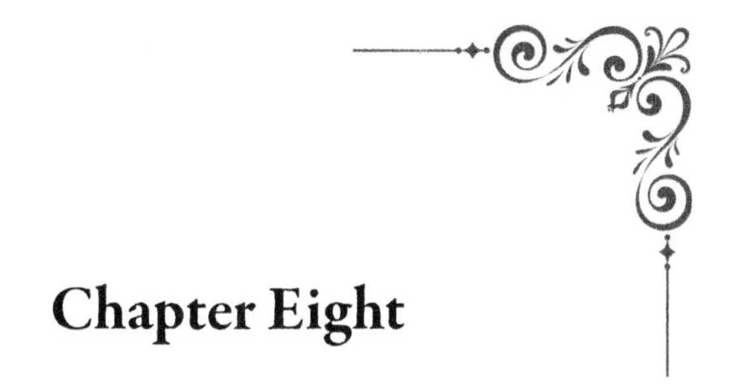

Chapter Eight

I AM AN IDIOT.

The laird of the McEwens, that beautiful man with the striking blue eyes, had kissed her. She hadn't been prepared for what surely must have been dragonflies dancing in her belly, nor actually feeling her heartbeat pound throughout every inch of her body, but she knew she liked those feelings. It was only unfortunate that these reactions had so completely befuddled her that she'd insulted him in such grand fashion that he'd carried her stiffly back to this cave and had ignored her fully since setting her onto her feet.

And all the minutes from then until now were spent trying very hard not to cry.

Maggie sat as she sometimes did, on her bottom with her knees drawn up to her chest. She'd clasped her arms around her legs and tried to keep her gaze away from the laird. And his lips. She'd spent several minutes watching him talk to Duncan at one point, watching his mouth move around his words, amazed that those very utilitarian body parts could so easily and effectively have caused such delight in her as they had only a short while ago.

Her face heated with a blush when she caught Archie staring at her with a narrow-eyed and contemplative frown. She didn't care what that cranky man thought. Laying her chin on her knees, she let the talk around her become muted, only noise in the back of her brain while she wrestled yet more with how superbly and effortlessly she'd managed to wreck the single most amazing event of her little life. She closed her eyes and tried to relive the entire encounter over and over, hoping to commit each second and sound and feel to memory, having been told there would be no repeat. A kiss shouldn't be a life-changing thing, she thought with a bit of a frown, but in some respect, she knew she was different even now.

She closed her eyes, impervious to the cold it seemed, adrift in her own tortured thoughts. When she opened her eyes, she found the laird's gaze upon her. She detected that his jaw was still, or once again, clenched. She tried to hold his gaze, hoped she conveyed properly her sorrow but could not be sure. Soon enough their contemplation of each other was interrupted by Archie's grousing as others began to find their beds for the night.

"Close quarters, lad, but you need no' be climbing on top of me."

"And where would you have me put my own legs, Arch?" Donal wondered with a rare irritation.

Maggie blinked and Iain removed his heated gaze from her. When Duncan found his pallet next to her, Maggie laid down as well, facing the captain tonight, not sure she could withstand the chief ignoring her straight on if she'd turned in that direction. He found his own bed within minutes and stretched the huge fur over her once again. This kindness only made her feel doubly wretched for how she'd treated him earlier.

She waited until all around was quiet, until the only sounds were those now familiar nighttime noises, various persons snoring and water dripping. Shifting upon the hard ground, she angled her face toward Iain and whispered, "There is only ever once a first time for something. I'm very sorry that I'd so foolishly destroyed my first kiss."

Despite the many minutes that had passed since he'd found his bed, his voice was not sleepy at all when he responded in a matching whisper, "It was not an irrational response. It remains, however, that I shouldn't have kissed you."

She needed a moment to gather the courage to press on. "And won't again?"

His reply was a long time coming, but then was really no response at all. "Go to sleep, Maggie Bryce."

There had been some discussion earlier, while she'd sat with her own miserable thoughts, about getting out early tomorrow, if the weather cooperated. They could be home by sunset, Duncan had proclaimed with some hope.

Too soon, she thought. She needed time to fix this, couldn't stand the idea of parting ways with Iain McEwen while he thought she disliked his kiss.

Maggie prayed for snow as she drifted off.

She was wakened hours later as she was shaken roughly. It took her only a brief moment to recollect her circumstance. Her next thought was that the trembling was her own shivering.

This was not the case. Iain McEwen was talking in his sleep, not pleasantly, and his hand—settled upon her hip at some point—was gripping the fabric of her skirt and jerking it angrily.

"Go on with ye!" He grumbled, the voice not his own, not low and deep and warm, but disjointed and nearly frantic.

Maggie turned around toward him, her skirts now twisted as he held her gown so tightly.

His eyes were closed and while his jaw was clenched, his teeth were bared. She understood in an instant that he was having a nightmare. This in itself was so...unreal—this huge and mighty soldier beset by nightmares? And to such a degree that behind the easy-to-interpret anger, she thought she detected either worry or fear.

Impossible. Iain McEwen, fearful?

It just couldn't be. More words came, but Maggie could not decipher them, but for thinking she caught the phrase "a wee critical something", which made no sense to her. Tentatively, she nudged at his chest, pushing her fingers against the leather of his breastplate. She jabbed several times, to no avail. The fingers at her hip began to dig into her flesh as he became more and more agitated by his night demons. At the same time, his speech became more and more unintelligible.

"Duncan," she called nervously, hoping the captain was wakeful, or made so by his laird's fussing.

He was not. There was no sound to indicate that any other McEwen was awake just now.

"Break his neck, go on then!" Iain growled quite clearly through his clenched teeth. His entire body began to spasm with his distress. The soft golden light of the near-dead fire showed beads of perspiration on his forehead, showed that his eyes remained closed.

"Sir," she whispered frantically, then once again, more harshly, trying to rouse him from his dream. "Chief McEwen." This seemed only to agitate him further and she thought his entire body might be twitching and jerking just now. And still he mumbled and cursed.

Some instinct lifted her hand further and she placed her palm against his cheek.

"Sir," she said softly.

His eyebrows lifted, as if he might hear her, but his trembling did not cease.

Maggie rose onto her elbow and moved her hand along his cheek. "Everything is all right."

The first thing to settle was the hand at her hip. His fingers no longer dug into her, though they still clung to the fabric of her skirt. Yet still, he growled low.

"Come back," she urged softly. "Wake up."

Perchance he would rouse now and be embarrassed for his night terror, because she had witnessed it. He did not wake though. He mumbled more and the hand at her hip jerked, drawing her abruptly against him.

Unafraid, knowing he only dreamed, she caressed his cheek more to quiet him. "Shh," she cooed. "'Tis but a dream." She brushed at the short hair at his temple, her touch soft and slow. "Shh." The lines on his forehead lessened. "Only a dream," she insisted in a silky voice.

His hand left her hip and moved up and over her arm, and settled on her face, his thumb under her chin. "Aye," he murmured gruffly. He threaded his fingers into her hair, around her nape, and drew her to him.

Maggie went willingly, let her lips join his, suddenly and once again made breathless by this man. He kissed her gingerly, almost reverently. She might have wept for this, a second chance at her first kiss. It wasn't that exactly, certainly not if he slept still and only dreamed he was kissing her. She didn't care, she let him do it, participated even in this splendor. It was so easy to push everything else aside. His mouth was wonderful, his lips warm, and his tongue hot.

But they were not alone, she was reminded soon enough that she pushed at his chest to end the kiss.

She pulled her lips from his. "You are dreaming still?" She guessed.

"I must be."

Maggie dipped her head but refused to allow this to dampen the small joy she knew just now. To her surprise, he pressed his lips to her forehead, this kiss slow and lasting several seconds. Closing her eyes, she felt only that, his touch, the sweetness of it. Wanting one more moment of this bliss, she laid her head against his chest and knew a larger delight when his arm wrapped around her, holding her close. Instantly she was imbued with a strong sense of security. There was safety here, and warmth, and something else she could not name but thought was lovely. The entire feeling of being wrapped so steadily in his sleepy embrace was both new and wondrous.

Sadly, she could not stay like this, she realized, and gently disengaged herself completely from him and settled once again at his side. She could make no sense of whatever it was she felt now for and about Iain McEwen. She only knew that if Kenneth Sutherland had looked at her the way Iain did, if he had kissed her the way this man had, if she thought for one minute he was capable of the same remorse Iain McEwen had shown at her initial, foolish response to his kiss, she'd never have run away.

IT DID NOT SNOW OVERNIGHT. In fact, the sun shone across a bright blue winter sky, Mother Nature offering a cheery apology for the storm of two days ago, it seemed.

Iain woke but did not move. Somewhere in the night, he and Maggie had both shifted so that they were now nearly nose to nose. Perhaps not exactly, but as his face was tipped downward and hers was slanted upward, it appeared that way.

She slept yet. He resisted the urge to sweep the hair off her face, was pleased to be able to stare unimpeded. Her lips were parted, her breathing even, her freckles on perfect display. He resisted as well revisiting certain events of yesterday. There truly was no need to hash it out anymore inside his head. What is done is done. A tragedy, to be sure, that there should be no more kisses between them, but then even this was immaterial, as they would likely part company this day.

His head pounded just now, as it so often did when he'd been plagued by nightmares. He wondered if he had been; he did not always recall them. He hoped he hadn't disturbed anyone, the lass most of all. Duncan had several times told him that he became quite violent when in the grip of those far off demons. He could bring to mind no snippets of any torment that might have plagued him overnight, was beset just now by only a memory of Maggie's kiss. Mayhap this was the cause of the ache about his temples. Unfortunate business, that. A shame to part ways with the lass with so much unsettled—indeed, conflicted—between them.

Her long lashes fluttered several times before they opened under his gaze. He did not look away, did not pretend he was not or hadn't been availing himself to a long and leisurely exploration of her adorable features. So then wasn't he surprised when she neither blushed nor demurred under the intensity of his regard. Instead, Maggie Bryce returned the scrutiny, looking over every inch of his face that he wondered he did not blush himself, never having been subjected to so thorough an examination.

"Will be a fine day for travel," he said, before color did rise on his cheeks. Or damn, before he made the mistake of kissing her again.

"Mm," she concurred. "A day for farewells, then, as you are headed north and I south."

He could not interpret the tone of her words. Acceptance? Resignation? Sorrow? "Hm." And then quiet, while he thought of this. Home to Berriedale while the lass walked in the opposite direction, toward the nunnery, where she might well spend the rest of her life, if he were to believe what she proclaimed.

The silence lengthened. Her gaze remained steadfast upon him. 'Twas a fairly intimate stare, felt somehow very tender, almost as if it should be reserved for two people who were better acquainted than Maggie Bryce and himself, all glorious kissing aside.

The rest of her life.

After several minutes, he cleared his throat quietly and murmured, "Of course, lass, you could always move on with us, take respite up at Berriedale. Mayhap only until all the snows clear." Instantly, he thought he should regret these words, thought them unwise somehow, but he could not.

She did not respond immediately that Iain thought to add, "By spring, should be no trouble to send you down to St. Edmund's in a cart, or take you there myself, if circumstances allow."

He could not name the emotions that skittered across her face, but he found himself rather holding his breath, simultaneously thinking himself the greatest arse that ever lived.

"I suppose," she finally said, "it might be an easier trek to St. Edmund's if I were to wait for more agreeable weather."

Iain breathed again. "Aye, it would be. The world's a dangerous place for a woman on her own."

Just one corner of her beautiful mouth curved upward. "But you could keep me safe."

Something inside him flipped contentedly at her wording, that she'd said as much as a statement, did not pose it as a question. A smile curved his lips. "Aye, Maggie Bryce, I think I can manage to keep one wayward lass safe and well."

"But would I be required to walk behind you and your men, as previously discussed?"

Ian grinned, felt his chest rumble with a bit of a chuckle. With this, her slight teasing, he thought she somehow had managed to put them on better footing, reverted to where they were before he'd dared to kiss her. At the same time, her seeming agreement to travel onward with him rather negated the untimely and unfortunate question she'd posed yesterday, *Am I in danger now?* So that he did now believe wholeheartedly that the query had been posed not with any fear of him, but with some surprise that he had kissed her at all.

"Nae, lass, we'll find you a nice seat atop the horse and no' behind it." She gave a nod and produced a contemplative smile that Iain dared further, "Seems a shame to leave unfinished this matter between us." This needed to be said—and to hell with what he'd told her yesterday—so that she had no illusions, that she could claim no surprise when next he tried to kiss her.

Iain was capable of more self-reflection than most men, he believed, but he did not at all examine his reasons for either the invitation or the bare cajoling. And yet, when she offered him another small smile, he found he was very pleased with this circumstance.

They rose shortly thereafter, as others began to wake.

"Let's get to it, lads," prodded Duncan.

Without further direction, the men gathered what few belongings and packs they'd brought in from the horses and kicked all of Maggie's beach and river stones over the still warm coals of the near-dead fire.

The lass had only her now empty basket to collect. She drew the long straps up over her shoulder and spent some time with the fabric of her wimple, once again arranging the creamy linen around and over her hair and head until all was covered completely.

Hew approached her, his own pack slung over his back, his sword returned to his belt. "But what will you do now?" Much worry was etched into his youthful face.

She told him with a pretty smile, "Your chief has invited me to travel with you to Berriedale for now."

She might well have said she'd been given the key to heaven, which she would now share with Hew, so delighted was his expression then.

Iain was anxious to be on the road, even as he understood they had no simple journey in front of them. At the same time, he felt jauntier than he had in days, and thought to have some fun with the lass, whom he still believed lied about her original destination.

Just as it appeared all were ready to depart the cave for the last time, Iain said to Maggie, "We like to say a prayer before we begin a journey." He was well aware of the scowls and confusion aimed at him.

"We do?" asked Donal, slanting a look of open-mouthed bafflement at his laird.

Iain ignored him. "Mayhap you would grace us with an invocation, sister? Seems we might stand a better chance of being heard if the beseeching comes from one so close to the Almighty."

"Oh," she said, without a trace of cleverness. "Um, of course." She wiped her hands nervously upon her cloak and considered the faces around her. "Very well. Um, gather 'round, I suppose."

"Around what?" Wondered Craig.

She jerked her eyes to him, frowning at him as if he'd done it apurpose, asked a daft question. "Around me," she said, which emerged more as a question than an answer.

Only Hew moved, stepping forward, his smile as earnest as ever, his cheeks uncommonly pink.

"Hmm," was her only thought about that. Iain stifled the grin that wanted to come, watching as she took a deep breath and presented, with a surfeit of quick thinking, he would later think, "Dearest God, almighty God, ancient of days, Lord of the land and sky and sea, compassionate and gracious God—"

"Long title, He has," said Donal, showing no shame at all for his irreverent quip.

"About as extravagant as your laird's, I should imagine," Maggie Bryce returned saucily, barely allowing time to fill the space between Donal's comment and her rejoinder. Several chuckles met this, some muffled, some abbreviated, Daimh's sounding as if it had burst out of him.

She went on, obviously intent on ignoring their further mischief. "The Lord shall give strength unto His people; the Lord shall give His people the blessing of peace. Be with us all this day, dear Lord; direct our counsel, govern our actions, guide our hands, and unite our hearts."

"Amen," said Archie, shuffling his feet, wanting to be moving toward home.

The lass was to be neither hurried nor quieted, it seemed, but kept on. This halted Archie, who had begun to move away from their very lazy circle. The old man pursed his lips and rolled his eyes, but he did fold his hands neatly before him again.

"And we beseech Thee, give us grace to improve Thy mercy to Thy glory; give us loud voices for the advancement of the gospel, the honor of our country, and the good of all mankind."

She was quiet. Yet no one moved, as she had not, but kept her own head bowed, her small gloved hands folded at her waist.

Iain grinned. The little brat.

"Harken unto my voice, O Lord, when I cry unto Thee; have mercy upon me and hear my prayer. Be it all in His name, through Jesus Christ our Lord, to whom, with Thee and the Holy Spirit, as for all Thy mercies, so in particular for deliverance this day, be all the glory and honor unto You, world without end. Amen."

"Amen," came the not at all harmonious chorus.

Archie was the first one to move then, taking his muttered, "Thought we'd no' ever get going this day," with him as he walked by Iain.

"Very nice, and thank you, sister," Duncan said with a good shake of his head, even as his mouth was pinched, as if he could not decide upon a smirk or a grimace.

MAGGIE UNFOLDED HER hands, and flexed her stiff fingers, happy to have that near-calamity behind her. She was quite pleased with how she managed to pull it off. But then, it wasn't as if the bible and prayer and the church's service were foreign to her; her mother, when she lived, had been enormously pious, and they'd visited chapel daily, and twice on Sundays. Maggie could still recall the exact nasally quality of the cleric's voice. Father Davidh had been a series of contradictions: his extreme size, most of it in girth should have lent itself to a deep and booming voice; his piercing little eyes, like crows' eyes, Maggie had always thought, should have housed some malevolence; his famously unkempt person, always suggesting he'd hastened through his dressing or mayhap had done it in the dark, should have been the convention of some slovenly person. And yet, Father Davidh had been soft-spoken and kind and orderly, perhaps the most gentle soul that Maggie might ever have known.

She said a genuine prayer of thanks to that lovely man, for unknowingly helping her to get through that prayer, and then followed the men out of the cave.

Only when they'd trekked down to the lower hut and stood waiting while Daimh and Donal sent out the horses, one by one, did Maggie wonder how an extra person such as she might be accommodated. She stood in snow which only reached to her ankles, as this path had been well trod over the last few days, squinting up as each man readied and mounted his horse. Duncan was the first to walk his down the hill, off this small shelf of ground, too narrow for all their mounts at once. She watched Craig and Archie follow him while Hew and the laird fussed with the huge saddles and attached their packs. Finally Donal and Daimh stood near their own mounts, making themselves and their horses ready.

She felt the laird's hand at her elbow then. In the bright light of day, his eyes were marvelously blue, creasing again with the grin he showed her. "I've said you'll no' be walking behind, lass. C'mon up with me."

Maggie returned his smile, happy for this situation, even if she did acknowledge some unease at the prospect of sitting atop so huge a beast. Iain pulled the strap of the basket off her arm and affixed this at the back of his saddle, opposite his own leather pack. Then he lifted Maggie by the waist and plunked her down sideways in the saddle. She grasped the pommel near her thigh, feeling instantly that her position was precarious. But Iain McEwen immediately swung up behind her and wrapped his strong arm around her middle, pulling her snug against him, and her worry evaporated.

"Have you never ridden a horse, lass?"

She shook her head, clutching the arm at her waist as he carefully directed the animal down the slope.

"We'll no' be running but you'll be sore later, nonetheless," he predicted grimly. "Nothing to be done about that."

Refusing to allow any apprehension to quell what should be vast excitement over her new circumstance, Maggie gave only brief life to the thought that her path was irreversible now. If she had carried on to St. Edmunds by herself, she might at any time have changed her mind and returned to the Gordon keep, pretending she'd never made any attempt to flee her own future. But now, with these McEwens, and their laird specifically, Maggie had some notion that she'd not be allowed any such luxury as a change of heart. They'd not simply say aye and let her off at the next cave, she knew.

She was going to Berriedale with Iain McEwen, the decision made in part by the prospect of more kisses from him, cajoled by his words, *Seems a shame to leave unfinished this matter between us*. A shame indeed, she thought with a secret smile.

They moved almost in a single line until they reached the flat land at the bottom of the Isauld Hills. No, they would indeed not be running, as the snows here still reached the horse's knees and hocks, making for a slow go. When they found what the laird called the Old Northern Trail, they shifted their line to ride two by two save for Craig in the lead. Maggie glanced around, wondering how they knew this was the road; everything was white, all the knolls and hills and scrub brush and trees. It all looked the same, in every direction.

There was a magnificent but eerie peacefulness to the quiet of the trail, the snow pristine until they marched over it, glistening under the early morning sun. Not a bird chirped, nor did any critter or beast show itself to them.

Maggie shifted several times, thinking she might never get on a horse again. The destrier did not lift each leg to march through the snow, but rather charged gracefully through it, and yet she felt each bump and step on her bottom, where it sat in the saddle between the laird's powerful thighs. Her discomfort must have been known to him, as he tightened his hold around her middle.

"Swing your leg 'round, lass. Astride will be less of a bother."

She did as he suggested, and quickly knew some relief and an even greater sense of security. Her shins were now bared to the cold, her gowns riding up her legs, but she thought this a trifling matter compared to the ache on her bottom.

There was not any talk among these men now, but Maggie would not know if that was in deference to the ghostly beauty of the quiet around them, or if it were their regular habit to ride noiselessly. And then, about an hour into their ride, Donal began to sing. His voice was deep but he kept it low. Maggie knew the song and instantly appreciated Donal's rendering of it, as he sang the usually jaunty verse much slower, rather hauntingly so.

"Foul weather, she'll be coming fast
Hear birdsong while ye can
How long comes the spring
When blossoms sing?
Make merry now, good man."

She was sorry when he stopped, as his voice was very pleasing, and suffered no qualms about picking up where he'd left off, hoping she did credit to Donal's version of it.

"Make merry while the sunshine lasts,
Hear birdsong while ye can.
When the nightingale sings
And blossoms spring,
Make merry now, good man."

It must have proved acceptable, as Donal turned around to grin at her while she sang. He joined her for the third verse.

"Whither think, fair weather hast
No birdsong o'er the land
How long comes the spring
When my heart sings?

Make merry now, good man."

From the second row, two lengths before her, Archie turned his head to the side and groused back at them, "Nothing like a little screeching in my ear to turn over my near-empty stomach."

"Aye, careful there, Arch," warned Donal. "I've an entire arsenal to keep you company on the drive. And I'm no' afraid to use it."

Maggie grinned and sang out a song for the grumpy old man, changing the words to suit her needs.

"I have a fair Archie
Far beyond the sea,
Many, many gifts does he send to me.
He sent me the thorns without any rose.
He sent me his scowl and now I am froze.
I have a fair Archie
Far beyond the sea
Why does he send these gifts to me?"

Of course, Donal and Daimh howled wildly at her little fun, and even Hew sent her an admiring chuckle, but Maggie's eyes were on Archie. He'd turned his face fully now and let her see just the beginning of a quirk in his lips.

"It's no' a lot of red in your hair, lass," he said, "but you sure do ken how to use it."

She didn't know exactly what that might mean, but she understood there was some positive in that statement.

"I think he smiled," Iain whispered at her ear, a chuckle in his tone. "An incredible feat you've managed there, lass."

They rode for a while within a strand of trees that darkened the day but did provide a trail bereft of the depth of snow they'd seen thus far.

"Outside these trees," Iain said, "we turn east and we're no' more than a few hours from home."

"Berriedale," she mused, liking the sound of it. She was about to ask him to tell her about his home, when Craig, at the lead, came to a full stop and let out a low clucking sound that halted everyone else.

Iain maneuvered the horse between Donal and Hew before them and they saw what Craig had. The trees opened up and an army stood before them.

Maggie's breath caught in her throat.

The bright green and gold and red of the Sutherland plaid, draped over more than half of the riders, was easily discernable even at this distance. There must be fifty men, she imagined with no small amount of horror, and was nearly choked by her fright when she spied Kenneth Sutherland at the fore. My God, he'd trespassed onto Mackay land to retrieve her. But how had Kenneth...? Had she been followed? Quickly, she put aside her questions of how, and dwelt on the belly-churning fear that gripped her now. She wanted to look away, hide herself from the coming army, unreasonably believing, if only for a second, that if she didn't look upon them, they wouldn't notice her.

Oh, but she had brought trouble to these very kind McEwens. *Oh, dear Lord*!

While the laird's attention was fixed on the sight before them, and when they weren't yet fully emerged from the trees, Maggie lifted his hand from her middle, swung her leg over, and dropped from the saddle. She landed poorly, fell forward and only thrust her hands out at the last minute to prevent herself from landing face first in the snow. Scrambling, she took off running, back across the tracks they'd only just made in the snow.

Chapter Nine

"HEW," IAIN CALLED LEVELLY, keeping his eye on the horde before them. "Fetch Maggie Bryce. Keep her out of sight."

Hew turned and frowned, his gaze having been fixed on the large number of riders before them, unaware that Maggie had dropped and bolted from Iain's horse. He yanked his mount out of formation and gave chase.

Iain moved further to stand his horse next to Duncan's.

"That's Sutherlands," his captain noted.

The mass of the encroaching army was scattered about the flat meadow before them. One man sat on horseback near the front of their sloppy columns, a big man, dressed finely enough to suggest he led this group. As Iain watched, another large man, older than the first, walked his mount forward, stopping near the first man. They gave the appearance of nonchalance, no weapons drawn, but Iain was not fooled. He'd play it the same way, he supposed, non-threatening until his purpose had been made known.

"And plenty of them," Iain replied. The lass had something to do with this, he was sure. A Sutherland would not dare cross the river onto Mackay land for no good reason. And a nameless, faceless fear would not have sent the lass scurrying away.

There would be no fight, whatever their aim. He wouldn't commit his men to death, and death it would be—the seven of them against what he assumed to be more than fifty. Twenty, he would consider taking on. Twenty, the lads would insist they could take on. But not fifty. He spied the bows, held casually in the hands of several of the Sutherland men. Fifty, including a dozen archers, while only Daimh and Craig carried bows and arrows in their party. 'Twould be naught but a slaughter.

"I am Iain McEwen," he called across the naked span of thirty or more yards, "Laird of Berriedale, kin to Donald Mackay, and you, sir—and your men—are on Mackay land now."

The younger man, the one Iain had guessed was the leader, urged his mount forward a few more yards. "Kenneth Sutherland," he called back. "Aye, I've trespassed. As have you, though you've hidden her now. Yet, I believe you are in possession of my betrothed."

"Christ Almighty," Duncan seethed without moving his lips. Iain would not know if this were in response to the lass being affianced, or to the identity of her betrothed.

Betrothed. It made sense now. *No convent after all,* Iain thought disgruntledly.

The older man, seeming almost too large for his smaller destrier, ambled forward. "Margaret Bryce is my daughter, and I want her returned to me this instant." His voice boomed across the space.

Iain knew several Sutherlands, had at one time fought alongside them, at Falkirk and at Stirling bridge, in the days when so many had marched to the ardent drumbeat of the great William Wallace. He'd heard the name Kenneth Sutherland, that was all, did not know any more of the man than what rumors had come to him, none of them favorable. But then, all news of a Sutherland that might reach his ears would never come in a positive light.

They must have been watching them, either had trailed them for days, possibly had been made immobile as well by the storm, or they'd happened to spy them today while out searching and had raced ahead of them. 'Twas his own fault, being attentive of the bewitching lass and not their surroundings.

"Which of you two fine gentlemen laid a hand on her?" The words were sent across the field before he thought better of them.

He quickly read Sutherland's expression, a quick but not overly concerned frown, which suggested more of an internal query of why Iain should care than a visible admission of guilt.

"I laid my hand on her," shouted her father without a trace of shame. He offered nothing else, no excuse, no reasoning, no justification. His tone actually suggested some daring, as if he only wanted to be challenged or reprimanded for his heavy-handedness.

Kenneth Sutherland slowly looked to his left and then his right, as if only to draw Iain's eye to follow, to remind him of the strength of his numbers. He faced Iain again, leaning forward over the pommel, and wondered, with a bit of a chuckle, "Are you to return my betrothed to me, McEwen, or shall I take her by force?" No sooner had the query come than Sutherland's archers drew on Iain and his men. "Seems a high price to pay for one woman."

"And yet, here you are," Iain returned, "venturing onto Mackay land to claim her."

The archers pulled back.

"Wait!"

Iain clenched his teeth when he heard Maggie's cry.

She came from the trees, calling out franticly, "I'm here! I'm here, Father."

Hew's frustrated and abbreviated call of, "Maggie, don't—" possibly did not reach the Sutherland army across the distance.

Iain turned his steed around so that his back was to the Sutherlands, so that he faced Maggie Bryce as she tramped toward the front of their line.

When she stood near to his horse, he ground out, "I specifically asked you if you were running from something that might bring danger to my men." His anger just now might more be the result of his own powerlessness. That she had lied to him, that he felt betrayed even as he barely knew her, that he could not save her from her own wedding, if that had been what had sent her running.

She was as pale as the snow, which highlighted starkly both her freckles and the remarkable green of her eyes. Damn her, but it was unfair for a lass's eyes to be that color!

She blanched before him at his dark tone. "I'm so sorry," she mouthed. He couldn't be sure, as she removed her gaze from him to reclaim her basket from the end of his saddle, but he thought her eyes watered.

"I thank you all for what you have done for me," she said to the rump of Iain's horse.

Inside he fumed, over this circumstance, over his own helplessness just now. But he said no more to her, his jaw tightened almost painfully to keep his mouth shut and his anger reined in.

Maggie Bryce lifted her gaze to him. Indeed, tears threatened. So many emotions were alive and glowing in her gaze, but he could read only anxiety and sorrow. She opened her mouth, but no words came forth. And then she turned away, lifting her skirts above the snow, and walked toward the Sutherland army.

Iain pivoted his mount again and did not take his gaze from her, even as he directed, "Craig, Daimh, draw on Sutherland."

"I became lost in the storm," Maggie called out with false cheeriness to her betrothed as she walked toward him. "These men were kind enough to offer shelter to me."

Daimh and Craig positioned themselves at the far left and right of their group, nocking arrows aimed at Kenneth Sutherland.

Sutherland steered his mount forward a few feet, his expression dark, possibly unaware that he was a target just now. "The storm was days ago," he challenged Maggie in a loud voice.

"And we," she returned, "were trapped in a cave, with snow to my hips." She was starting to pant heavily, either from her exertions traipsing through the snow or because of a fear that her lies might be exposed, Iain could not be sure.

"And he has now attempted to hide your presence from me," Kenneth Sutherland pointed out.

Iain heard her scoff breathlessly and say, "Laird McEwen sought only to hide my presence from an approaching army. Of course we had no idea that it was you. The man was intent only with keeping me out of harm's way. You should be thanking him for such care he—all of them—have shown me."

Iain's jaw tightened yet more. The bastard made her walk all the way to him, did not come to collect her, though it was obvious to all that she was too small for the deep snow.

She continued to talk, giving more defense or possibly sweet-talking her future husband, but Iain could no longer hear what she said.

Next to him, Hew ground out quietly, as ferocious as Iain had ever heard him, "Do not let her go with them. She obviously didn't want to marry him, or she wouldn't have lied about going off to St. Edmunds."

"'Tis no' our business," said Duncan sharply, his gaze trained on the archers, "between a man and his betrothed, certainly no' a Sutherland union."

Iain felt his heart lurch. He clamped his teeth tight.

"Sutherland lass," Donal said behind them, disbelief shading his tone. "She dinna act like one."

"God damn you," Hew cursed at Iain, ignoring Donal. "You coward."

Iain nodded. What else could he do? The lad would understand. At some point, perhaps. It would serve no purpose to object, when they were only seven men. They would be cut down, mercilessly, and for what? The lass would still be leaving with Kenneth Sutherland, when they were dead.

"Archie, get him out of here," Iain said tightly. His fingers curled slowly into fists as he watched her walk across the space that separated the Sutherland ensemble from his Mackays, his expression grim. A sickening ache rumbled in his chest and stomach, while his nostrils flared with disgust at his own weakness, and at that part of him that for a brief moment actually considered calling her back to him anyway.

Hew spat at Iain, his saliva landing on Iain's thigh before Archie shifted his horse and collected the bridle of Hew's. Iain caught only a glimpse of Archie's glowering red face before he pulled Hew away from the scene.

When Maggie had reached the army, Kenneth Sutherland raised a hand, summoning a young lad forward. The lad dismounted and helped Maggie into his saddle, not without some difficulty. When she was settled upon the horse, Kenneth Sutherland faced Iain again and called out, his voice painted with condescension, "I ought to cut you down where you stand, McEwen."

Maggie Bryce had kept her head bowed in shame upon mounting, but now cried out and glanced up sharply at her betrothed.

Jaw tight, Iain ignored her and made a point to look left and then right, as Kenneth Sutherland had done a moment ago, alerting the man that he was in the sights of two archers himself. "Trained on you, Sutherland," he called out. "You'd be the first to drop. Think your archers can hit 'em before they let loose?"

There was still quite a distance between them, but Iain was sure he saw the man's lip curl.

Iain and Kenneth Sutherland exchanged stand-off glares for a full moment before Sutherland made a motion with his hand that began to move his army away from the meadow, headed west. Even when Kenneth Sutherland steered his own mount away, he continued to scowl at Iain.

"We'd do best to make ourselves scarce as well," Duncan said beside him.

"No' until they're out of sight."

The meadow was wide, and the Sutherland army had a way to go to reach the trees which would remove them from the open space. Iain and Duncan watched until the very last Sutherland disappeared into the dense strand of pines.

Craig and Donal lowered their bows when the last Sutherland had disappeared.

Iain dismounted while he waited, stretching his legs to ease the tension coursing through his entire body. Some sound made him turn, just in time to see young Hew charging at him, his face still contorted with his anger at what he perceived to be Iain's spinelessness.

Duncan sprung from his saddle and yanked Hew back by the collar of his fur.

Iain met the accusation in Hew's glare while Duncan upbraided the lad.

"Be done with it!" Duncan snarled at him. "It's no' as if she'd give you the time of day, Hew," Duncan spat out, needing the lad to understand he hadn't lost anything, really. "You think she'd have looked twice?" Duncan ground out, shaking Hew's shoulder, holding him close to his heated words. "Think you finally met the one who might notice you? Did you ken that—"

Hew pushed off him, an unprecedented amount of strength and fury shown as he shoved both hands against Duncan's broad chest, startling the older man, sending him reeling.

"I never said she—I dinna expect anything!" Hew cried out, spittle following the impassioned rush of words. "I dinna think anything! I dinna hope for anything! I just wanted to—" He stopped suddenly, his perpetually pinkened cheeks bright red just now. He lost his shout, lost the heat of his anger, that he finished in a wobbly voice, "I just wanted to ken her."

Iain nodded, fully comprehending Hew's dismay.

"She was no' ours, lad." He said after a while, shifting his jaw to accommodate the delivery of those bitter words.

Iain waited, but Hew said no more, so that Iain gained the saddle again and began moving in the opposite direction the Sutherlands had taken, headed east. Of course, he need not look behind to know his men followed. They must move quickly now, put a good amount of distance between them and the Sutherlands; he'd never trust a Sutherland to let that simple leave-taking be that. With his jaw tight, he refused to allow himself to dwell at all on the lass, or Hew's reaction to her leaving, and certainly not his own.

He was surprised by a sharp and curt whistle from behind him. Iain turned in the saddle. All had followed but Craig, who had wandered to where the Sutherland army had made their stand. Craig crouched in an area of well trampled snow, his forearms on his thighs while he waited for Iain and the others to come to him.

Iain did not dismount but circled around Craig.

Before he spoke, explaining his departure, Craig shook his head. He pointed to the beaten down, hard-packed snow in one spot. Iain lifted one hand, wondering what he was supposed to be seeing.

"Jesus," Duncan breathed next to him, obviously understanding before Iain did.

Craig said finally, "The print." He pointed to one very clear horseshoe impression in the snow. "Seven nail holes."

The blood drained from Iain's face and chest, pooling in a dreadful pit in his belly. "Nae," was all he said, unable to believe what this implied. Woodenly, he dismounted, needing to verify this with his own eyes. And there it was, directly below Craig's knee, a clear print.

Hew emitted a strangled and hoarse cry, drawing Iain's gaze to him. He felt every bit of the hateful recrimination in the lad's foul glare.

Iain glanced down at the print again and then up at the trees, through which Maggie Bryce had just ridden off with her betrothed, Alpin.

THEY ARRIVED AT THE Gordon keep in time for supper. The entire ride had been miserable, with Maggie beset by so much sorrow to have been taken away from the McEwens, the laird specifically. Beset as well by so much dread, because every time Kenneth Sutherland happened to glance her way, there seemed to be some promise of an unpleasant reprisal in his gaze. He hadn't spoken another word to her since their leave-taking of the McEwens, but Maggie worried that he did not, after all, believe her tale.

When their party crammed into the Gordon's snowy and muddy yard, Kenneth himself came to collect Maggie. Without care, he yanked her by one hand from the horse, ignoring her stumbling upon the ground, and marched her into the keep. Ignoring Elizabeth's fretting that she was safe, Kenneth took to the stairs and barked, "Which one?" as he contemplated the doors to the family's chamber.

"Next floor," came weakly from Maggie, and she was hauled up another flight of stairs.

There were only two doors on this floor that Kenneth easily ascertained which was hers by poking his head into each. He shoved her ahead of him with such force that she nearly fell to the ground inside her own chamber. Maggie's chest banged with the same thud that accompanied his slamming of the door behind him.

He approached her slowly, all his menace shown now, his mouth distorted to ugliness, his brows angled low, his eyes soulless.

When he was close, he thumped his forefinger into her chest. His voice was absurdly velvety as he said, "When next you try to run from me, I suggest you get further away."

"But I didn't—"

"If ever I have to chase you down again," he continued, ignoring her feeble defense, "I will make sure you are not fit to walk across a room, let alone away from me."

"'Twas the storm—"

The fingers at her chest suddenly crimped into the folds of her closed cloak, twisting and pulling her close. "When I am speaking, you are not." This was ground out with a barely restrained ferocity. And all the words that followed only grew louder and more ominous. "You are nothing to me, but I'll be damned if I'll be made to look a fool by you. Your role will be one of a slave. To me. To my needs. To my wants. For every moment of grief you cause me, I will visit thrice as much upon you. You will learn right quick that I will suffer no whims of disobedience or rebellion. Am I making myself clear?" He shouted this last, rattling his hand inside her cloak, shaking her up against him.

Maggie nodded vigorously, wordlessly, truly terrified by the vengeance promised. With one more sneer, he pushed her away with such force that she was knocked off her feet, landing on her backside on the timber floor.

Her soon-to-be husband towered over her, still a snarl about his face. "We are not even wed yet and I am disgusted with you. You would do well to make sure my mood improves."

Late that night, Maggie stared out the lone slim window in her chambers. 'Twas a fine view, over the picturesque winter landscape of rolling hills and forests, but Maggie's heart was heavy. She pictured the McEwen chief and his men riding home to that place called Berriedale and cried for most of the night that she was not with them, and never would be again.

Chapter Ten

THE REMAINING DRIVE home to Berriedale was tedious, and for so many reasons. They did not make good time, Donal's horse having gone lame that they were forced to put it down and the brothers rode Daimh's horse together, which slowed them down yet more; it began to snow again, late in the afternoon, that Duncan raised his fist to the sky and shouted, "What now, you fecking bitch?" seemingly addressing the mother of nature, exposing his own sour mood; and Hew's temperament had not improved and the lad was often found lagging far enough behind that they were twice compelled to stop and await him catching up. After the second time, Archie grumbled heatedly to the lad, "We'll no be waiting again. Get over your fecking snit or find another destination."

They barely spoke, hadn't said much after Iain had convinced them that it was only begging for their own deaths if they charged after Alpin and the Sutherlands now. They needed to get home to Berriedale and regroup, call up the McEwen army, send notice of Alpin's identity to Donald Mackay, and make a plan first.

Iain wrestled with his thoughts regarding Maggie Bryce for quite some time, vacillating between believing her as innocent as she appeared and truly intent upon escape, and wondering if there was any possibility that she might be working with Alpin. Did she lay traps with her bewitching smile and winsome personality? He wondered if any of his men also grappled with the same irrational thought that because of her falsehoods she had somehow betrayed them, that it was personal.

However, by the time he rode through the gates of Berriedale, Iain had settled all the disquiet in his mind, had categorized each component of the day and all this new information. He'd exonerated Maggie of any complicity in Alpin's crimes. He excused her lies and her flight as self-preservation. And he knew he must somehow save her from Alpin even while he destroyed the monster. All of this was considered and decided with some back-of-the-mind certainty that if they'd not discovered that her betrothed were Alpin, he'd have purposefully wiped his memory clean of her, unable to completely exonerate her of her falsehoods, even as he was able to justify the reason behind them.

They did not reach Berriedale until just before midnight, pushing on when the sun set, rather than wisely hunkering down somewhere as they had the previous three nights. The hour precluded any great reception, for which they were all privately thankful. The men went off in different directions, the twins and Hew to their mams in the village, the others to the soldiers' barracks, and Iain to the keep.

Artair was the first person Iain saw in the morning. The old man had served as both bailiff and steward to Berriedale for longer than Iain had been alive. Iain did not ever recall a look upon the man's weathered face that was not tranquil, and this was no exception, as Artair showed no surprise to see his laird returned and breaking his fast quietly and contemplatively within the hall.

Folding his hands into the voluminous sleeves of his customary gray robe with the wide cowl, the perpetual ledger within his arms, Artair only shifted his direction upon spying his master and came to stand before Iain at the family's table.

Iain acknowledged the steward with a nod, taking a swig of the ale to chase down the sweetbreads, which seemed a veritable feast to him after so many months on the road.

"Your mother will be pleased for your return, Chief," the old man intoned gently, "as will all."

"Aye, and I'm sure you'll be wanting some time with me, Artair, but I'll beg a few days to set some other matters to rights first."

"As you wish, lad."

Only Duncan, Archie, and Artair could get away with calling their chief *lad*. Iain thought only Archie's age, almost double his own, granted that man leave to use so informal an address; Duncan's permission came nobly and hard fought, mostly at Iain's side; Artair's use of the label had been earned by way of his steadfast loyalty to any McEwen and the constant poise in the face of so many challenges to Berriedale and its family over the years.

"You are solemn today, lad," Artair commented. "I take it your quest did not end well."

Iain considered Artair with a big sigh. There was something reassuring in the man's quiet presence, the very familiar gray eyes and thinning hair. The top of Artair's balding head was wider and rounder than his cheeks and chin, which narrowed to a square point. There wasn't anything about the man that did not suggest patience and an aged wisdom, in which Iain normally found great comfort.

"It did no' end well at all, truth be told," was all that Iain said just now. He wasn't of a mind to discuss the entire disastrous news, the identity of Alpin, and the ramifications that must follow. Not yet.

His mother shrieked when she saw him as she entered the hall a short time later. Iain smiled at her and allowed himself to be engulfed in her embrace, acknowledging how truly wonderful it felt, this time returned. When she was done squeezing him, she took his cheeks in her hands and looked him over with misty eyes.

"Too long gone, my darling," she cooed.

Iain covered his mother's hands with his own. "You dinna know the half of it, Mother."

She was an amazing woman, who still had the uncanny ability to make him feel five years old even while she mostly championed and applauded his decision-making and ruling style.

Glenna McEwen, sister to the great Donald Mackay, was tall and willowy and shared the same blue eyes as her son. She somehow managed to look a full ten years younger than her half a century of years, improbable for the harsh life she'd known thus far; her husband had been gone for more than ten years; she'd buried two children, one a babe, another a sister Iain barely recalled as he'd been naught but a child himself when Anna had been taken by a fever; and Glenna herself had suffered some misfortune years ago, which she never discussed, but that had left her with a pronounced limp and a brutal scar across her left cheek.

He spent some time then with both Glenna and Artair, mostly listening to their updates of Berriedale, pleased that no specific issue called his attention immediately, as his mind was yet occupied with retrieving Maggie Bryce and apprehending the criminal, Alpin. When his mother departed, intent on some business in the kitchens, Artair brought other news to Iain.

"I've since burned it to preserve security," Artair said, "but there was a missive from the king."

This captured all of Iain's attention.

"He will return, as we suspected, and hopes the McEwens will be available to him. Our king will arrive further south but plans to set his brothers down at Loch Ryan with eighteen galleys. Bruce will reach out once he's landed."

"Do you have any sense of timing?"

Artair consulted the topmost sheepskin parchment in his file of papers. "The missive is now fourteen days old. Of course, there was no date given for his arrival, but my sense was that it would have been within the month."

Iain nodded. "And that was all?"

"That was all, lad. Needs only waiting further instruction."

"We have identified Alpin and will want to have a go at him."

This seemed to impress Artair, who lifted one gray brow. "Can it be done inside a week?"

Iain shook his head. "I'm no' sure."

"Thus, you must qualify: your king or the serpent, Alpin."

"Always king," Iain believed.

Artair nodded. "And yet Alpin has wreaked havoc here in Caithness to rival that of what the English have done in the south."

Iain considered this. "Alpin is but half a day away. If we go and are delayed, we might quickly be summoned if the king reaches out for us. But aye, my only advantage over Alpin just now is that he dinna ken that I am aware of his identity."

"An advantage that will be lost if you are called away in the midst of your pursuit."

"It's a risk worth taking, I'm thinking," Iain deliberated aloud. "The Bruce might no' call for a month and how many others would die by Alpin's hand in that time?"

"I agree."

There was some comfort in the old man's accord, though it would prove meaningless if what they feared—the king summoning the McEwens while they hunted Alpin directly—came to pass.

He asked Artair to stay when Duncan and the others joined him in the hall shortly thereafter. This family table, at which Iain and Artair now sat, had seen its share of military and political discussions over the years.

Iain was surprised when Daimh—not Hew—pressed almost instantly, "We're going to retrieve the lass, aye?"

Iain nodded, but made it very clear, "Presently, we have three priorities." He ticked off on his fingers. "Robert Bruce. Alpin. Maggie Bryce."

"The king?" Archie asked.

"Aye," answered Iain. "We've had a missive from the Bruce, with some instruction to be available for his coming. He wants to move against the English at his signal; thus, whatever we decide about Alpin, we must act quickly. Alpin is no' to be left unchecked, but our first priority is to our king."

"We can hit up Sutherland's Blackhouse," Archie surmised, "assume a two to three day stance unless we were lucky enough to catch 'em completely off guard. Chances are, if successful, could be gone and back inside a sennight."

"You want to lay siege to Blackhouse?" Hew threw up his hands. "With Maggie within its walls?"

"Hundreds within the walls," Archie argued. "No' all of them guilty of Alpin's crimes either. Always casualties, lad."

Hew faced Iain. "How can you be so cavalier about her life?"

With some frustration for the lad's mistaken assumption, Iain thought first to defend, "I'm no' cavalier about any life, no' the monks at Wick nor those poor bastards near Helmsdale that we buried."

Into the charged air that followed this, Artair wondered, "Who is Maggie Bryce?"

Iain would forever wonder why so much silence had followed Artair's simple query, why he and Hew only seethed at each other, as if waiting to see how the other might explain Maggie Bryce. Or why Donal and Daimh ducked their heads to avoid Artair's moving, questioning gaze, or why Duncan blew out a frustrated sigh.

Who was Maggie Bryce? What was she to them?

It was Archie who finally answered, his voice gruff, "She's a wench we met up with along the way. Turns out she's set to marry Sutherland...Alpin."

"Aye, and now she's merely a wench." Hew threw up his hands.

Duncan scoffed at this as well. "Not at all a pitiable creature," he mocked. "We should spare her no thought, aye, Arch? Obviously, the lass took to the road sheerly out of spite and malice, to do naught but aggrieve her betrothed. Aye, she braved a storm, and on foot, and begs to hie to St. Edmund's," his voice grew in both speed and anger as he continued, "and her face turns that shade of white when the man finds her, that the only thing remained of color were those damn freckles!"

Iain wasn't sure why the last of Duncan's fury was directed at him; nevertheless, he felt the need to point out, "I've said we'll get the lass. But it has to be done right, has to be planned properly."

"Canna just charge in there, willy-nilly," Daimh concurred.

"You met her on the road?" Artair desired clarification.

It was Donal who spelled out the particulars of how they came upon Maggie Bryce. "We found her near frozen solid in the bothies, and she stayed with us for those few days we camped out there. Told us she had visited friends but was planning on walking to St. Edmunds to take the cloth. Never said she was betrothed to Sutherland, dinna ken that part until the man and his army of fifty found us out near Glut."

Artair turned his speculative gaze to Iain but said nothing.

Duncan clarified gruffly, for Artair's sake, "We dinna ken Sutherland was Alpin until after he'd ridden off with the lass."

"He let her go," Hew accused of Iain, adding scornfully, "Wouldn't allow us to chase after her once we ken who Alpin was."

Iain stepped forward and jabbed his finger into Hew's chest. "That's the last time you make that remark. It would have been death, for every one of us."

"He understands that," Duncan said on a sigh. "Frustrated, that's all."

Silence reigned for several long seconds.

Artair spoke again then. "So many of the persons inside the walls of Blackhouse will be innocent, of course. Arch speaks true, there are always casualties. I'm not sure an exception should be made for *one* person, when so much is at stake." When there was no response to this, he added pointedly, "No matter the impression she made upon you."

Quiet scowls were all that confronted Artair at these words.

"You dinna ken her," Hew said quietly, shaking his head.

"Make a decision," Duncan prodded Iain.

Nodding, Iain said firmly, "We'll commit to some reconnaissance aforehand, ascertain if there's any chance to get her out before we lay siege."

While the soldiers nodded in unison their agreement to this, Artair advised, "You'll want to clarify that you might well make an attempt to save this lass, but that the capture of Alpin must take precedence."

Iain met Hew's bright blue gaze, while his own jaw tightened. "Aye."

He couldn't very well commit his men to saving the life of only one person—*no matter the impression she made upon you*—and likely he wouldn't have to coerce half of these here now. Privately, however, Iain vowed that he would do whatever was necessary to get Maggie Bryce away from Kenneth Sutherland.

IT TOOK TWO WHOLE DAYS to gather the number of men Iain required to pursue Alpin and prepare the logistics of their travel and their plan for the assault on Blackhouse Manor. Iain was generally a patient person, understanding fully that mistakes were made when the preparation was hurried, but even he bristled with exasperation that they did not—could not—ride out of Berriedale sooner.

When they did finally march toward Blackhouse, Iain led an army of over one hundred men. Behind him rode some of the best warriors in Scotland and the personnel necessary for the possibility of a long siege—the best archers, skilled carpenters, blacksmiths, and Berriedale's own engineer, who would oversee the building of any war machine on site. Carts laden with thick, freshly chopped logs plodded along at the rear of the moving pack, followed by a dozen more carts that transported all necessary implements and gear.

The snow was no more a hindrance, having shrunk further in the last few days; yet they were committed to a ponderous journey across the rugged landscape, owing to the number and weight of those burdened carts. Iain, Archie, and Hew rode on ahead, intent upon spying upon the keep to evaluate their options for their twofold intent.

Watching the keep from atop a low hill, it didn't take long for them to realize that Blackhouse was deserted. Dumbfounded and angry, Iain stood tall from his crouched position and squinted with fierce recrimination at the manse. And it took everything he had to await the arrival of the rest of his army before he charged through the open gates of Blackhouse.

They found only a few persons milling about the keep. Blackhouse's steward gave up information, at Archie's persuasive coercion, that all who were housed inside Blackhouse had been removed to another Sutherland property, Halliwell. Further, vigorous interrogation revealed that this unlikely move had been prompted by Kenneth Sutherland having been called up by Dungal MacDouall to make war against Robert Bruce and his cause.

"Where is Maggie Bryce? Is she gone to Halliwell?" Iain wanted to know.

The middle-aged steward, Oswald, sent frightened eyes to Iain, holding his hands up defensively before Archie. Trembling, he shook his head and cried out, "I dinna ken a Maggie Bryce."

Archie leaned into him. "Margaret Bryce, betrothed to Kenneth Sutherland!"

Only slight relief tempered the man's features, for his understanding. "Aye, aye. The lass he's to wed." Fear climbed again into his face. "But I dinna ken where she's kept."

"You're steward to the man and dinna ken where his bride is?" Iain barked with skepticism.

Archie tightened his fist in the man's cowl.

The steward cringed, tugging at Archie's hands helplessly. "I dinna ken, I swear. I never met the wench. The betrothal was only announced a sennight ago."

"She's no' a wench," Daimh sniped at the man before taking leave of the stables, where they'd found the steward hidden.

"Find out what he knows about Alpin's activities," Iain said, and he left the stables, and the matter, to Archie and Donal and Craig, who remained.

Iain glanced around the empty courtyard of Blackhouse, taking long and deep breaths to calm himself. A muscle ticked in his neck, and another pulsed near his temple. Where in the hell was Maggie Bryce?

MAGGIE HUDDLED INSIDE her heavy wool cloak, stiff and cold, but using all her remaining strength to not glance back with any hope or even despair as the Gordon keep faded into the distance. She wanted to cry, again, but could not. Apparently her body had exhausted all its tears in the last forty-eight hours, even if her mind had not.

They been married two nights ago, and it had taken her new husband but a short amount of time to show her exactly what kind of monster he was.

"You won't need that," he'd said when he'd come to her borrowed chamber after their vows. He'd pointed dismissively at the dressing gown she'd donned only moments before.

Elizabeth had kindly helped her ready herself for her wedding night, her face grim and her words few, which had only heightened Maggie's unease.

Apprehensive about stripping bare before him under the light afforded by many softly glowing tapers, Maggie had hesitated. That had been a mistake. Her new husband, with little patience and even less finesse, had rent the gown cleanly from her body with one quick and forceful swipe of the fabric at the neckline.

Her fears, all her trepidation over her wedding night, had been justified, she'd learned quickly enough. Their first coupling as husband and wife had been horrendous, Kenneth Sutherland proving swiftly that he lacked any shred of human decency, and that he held a very low opinion of his new bride.

In the light of day, with her husband riding his own steed and not confined to the vehicle with her, Maggie chose not to review every gory detail of her initiation to sex or even the next night when the nightmare was repeated. When next she cried, it was with a tremendous amount of dread, that she'd closed her eyes through much of the ordeal, and that she'd brought to mind the image of Iain McEwen. At the time, she'd considered it necessary; it might have been the very thing that had seen her through it. In hindsight, however, she was very afraid that she had attached that awful act to Iain merely by invoking his image that she might hold onto something good, something sure and safe.

After quite a lengthy span of fitfulness, Maggie glanced out over the moving scenery, though had little appreciation—indeed, little awareness—of the snow-capped hills or trees or the gently rolling pastures. Kenneth Sutherland saw no need to inform his bride of their travel plans, that Maggie had only learned from Elizabeth that they had been summoned by someone named MacDouall, and that Kenneth was to bring a large portion of the Sutherland army with him for whatever purpose.

"But why must I go with him?" Maggie had asked dear Elizabeth. "Why would he want a woman anywhere around an army?" She had to assume that some campaign, related to the ongoing war with England, was their destination.

Elizabeth had grimaced at Maggie, but did not mince words, "He is newly wed. He will want to avail himself of his new bride."

Maggie couldn't at this time have said what her response might have been to that. But she recalled well Elizabeth's pinched face look, as if she were sorry for her, but also anxious to rid herself and her household of all the wretchedness that was Maggie's marriage.

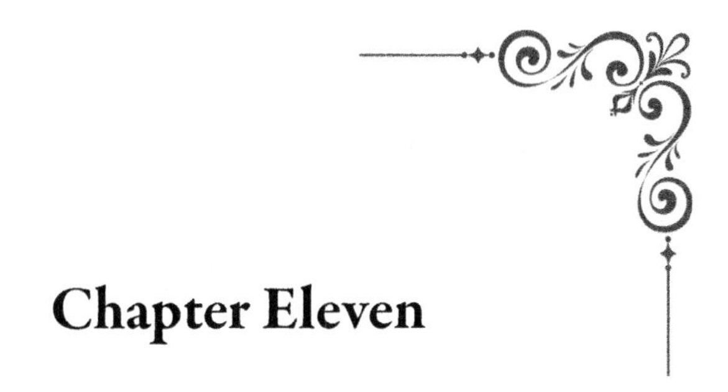

Chapter Eleven

May 1307

MAGGIE PRETENDED SHE was sleeping for the first several hours of the trip. It was simply easier than either the effort she would need to expend to ignore her traveling companion or worse, actually making conversation with the woman.

She'd not dared to show any emotion to her husband when he'd announced she'd be sent to Blackhouse while he remained in Carlisle, but oh how she had cried with joy inside.

A few days had passed since then, and she'd begun to fear that he might have changed his mind. She hadn't asked if this was so, not of a mind to fuel any irritation in the man, something she'd learned quite early on she would be wise to avoid at any cost.

Why he'd ever brought her to Carlisle with him would forever be a mystery to her. It had been a miserable few months, where she'd rarely been allowed to leave the rooms they'd let in the city, only made slightly more bearable by the one sitting across from her now.

Maggie finally opened her eyes and immediately met the dark gaze of Ailith. They traded unblinking stares, never having much cause for conversation. Ailith, with her pouty lips and raven black hair, was her husband's leman, and thought herself better than Maggie. Ailith's gown was made of a soft plum linen, the sleeves and bodice embroidered prettily with golden threads. Over this she wore a mantle of red, lined with soft yellow sindon, while Maggie owned no mantle at all, donned still the same gray cloak she'd known and had worn for years. Of course Maggie did not like her, but she could never argue that Ailith's presence in her husband's life had taken some pressure off herself—not all, certainly not as much as Maggie would have liked, but the woman did serve a purpose. Honestly, Maggie had no cause to feel any acrimony toward her, save that Ailith always behaved so abominably toward Maggie.

"It's all your fault," Ailith said now, "that we've been sent away."

"I'm quite sure you've set your own path, Ailith, as have I," Maggie said. It was only her own wretchedness that made her add, "Mayhap you didn't work hard enough to keep his attention away from the good ladies of Carlisle Castle. You gave up fairly quickly, to my thinking, with the coming of those English ladies."

"You are his wife," Ailith shot back. "It was your duty to assure he had no use for those monsters."

Maggie smiled grimly at her. There was no point in arguing with her. Ailith had proven more than once that she was capable of physical violence against Maggie; she had no wish to repeat any of those occasions. She did dare to ask, as she had often wondered, "Why did Kenneth not marry you, Ailith? You've been his whore for years, if I understand correctly? Have several bairns, do you not?"

Ailith clamped her lips and skinnied her eyes, possibly wondering if any animosity attended Maggie's' query. When she didn't answer, Maggie said, "I was only curious. You seem to have some feeling for him, or at the very least a desire for his company, his interest."

"I haven't any lands, of course," she finally answered curtly.

Maggie nodded, having suspected that. "But I am not your enemy. I neither sought nor wanted to be married to him."

Ailith favored her with a scornful frown. "How could you not? He's handsome and monied. He's a fine bedmate." She pursed her lips while considering Maggie. "Aye," she said with a smirk, "he said you dinna like it, dinna ken how to please a man. Said you squealed and cried the first time—you ken that only riles him up, aye?"

I know that now, Maggie thought dispassionately. "I only wanted to impress upon you that you and I want the same thing. You want him and I don't." An idea, which she'd toyed with for weeks, was put into words. "Our wedding gave him—and the Earl of Sutherland—the lands my father traded, but honestly what other use does he have of me, but to torment me? Bairns? He can have those by any woman, as you've shown. Perhaps if I were away, he might now wed you?"

Ailith gave her another long stare. She was many things, but she was not obtuse; she knew exactly what Maggie was proposing.

She smiled finally and Maggie slowly released her breath.

"You want me to help you escape?"

Maggie nodded. Her hands fisted in her lap.

Ailith nodded in return, her smile becoming oily. "I'll be giving that some thought."

Only allowing a small sense of hope to blossom within, Maggie inclined her head and closed her eyes once again, settling in for the remainder of the drive to Blackhouse.

As happened so often, when she closed her eyes, she saw Iain McEwen. Possibly, the image of him, the memory of him was all that had kept her sane these last few months. Not only him, but his men as well. Those few days with those seven men had, inexplicably, been some of the happiest of her life. This bespoke of one of two things: either that her little life was so woefully pathetic that being trapped in a snow storm with seven strangers had seemed wonderfully idyllic to her, or that Iain McEwen's kiss had been a larger experience in that dreary life than she'd known at the time. Perhaps both were true.

His eyes are blue, and his hair is dark. His smile is beautiful, and his arms are safe.

Sometimes she chanted this in her head, to keep it alive. She bemoaned the staleness of memory, that each day brought her further away from something so amazing. At this point, many months removed from him, she feared she recalled only that being in his arms, however briefly and sleepily, had felt warm and solid and right, but she could no longer imagine those strong arms around her, could not feel him press his lips to her forehead anymore.

Of all the things she missed, things she'd lost since marrying Kenneth Sutherland—her innocence, her sometimes fearlessness, her sense of self, hope—she was most sorrowful over the loss of memory.

She recalled some mention of an unfinished matter between them, her and Iain McEwen, but could not rightly bring to mind the exact words; she remembered Hew's earnest face watching her, and Archie's grin when she'd sung a song for him; she knew that the twins were beautiful, but could not recall if it were Daimh or Donal who had carried her up to the third hut; flashes of Iain's blue eyes were strong thankfully, but she could no more call to mind the exact shape of his smile, was only teased by some memory that suggested it was lovely.

However would she manage sanity when it was all gone?

They arrived at Blackhouse shortly before dark. Maggie had actually dozed, which allowed Ailith to scamper first out of the carriage. There were few to greet them, Blackhouse having been left almost completely vacant when the chief had taken his leave months ago. Maggie alighted and saw Ailith rushing over to a rotund and bald man, speaking quickly to him, pointing a finger at the man with some intent. The man lifted his gaze to Maggie, eyes thinned under his heavy scowl, at whatever Ailith was saying to him.

Several soldiers, who seemed not to be guarding anything, appeared from the barracks. Maggie cast her gaze around the bailey. 'Twas a sloppy yard, mud puddled in so many places and piles of chopped wood stacked so lazily that it accounted for much more ground space than it needed; a walkway above the hall, which overlooked the bailey, was missing several rails and one cut timber of the rail, having lost its hold at one end, dangled precariously close to the door that one would have to skirt it to avoid walking into it when entering the hall.

They approached, Ailith and the heavyset man. Neither of their expressions suggested Maggie should not suspect some trouble brewing.

So much for hope.

Maggie straightened her shoulders and announced, "I am Lady Sutherland, sir, and I—"

"She needs to be locked away," Ailith cut in, "as she has plans to run from our chief and their marriage."

"Escape your laird?" The man said, with a tsk-tsk that made Maggie's stomach turn. "We cannot allow that. You might have the right of it, Ailith, under lock and key to protect what belongs to our chief."

Cringing inside at what this might mean, Maggie felt soldiers move around her and at the plump man's behest, take hold of her arms. She went meekly with them, having learned over the last few months that her screams would go unanswered.

June 1307

FOUR MEN GATHERED ROUND the table in the great hall at Berriedale, the first time they'd met as such in many a month. No one spoke while they waited on Artair. Duncan stood at Iain's side, his arms crossed over his chest, his mouth tight while he stared out at nothing. Donal hovered near the end of the table, seated, pointing his dagger this way and that to catch and reflect sunshine from the windows. Archie sat near Iain, the chair pushed back, his elbows rested on his knees, head bowed.

"We should expand your officers' field," Duncan said after a while.

Iain did not turn, seated at the chief's chair, his forearms on the table, his gaze on the hearth across the hall. He'd thought as much recently. Since their numbers had dwindled, he would need to replace what they'd lost. He needed a tracker and a logistics man, among other things. "Bring up whomever you regard fit," he said, leaving the matter to his captain. He thought to intercede only so much as to command, "But no' Rhys. He gets under my skin." He tapped his tankard absently on the smooth wooden table top.

"Too much ale in that one," Archie added, seeming to concur.

"Boyd had spent some time with Craig," Duncan mused. "Might be growing pains, but he'll do fine for tracking."

"Eideard's got a good head," Archie noted, fine praise from one who rarely offered any.

Iain and Duncan nodded, and they were silent again, the very need for this discussion souring them further.

It was another ten minutes before Artair joined them, his leather binder of notes in hand.

"What news, Artair?" Iain asked of his steward, straightening in his chair.

He'd charged the man with putting out discreet feelers to find out where Kenneth Sutherland was at this moment. It had been a hell of a few months, gone from one battle to the next, it seemed. After their near siege on Blackhouse in early February, they'd been summoned by the king and had managed to locate and join Robert Bruce's force. The king's army, at the time, had been comprised mostly of men from the Isles, and what few dozen he'd gathered, having returned to his Carrick lands. The Bruce had been all too pleased to welcome the Mackays and a few other smaller chiefs into his fold, which more than tripled his numbers.

Sadly, they'd not been with the Bruce but days when they'd received the sorry news that the king's own brothers, having returned to the mainland from Ireland, had been met by the hostile force of that damn MacDouall—likely Sutherland, too. Their small force had been quickly overwhelmed by MacDouall and company, the brothers captured and taken to the English in Carlisle. It had been weeks before they'd been given the grim news of the sad and grisly deaths of Thomas and Alexander Bruce, under the order of Edward I.

At the time, they'd had some intelligence that suggested that Kenneth Sutherland had been a party to the transport, but they had lost track of him since. Thus, upon his return to Berriedale last week, Iain had set Artair the task of finding Alpin. Over the years, Artair had said repeatedly that information was power, and had once confessed to having what he called *rows of crows*, covert sources of intelligence throughout Caithness and further south, which had sometimes played a vital role in the safety and security of Berriedale.

"Kenneth Sutherland," Artair told Iain and his men, setting his papers down on the table before him, "and the Blackhouse Sutherlands did indeed conduct the Bruce brothers to Carlisle, alongside a party of MacDoualls. It is my understanding that Sutherland found favor with Edward I and some liking of Carlisle Castle and has remained there."

This was not the news they'd wanted to hear. They'd hoped to return to Berriedale and continue the pursuit of Alpin.

Artair folded his hands into his sleeves, as was his way, and added, "There was some news—its reliability cannot be verified—that young Sutherland sent his bride home to Blackhouse, possibly as long as a month ago."

Duncan, Iain, Archie, and Donal exchanged glances. That she was married to Sutherland was old news by now, Artair having managed to get that and other information to Iain while he'd been with the king. It sat no better with him now, even months removed from first hearing of it.

Duncan put out what many were thinking. "So the lass is now at Blackhouse and her husband hundreds of miles away."

"That *may* be correct," Artair allowed, his tone filled with caution, which not one man heeded.

"Sutherland's no' at Blackhouse, but we could be," Archie suggested, "in half a day, if we ride hard."

"Wouldn't need the whole army," Donal reasoned, "if only the lass and only a small retainer returned."

Iain glanced around the men, assessing the willingness of each one, which he found to be equal to his own. He nodded and just like that, the decision was made. The men quickly disassembled, anxious to be about the business of readying for the excursion.

Artair gave him a stoic nod, knowing he would go to Blackhouse, with or without his approval.

"This, then, would have nothing to do with the apprehension of Alpin," Artair reasoned when the men had departed the hall. "Is she worth the risk? You canna expect to steal a man's bride without reprisal."

Iain shook his head, not quite knowing how to justify their obsession with saving Maggie Bryce. He tipped back the rest of his ale, setting the tankard back down with uncommon slowness.

Thoughts of Maggie Bryce and the image of Maggie Bryce, the very sound of her velvety voice had been with him for months. He'd waffled between anger over her lies to him, regret that he'd let her go with Sutherland, and admittedly, some acknowledgment that he'd been right smitten with the lass. His emotions regarding her were all over the place. At some point, months ago, he'd convinced himself that his sentiments concerning her would not have been so dramatic if she'd but remained with them, that it had been the loss of her—and knowing with whom she'd ridden off—that had accentuated everything he'd felt. But then Hew...

He shook his head now.

Looking into Artair's solid gray eyes, he explained as much as he understood. "Seems our lives are split into two halves: before Maggie Bryce and after. But I canna figure the why of it."

Artair nodded thoughtfully and moved around the table. He took the chair beside Iain, pushed out a bit so that he faced Iain with his elbows on his thighs, his head bowed as Iain stared still across the hall.

In his low and calm tone, Artair said, "Of course, I did not have the privilege of meeting the girl, but I hope to one day, as she cast quite a spell upon you...all of you. Likely, you felt as if you failed her, mayhap thought you lost something when you couldn't pull her from Sutherland's grasp before it was too late. That was the beginning of a number of unfavorable turns. And then you rode off to your king's side and you lost Hew at Glen Trool and Craig and Daimh at Loudon Hill. More loss. It weighs heavily, I imagine." Artair sighed. "And it has not escaped my notice that the unit—your close circle, the officers—are not at all the same. They are, all of you, more somber...different men, every one of you. Even Archie—I didn't think he had but one or two emotions, truth be told—is more complex these days."

Of course, the loss of Hew and Craig and Daimh weighed heavily upon Iain, more so than had any deaths from earlier battles over the last decade. But how was it related to his inability to free the lass? Iain could not understand. Hew's death, with thoughts of Maggie as his last, had indeed returned Maggie to the fore of Iain's thoughts, as if clinging to the memory of her somehow kept Hew close as well.

Artair guessed, "And now you feel if you recover the lass, you'll somehow get back to where you were. Then."

Iain shook his head. "But it canna. Hew and Daimh and Craig will still be gone."

"You couldn't save them. But you can save the lass. That is what drives you now."

Iain tightened his jaw to keep his lips from trembling. "Last thing Hew said was to no' forget Maggie Bryce."

"Aye," Artair nodded sadly. "Arch said as much. Said Hew made him promise, hence Arch's sudden zeal to recover her."

Iain turned his head on his shoulder to consider Artair beside him. "Will it work? Will it fix anything?"

The old man shrugged, his lips thinned. "It won't bring them back, lad. Aye, but you know that. Yet, you've never been one to leave things undone. Go on and get her. You'll have done your duty to one without recourse. And mayhap—if she's all that you believe her to be—she can bring some joy back to Berriedale."

They sat quietly for a moment.

Artair touched the sleeve of Iain's tunic. When Iain faced him again, Artair said, "It's not your fault. You're not to blame. Bruce is not to blame. It is just war, lad. 'Tis all it will ever be. War. Love. Life. Over and over again until we die. We do the best we can. Never less than that."

Chapter Twelve

IAIN AND DUNCAN FOLLOWED Archie up to the lookout point and watched Blackhouse Castle for more than an hour. They'd ascertained quickly enough that Blackhouse—or any valuable commodity within—was ripe for the plucking as so few soldiers seemed to be in residence. 'Twas only their own disbelief that made them continue to watch, waiting it seemed, for the Sutherland army to appear from...somewhere.

"Jesus," Duncan mused, "almost as if he's inviting us in. Nary a guard atop the wall."

"It canna be this easy," Archie said, with his usual pessimism.

But then, "This is Sutherland land," Iain reasoned. "No reason to close the gate during the day."

Sutherland land indeed, and none would dare attack. Or none should dare, but half an hour later saw Iain McEwen and his party of twenty charging at full speed through the open gates and into the Sutherland yard, swords drawn as soon as they passed under the gatehouse.

Donal and the since promoted Eideard and several others pranced their mounts near to the door of the soldiers quarters as planned, should they be surprised by anyone thinking to become a hero today.

"Maggie Bryce," Iain called so loudly, it nearly echoed through the yard and keep.

"Maggie!" Duncan added his own cry.

The door near to the gatehouse did burst open but the three soldiers who'd erupted from the barracks were quick to drop their swords when they realized they were outnumbered. Another man, atop the battlements, leaned over with arrow nocked upon his bow.

"Daft bugger!" Archie shouted up at him. "No blood spilled—unless you start it! C'mon down."

"Maggie Bryce!" Iain called again. He dismounted, keeping his sword aloft and prepared to storm the hall when the door opened.

A woman stepped into the yard and plopped her hands onto her hips. She glared directly at Iain, brown eyes flashing. She must be kin to Sutherland, dressed as finely as she was, her brightly colored gown incompatible against the backdrop of the earthen browns and grays of this yard. She was followed into the yard by the overweight steward, whom Iain recalled. That man's skinny little eyes met with Arch and his jaw gaped.

"Who are you?" The woman asked.

"I've come for Maggie Bryce," was all Iain offered, moving forward still, knowing Duncan and Archie followed. The woman and the steward moved out of his path as he took the hall, but the woman recovered quickly, dogging his heels.

"Maggie Bryce!" Iain called again.

"She's no' here!" The woman screeched behind him.

Iain stopped in the middle of the hall and surveyed the room, noting the three different passageways that led from it. He turned on the woman, towered over her, intimidating her with his size and the fierce scowl marring his features. And even while he glared down at her, he said to Archie, “See what the good steward has to say about Maggie Bryce’s whereabouts.”

The steward, having followed them into the hall, made a sound that was peculiarly animal like, a yip of fear, perhaps with cruel recollection of Archie’s previous methods for extracting information. He turned, made to dash away through the open doorway. Donal stepped forward from outside, attuned to both the goings-on in the hall and the nonexistent resistance in the yard. He blocked the opening with the tip of his sword, thrust within.

The obese steward backed up, bumping into Archie’s chest, startling, shrieking, and turning.

“She’s locked away!” The steward was quick to give up then. “But it was not my idea! I dinna want to lock her up!”

“Point!” Arch insisted, bearing down on the fat man, forcing him back towards the doorway.

He did so, indicating the northern most corridor with a wobbly finger.

Iain gave one last lip curl to the brazen woman and heard Duncan instruct two of his men, “Keep them here,” before Iain, Duncan and Archie took off through the corridor. Several doors along the passageway opened only into storerooms, an office, and the garderobe, but there was no Maggie. At the end of the corridor was a set of stairs, but they led down and not up.

“I’ll kill him,” Iain seethed, grabbing up a torch from an iron ring in the wall and taking the narrow stone steps two at a time. The stairs turned twice and brought them to a small opening under the castle that was surrounded by three iron-gated, black-as-pitch cells. “Maggie,” Iain called, softly now, detecting no movement in any of the dungeon compartments. He stepped forward and held the torch near the bars of the first and then the second. A flash of movement at the far interior of the second cell caught his eye.

"There's no key," Duncan said behind him. To Archie, he said, "Get on up and get that key—"

Iain thrust the torch at Duncan, cutting off his instructions, and lifted his sword over his head, crashing the hilt down onto the lock mechanism on the gate. It took two swings, but the lock was cleaved away and clanked to the damp ground, the echo of it bouncing around the dank chamber. Sheathing his sword, Iain pulled open the gate and stepped inside. He had to duck to do so, the cell not being more than five feet tall.

The figure at the back of the cell cowered further into the corner.

"Maggie Bryce, I've come to take you away."

Duncan moved forward with the torch, the light slowly revealing the face of Maggie Bryce to them.

Wide and dull eyes greeted them, showing no recognition at all, before they narrowed against the onslaught of the soft glow of the torch. She was garbed in a filthy wool kirtle, one barely fit for a peasant, stained and torn. Her bare feet, sticking out from under the hem, were brown and muddied. She lifted a hand, held it up defensively before her, the fingers and palm as grimy as her feet.

"That bastard," Duncan frothed.

Iain went onto his haunches before her, sorry that she cringed and shrank yet more. He thought he detected some acknowledgment and furthered this by saying, "It's Iain McEwen, lass. I ken we're late coming, but I've come to take you away." He lifted his hand and moved the clumpy, tangled strands of hair away from her face.

"No." She shook her head back and forth. She did not slap at his hand, but slowly pushed it away from her. "You must go."

Everything stopped. Or it seemed as if it did. Iain stared, dumbstruck. Of all the possibilities of resistance he'd imagined he might encounter at Blackhouse, this had never been one he'd considered.

"Holy mother of God," Duncan breathed, as dumbfounded as Iain.

"You dinna want to leave?" Iain clarified.

"No, but thank you," she said, her voice so small he barely heard her.

Iain exchanged a perplexed look with Duncan.

His captain addressed Maggie. "You want to stay here? Married to Sutherland? Do you know what he is capable of? Dungeon aside, lass, he's—" He stopped when Maggie swung her gaze to him.

Her expression, eyes jerked to Duncan as if she were surprised *he* knew of Kenneth's violent tendencies, spoke volumes. *Jesu*, she was terrified.

"He will kill you," she murmured softly. "And me. All of us."

Archie moved from the other side of Iain, grousing, "Aye, and that's enough of that, Maggie lass." He bent at the waist, hands on his knees until he was eye level with her. "C'mon, now—willingly or by force. We're no leaving without you."

Maggie Bryce continued to shake her head, wrapping her arms around her bent knees. Iain just now noticed the tremors about her, moving all of her slim body against the damp wall.

Archie stood up and grabbed Iain's tunic sleeve, advising tersely very close to Iain's face, "Grab her and go. We canna fix her now, nor explain anything. No time now."

"Aye," Duncan agreed.

The two men stepped out of the cell. Iain blew out a harsh breath and reached for her. She reacted immediately to his touch, her hands swatting left and right, smacking into his chest and face, her nails digging into his scalp. She screamed and twisted until Iain managed to pull her to her feet and out into the common area that he could stand fully. She continued to fight him. He wanted to soothe her, but Archie was right; who knew how much time they had until a unit or the entire Sutherland army returned to Blackhouse? With little choice, he bent and grabbed one of her still-flailing arms, pressing his shoulder into her stomach, lifting her up and over his back, circling her legs with his other hand. He followed Archie and Duncan out of the dungeon and up the steps, steadying himself with a hand against the wall of the narrow stairway while Maggie Bryce's fists pounded into his back and buttocks.

Iain held her tight and cooed as they reached the ground floor "Shh. It's fine. It's good, Maggie Bryce."

In the hall, the brightly garbed woman screeched when she saw them returned, more probably when she saw Maggie Bryce draped over his shoulder. The woman charged at Iain, seemingly oblivious to Duncan's heavy hand catching her, bringing her to a shaky halt. Within two feet of Iain, she shouted, "Who are you to take her? What do you want with her?"

Settling his palm against the hilt of his sword, Iain scowled down at her. "Who are you to say I will no'?"

Maggie had stilled at the sound of the woman's voice. "Ailith?" Maggie murmured weakly from his back, a vague question in her tone. As she had calmed at the woman's voice, had quit her pounding on his back, Iain lowered Maggie onto her feet. He took both her hands in his as her legs wobbled instantly.

"Does she require removal as well, lass?" Iain asked of Maggie, sorry for the pale and bedraggled figure she cut just now, nearly cowering before him. She did not meet his eyes, but stared at the woman, held out of reach by Duncan yet.

Maggie shook her head. "S-she is my husband's whore."

"Aye, then," Iain said and, ignoring the woman's affronted outcry, asked of Maggie, "Is she to be treated as you have been? Arch'd be happy to stuff her and the fat man in the cells."

She met his gaze now, crinkling her brow over her green eyes. God, she was a mess. Not at all the Maggie he remembered. No fire lit her eyes, no smile teased at her lips, no color tinted her cheeks. He owed her nothing, he realized, yet acknowledged the guilt that chomped at him. He vowed to himself right then that he would never fail her again.

Her shoulders lifted in a sparse and nervous shrug. Her fingers dug into his palm. In a low voice, with a nervous glance in the woman's direction, she said, "You are truly Iain McEwen?" Tears glistened in her dull green eyes when she faced Iain again.

His expression softened. "Aye, lass."

She caught her breath and her lip trembled again. "He will kill you."

"Never happen," Archie grumbled from somewhere behind them.

It was Iain's turn to shrug. "I'm no' leaving without you, lass."

The nod that came was slow and small.

"And let's get to that," Archie insisted, moving toward the door, knocking against the steward with such force to send the man onto his generous backside.

Iain and Maggie followed, he holding one of her hands still. She shielded her eyes against the sun when they stepped into the yard. One of his soldiers walked his horse over to him while Iain's gaze scanned the bailey. More people of Blackhouse had gathered, idling about and whispering. Ignoring them, Iain lifted Maggie into the saddle and climbed up behind her, pulling her tight against him, his arms close around her, the reins held in front of her.

The woman Ailith had followed them into the yard and was screaming as all his men mounted. "Take me! Damn you! Take me, too!" She beat her fists against Donal's leg, as he'd sat closest to the hall upon his destrier. She clung to his boot while he fought to kick her away.

Iain called out to the woman, and anyone else who might record his message. "You tell Kenneth Sutherland that Iain McEwen has taken his wife. And you tell the bastard he'll no ever get her back."

The grumbling crowd grew more boisterous. A missile of horse dung was flung at one of Iain's men. Somewhere another woman cried out. The twenty Mackays, inside the small yard with their large destriers, took up so much space, and made for good targets if these people found the nerve.

It was Archie who put them to rights. "Let's go, lads! We've got what we come for!" And he jerked his mount around and dashed through the gate. Duncan gathered himself and tilted his head at Iain, who kicked the horse forward as Maggie began to cry in front of him. Donal finally removed himself from the woman's cloying hands and he and Duncan raced out of the bailey behind Archie and Iain, followed by the remainder of Iain's small party. Eideard and Donal stayed near the keep, just outside the gates, until the rest of the party was out of sight. But no Sutherland soldier took to the wall, to heave arrows through the air at the escaping kidnappers.

Maggie continued to whimper in his arms. She rode sidesaddle and clung to him, her face buried against him while she keened softly into his chest. Occasionally, over the thundering galloping of nearly a dozen horses, he heard her mumbling. Tears of relief, or of joy, Iain hoped.

Iain shifted the reins to one hand when they were far enough away, when no reprisal seemed to be forthcoming. He cradled her more tightly against him and pressed his face to the side of her head.

"Close your eyes, Maggie Bryce. You're safe."

THERE WAS NO WAY MAGGIE could unpack and explore all the emotions surging through her as they rode away from Blackhouse. Chief among these was relief, though admittedly this was tainted still with fear until they moved farther and farther away from her home.

Her home no more. Not that it ever had been. Not that she'd ever wanted it to be. Her bare knowledge of Blackhouse consisted of her many weeks in the cells below the ground, cold and hungry and afraid.

Iain Mackay had come to rescue her, she mused, still stupefied by the very idea. She'd not ever dreamed it, had given up on dreams long ago. Truly, she couldn't say she'd even thought of him since arriving at Blackhouse, but then, she'd thought of very little, her sanity kept only by chanting hymns and reciting what little she recalled of prayer, refusing to give up on that, her only hope.

But then Iain McEwen had come to rescue her. She sobbed anew with this wondrous turn of events, even as part of her feared yet some retaliation from Kenneth Sutherland. Would he miraculously show himself ahead on their path, as he had once before? Would he return home to Blackhouse, find her gone, and pursue her? Would she ever truly be free?

Close your eyes, Maggie. You're safe.

When her sobs had quieted after a while, sheer exhaustion shuttered her eyes and her mind, and she slept. Maggie woke when the motion beneath her stopped. She startled at first but quickly recalled her circumstance. Sitting sideways, half across Iain McEwen's lap, Maggie tipped her head up against his chest. He did not look down at her but stared out ahead. Maggie turned her face and followed his gaze.

"Berriedale," she breathed, not quite sure why the name of his home had stayed with her.

They sat upon a narrow stretch of high ground, bracketed closely by steep slopes of rock and on one side, a lazy river. At the end of this flat ground sat a small building of stone, its shape suggesting a chapel. Beyond that, past a massive wooden planked bridge, sitting upon a tongue of rock that projected out across the mouth of the river where it met the grand sea, sat an imposing castle. The stone of the castle and walls was a muted red color, showing an inner and an outer wall and a large courtyard dominated by a substantial keep and many outbuildings. The outer crenellated wall was two stories high and ringed the very edge of the rocky promontory on which sat the castle, showing naught but a straight cliff beneath on the river side, and slanted rocks on the southeast side that dipped into the sea. Another wall, inside this one, dissected the front quarter of the main wall.

They crossed the first bridge, which spanned a depression between the high ground and the rock of the castle's land. The horses' hoofs clicked steadily over the timber before they reached soft grass, which led them to a deeper drop-off, which was met on the opposite side by a gatehouse at the south end of the oval wall. As Maggie watched, the drawbridge of the gate was lowered until its peak settled upon the ground at their feet.

"Aye, lass. Berriedale," Iain said as he marched the huge steed over the bridge. "Home."

The first courtyard beyond the gatehouse seemed to have no purpose save for growing short green grass. They rode through another open gate, this one of thick wood and a square top, and entered the main yard of the castle. The keep itself had been built just inside the northwest section of the enclosed wall, on the river side, its peak being four stories high.

Maggie knew immediately that more than sunshine brightened this castle and its denizens. The yard was neat and orderly, the buildings well-kept and tidy. Those few peasants who milled about, a handful or so, showed only joy to see their chief and the McEwen men returned. The walls, both the inner and outer, were manned by attentive guardsmen who tipped their heads respectfully as their chief passed under them.

In front of the keep, Iain dismounted. Her gaze was still moving around this pleasant yard but was returned to him when his hands settled at her waist to bring her down from the saddle. Several lads came running out from one section of the long and low building opposite the keep, taking charge of all the soldier's steeds.

"I'll take you to my mother, lass," he said, taking her hand.

Maggie tugged at her hand, a girlish panic taking hold. When he turned to her with a frown for her slight resistance, Maggie enlightened him nervously, "I cannot meet your mother—any person—as I am." She plucked nervously at the loose and beyond filthy bodice of her sad kirtle.

"A bath first then," said a voice behind her, while Iain seemed to not comprehend what she fussed about.

Maggie turned and found Duncan, the chief's captain, approaching. Behind him, Archie and one of the twins hovered. She almost started crying again. She'd known they were among those who had come for her at Blackhouse, but the quick escape and the ride to Berriedale, most of which she'd slept or cried through, had prevented her from acknowledging them. But these were some very dear, wonderfully familiar faces. Reaching out, she meant to touch her dirty hand to Duncan's forearm, but pulled it back quickly as the light of day showed how filthy her fingers actually were. Still, she offered a wobbly smile, and let her gaze include Archie and the twin when she said, "I now owe you my life twice, it seems." Flattening her dirty hand against her heart, she added, "I am forever indebted to you."

"Aye, but you're a sight for these sore eyes, lass," said the captain.

"Well, I'm a sight, I'm sure," she returned with a nervous laugh. It sounded at once both foreign and beautiful to her ears. "But where are Hew and Craig and," she pointed at the twin, thinking he was Donal, recalling as she hadn't in the past few months that the hair at his forehead was thinner, "and Daimh?"

Duncan made a face just as Iain tugged at her hand.

"Aye, let's get you a bath first, lass," Iain said. "Time enough for catching up later."

Duncan and Archie and Donal seized happily on this.

"Och, you'll feel brand new after a good hot one."

"I'd wager the mistress can find you a clean gown, even."

Thus, Maggie was led up a set of stone steps that sat adjacent to the wall and led into the keep's hall. She hadn't visited many halls in her life but thought this one very well-appointed. Long and wide, it housed not one, but two hearths set in opposite corners. At one end of the room, a beautiful carved wood table sat on a raised stone platform; behind this table sat seven chairs, carved with equal finesse as the table; the stone wall beyond the table was decorated with many shields and weapons, some painted and some not, depicting ships and a dragon and the colors of the Mackays; the other end of the room showed a wooden screen, only half as high as the arched ceiling, with two openings, presently covered in a burgundy draped fabric; the arched ceiling was made of stone as well and was framed majestically by huge timbers of dark wood.

Iain had let go of her hand, but Maggie continued to follow him as he led the way up a wooden staircase on the exterior wall. "'Tis only my mother and I to use the family chambers," he was saying as they reached the next floor. He pushed open a heavy arched door at the end of the corridor. "This one'll be fine."

Iain stood just in the doorway, waiting for her to enter. Maggie didn't even bother to glance inside.

"I cannot take up a family chamber," she protested, aghast at the very idea. "I-I just cannot. Have you no servant quarters? Or mayhap a—"

He grinned, which quieted Maggie.

"Servants come from the village. Only two or three that reside inside the keep. But there are no more bedchambers, lass. Only these, for guests, which you are." He waved her inside, his grin now rather indulgent. "C'mon then. You're no' a servant, Maggie Bryce."

Slowly, Maggie moved by him as he remained in the doorway and stepped into the room. The chamber was very pretty, with tapestries on the walls and inside the shutters of the two windows. A beautifully embroidered coverlet of soft brown covered what appeared to be a very plush mattress on the raised bed. A short table stood beside the bed, supporting an ewer and basin, and a tall cupboard took up the wall space between the two windows.

More tears threatened, over the joy of her unexpected good fortune. Still, she demurred. "This is meant for finer guests than me," she guessed.

Maggie sensed him moving behind her, away from the door and then was startled by the touch of his hands, fixed upon her upper arms, that she stiffened in response. There was something soothing about this action, his touch, some familiarity that they truly couldn't claim but which she embraced inside for the peace it brought her. Possibly it was her stiffness that made him drop his hands after but a moment. Maggie was not sorry for the loss. Having some of her wits returned to her since leaving Blackhouse, she knew she did not want to be touched.

"It's for you. I'd think you'd be pleased with the comforts of it, after..."

Maggie nodded. "You'd think." It was gorgeous, every inch of the room, but was too grand by far for her.

He moved around her and bent near the small hearth to make a fire. "We haven't too many guests way up here, lass. Actually, I'm thinking my mother will be pleased with your coming."

Maggie turned and stared at his back. "Does she...know who I—does she know I'm here?"

"She will. She's no complicated, lass. Dinna fret."

Maggie covered her face again, willing tears to hold. His kindness, his very easiness, might well undo her. How did this happen? How did she come to be here? *Oh, please don't tell me I'm dreaming.*

"I don't understand," she cried, lowering her hands. "I don't know how—why—you came for me."

"Shh." He stood from the hearth and faced her.

"And what's going to happen," she continued, her fears too much to contain just then, "when he comes for me. Am I...?"

It looked as if he might step forward. Maggie automatically stepped backward. He didn't move then but he did shutter his expression.

"You'll no be fussing, lass. We've got all evening to talk and straighten it all out. You have your bath now and then you come down to the hall."

"You're going to require a bath as well," Maggie said and sniffled. "I can smell myself. Oh, God."

He chuckled at this, the sound insincere, she thought, more awkwardness forced between them. "Aye, you are ripe, lass." He indicated the lone chair that sat between the small table and the hearth. "You wait here. I'll send up the lads with the bath, and probably Edda to give you aid."

Maggie nodded and watched him leave, unwilling or unable to allow herself to feel hope. She waited then for the blessed bath to come, her gaze transfixed by the mesmerizing flames of the small fire Iain McEwen had made for her.

Chapter Thirteen

THE NEXT PERSON TO enter the bedchambers was certainly not any person meant to deliver her bath. Maggie knew immediately that this must be the laird's mother. The woman was lovely, more handsome than pretty, Maggie thought, adorned perfectly in a sleeveless blue gown over a long-sleeved kirtle of soft gray, the lines of stitching so fine as to give envy to any seamstress. Maggie had some success not staring at the deep and old scar that sliced across the woman's cheek but did little to diminish the fact that she was striking.

Jumping from the chair, Maggie dipped a quick curtsy then waited while the woman took her measure. She stared at Maggie for a long moment, possibly trying to see beyond the filth and grime before she walked around her to set down on the tabletop a bundle she'd brought with her.

Maggie rather scampered out of the way, moving along the hearth to stand at the opposite end. This seemed to suit the woman, who then sat in the chair Maggie had abandoned. Her limp, like the remnant on her cheek, had not gone unnoticed.

She faced Maggie, her position rather manly, hands on her knees, her back straight and tall. Finally, she tilted her head and said, "So you are Maggie Bryce." Any coolness Maggie might have suspected because of her silence for the first few minutes of coming to this chamber evaporated instantly at the kindness in the woman's face now.

Maggie shifted her weight onto her left foot and lifted a fisted hand against the stone of the hearth. She nodded.

"I can see that you are very lovely—underneath the filth, that is," the woman said, her smile aged and soft. She shook her head and the smile widened. "But you must be more than that, I imagine, to have captured the minds and hearts of Iain and so many of his men."

While she did not feel as if she were particularly being accused of something, Maggie was quick to counter, "Oh, no, mistress. I assure you, I've...captured nothing." And damn, but why did she want to cry so many times today! "But they are...I don't know if they're truly and always wonderful, but they have been to me."

The woman came immediately to her feet and rushed to Maggie. "Oh, no, my dear. Please don't cry. Of course, they're wonderful. As I'm sure you must be." Without a care for her fine garments, she wrapped an arm around Maggie's shoulder, standing nearly as tall as her son, and squeezed her tight. "Now, now, we're done with tears, lass. All that was bad is done. And now you move forward."

Maggie nodded jerkily, eager to please. "It's not fear, mistress. It's not anything but happiness that brings the tears, I think." More falseness, unwilling to explain to this woman that she could find no joy yet, knowing her husband would find her eventually. And that she would pay for an escape she had nothing to do with.

"Well then, that's a wonderful thing. You cry away. Ah, here is Henry with the bath. The water cannot be far behind." She pointed to a spot near the front of the hearth and the lad lowered the wooden vessel from his shoulder and scampered away. Addressing Maggie again, she said, "I'm Glenna McEwen of course, the laird's mam. I know only bits and pieces, to be honest, but you can fill me in with the details." At Maggie's sigh, she said kindly, "When you're ready."

More lads came, bearing buckets of steaming water, which was efficiently emptied into the tub. This process was repeated twice by the three lads, until the bath was filled to more than half. Glenna McEwen shooed the last boy away and closed the door behind him. Turning to Maggie, she beckoned with her hand. "Come along, my dear."

Maggie's eyes widened. "Mistress, you cannot—*should not*—attend my bath."

"Dinna fuss, dear." Without warning, she stood before Maggie and began lifting her tired gown up and over her head. "We haven't a huge staff here, and very few women. Between you and me, makes for a much smoother running household. However, the drawback is that we must see to ourselves, which you'll get used to."

"I've never had a lady's maid, mistress," Maggie admitted. She kicked off her pitiful shoes and dropped her hose to the floor as well and climbed into the bath, happily sinking back into the gorgeous warmth.

The mistress of Berriedale bent and plucked up each piece of Maggie's discarded wardrobe and said from the door, "Take no offense, my dear, but these will be burned. And I'll fetch the soaps, which the lads apparently have forgotten. You rest, enjoy the glory of it."

Maggie did relish it, but Glenna McEwen returned in good time and the serious work of getting herself clean began. By the time she stepped from the bath into the cozy linen towel, almost an hour had passed since the woman had walked through the door. Maggie was invigorated by the lovely lilac scented soap Glenna had supplied and was thankful their conversation had not encompassed anything more than information about Berriedale.

Glenna McEwen was the sister to the laird of all of Caithness, Donald Mackay, and had married Ilagan McEwen when she was but sixteen.

"He was a very fine man," she said wistfully. "Very easy on the eyes and a true son of Scotland, died fighting for her freedom."

The laird's mother then set herself the task of untangling the mass of Maggie's thick but now clean hair, using a bone comb that she was quite proud to say had come from France, via her brother.

Standing behind while Maggie sat again in the sturdy chair, Glenna McEwen tediously worked out the knots and said, "Now we'll get the story out, Maggie Bryce. I do not like not knowing a person who resides in my home." When Maggie nodded, she added, "My son is wonderful in many regards, but does not always tell his mother everything. What little I know comes from what I've coaxed out of Artair, Berriedale's steward."

Maggie shifted on her bottom and pulled the linen towel more securely around her. "Shall I begin at the beginning, when I met your son?"

"No, unless there's more to it than they found you near frozen in a cave, but then you were put upon by Sutherlands and you were taken away."

"That's it, essentially," Maggie admitted. "Except...except that I lied to Ia—your son. I was running from the betrothal to Kenneth Sutherland when I was caught in the storm. But I told your son that I was headed to St. Edmund's—"

"The cloister?"

Maggie nodded. "Which wasn't exactly a lie, as that was my destination, when I decided I didn't want to marry...him."

"Not exactly a lie at all," Glenna McEwen graciously allowed.

"But then I put them in danger—they might have been killed. For that, I am very sorry."

"But they were not. And Iain and the lads never met a battle they didn't like," she said with a small chuckle. "Such men. Happiest when engaged in any bloodshed."

"He was so angry at me," Maggie said, recalling the glower he'd given her at the time, how her heart had broken. "So I don't understand why he came for me now, after all this time. Nothing makes sense."

"But it is my understanding that they went to—Blackhouse, is it? Yes, they went there only days after you were retrieved by Sutherland. Went with his whole army. Of course, you were not there. And then...then they were called away in service to the king."

Maggie's jaw gaped. She might have whipped her face around to Glenna, but that the woman had flattened her hand against the top of Maggie's head while she worked out the tangles below.

"They went to Blackhouse?"

"As I understand it. Which says so many things to me, but most of the answers you'll now be seeking must come from Iain. Oh my, are you crying again, my dear?"

Maggie nodded. "I'm a mess. I know. I just don't understand the kindness of one, and to a near stranger, in contrast to the evil of another, who is...my husband."

Glenna came around the front of the chair and went down on her knees, drawing Maggie's watery gaze to her. She clutched at Maggie's fisted hands and insisted, "Kindness and the other have nothing to do with proximity or relationships. A person is good or not, and that is all. I will act just as kindly to a stranger as I would to my own son, because I am good. Your husband is a monster and is likely evil for the very sake of being evil—some people are just born that way. It has nothing to do with you, but for your unfortunate relation to him. But now that's done. Do you hear me, Maggie Bryce? It's done. I still don't know everything, but if my son drove twenty men half a day to find you and rescue you, I'd bet my good leg that he's not going to give you up. Not ever."

Maggie tried to smile. But she just could not.

Glenna stood and finished with Maggie's hair, managing two long braids, which she rolled up and pinned to the back of Maggie's head.

"There," said Glenna, "now let's get you dressed."

THE HALL HAD STARTED to fill as the supper hour grew near but went completely still and silent when Maggie Bryce and Glenna McEwen entered.

Iain, standing with several of his soldiers, had just taken a swig of ale when Duncan nudged him and tipped his head toward the stairs. Iain gulped and choked and coughed at the sight of her. Duncan laughed and swatted him heartily on his back.

Maggie Bryce, frozen in the cave, overdressed in many layers, including the shapeless cloak and perpetual wimple, had been beautiful. Maggie Bryce of the dungeons, gaunt and pale in her filthy kirtle and smelling of only-God-knew-what foulness, had somehow still been very appealing.

But this Maggie Bryce, fresh from her bath and garbed in a fine gown of rich blue wool, which hugged her curves so lovingly, was...exquisite.

His mother, not one to let a silence have no purpose, called out cheerily, "Friends, it's not as if you've never set your eyes upon a beautiful woman before! After all, I've lived here for years!"

And the silence was further undone with the cheers and laughter that followed this, so that the remainder of their descent, and their walking through the crowd seemed not so singular an event after all.

Iain knew some pleasure that Maggie's eyes had so quickly, even at the top of the stairs, sought him out. It was unfortunate then, that the initial quieting of the room had sent her anxious gaze to her own chest. And neither his mother's quip nor the happy laughter that followed had wrested her gaze from her own person. Shades of the sprightly Maggie Bryce he remembered from the cave, remembered quite often if he were honest, were nowhere to be found.

In the next moment, she stood before him, delivered as it were to him and Duncan and Archie as they stood near the center of the hall. His mother departed, off to the kitchens no doubt to be assured the meal would be delivered promptly and beautifully.

Possibly Maggie had no interest in all the goings-on of the hall, but she pretended she did, her eye scanning the hall, giving no individual attention to any person, not even this circle of people she knew. He hadn't forgotten how green her eyes were, of course, but damn, he hadn't recalled properly, that was sure.

Meeting Duncan's gaze, Iain saw that he noticed it as well, that she was not at all the same Maggie Bryce they'd known. She was neither wide-eyed nor curious, her roving gaze filled only with dread, he thought, swiveling often to the door of the hall, as if she expected at any moment the portal might be kicked in by an army.

Her husband, he supposed she feared.

"Aye and that's a lot of promise fulfilled, lass," Duncan said cheerily beside Iain. "Thought you were bonny in the caves, but that dinna compare to this, now."

Her gaze spun from the door to his captain and she required several seconds to digest his words, it seemed, but then only offered a wee smile, though said nothing so that Duncan blew out a breath and searched for more conversation.

Cheerily, he said, "Summer is nigh, Berriedale is healthy and its laird in residence, war has paused for the while—all is right in our little corner of the world." He lifted his tankard as a toast.

Arch and Iain followed suit, tipping the ale back just as Glenna returned to them.

Maggie said nothing.

Iain saw Artair approaching, inclining his head to persons as he passed, his smile slight but friendly. The old man stepped into the space between Duncan and Glenna, making no effort to remove his curious gaze from Maggie. Iain didn't understand why it was so important to him that Artair appreciate the lass, or why he was nervous about an introduction, but recognized some anxiety within that the old man approve.

"Artair, may I present Maggie Bryce? Lass, this be Artair, Berriedale's fine steward."

Artair stepped forward, closing the space between them, his keen gray eyes giving no hint to his thoughts. He lifted Maggie's hand in his, holding it lightly, patting the top of it with his other hand, while he held her gaze and measured her person.

She fisted the fingers of her untouched hand at her side.

"This is indeed a great pleasure," he said in his polite way. "It'll be no secret that your name has come to my ears more than once, lass. It's nice to put a bonny face to the name."

"I am very pleased to meet you," Maggie replied earnestly with a briefly bowed head. "Mistress Glenna says you've been with three Berriedale chiefs now."

Artair gave one of his slow smiles. "Which is her polite way of having informed you that I am as old as dirt, lass." Before Maggie could gainsay this, he patted her hand again and advised, "But yes, three lairds I've now proudly served."

Her response was naught but a nod and she pulled her hand away from his. Iain saw those fingers as well clench and disappear into her skirts.

The kitchen staff appeared then, bearing trays and platters of food.

Glenna shooed everyone to their seats, leading Maggie Bryce to the head table with them. Maggie's halting, "Oh, but I couldn't," was dismissed by his mother with a negligent, "But you will," as she directed her to sit in the chair beside Iain.

"Begin as you mean to proceed," his mother said to him when he threw a questioning glance her way, over Maggie's head.

He had no quarrel with Maggie sitting at the head table, only supposed it might send the wrong message about her position at Berriedale. But then, as she *had* no official position, other than a guest he supposed, he didn't worry overmuch about it. Berriedale's people were generally good-natured and welcoming—Glenna and Artair would never allow for anything less.

However, he did somehow need to explain her presence to one and all and did so with a toast before they dined.

"We have much to celebrate tonight. This is Maggie Bryce, ladies and gentlemen. Treated poorly by the Sutherlands, she comes to us with much to offer and with hopes of a fine welcome. Now, dinna ask her to tell you any jests, as she's no' a good mummer." While the people inside the hall laughed at this, Maggie only stared straight ahead. "Welcome her kindly, if you please, for by the grace of God, she's one of us now!"

MAGGIE MIGHT HAVE ENJOYED the meal and the company tremendously, watching all that went on while listening to the conversations of Iain to her left and Archie to her right. The hall really was boisterous, and the food was very finely presented. Sitting before the laird was one of many roasted geese, stuffed with savory and pears and quinces. There came platters of spiced cabbage and minced pork and raisin tartlets, followed by a dish that widened Maggie's eyes—boiled dough pieces baked with cheese and butter, which Iain told her was called macrows, and which Maggie decided was her new favorite food item.

If only her stomach would allow her to appreciate any of it.

When the kitchen wenches and lads began to clear tables, a woman sat down in the far corner of the hall and began to play the rebec, the jaunty but low-keyed notes a perfect backdrop to the chatter in the room.

Suppers in Torish, even when her mam and siblings were alive and home, had been quiet and quick, the food given as nourishment, and swiftly consumed that they might return to their labors. Dining at the home of the Gordons, in the short time she'd been housed with them, had been more leisurely, but very sedate, only the Gordons and she and occasionally her father in attendance. And then Carlisle. She'd been a guest only once in the grand hall of the castle, very soon after her wedding and their arrival. An English soldier had inquired of her circumstance, of her family, when her husband was away from her side. Kenneth had returned to find his wife quietly answering the man's polite inquiries. She'd been whisked away from the hall, his fingers tight around her upper arm. She'd paid dearly for the few words she dared to speak to a kind stranger and was subsequently banned from the dining hall by her husband after that, taking her meals alone in the prison of her grand chamber.

But this now, this hall and these happy people, was unlike anything she had ever known, for exactly how cheery and relaxed this entire room and this supper event were.

She leaned over to Archie once again. He'd finished eating and only sat back, his ale still in hand, seeming content to linger and enjoy the din of the room as she did. "Everyone is so...lighthearted."

Archie nodded agreeably after considering her curiously for a moment. "Berriedale is generally a happy place." He shrugged a bit, tipped his tankard of ale on the cloth covered table. "No' that it hasn't seen its share of woes through the years. But aye, you've landed well, lass."

"Less landed, I imagine, than was delivered. But where is Hew? Is he on watch? And Daimh and Craig?"

Archie made some inscrutable face and said vaguely, "Aye. Soon, lass." He leaned back in his big chair then and made another mysterious face. Maggie turned and saw that Archie was holding the gaze of Iain, who gave a curt nod and stood.

"C'mon then, lass," the chief said, holding out his hand to Maggie. "We'll take a nice stroll around the yard."

Maggie understood she was expected to rise but pretended not to notice the proffered hand. She stood at the back of the dais and lifted her eyes to him. He showed a tight smile and pointed to his left, indicating she should step away from the family table and off the dais. He then led the way, single file through the rows of trestle tables, and then out of the hall.

Out in the yard, aglow in a soft orange haze from the setting sun, Maggie folded her hands in front of her and followed as he led her in the direction of the inner gate.

"Your mother is lovely," Maggie said when conversation seemed not to be on his agenda.

"Aye," he said. "A great lady, she is." He gave a nod to the men atop the gate, the watchmen, and led them out into the outer yard through the open gate.

Maggie turned, walking backwards, searching the helmed figures of the men upon the elevated walkway, looking for any familiar face. She saw none, turned forward, and focused her gaze on the battlements above the outer gate as these men acknowledged their laird's passing through and his call of, "We'll no be long, back in time for gate closing."

Maggie sighed a bit, having hoped for a glimpse of Hew.

They walked further, over the lowered drawbridge and across the grass until they came to the timber-planked bridge. There, Iain pointed to the edge of the bridge and sat with his legs dangling over the side, above the slight depression of ground beneath. Maggie did likewise, sat beside him, her eyes following as he steered her gaze toward the west.

This presented a clear view of the river that met the sea and beyond that, the beginnings of a magnificent sunset, the sky a multitude of colors, streaked with thin orange and blue and purple clouds.

"He's no here, lass," Iain said, his voice somber and low.

Maggie pulled her appreciative gaze from the sunset and fixed it on Iain. "Who's not here?"

Iain pulled at weeds and vines that grew up from the ground beneath and snaked through spaces between the laid timber of the bridge. "Hew."

Frowning, she watched his hands, stripping the plucked vine of its leaves in his lap. She was afraid to query further, advised of the answers to any questions she would have had by his suddenly solemn mood.

"Or Daimh. Or even Craig."

Maggie's bottom lip fell. She stared at him, even as he kept his head lowered, his hands busy with the weeds. Eventually, her shoulders slumping, she turned again to the masterpiece God made in the sky. Now, curiously, amazingly, she seemed to have no tears to shed, even as her chest tightened painfully and a heat gathered in her throat and cheeks.

"They are gone, then."

"Aye."

She sighed with a great sadness but couldn't honestly say she was shocked...but that all three were gone. "I rather thought Hew might have...it makes sense, then." Iain turned now and frowned at her, until she explained, "I dreamed of him, a few weeks back. Hew. Maybe months, I'm not sure. He was just there, smiling at me, no flush to his cheeks. Just...happy to see me." She shrugged, unable to explain it properly. "As was I...happy to see him. His features were so peaceful, not a wrinkle in his brow. And...I don't know how, but I knew he was gone."

"Gone upon the Steps of Trool," Iain said. "Then Craig and Daimh lost at Loudon Hill."

"Loudon Hill?" That place was familiar to her or stirred some memory. "I'd heard Loudon Hill mentioned when we were in Carlisle. The entire court spoke of it for days—whispered really, as none would dare say the words too loud. The English King was incensed at the loss there."

It was Iain's turn to show surprise. "You met the English King?"

She shook her head. "I did not. I spied him from some distance one day, unable to believe that so sickly and feeble a man was the same who had rained such terror and brutality over Scotland for so long." She gave some thought to that lone sighting of the man his own subjects both revered and feared. "He could barely stand. But his voice, when he spoke, was strong and vital."

"Rumor claims he's no long for this earth."

"I couldn't believe a man who looked like that—all magnificent robes and finery aside—was a living and breathing thing."

"Did you enjoy the royal court?" he asked, adding almost as a postscript, "Nonetheless?"

At first, Maggie thought the question odd, and let her expression tell him as much. Quickly, however, she supposed so many people would have been enthralled by the once in a lifetime chance to walk within arm's length of the lady Queen in the halls of Carlisle's priory, to rub shoulders with the most powerful people in the land, to see such splendid persons and clothes and trappings and food. Perhaps Iain McEwen supposed she might be one of these people.

"Not at all," she said. And then, returning her focus to the loss of those men who had been so kind and dear to her. "But Hew and Daimh and Craig. It's just awful." She glanced up at Iain, who favored the sky once again with his gaze. "I'm sorry about your friends. I'm sorry that is your life, that on any given day, you might be called to arms, and you might lose friends and family and loved ones."

He nodded, bleakly, she thought, pursing his lips a bit. "Aye, and I'm sorry you had to marry such a one as Sutherland."

"Of course, that was not your fault...not your doing."

He shrugged. "And Hew's death was not yours," he countered. "But sorry circumstances deserve some recognition."

Maggie considered this but gave no reply.

He lowered his head, his chin almost to his chest, while he played with those stripped vines again, and inquired, "Do you want to talk about it?"

Maggie jerked her gaze to him. "Talk about being wed to Kenneth Sutherland?" She was rather confounded by the question. Why ever would she want to relive any of that awfulness? she marveled. Her freedom was new yet, and she grappled still with a fear that it was not to be a permanent condition, that her husband would find her. She would pay dearly when he did, she dreaded, and gave some thought to wonder if this precious bit of freedom now would be worth the punishment that would surely come.

Iain McEwen surprised her again, giving a fairly sheepish chuckle before he said, "Mother and Artair are forever insisting that we mustn't keep our sorrows inside." There was some mocking sentiment to his tone, as if he quoted either of them but did not entirely agree with the observation. "We must visit them and review them, our sorrows and our grief, to better exorcise them from our minds and hearts."

Maggie reflected upon this recitation, though was of no mind to share with this man the horrid details of her short marriage. Her marriage, for all its brevity, had been the substance of nightmares. Perhaps—if—one day she was assured of a more permanent sense of freedom, she might well do herself a favor and address it internally. But...not yet.

"I don't think I need to," she said finally and thought to include, "but thank you." Maggie supposed she sensed some relief in him then and returned her gaze to the glorious sky, the light and colors having changed so much in just the few minutes they'd sat. Taking a deep breath, she said to him what had plagued her most in the last many months. "I apologize for lying to you, for not telling you I was indeed betrothed to him. You asked. Repeatedly." She ducked her head in shame and mumbled her only feeble excuse. "I...I just...I never thought for a minute that he would find me."

He nodded though did not look her way. When enough time had passed that she began to wonder if he would respond at all, if he would forgive her, he finally said, "You owe me no apology, Maggie Bryce. You did only what you thought you needed to."

She read no forgiveness, in either his tone or his words, that she pressed on, "But now you have saved me, again, that I feel doubly sorry for what little faith I'd placed in you."

He gave a cheerless chuckle and tossed the bare stem aside. "You dinna ken me at all. You were right no' to trust a stranger with that truth."

Her shoulders slumped, sorry now that she had resurrected this between them. "Although I did trust you, oddly enough. Truth be told, by the time...we parted, I felt we were not strangers."

This brought his gaze back to her. She could read nothing in his dark eyes and was quickly unnerved by the intensity of his stare that she lowered her face again.

"No' strangers by then, no." He lifted himself to his feet then. "We need to get back, that they can close the gate."

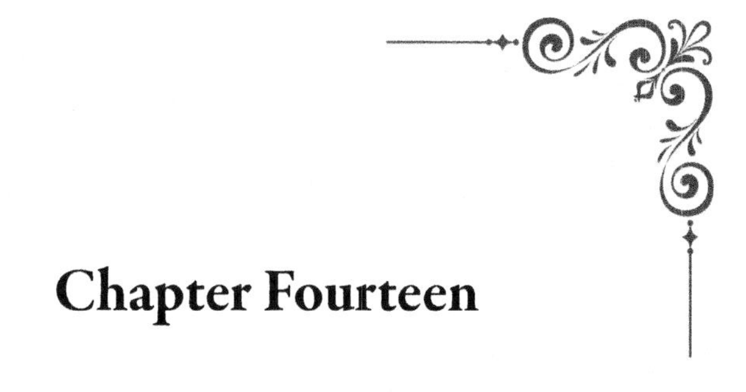

Chapter Fourteen

THE VERY NEXT MORNING, her first full day at Berriedale, Maggie shadowed Glenna around the keep, meeting first all the kitchen staff as Glenna's day began there. The mistress and the cook, a sour-faced though pleasant woman curiously named Rabbie, dealt quickly and efficiently with the meal plan for the day and what preparations they would plan for the next week. Maggie half-listened, glancing around the bustling room, which seemed to employ mostly children, girls and boys all younger than herself. They were positioned at various places and jobs around the kitchen; two girls chopping leeks upon a prep table, both small enough that they stood on short stools to be of a good height to apply pressure to the large knives they used; a young lad swept out one unlit section of the large hearth, using a short-handled broom to sweep ashes into a bucket; through a door at the end of the kitchen, Maggie spied another pair, a lad and lass, sitting on more short stools around a tub in the scullery, cleaning kitchenware from the day's first meal. She frowned at these two, thinking neither of them older than ten years of age.

Glenna followed her gaze and said, "Never too young to work."

Maggie faced Glenna, a bit of guilt tinting her face for her judgment that indeed, they were too young.

Glenna explained, "No one is idle at Berriedale. The children of the keep—and even from the village, if their parents desire—labor for two hours every day. Never more."

This relieved Maggie somewhat, having worried that they were too young for a long day of labor.

Glenna grinned. "We're not monsters, lass. But truly, idle hands will only beget problems."

Rabbie, having finished her meeting with Glenna, had moved on to beginning preparations for supper. From a basket at her feet, she lifted a long salmon onto the counter and neatly chopped his head off with one swipe of her sharp cleaver. The severed head was pushed to one side and the body to another, and another salmon was brought up for execution.

Maggie winced as the knife chopped again, the thud and squish of the death blow turning her stomach. Grimacing, she pressed a hand over her belly and tightened her lips. When the third fish was relieved of its head, Maggie darted away from the counter, toward the back door, covering her mouth as she ran.

To her great mortification, she had barely made it through the door when she retched and heaved her morning meal into the dirt of the rear bailey. Bent at her waist, she felt Glenna's hand on her back.

"Maggie dear," she said with some sympathy. "Oh, my."

Maggie straightened, having no idea what just happened. She had not been unwell, had not the slightest rumble in her belly all morning. With an embarrassed grimace toward Glenna, she could only murmur, "Apologies, Mistress. I'm not sure how...why—"

Glenna took her hand, squeezing her fingers around Maggie's, bringing her uncomfortable gaze to her own concerned one. "Had you not felt ill?"

"Not at all," Maggie replied. "A bit nervous, mayhap. My first day at Berriedale."

"But certainly not enough to have caused that," Glenna surmised, throwing a glance at the mess in the dirt.

"I am so sorry. I will clean that—"

"You will do no such thing," Glenna returned with a frown. She sighed then. "When did you last menstruate, lass?"

Perplexed, Maggie showed a frown of her own. She glanced around, happy there was none to witness this unseemly conversation in the light of day, in the open bailey. Shaking her head, she tried to recall, and said to the mistress, "I suppose when we first arrived in Carlisle."

Glenna's eyes widened, frightening Maggie, who was beginning to have an inkling why Glenna had asked so personal a question. "Goodness, lass! That must have been months ago."

Maggie nodded, her lips trembling. Disjointedly, she tried to deny what might be true. "But then—Blackhouse...and the cell—" she said, glancing up with a mixture of despair. "Surely, only anxiety...has wrought its absence."

The mistress made a face, allowing this might be possible. Squeezing Maggie's hand, she said, "While that is wholly conceivable, we must brace ourselves for the probability that it is not the case."

This withered Maggie, whose legs seemed to buckle under her. Glenna yanked at her hand as Maggie sank. But it wasn't enough to keep her upright.

"Whoa!" She heard called just as she was secured by hands stronger than Glenna's. She recognized Iain's voice and while she froze at his touch, she hadn't the strength to resist it, her wits and vigor being sapped by the idea Glenna had so regrettably planted.

With a lightness that Maggie vaguely assumed was manufactured, Glenna rushed out with a laugh, "The poor dear apparently has no stomach for the preparation of our favorite salmon."

"I'm fine," Maggie said, the weakness of her voice fashioned from a staggering fear and disbelief. Slowly she straightened, willing her legs to hold her. She pushed Iain's hand away from her arm.

He, too, must have come from the kitchen, the door still ajar behind him. Maggie was not unmoved by the concern darkening his features but insisted, "I really am all right." She pressed her hand to her belly and tried, as Glenna had, to make light of it. "How silly of me."

Glenna assisted with a collaborator's grin. "How swift and brutal was Rabbie's swinging hatchet."

"Aye," mumbled Maggie, removing her gaze from Iain's.

Seemingly satisfied with their suggestion for Maggie's upset, Iain said, "C'mon then, lass. We'll take some greater fresh air down at the beach."

Wide eyes greeted this suggestion.

Glenna was quick to object. "Nay, son. The lass should rest a bit, get her humors restored."

In good cheer, which Maggie thought was falsely increased, he gainsaid the mistress. "No better way to correct humors than salt air in your lungs and sand between your toes." When it appeared his mother might argue yet more, Iain laughed and stepped away, beckoning Maggie to him. "You'll get her back in no time at all."

Maggie sent an anxious glance to Glenna, hoping for yet more assistance so that she didn't have to go with him. But his mother only nodded, her mouth pinched with some whiff of an expression that Maggie read as saying, *pretend all is well.*

"I'd come to collect you," Iain said, when she walked toward him without any eagerness, "thought you might want to discover the beach."

"That was very kind of you to consider me," Maggie allowed sincerely, "but I shouldn't like to be gone too long." At Iain's questioning look, she added, "I've barely been at your mother's side an hour and truly wanted to learn what I might to be helpful."

"Plenty of time for that, lass."

They walked toward the far end of the curtained wall, the end opposite the main gates from which they had come upon Berriedale yesterday. Here, at the northeast side of the castle, there was only a man-sized door in the wall, which stood half open. Iain pushed it further open and led Maggie through.

The sea was the first thing Maggie saw, no less fascinated with the sight of it now than she had been yesterday. Sunlight danced in the waves, glistening so bright as to render all the water in a shimmery summer haze. The ground here, outside the wall, was mostly rock, even and spattered here and there with bits of green growing things. Iain closed the gate behind them and walked straight forward, toward the cliff.

"Bit of a dip here," he said, leaping forward, down a drop of three or four feet.

The cliff here was not as steep as the northwest side, which faced the river. Here the ground gave way to a gentle decline of sea grass and thistle that meandered down to the beach. Iain stood below, on a well-worn path of sand and stone, offering his hand as Maggie meant to navigate her way down. She declined his help, with what she thought was a politely given, "I'm fine," and carefully picked her way through the rocks and dunes. She stopped at one point, to consider the vista, surveying the land and the sea, and the beach itself so far below. 'Twas not a large or grand beach, but a triangle plot of sand at the bottom of this hill that possibly measured in both width and length the exact dimensions of the bailey above.

Several people and two small boats were visible below. Maggie recognized Archie's dark head of hair and beard; saw him assisting several others, hoisting the boat up onto the beach, as if they'd just come ashore. They descended, Iain well ahead of her now. Maggie could not deny that she was enthralled by the sea and the sound and the salty air. The wind whipped up her hair and even the hem of her blue and borrowed kirtle, but she knew there was wonder and solace and joy to be had here, even with so many people below.

It was indeed Archie with the boat, though Maggie recognized no other man. They'd shoved it far up into the sand, almost to the bottom of the hill.

"Were you fishing?" Maggie asked when she stood beside Archie. She had to lift her voice over the small, but noisily crashing waves.

If Archie were surprised to see her, he gave no indication. He shook his head, and included Iain in his answer, as if giving a report. "Nae, lass. Just out and about, but there was naught to see."

To Iain, he said, "I'll get up top with the lads." He followed the five other men from the boat as they climbed the hill to the keep.

Maggie watched them for a moment, taking note of how easily the younger lads scampered up the hill. Turning back to the sea, she moved forward, giving some thought to Iain's earlier words, about toes in the sand. She glanced down, pressing the hem of her gown near to her legs, showing her slippered and hosed feet. 'Twould be too much trouble, she supposed, and likely unseemly, to remove the hose and shoes. Perhaps if she'd been alone....

"Aye, go on, lass."

Lifting her gaze showed Iain perched in the sand several yards away, doing just as she contemplated. But then, he had only his leather boots to remove, appeared to wear no hose.

"We dispense with the formality of hose so often for just this purpose," he advised.

She couldn't—wouldn't—she knew.

He rose and swiped at his bottom, sending sand skirting away, and gave her a funny look.

"Lass, you must let go of everything you ken," he said. "Berriedale is easy and different. We work hard. We play hard. We don't hold with too much convention that interferes with either."

She might have stayed. She wouldn't have abandoned herself as he had, but she might have enjoyed watching him. She still couldn't quite believe that he was Iain McEwen and that he'd come for her and that she was with him now, and that he was as beautiful as she had never allowed herself to forget. She might have stayed, but for the resurgence of her curdling belly. Dread flooded her features while his boyish abandon vanished instantly at her sudden upset. Maggie began to back away from him, breathing heavily through her mouth, fearing she might hurl right in front of him.

"Maggie?"

Shaking her head, still moving away from him, she mumbled an apology and turned and began to march swiftly toward the hill that would see her back to the keep. Any hope that she might contain the illness until she was alone in her chambers was slim. She had no idea that walking swiftly through sand was such a chore.

Of course, Iain McEwen would not let that be that. She whimpered when she heard him call her name, his voice carrying over the sound of the tide. *Please don't follow me.*

But he did, catching her arm—not harshly with any recrimination for her hasty and unexplained departure, but with concern, for her ashen pallor and need to be away. Still, Maggie jerked out of his grasp.

"Oh, please," she begged when he bolted in front of her then and stopped her forward progress.

He wouldn't let her pass, shifted left or right as she tried to move around him. "Maggie, what is wrong?" His beautiful blue eyes were dark and etched with concern. And that was when she lost control of her roiling belly and heaved its contents outward once again.

Iain's jaw gaped, glancing down first at his breeches, which had borne the brunt of the assault, and then back to Maggie.

Her mortification was complete, then. She glanced up at him, her face colored and twisted with abject humiliation, but just for a moment before she vomited yet again. This time, she managed to turn away, falling into the sand, making more of a mess at his feet.

The wind had done some dastardly things to her hair while she'd been out, and she made to gather the loose and flowing strands out of the way near her shoulder. Another wave of nausea overtook her, and Maggie pressed her hands into the cool sand instead, balancing herself above the chamber pot she'd just made beneath her face.

Tears dribbled down her cheeks when she felt Iain's hands, collecting her bothersome hair, holding it out of the way. He must have gathered it into one hand as he then placed the other on her back, rubbing softly up and down. Instinctively, she curved her back away from his hand and it was removed.

It was several minutes before Maggie was relatively sure she would heave no more. Straightening so that she sat up, she glanced up at Iain, who now crouched at her side, still holding the thick mass of her hair.

"I-I think your mother might be right," she said miserably.

He frowned. "About what?"

She didn't want to see his reaction and yet could not look away. "That I might...might be with child."

To his credit, his eyes widened only briefly before he reined in any further reaction. And yet his jaw was tight when he said, "Bound to happen, I imagine. Marriage has a way of doing that."

Closing her eyes, Maggie concentrated on the bare sound of the wind, the feel of it against her flushed cheeks. She curled her fingers further into the sand, discovering that beneath the dry and sloppy top layer, the sand was cool and compact beneath. She heard a bird caw close by, listened to the crash of the small waves upon the shore—concentrated on anything that was not her predicament, not her woeful life.

"It'll be fine, Maggie," he said. He'd lowered his voice, his tone giving some hint of an attempt to convince himself as well.

Nodding, she opened her eyes, taking only another spare moment to decide that her belly might have settled now, rubbing her hand along it.

Good God, a babe.

Despite the horror of her few months as Kenneth Sutherland's wife, she felt as if she were naught but a child herself yet. A frightened, hopeless child bereft of family or support or love.

Maggie turned her gaze again to Iain.

Tears gathered in her eyes—perhaps her overwrought emotions of the last few days were now explained. "You must send me back to Blackhouse," she guessed, her heart dropping.

He frowned at her, his blue eyes flashing in the morning sun. "Send you back."

Maggie could not decipher if he'd repeated the words as a statement or as a question.

"You cannot have a Sutherland child living here at Berriedale." His frown deepened and she rushed out, "And if he knew...if Kenneth knew, he'd not stop until the babe was claimed. Returned to him."

Blowing out a sigh, Iain explained, "You'll no' ever be returned to Blackhouse, lass. You'll no' ever be returned to Sutherland—child or no."

While that offered her some relief, even as she wasn't quite sure Iain McEwen would be able to keep that promise, Maggie was just now beginning to understand the severity and full detriment of her condition. All her future choices were diminished now. Whether she might have stayed here at Berriedale or have gone on to St. Edmund's as had been her original intent months ago, everything was changed. Neither of these choices seemed a viable option now. Either one might have suited her....

But for a child. She would not be allowed to take her child with her to the cloister, but then wasn't sure she could imagine giving up her own flesh and blood, no matter that his father was a monster. She also could not conceive that a Sutherland child would know peace or find love at Berriedale, despite how kindly these people had thus far been to her. She was, once again, at the mercy of fate. And fate, she'd decided months ago, had no love for her.

"He will come for me," she predicted, "and he will learn of the child." And there will be no escape.

"Aye, he might," Iain concurred. "But he'll no live to see any child raised, Maggie. He's bound to die, and by my hand. The reasons outweigh rationale. He betrayed our own true king; he has visited unimaginable crimes upon the people of Caithness, and no' least of all for what he's done to you."

As afraid as she was of Kenneth, she admitted, "I-I would not want his blood on your hands...not for me." She hadn't the heart or the energy to tell him he would never emerge the victor, if he were ever to come up against Kenneth Sutherland. He could never hope to outwit, survive, or overcome such malevolence as was her husband.

Iain's lip curled. "Then I'll do it for Robert Bruce or for the monks near Wick or the poor bastards near Helmsdale. Dinna matter for whom, the man will die."

"The monks?" She frowned at him.

Iain stared at her until a dawning of understanding overtook her features, her mouth opening, her eyes widening. She clapped her hand over her mouth and shook her head in horror, having some recollection of the tales of the one named Alpin from her time with the McEwens during the storm.

"'Tis true," Iain assured her while she blanched.

"I am wed to the devil."

Iain tilted his head and showed a measured amount of sympathy. "But you ken that already, aye?"

Maggie nodded.

GLENNA PUT MAGGIE TO rights the next morning. Or, as right as she could, in a stern and motherly fashion.

"Now that's enough of that, Maggie Bryce," said the woman while they met in the hall after the morning meal. Maggie had arrived late, not at all hungry, having another bout of illness upon waking.

She'd just revealed to the woman who—what—exactly her husband was, and how she couldn't bear to bring a child into the world who might have any of his father's tendencies, any of his evilness.

"Children aren't born that way, of course," Glenna said. "They are made into monsters by the people and circumstances that surround them." She shook her head. "I am not about to listen to many months of you whining about a monster growing inside you."

Taken aback by Glenna's harshness, her complete lack of empathy, Maggie made to argue in defense of her fears. Glenna would have none of it.

The older woman held up her index finger at Maggie. "I mean it. Never saw an easy pregnancy when it was shrouded in doom. You're here. You're safe. Your child will never know his father. Let's move on."

And that was that, Maggie guessed.

"How is your needlework, Maggie?"

Maggie blinked, a bit befuddled by the complete change of subject and wondering about the purpose of such a question. "If, mistress, by needlework, you mean trifling compositions upon fine linen that might never serve any purpose but to amuse a lady, then consider mine poor. If you refer to mending, I have passable capabilities."

Glenna smiled. "Passable will do. Since you've no stomach to be of any help in the kitchens, I thought you might take over some of the mending. 'Tis only household items, and some personal wardrobe pieces that need attention."

Thrilled to be given some occupation, Maggie eagerly accepted.

They spent the next few hours in Glenna's solar, a private chamber on the second floor near the bedchambers. The room was not used very often, Maggie thought, taking note of the dust covered furniture and the dampness, which suggested it saw few fires. But the chairs were comfortable, padded with tapestry covered cushions, and the light was good, this window facing the spot where the river washed into the sea, being larger and wider than most of the thin openings in the stone throughout the keep.

At Glenna's urging, Maggie explained how she came to be betrothed to Kenneth Sutherland, that her father was one of the larger landholders, that he surely saw more benefit from the union than she had.

"But isn't that the way of it?" Glenna suggested, her hands nimble and efficient upon the table linen she worked on, the previously shaggy hem of one corner completely unnoticed now under its mistress's ministrations. "Men make all the decisions, direct every aspect of our lives as if we are not persons, all with the same hearts and minds and eyes and ears."

This raised Maggie's gaze from kitchen aprons she'd been tasked with mending. "Were you sold in marriage then as well?"

Glenna grinned, which crinkled the scar on her cheek. "Aye, sold. I wouldn't have chosen Ilagan McEwen of my own accord. But then, wasn't I simply the luckiest of persons, to have been loved by that man. My, but he was easy on the eyes."

Maggie grinned with wistfulness, at Glenna's soft tone. Mayhap the son took after his father, *easy on the eyes* and having women imagining themselves lucky if they were to be loved by him.

Apparently happy to reminisce, Glenna added, "He saw past my face and my leg and...just loved me. Oh, and he was very good at it."

Possibly it was impolite, but Maggie was curious and asked, "How did you...did you have an accident?"

"I had a drunken wretch as a suitor," Glenna answered, her tone suddenly acidic. "who thought to take some liberties one day inside my father's stables. We fought, he struck me, and I fell and struck the corner of the stall" –she pointed to her cheek—"that's this, and then my leg was impaled on the iron prong of the pitchfork. That scar is not so ghastly, but the injury must have done some damage inside that I never was able to walk smoothly again."

"But how awful," Maggie said. "What happened to that man?"

Glenna shrugged. "Nothing, I suppose. He was the son of the local gentry. My father made a complaint, but I don't think anything was ever done about it."

"But then you met your husband," Maggie said, urging her to share more.

"I cried for days when my father told me he'd betrothed me to some man I'd never met." Glenna rolled her eyes. "So much unfounded worry, what a waste. I'd been so afraid the man would take one look at me and denounce the entire affair. He did not, of course. Instead, he told me I was beautiful." She laughed, sounding much younger than her years. "I thought, good heavens, this man must really need to marry, must really need the land and sheep that came with me." Her entire posture softened with her memories. "We married, of course, and honest to God, there was never a day that he lived that I didn't feel beautiful."

"How long ago did your husband—"

"Too long," Glenna answered sharply, as if she bore yet some resentment that he'd died at all. "Iain was not yet a man, that Duncan and Artair managed Berriedale for many years." She was quiet for a wee bit, staring blindly at the fabric and thread in her hands. "I love my son, but honestly, Maggie, it's a bittersweet thing, him so like his father. Seems everyday I am reminded of what I no longer have."

"But how lovely," Maggie supposed, "to have loved, to have been loved so wonderfully."

Another grin, a happy one, despite the subject matter, answered this. "Of course, you are right. Only that it makes the loss of him that much more powerful." With a pointed look at Maggie, she said, "Be glad you've no mourning to accompany your removal from your husband." And then she shrugged. "I survived that—the bounder's attack on me, the loss of Ilagan—and everything before and all that came after, none of which is insignificant. And you will, too, Maggie Bryce."

Chapter Fifteen

IAIN MCEWEN WAS A VERY busy man, Maggie realized. Despite what he had said to her on her first day at Berriedale, that he worked hard and played hard, she saw little of the latter. But then, she saw so little of Iain.

Weeks went by and while Maggie was pleased to have been so well received at the McEwen keep, and while she enjoyed tremendously Glenna's company, she wondered at Iain's noticeable absence. He'd sought her out that first day, had taken her with him that she might enjoy a bit of leisure at the beach.

Then he'd learned that she was with child.

And he'd not requested her company since.

So, while she was pleased beyond measure to have escaped Kenneth Sutherland and the dungeon of Blackhouse, she considered that she only lived with different kinds of despair. First, despite the time that had passed, she could not completely abandon the fearful notion that her husband would find her, that her freedom was to be short-lived and that his retribution would be gruesome. Next, she had yet to fully accept that she carried a child. True, she'd not bled in many months and she knew, she understood that undoubtedly a life grew inside her, but she had yet to comprehend—had yet to fully allow for any reflection—what this meant to her and for her. She was not in denial, she convinced herself, she just wasn't ready to acknowledge it completely. Regularly, she decided that she would think more upon it tomorrow. Always tomorrow.

She didn't blame Iain McEwen one bit for avoiding her. This was the height of irony, of course, that she'd clung so feverishly to the image of him over the past several months, that she'd made fine use of her memory of him to protect her own sanity. And now she was with him, he'd come to save her, and she found herself in no way interested in knowing him again, so afraid of what he might want of her.

Actually, it was not only her he seemed to avoid. He was gone regularly from the keep, training during daylight hours with large portions of his army. The training field was located outside the keep, which meant the castle and yard, during the day, were mostly quiet and empty. Sometimes, Iain and several others, which mostly included Duncan and Archie, went off for days, "scouting," Glenna had told her with a shrug that suggested either she really didn't understand what they were about or that *scouting* was all Maggie needed to know.

Maggie continued to assist with the mending, but pretty soon, her regular attention to this—as she had no other occupation—meant that the work was all done. Still sometimes plagued by morning sickness, she was not yet allowed to return to the kitchens. But she was eager to help in other ways and offered as much, so that one day when the bulk of the McEwen army had been gone for more than a day and a night, she was tasked with assisting Edda, the occasional kitchen girl, with the delivery of all the saved bone and antlers of the castle down to Edgar, the boneworker in the village. Just outside the doors to the kitchen of Berriedale sat a wooden, lidded box, where bones and antlers and horn, removed from the slaughtered dinner meats, were stored and removed down to Edgar as needed, when the box was filled.

"He's clever—more clever than any of the other local lads," Edda was saying. "He's no' as handsome, of course, that would be the twin or Eideard or even Simon who are handsomest. But I think he's going to speak to my da' soon."

They been walking and talking for the past ten minutes, or rather Edda had been doing all the chattering, telling Maggie all about her budding romance with the soldier, William.

"But do you like him?" Maggie asked. As of yet, the girl had imparted only that he was a soldier, and likely earned more coin than any of the village laborers, and apparently he was 'clever', but hadn't given any hint of his character, or if this was even a consideration. "Is he nice?"

"I guess." Edda said with a shrug, answering many questions Maggie might have had.

Though several years younger, Edda was taller and broader than Maggie that she struggled not at all with the smelly and lumpy drawstring burlap bag. She held the pulled strings at her shoulder, the weight of the bag bumping against her back with each jaunty step. She seemed not to mind that her loose blonde hair was draped over the bloodstained bag. She talked almost non-stop, prattled really, while Maggie struggled with her bag, trying not to touch any parts of it to herself, hoping the odor did not upset her stomach, which had been very kind to her today. At some point, she gave up and simply dragged the weighty bag along the sheep path, quite pleased then that this put the odor behind her as well.

"What do you and William do?" Maggie wondered, trying to learn more about both Edda and the lad. "How does he court you?"

Another shrug preceded her answer of, "I watch him when he's training. And," she said pointedly, drawing Maggie's gaze with her drawn out tone, "we meet down by Loch Liddel some nights."

Maggie gasped. "At night? What for?" Edda's giant smirk and the saucy turn of her one shoulder answered for her. Maggie resisted rolling her eyes. "Have you and William talked about wedding?"

Another smirk. "We're so often too busy for much talking."

Maggie kept her gaze on the path and kept her opinions to herself. She liked Edda; the girl was friendly and worked hard inside the keep. She wasn't going to be the one who disillusioned her. And what did she know? Maybe Edda was only trying to impress her with her worldliness, by suggesting what she had. Mayhap the lad was truly keen on her.

"And do your parents know that you meet him at night?"

"Och, no! My da' would kill me. And that'd be after he killed William."

For the life of her, Maggie couldn't remember where this bit of advice came from, but she had thought about it over the years, and thought now to share it with Edda, hoping it made some dent in that over-confidence, which seemed sorely misplaced in this circumstance.

"I'd always heard that nothing right or good should ever need to be hidden."

They continued to walk, moving just to the top of the hill, that the village appeared below them. Edda had turned though, away from the charming view to frown at Maggie, her thick dark brows lowering over her pretty eyes. Maggie glanced up at her just as Edda made her eyes skinny with some deliberation about Maggie's words. Shrugging, hoping to lessen the impact just a bit, Maggie gave the impression that it was only something that she'd heard, that maybe it didn't need to be taken as gospel.

The village below was laid out in a half-moon shape, with several roads of thatched cottages dissecting across. At one end was the largest building, what Maggie suspected was the tithe barn, and at the far west side sat what looked like a small church with a square, fenced yard beside it. Several of the homes showed attached outbuildings, likely workrooms of the potter or the boneworker or the tanner.

Beyond was a meadow, dotted now with fluffy white sheep, and in the distance, far off to the east and fringed by several copses of trees, was a pear-shaped loch—possibly the place of Edda and William's trysts—the blue water shiny and reflective under the midday sun. Every other bit of land visible from this vantage point was a field, plowed or fallow or blooming. The cottages were spaced generously that no one cottage sat atop the next. Three of them were built into the bottom of the hill on which they stood. Edda pointed directly below to those houses and down they went, Maggie still lugging the burlap on the ground behind her.

They strode between two cottages and turned around the front of the largest one, which put them immediately in front of a tall and narrow shed. Inside was a man, younger than Maggie would have suspected the boneworker to be, but large, possibly wider and taller than even Iain McEwen.

"Aye, Edgar," Edda called out, swinging her bag down onto the ground next to a table in the middle of the shed.

He turned to them, taking up so much space inside his workroom. Edgar the boneworker was quite handsome, with thick auburn hair and soft brown eyes. A gentle giant, Maggie thought instantly, having no idea if he were in fact gentle, only that he looked as if he might be.

He nodded and set his gaze with some curiosity onto Maggie, moving forward, away from the gloom of the rear of the shed.

She deposited her haul as well and bid the man a good day, also announcing, "We're to request a half dozen drinking horns and an equal number of handles to be given to the smithy for spoon making."

Edda winked at the silent boneworker. "And we'd no' refuse a fine cloak pin, if you were of a mind to make a lass feel pretty."

His gaze stayed with Maggie. "Aye, I might be." His voice fit him perfectly, the words given slowly and deeply.

"That's Maggie Bryce," Edda said, following his gaze. She picked up a piece of bone on his work table and turned it over in her hands, as if she had some interest in the chunk. "She's the one from the Sutherland's Blackhouse."

He nodded again and began to open one of the bags.

Maggie glanced around. His work shed was not much more than three walls of shelving, packed with bones in various shapes and sizes and antlers, stacked and tangled all about one section. In the middle of the dim shed was the table, the top covered in dust and shavings, and tools and half-worked projects.

When she turned back to Edgar, he'd emptied some of the bag and then upended the whole thing, shaking it until all the bone and horn fell to the ground. "Do others give or trade bone with you? Or do you mostly collect it yourself?" Maggie wondered.

"Only the castle sends down bone," he answered. "I'll scavenge the woods for more if I run short—that might only happen in the winter, but rarely."

"What needs to be done to those pieces"—she pointed to the bags they'd delivered—"to get them to look like those?" She moved her finger to the shelves, where all the pieces were clean and dry.

"If I need them immediately, I'd boil them clean," Edgar answered. "Mostly though, I just bury them, let nature—ground and bugs—do all the work."

"Oh."

Maggie wondered if she and Edda might depart now, their task completed. Instead, Edda appeared to be in no hurry, content to investigate his wares, handling one piece and then another.

As the boneworker did not seem to mind their company or Maggie's questions, she pointed to a strange tool upon the table, which seemed to be made of metal and bone. "What is that?"

IAIN REINED IN AT THE top of the lane, dismounting smoothly and tying off his steed at the corner post of Soerlie McEchrine's front walk. His business with the man was quickly forgotten, however, when he spied Maggie Bryce a few houses down, standing just at the corner of the bonemaker's shed. Curious as to her industry within the village, and specifically with Edgar, he ambled slowly toward her. Coming from further down the lane, he was afforded a view of only a bare portion of her profile, his gaze initially captured by her bright and shiny hair. The head of the giant, Edgar, was bent down toward Maggie as he showed her the wood plane, describing how it worked, turning the tool over to let her see the iron sole underneath.

Maggie tapped her finger on the tool when Edgar turned it upright. "What is this made of?"

"Aye, that's horn, Maggie Bryce," answered Edgar, his voice as deep as Maggie's was soft. "We have others made of wood themselves—beech or yew, maybe—and some made of bone, too, but those dinna keep so well."

"Horn? An antler?"

Patiently, Edgar explained, "Nae, lass. The antler belongs to deer, the red or the roe deer. Horn, see, comes from the sheep or the cattle, and we've got plenty of them, aye?"

"I see." And Maggie picked up another tool from the table. "What is this one?"

Edgar took that tool from her hand and identified and explained the purpose of the awl. He towered over her to such a degree that she appeared only a child next to the boneworker.

Iain brushed aside the dislike that had surfaced when he'd heard Edgar refer to her as he sometimes did, as *Maggie Bryce.* He brushed aside as well how completely at ease with the man Maggie appeared; the mammoth man did not intimidate her, it seemed. She stood very close to him, tipping her head up to him, listening intently.

It had only been a few weeks since they'd recovered her from Blackhouse, but Iain had yet to see so much of Maggie Bryce of the winter caves. When first they'd met during that storm, and after her initial fright, he'd been captivated by how blithe and enchanting she'd been, how engaging and merry. In retrospect, he'd thought it quite absurd that a person should have been so lighthearted in the midst of an escape from a future she did not wish.

That girl was gone. He thought that possibly none of her remained, that all of her must have been obliterated by Kenneth Sutherland. He hadn't spent too much time in her company of late, save for suppers when he was home, where she'd somehow managed to assume a different seat than the one she'd originally taken next to him. She now sat on the other side of Archie at mealtimes, content it seemed to keep company with him and Donal on her far side. But it had not escaped his notice that she was different now, a subdued lass who offered only rare smiles that never quite reached her eyes. There was a quietness about her presently that any who had met Maggie Bryce before she'd wed might find sorrowful.

He hung back now, not entirely sure that any intrusion from him would be received as welcome, certainly when he'd avoided her for the past few weeks.

It actually hadn't been intentional, not at first. He'd been called down to Stonehaven to meet with Gregor Kincaid and Jamie MacKenna, for a wee covert discussion about gathering more troops for Bruce's army. When he'd returned, and since, as now, he felt some unease, not sure how to approach her, what he might say. His mother had told him that she had yet to accept the pregnancy as either possible or agreeable, that she didn't want to even talk about it. And he was not impervious to the fact that on the very few occasions that he'd made any contact with her since bringing her to Berriedale—taking her hand, touching her with only the intent to direct her or reassure—she'd flinched or bristled. Like the thinnest glass she was at those times, fragile and likely to crack with even the smallest bit of pressure.

Contrarily, just being in her presence—even this creature, who was but a shadow of the Maggie Bryce he'd known so briefly—put him in mind of what he'd discovered right quick last winter, that he didn't know how to be around her without craving some small and pitiful contact with her. But *Jesu*, that was the last thing the lass needed now.

He debated backing away, getting about his business, but Edda stepped outside the work shed, noticing his presence. She squeaked and asked, without an actual greeting, "The army is returned then?"

"Aye," he said.

This turned Maggie Bryce and Edgar toward him.

Edda's cheeks pinkened. She nearly bounced on her toes. "Maggie, you can see yourself back to the keep?" And without waiting an answer, she was off, around the shack and back up the hill.

Iain and Edgar exchanged nods as greetings while Maggie Bryce only stared at him, her green eyes showing no expression from under the shadow of Edgar's large frame.

"I'm headed back," Iain lied. "I'll take you up."

Curiously, while Maggie looked as if she might refuse, Edgar also appeared to want to reject Iain's offer.

Of course, she could not refuse, having no reason to do so. She nodded vaguely and stepped further out of the shed. She smiled up at Edgar—a smile that Iain judged to be quite warm—and then followed Iain's direction, his raised hand indicating his mount not far away.

"Good day, Maggie Bryce," Edgar called after them.

Maggie turned and waved. "And to you, Edgar." Her smile widened, but only until she faced the lane again, and then it disappeared altogether.

When they reached his horse, Iain wondered how she might stand riding with him upon the saddle meant for one, when she clearly abhorred any contact—was it only with him?

"Might we walk?" She asked stiltedly.

Much better, he decided, than her sitting so stiffly in front of him. "Aye," he agreed and led the way around the corner of the lane, and toward the hill. He pulled the reins of the horse, who ambled along behind them.

"You were gone a little while," she said by way of conversation, "and your mother is fairly guarded with any information. Am I not supposed to know where you go or what you are about?"

He shook his head. "No secret, really. We were gone to Stonehaven for a bit—that's Gregor Kincaid's land. A few clan chiefs met there, discussing raising more troops for Robert Bruce. I'd like to take you down there sometime. You'd like Gregor's wife, Anice."

"Hm," she said, noncommittally.

"Then we went up to Uncle Donald—the MacKay—for the annual Caithness council."

"Oh."

She'd asked the question but did not seem very interested in the answers.

"I was surprised that you left with so few to actually guard Berriedale," she said.

Iain turned toward her even as they continued to walk up the hill. Ah, now he understood. This, stated with such connived indifference that he could only supposed this, then, was the heart of the matter.

Iain stopped and waited until she did as well. She did, after a few more steps, that she was further up the hill and nearly eye level with him when she faced him.

"Maggie, you're in no danger here. I'd no' leave if I thought you—any of Berriedale—were at risk."

"But how can you know that?"

"I've got a unit embedded down near Carlisle. And Artair has a system of intelligence throughout most of the Highlands. Kenneth Sutherland wouldn't be within a day of Berriedale before I ken it."

"Can you be sure?"

"I can. I am. Settle your mind in that regard, Maggie Bryce. He's no' anywhere near you. And when he comes, we'll be ready."

He hoped to see some relief in her features, hoped maybe this was what had kept her so standoffish. Her expression changed barely at all, though she nodded, accepting *his* belief in the words, if not her own.

Iain sighed and followed as she turned and resumed the uphill trek.

Thinking a silent return to the keep might seem to drive the unaccountable wedge between them yet deeper, he asked, "What have you been keeping yourself busy with?"

Shrugging a bit while she climbed ahead of him, her skirts lifted out of the way, she answered, "Whatever your mother needs help with. Mending, mostly, but I've finished all that for now. I'm not sure what I might get about this afternoon, if she hasn't another chore for me."

"You take some time for yourself then," he advised.

She'd reached the top of the hill ahead of Iain. She didn't stop and wait for him, but he thought she slowed her pace that when he reached the peak as well, they strode nearly side by side.

Ignoring his suggestion about enjoying some idle time, and while keeping her gaze on the path ahead, she said, "Your mother had said she might travel down to some place called Hawkmore and spend some time with her friend, Diana Maitland. She said I might go with her. Would that be...allowed?"

Iain's brow crinkled. "Aye, mother and the Mistress Maitland are verra friendly, cut from the same cloth they are. They visit, here or there, at least once a year. But Maggie, you dinna need permission. You're no' answerable to any but yourself."

"I just didn't know if..." she began but left it unfinished.

"When will you embrace this?" He wondered, a bit of starkness in his tone.

This stopped her, turned her toward him, her own drawn brow matching his. "Embrace what?"

"You're free, Maggie. Subject to no one. Threatened by no one. In no danger. I've given you my word."

The smile she showed him then only attempted to be kind, but without great success. "Apologies, sir. I do not seek to—"

"Enough," he bit out. "I am Iain and you are Maggie. I've held you in my arms and I've kissed you and it was your face I saw when the war was brutal, and I needed something to cling to...so that...." He shook his head. "And I came back for you, and I took you from Blackhouse because I couldn't let you be...stay married to him. And no' a day goes by I dinna wish I'd fought for you then." He closed his mouth, clamped his lips even.

Maggie bit her lip. Mayhap a bit of remorse played across her features, colored her cheeks.

Iain stepped forward, reached for her hand.

She didn't back away, but she did curl her fingers into her palm.

Iain withdrew his hand.

"That would have only served to see all of you killed, of course," she said stiffly, her expression distant now, purposefully so.

"Aye, and I still wish I'd no' let you go then."

Her slim shoulders lifted slightly. "What's done is done."

Aye, and that was the problem.

Chapter Sixteen

HE HADN'T SLEPT WELL, his mind hammering incessantly with Maggie's unbearably sparse and gloomy conversation of the day before. She'd been at once skeptical of either or both his ability or his interest in keeping her safe, and then cool and nearly vigorous in her attempt to remain aloof. Possibly the most disturbing part of their stilted chat was his certainty that he was the only one thinking about kissing whenever they were together. This was especially bothersome because the lasting image he'd carried with him for months last winter was the look on her face after he had kissed her so long ago. Before she'd questioned if she were in danger, she'd been filled with wonder, he was convinced, neither immune to his kiss nor undesirous of his attention.

But that was then.

Now, she could barely make eye contact with him. And while he was well aware of how much space she took up in his mind, rearranging things inside there for so long, he wasn't quite sure that he had likewise managed to carve out even some tiny temporary residence in her head.

Today, he meant to change all that. Naturally, his awareness in how she fared, how she thrived—or did not—at Berriedale were related to his other interest, of kissing her. Somewhere deeper, however, he knew that regardless of whether the spark that had once been lit between them was ever reignited or not, he wanted her to flourish and to find peace at Berriedale.

With that in mind, he sought her out shortly after he'd broken his fast, determined that he would not allow her to gainsay his plans for her this day, though he was fairly certain she would try. Admittedly, he was a wee bit surprised to hear from his mother that she'd gone down to the beach already and was not yet returned.

"Gone to the beach for what?" He wondered.

Glenna raised her brows, ignoring for the moment Rabbie and the conversation her son had interrupted. "Is that not allowed?"

Iain favored his mother with a roll of his eyes, to which she was particularly well accustomed. "I dinna say that, Mother. I asked about the purpose."

"She's collecting seaweed with young Giric."

"Thank you, Mother," he said and pivoted. He called over his shoulder, "She'll be gone the rest of the day." He exited the keep from the kitchen and made his way down to the beach.

He saw her at once, on her knees with the lad, Giric, their heads pressed together over something in the sand. Giric's unruly hair was nearly the same hue as Maggie's, light and dark, rosy and blonde, that he could not rightly say where one head ended and the other began.

He made his way downward, the wind billowing his tunic and plaid, curious about what held their attention. Seaweed, he thought, would not have captured such rapt and close scrutiny that they were unaware of his presence until his boots crept into their periphery.

They both startled at once, lifting their heads, sitting back on their legs. Maggie covered her heart with her hand, very startled indeed. Giric squinted up at Iain, his face scrunched up and revealing a recently lost tooth.

Iain sent his gaze quickly over the basket, filled to capacity it seemed with their haul of seaweed. He looked into the sand then but saw nothing at first, until Giric pointed specifically to a small dimple in the wet, but not puddled, sand. Giric didn't touch the sand but it moved.

Frowning, and more curious, Iain went onto his haunches between Maggie and Giric and watched more closely. It did it again, sent up a little bubble of sand that burst lightly and settled quickly.

"What is it?" Maggie wondered.

"Is it a monster underneath?" Giric asked.

"It's *something* underneath, I would guess," Iain said. To Maggie, "Air being forced upward. Likely a critter." He swiped at the sand, removing several inches until his fingers met with a solid but moving thing. He moved more sand away to reveal just the claw of a crab. This quickly disappeared as the animal burrowed further.

"Crab," Giric said, his disappointment evident.

Iain grinned and covered the critter again before standing. He offered his hand to Maggie, who amazed him by taking it, allowing him to pull her to her feet. While she dusted off her skirt, he collected her basket and met her gaze. Perhaps she was a bit less wary of him, her green eyes bright under the morning sun, meeting his, not looking away. She was, as ever, impossibly bonny, freckled and sun-colored, the bulk of her hair twisted into a serviceable knot at her nape, mostly unmoved by the wind save for small and curling tendrils near her cheeks and ears. He would never not be fascinated—enticed, he supposed—by the shape and color of her mouth, her lips perfectly pink and full.

He lifted the basket of seaweed. "Done for today?"

"Aye," She answered. "We were headed back."

"Good. I've taken over your schedule for the remainder of the day."

"Wait. What?" She called after him as he began walking back toward the keep.

"We're off to Dunbeath," he called, handing the basket to Giric with instructions to get that to Rabbie in the kitchen. He watched the lad dash up the hill and turned to face Maggie, sensing that she'd stopped. He set his hands onto his hips, prepared to argue or cajole or persuade, as needed.

Maggie lifted her hand to her forehead, putting her eyes into shade. "Who's off to Dunbeath? And what's in Dunbeath?"

"The market's in Dunbeath. We'll take the cart, pick up some wares." While this was true, he did acknowledge to himself that he'd rather intentionally made it sound like a chore, like a castle need, having some idea she would not refuse a task. She might well have denied the invitation if he'd revealed its true purpose: getting her away, having her to himself, making her smile. "Eideard's unit will accompany us."

"Oh." And then, "Very well."

Iain made sure not to dissect that response, wasn't sure he wanted to know if she'd agreed because they would be safe with the armed retinue, or if she'd consented because she expected that the armed guard meant that she wouldn't be alone with him.

Ten minutes later saw them seated side by side upon the bench seat of the small wagon, passing through the inner and outer gate and rolling over the small bridge, leaving Berriedale behind them. Eideard and another dozen or so men followed at a similar leisurely pace, leaving a bit of distance between themselves and the cart.

"Have you ever been to a large market?" Iain asked of Maggie.

"We had a weekly market in Torish, but that consisted of only the locals, hawking their wares. Mostly it was a trade fair, as people used their own goods to barter for things they didn't make or couldn't otherwise afford. I suppose it was not very large, though."

"Aye, then you'll like the market at Dunbeath. It's held monthly, and is governed and promoted by the MacKay council, so that it draws vendors and merchants from further afield. There have been occasions that tradesmen from as far as France and Italy have made their way to the market."

They sat fairly close, that every little bounce or jig of the cart brushed his thigh across the skirt of hers.

"What did they sell?"

Iain chuckled. "One fine man, I'll no' ever forget his name—Foulques de Merle—sold wine. Once. That was disallowed ever after, too much sampling right there in the market, no' even waiting until they were away and home. Turned into one big brawl," Iain said, fondly recalling his own eager participation. "The wine was tasty, I do recall."

She turned quickly, steadying her gaze on him. "Did you partake of both the drinking and the fighting?"

"I may have, but dinna ask me if I ken what the fighting was all about. Was years ago. At that time, if I saw fists flying, seemed only right to join in."

"Boyish misdeeds?"

"I prefer to think of it rather as youthful exuberance." He shrugged, aiming for innocence, but it was perceived more as devilish.

Warming to their chatter—sooner than Iain might have dared to hope—she asked, "Would you say that you've outgrown that? That natural exuberance that dances around so much of our youth?"

He spared her a glance, appreciating the intriguing lift of her brow, and the fact that she met his gaze with little reticence.

Cheerily, he said, "I'm no' sure. I'm feeling fairly spry today."

"Must I plead for no fisticuffs then?"

This elicited another chuckle. "Haven't heard that word in a while. The old MacBriar—he's chief down at Swordmair, where I summered a few years—liked that word, was constantly admonishing his son and I and another friend to *leave off with the fisticuffs*."

"Somehow that doesn't surprise me," she said, without rancor. "As far as I can tell, you are pretty even-tempered and...affable. I suppose that comes with a pleasing childhood?" She sent a narrowed and suspicious glance up to him, though it was cloaked in good humor. "Were you the spoiled child heir, who could do no wrong? Mayhap a mischief-maker?"

Iain could not deny this. "Aye, likely someone should have taken a strap to me more often. But I liked my fun, didn't seek to harm others, yet got in my fair share of trouble. Archie used to say he couldn't wait for me to outgrow my energy."

"Have you?"

"Mayhap all those boyish ideas in my head were only supplanted by duty. Life happens...some parts better than others.

You ken it yourself: you're forced to grow up right quick, sometimes in the midst of a...horrific experience."

He was immediately sorry that he'd revealed so much, and then sorrier still when she quieted, her face lowered to her lap. *Damn*, he'd been specifically speaking of his own life events, but she either imagined he referred to hers, or it brought her dreadful marriage to mind.

Not of a mind to let a pall be cast over what was so far a very pleasant, and remarkably easy conversation, he nudged her arm and pointed off the path into the trees.

"What is that?" She stared at a door—an actual tiny door—added to the bottom of a thick yew tree. It hadn't been carved into the trunk, but fashioned from another piece of wood, arched and sanded smooth. It had been fixed into a hollow at the base of the tree and was complete with a small window and even a door knob, being in total no taller than Iain's forearm.

"Faerie house."

Maggie gave him a dubious look. "It is not."

"Aye, but it is." He kept his grin in check.

"Does the door open?"

"Of course."

"Did you do that?"

Now he laughed. "I did no'. It is no' wise to court the faeries."

"I thought they didn't like to be called faeries."

"Aye, the fair folk they be," he acknowledged but then whispered, "but you ken they dinna really exist?"

"I do not ken that and neither do you."

"Fair enough," he allowed.

"My mam used to tell me stories at night, or anytime we were alone. Magical tales of the faerie realm, and all its inhabitants.

She gave them names and narratives, impossibly never forgetting little details she'd presented or what they had or were about to do. It was like a running tale, she just continued to add to it."

"Do you recall any of it?"

"The specifics?" She made a face. "Sadly, barely at all. The faeries were most often associated with water—wells or lochs and even the sea. Each waterway had its own faerie protector. They are very sensitive to humans, enjoy observing us, but do not want to interact with us. Oh, I just remembered—Cailean was the name of the faerie king."

Her voice had become wistful and soft.

"You were close with your mam. You miss her?"

"Every day." She chewed her lip for a moment. "I cannot imagine there exists a girl who doesn't crave her mother when she finds her own self with child."

"Like as no."

It took more than an hour to drive to Dunbeath. They engaged in constant chatter, covering mostly generic topics, but Iain was pleased with even this small progress. A fine step forward. Eideard and the rest of the soldiers hung back, allowing for plenty of privacy.

Dunbeath was a fishing village, sitting at the mouth of the Dunbeath River, which widened considerably before spilling into the North Sea. The market was held on the cliffs of the south side of the river. There wasn't much to recommend the area, no large town or burgh or castle, but the deep harbor served as a fine port for merchants arriving by sea. Today saw only a half dozen or so boats lined up near the spare harbor, which was no more than a narrow dock built into the side of the cliff.

MAGGIE UNCONSCIOUSLY took Iain's hand as she alighted from the cart, her curious gaze held by the goings-on. Indeed, this was far larger than any market she'd ever visited, with a variety of stalls and booths set up in several aisles along the stretch of earth that jutted out toward the sea.

When her feet touched the ground, she spun around, seeing mostly green and brown, earth and grass and trees, all about, intersected only barely by six permanent buildings further back from the water. Likely, when no market was operating, this was only a very quiet place. But now, with dozens and dozens of vendors, the place bustled with people, men and women from every layer of society, it seemed; she saw ladies in fine wools and lace and so many different colored plaids; children darted here and there, some dressed raggedly or modestly, announcing their crofter status; one man and woman appeared in matching wools of bright blue, which was both striking and curious, Maggie thought.

They left the cart where others had parked their horses and vehicles, in a fenced area outside the main market. As Iain led the way toward the stalls, Eideard and the others were just entering the area. Maggie waved to Eideard and then rushed forward to catch up with Iain. They walked up the main road, which appeared to be the middle aisle. Though there were plenty of people, hundreds maybe in this relatively small space, the general din was tempered, polite and quiet. Only the raised voices of vendors, calling out their wares, disturbed the low-key clamor.

"It's rather subdued," she noted. "I take it there's no wine merchant today."

Iain turned and gave her a handsome smile. "A shame, that."

When they passed the first stall, selling a very non-descript variety of crocks and jars, Iain grabbed her hand, steering her toward the right as the crowd thickened. As it seemed a perfectly utilitarian gesture, Maggie minded not at all.

"Are we here for anything specific?" She asked, peering into the second booth, a very tidy unit displaying woodwares, trenchers and bowls and cups, meticulously carved and oiled to shine so attractively, the grain of the wood enhanced by the oil.

"A few more furs for the keep," Iain answered, and sent her a smirk. "Archie claims his knees are telling him we're in for a rough winter." He shrugged and added, "Rabbie would like a few bushels of pears; Berriedale's pear trees suffered a blight this year and bore no fruit at all. And Mother has tasked me with finding a different variety of grapes, to expand that part of the orchard."

"Archie's knees dictate your market list?"

"They've proven verra reliable in the past." His grin was a beautiful thing to behold.

There was so much to see. Booths with handicrafts of wood or lace or cloth, and sheds of game and meat, the fresh carcasses hung from heavy hooks all around the perimeter; many of the sellers offered fruit, as it was the growing season; furs and fabrics and furniture were well represented; and there were several occasions when Maggie needed to stop and handle the wares, unable to identify them by sight.

The first of these was inside a tent draped with bright cotton and silk fabrics, the brightest colors at the market. The wares being presented, set beautifully onto tables covered in more jewel-tone fabrics, appeared to be only an assortment of flasks and strange, oblong stones.

The woman inside the tent, behind the tables, was garbed in a rich red silk, so perfect against her deep skin tone and black eyes.

Maggie frowned over one of the stones, no bigger than her palm, and lifted it to inspect it, under the watchful gaze of the woman. A cork stopper plugged one end of the stone.

The woman grinned—Maggie would have called it provocative, her smirk—and possibly understood that Maggie had no idea what she held. The vendor spoke to Iain, though, her pouty lips issuing each word slowly and suggestively. "Ah, you've not indulged your lady with such luxuries?" Her voice was thick with a foreign flavor.

With a short laugh, and without explaining that Maggie was not his lady, Iain only said, "I have not."

The merchant stepped forward and lifted another flat-bottomed stone piece from the table. She pulled out the stubby cork and waved the piece under Maggie's nose.

Maggie's eyes lit up at the scent that drifted near her. She glanced to Iain at her side and said with much delight. "It smells of lavender."

He smiled.

Maggie uncorked the stone bottle she held and sniffed, her lips parting and her shoulders dropping with her thrill. She fluttered the cork under Iain's nose. "Ooh, lemon."

"But lemon is not your scent," the woman said.

"It isn't?"

"Non," the woman said and reached for another perfume bottle, this one made of clay and carved with a leaf motif. She shook the piece and beckoned Maggie forward over the table.

Leaning in, Maggie inhaled the sensual and dreamy scent and allowed the woman to rub the cork over her neck by her ears. Closing her eyes, she breathed deeply again, and proclaimed absently, "I am in love."

"Sandalwood," the woman explained with a husky chuckle. She waved her hand around in front of Maggie's face. "Very exotic. Lemon and lavender?" She pursed her lips and shook her head. "Not for you."

While Maggie investigated other scents offered, the woman dedicated her attention to Iain, at times speaking a language that Maggie did not understand but that Iain apparently did, as he responded with similarly foreign words. And before she might have protested, Iain was handing coin to the woman and was given the sandalwood perfume in a small hemp bag.

"No," Maggie argued, when she realized what was happening. "Are you buying that for me? Please do not."

"It's no' for me, lass," he said and tucked the bag into his tunic. "I try no' to give the lads too much ammunition."

Ignoring his quip and thinking of the coin he'd just spent on her, Maggie insisted. "Truly, I wasn't—you shouldn't have done that."

"I had to," he defended. "You smell...delicious."

She should have been outraged, or at the very least made uneasy, but she found herself bursting out with a laugh. *Delicious* was not a word she would have associated with the sandalwood scent, being a strange way to describe the perfume. With a sigh, she tried to gracefully give her thanks. "That was very kind of you, though unnecessary."

"Simple pleasures, Maggie Bryce. Life should be peppered with them."

She could think of no argument to upset that august notion.

They thanked the purveyor and moved on. Maggie saw Eideard and some of Berriedale's soldiers here and there. They were close enough when the pears and furs were eventually purchased that the lads carried them back to the cart.

It took them over an hour to get through just one aisle, Maggie keen to inspect almost every booth. It was a beautiful day, the skies clear and the sun warm upon her head that she enjoyed sometimes ducking under the canopies of the stalls to escape the heat. This might have been what prompted Iain to pull her toward the booth teeming with straw hats. There were hundreds of them, stacked and hung, all similarly colored, pale and wide brimmed, some more ornate in shape than others.

"Pick out a hat," he instructed.

"I do not need a hat," she said, having no wish to see any more coin leave his person for her needs.

"Aye, you do," he insisted pleasantly, reaching past her to grab one from a pile on the table. It was possibly the ugliest one displayed, the crown being more square than round and the brim fringed instead of trimmed neatly. "Either you pick one you like," he said, placing the monstrosity on her head, "or I will." He smiled at her.

Rather petulantly, hoping to change his mind, she said, "I don't have moneys to repay you, as well you know."

Iain met her gaze, brushed the hair behind her ear, under the ridiculous hat. "I dinna want your coin, Maggie Bryce." And then he grimaced and pulled the hat from her head. "But then, I dinna want you donning that eyesore."

Grinning and game—she'd never owned her own hat—Maggie complied and began to try on different ones. She turned to Iain at one point to get his opinion and found him leaning against the corner post of the booth, wearing the ugly hat he'd first plunked on her head.

"Suits you perfectly," she said. She tipped her head, with the very plain but serviceable hat upon it, round of crown and brim, the straw uniform in color.

"Needs a ribbon," Iain said, pulling that square piece from his head.

"There's plenty of ribbon at Berriedale," said Maggie.

But Iain ignored her, pointing to the center of the booth, above the silent merchant in a comfy chair. There, ribbons of every color and fabric imaginable, long and short and in so many different widths, hung from the rafters.

"Green, of course," suggested Iain.

"Why, *of course*?"

"To match your eyes," he responded casually, indicating to the vendor his choice, a fabulous length of silk the exact shade of the sea when it was calm and bathed in sunshine.

"Silk is not very practical."

"The hat is practical, lass," Iain contended while the merchant rose and fetched the ribbon. "The silk can be frivolous."

Half an hour later, Iain and Maggie sat under a wide oak tree, just outside the market perimeter, snacking on food stuffs he'd purchased, sweet breads and nuts and ale.

She wore her new hat, tied under her chin with the silly silk ribbon, and smelled of the decadent sandalwood and thought this might be one of her favorite days ever, in all her life.

"Thank you," she said to him.

"Stop saying that, Maggie Bryce. Eat your sweets."

They sat on the ground and Iain had laid their small feast between them, having spread wide the cloth the sweet breads had been wrapped in.

"Am I allowed to voice my appreciation to you, for bringing me to Dunbeath today?"

He was stretched out, propped up on his elbow, one ankle crossed over the other. He tossed a handful of nuts into his mouth and observed Maggie silently, thoughtfully, while he chewed. When he swallowed, he said, "It's good to see you smile, lass."

"You...had an agenda, then?" She asked.

"Aye, I'll no deny it."

"Why? What agenda?"

"Several reasons," he admitted. The grin that followed, the one he showed to her, tipping his face toward her was both charming and sheepish. "You want all the reasons then, or just the main parts?"

"I'm not sure. What do you think I might want to hear?"

"How 'bout I test some answers out on you? They'll all be truthful, but some might be more...revelatory than others, might make you uneasy. You can stop me at any time."

"Mayhap I don't want to know the *why*."

Now he lifted a brow at her. "Truly?"

Anxiously, she said, "Fine. Start with one, a simple one."

"Verra well. I'm the laird of Berriedale and all its denizens, thus responsible for the welfare of the people. I believe you are unhappy and I am bound to change that."

"So you've taken others—unhappy or dejected or...even troubled persons—out for the day to...what? Cheer them up?"

He chuckled outright now. "Well, I've no' ever loaded up the cart with a person in need of cheering, but I'd once traveled to Glasgow to bring home Ester Herman's son. He'd been lured away by a woman—I use that term loosely, as she was—and his mother was struggling in her croft without him."

"So you meddled with love—"

"It was no' love," he said, making a distasteful face, "unless, of course, you consider the exchange of coin to be part of affection."

"Oh."

"Aye." He leaned over and grabbed another handful of the almonds. "When the brewer's husband was ailing, I sat with him every afternoon for several weeks; Agnes needed to work, but dinna want to leave him alone. He was a good man, was Martin, but I didn't need to be there every day. So you see, this is not unprecedented, what I'm about with you today."

Maggie bit her lip and gave her gaze to a bird, flying low over the market before ducking low and out of sight. Cautiously, she asked, "But there is or are other reasons for bringing me to Dunbeath?"

"You needed a hat."

"Hmm," she murmured with some suspicion.

"Aye, and I like being with you."

"Why?" She asked, rather than thinking it through. Glancing briefly at him, she explained her harshly given response. "I mean only that...sometimes I don't even like being with me."

"But you're hoping to change that, aye?"

Shrugging, which all but admitted she hadn't really thought about it, she said, "I guess so."

Wiping his hands against each other, he laid onto his back, with his arms under his head. "I've got more work ahead than suspected, then."

Maggie allowed a grin for this response. With more lightness than she'd known of late, she said, "Very well. There's a few stated reasons for shirking all your duties to spend the day with me, and I don't yet feel a bit uneasy."

Iain turned his head on his arms and looked at her, his regard measured and compelling. "There's more. You want to ken it?"

Her heartbeat quickened. "Do I?"

The corner of his mouth lifted. "I want you to ken. I canna believe you dinna already."

Maggie began to shake her head. "That's enough then," she said, her voice small. "You are a good chief to your people and for some mysterious reason, you enjoy my dreary company. That will suffice for now."

"Lass, I'm pleased to ken that you are decidedly undreary today."

"I do not think that *undreary* is an actual word."

"I just used it."

"That doesn't make it real."

"Did you ken what I meant?"

"Well, yes, but—"

"Must be real, then."

She didn't know why this struck her as funny, but it did, that she let out a disbelieving giggle, that he should have used such a fantastically nonsensical argument that essentially won out.

A very good day indeed.

Chapter Seventeen

WHEN THEY RETURNED to the market after their small lunch, they met with Eideard and several soldiers, who enjoyed their own purchased nuts and sweets while they walked. She noted that several lads, Eideard included, had other hemp or linen bags tied to their belts and wondered if they'd bought gifts for their sweethearts.

Iain made several other purchases in the afternoon, including two new iron kettles which he insisted were of good quality and reasonably priced, and then several leather flasks and a very fine quality saddlebag, with intricate metal detail on the light auburn hide. He haggled not at all, paid whatever the seller asked or stated, and when Maggie inquired of this, he explained, "Berriedale can afford it presently, and it's good business to purchase here, ensures the market will continue and the vendors will return."

By the time Iain told Eideard to round up the lads to head home, Maggie thought they might miss supper, as it was so late in the afternoon. Iain kept them to a steady though not particularly fast pace as they drove back to Berriedale. She still wore her new hat, and held her perfume in her lap, feeling as if she now owned luxuries. The bed of the cart was laden with the rest of the items bought, but Maggie thought it was not so heavy to distress the palfrey.

They weren't very far gone from the market when their ride was interrupted by a flock of sheep crossing the narrow road in front of them. Iain reined in and they waited, the soldiers moving ahead of them to give some assistance to the shepherd moving his sheep.

"Just be a moment," Iain advised, holding the reins firmly that the horse and cart remained still.

Turning toward Iain, she said absently, "I either wish we'd saved some of those sweetbreads for the drive home, or I hope Rabbie has them on the menu tonight."

He began to grin at her, but it dropped suddenly, his eyes on her hat. "Don't move," he said firmly.

She did as requested, held very still, but needed to know, "Is it a spider?" She closed her eyes tightly. She hated spiders.

He said nothing but put his hand on her arm and reached across to her far side and swiped at something above her. He slapped several times actually, mumbling a curse, which caused Maggie to shiver and jerk with each attempt to rid her of whatever threatened. She expected to feel some creepy crawly thing touch her skin at any moment.

"Gone," he said when he'd stopped swiping at her hat, which was now crooked, and only covered the back of her head.

Maggie opened her eyes and exhaled.

Iain was very close, adjusting her hat as Maggie reached to do the same.

Their hands touched. At once, they stilled. Maggie stared at his lips, so close to her face.

"Was it a spider?" She asked, unaccountably breathless.

"Aye," he said slowly, lowering his hands.

Maggie lifted her gaze, found him watching her with an intensity that was not completely unfamiliar to her. *Oh*.

"Was fairly large," he said softly, his scrutiny splitting time between her eyes and mouth.

"I do not like spiders." Her breathing difficulties were exacerbated by his heated regard. Somewhere in her distant awareness was the sound of the soldiers moving the sheep, "hi-yah!" and "get on, sheep!" penetrating her consciousness.

The corner of his mouth lifted. "Nor I." He leaned forward, dipping his head toward her.

Maggie drew in a sharp breath, bracing herself, her gaze locked on his beautiful blue eyes and the purpose shown in them just now as he closed in on her.

"All set, Chief!" Someone called out.

This effectively broke the spell. Iain swung his gaze forward and Maggie released a rush of breath.

Primly, she shifted and straightened, sending her gaze out ahead of the cart, now clear of the entire flock, the shepherd and the smallest sheep having just reached the other side of the path, disappearing down the hill.

Iain adjusted the reins in his hands but did not engage the palfrey to move. Maggie held herself very still, knowing his regard was once more returned to her.

Please just drive. She closed her eyes briefly, unwilling to say what her response might have been to his kiss, which had clearly been his intent.

It was a long time until her heart stopped racing, until her belly settled.

This made for a very awkward return trip. Maggie was quite sure he was as disturbed as she by the near-occurrence of a kiss, as he made only small efforts toward conversation. Like her, he seemed to hold himself rather stiffly now, making sure his thigh did not at all brush against hers as they drove.

Maggie stared straight ahead, so very happy when Berriedale came into view almost an hour later.

Inside the yard, Iain exited the seat with some haste. She knew she did not mistake the great breath he drew in before he helped her alight, but she couldn't decide if it were the beginning of a large sigh or a buoying inhale.

But then he did not release her hands when she was standing on the ground next to him, even though Archie and Duncan were crossing the yard to them, possibly intent on helping unload the cart.

"Dinna be uneasy now, lass," Iain told her. "That's just more unfinished business between us."

Maggie didn't know what to say to that, so she only nodded abruptly and pulled her hands from his.

As she walked toward the keep, she knew some apprehension, expecting that Iain watched her. This was nearly confirmed when she heard Archie say to his chief, "What's got you grinning like that kind of idiot?"

She tamped the smile that wanted to come, and ignored the frolicking butterflies in her belly.

THE NEXT AFTERNOON, Maggie found Artair in the hall and asked him if she might be of some assistance to him. She had already spent some small time in his company, mostly by way of Glenna's meetings with him, and found that his serenity was constant; the man was the height and breadth of all that was calm and reassuring.

He was surprised by the query, she sensed. Seated at the family's table, he lifted his nearly bald head from the parchment upon which he'd been writing and showed a bit of startled pleasure in his placid gaze.

"You do not like to be idle, do you, lass?"

Maggie scrunched her face and shook her head. "The day is just too long then."

"And leaves the mind with too much temptation?"

Maggie nodded. "I'd much rather not be left to my own devices, and my own thoughts."

He didn't question this, didn't ask what troubles might harass her, but asked, "Do you know how to read and write, lass?"

"I do, a bit, and wouldn't mind improving the skill." At Artair's further surprise, she explained, "At my home in Torish, my friend Marta was taught, as her mam had been very well educated." With a shrug, she said, "I was curious, and Marta was willing to share what she'd been taught."

Artair held up his hand and showed what was normally hidden in his sleeves, that his fingers were bent awkwardly and severely into his palms. "Getting more and more difficult for me to write, lass."

"Then my timing might be auspicious?" Maggie wondered, with some small bit of hope.

The steward smiled kindly. "Aye, it is at that."

"I thought I had heard Glenna make some mention that you had your own office, Artair," Maggie said as she walked around the table to sit next to him, which put her in the same chair she normally occupied at supper each evening. "Yet, you sit here in the hall."

Artair moved the small ink well closer to Maggie and laid the quill in front of her on the uncovered table. "Aye, lass, my chamber and my wee office sit there between the larder and the scullery. Truth be told, it's dark and dank at that end of the keep. I enjoy the better light and fresher air of the hall."

"Artair, I think the same thing sometimes when I'm in the solar above stairs. Mayhap I'll do as you have when next there is mending to attend, bring my work down here." Maggie picked up the quill and was quick to add, "If that would be all right?"

"I decree that it will be," he allowed, "and I would enjoy the company."

Artair then explained to Maggie what he'd been doing, keeping a log of all the household expenses. There was a pile of little notes, some in Artair's own script, which matched the words and numbers in the ledger. "These are either receipts for goods purchased or monies spent, or notes I've made of any expenditures that I then log into the ledger. And this stack here," he said, indicating another pile, "are income notes, if we've sold sheep or collected rents or the tithes. See how there are several columns? Incoming and outgoing." He further explained, "And next month, when harvest begins, there's a separate journal for that, year by year, where all is recorded."

"So where shall I begin? Your last entry is for two yokes at four shillings and then one augur, three pence."

Artair nodded and consulted the notes, moving aside the corresponding notes from those entered. "So, here we are," he said, lifting the next receipt. "Draught horse, twenty shillings."

Maggie dipped the quill carefully into the ink and began to record all the expenditures from the last week as Artair read them. Tools and implements such as anvils and bellows, and kitchen necessities of pepper and sugar and saffron were listed in groups depending on where they were used, the keep in general, the kitchen specifically, the yard and grounds, or outside the castle.

"Spinning wheel, ten pence," Artair said, turning over the last of his own hand-written notes.

"Is the spinning wheel for the household then?"

"No, that would be for Alice down in the village."

"And the castle pays for this?"

"Aye. Alice needs the device to maintain a living, so we provide it. And she repays the cost of the wheel by providing thread and yarn to the castle, one tenth of her production per month for the next year."

"That's very reasonable, I should imagine." Maggie recorded this, pleased that she'd kept her script as small and as neat as Artair's.

Artair nodded. "She wouldn't be able to purchase the wheel outright by herself, and we cannot have any person of Berriedale in need or wanting. And, of course, we are paid with the threads and yarns, which are very useful as you know."

"A satisfactory arrangement for all parties, then," Maggie concluded. "But how did you know she needed a spinning wheel?"

"We have several gatherings in the hall each month," Artair explained. "Once a month, the chief sits as judge over a court to hear cases of small crimes and grievances. And then once a month, he receives requests for benefice. So last month Alice made the petition for the spinning wheel and it was determined that the need was worthy, and the arrangements were made."

"Can anyone ask for anything?" Maggie wondered.

"Nae, lass. We do not entertain frivolous requests and we only hear petitions from wards, family, or inhabitants of Berriedale. They must live and work within our borders and they must demonstrate a genuine need."

"That makes sense."

Artair's brows lifted slowly. "But, Maggie, might you be interested in attending the next court? My sorry fingers would be thankful if you would be so kind as to take the notes from the meeting."

Maggie had no idea what all that might entail, but she was eager to be of service to Artair as she was rather enamored with his soft-spoken manner and very kind eyes.

"I would be very pleased to do so," she agreed. "But Artair, you've seen how slowly I make all the letters and numbers. I feel I might get lost, or not be efficient enough."

Artair waved this off. "I can show you those journals, where I record all that is argued and said, and all determinations made. It's all very succinct. I do not put to paper every word said, just a summary."

"Very well, I would be delighted to help you while I am here."

Artair turned curious gray eyes onto her. "Are you going somewhere, lass?"

Realizing what she'd said, what she'd admitted, Maggie scrambled for a reply, explaining disjointedly, "I haven't any plans—that is, I'd be pleased to remain at...but of course I know that my...my—"

Artair covered her hand with his, which effectively silenced her. "You are safe, Maggie Bryce." Those few words were given with more vigor than any others she'd heard yet from the steward.

Nodding, trying to smile for his wish to see her composed and unafraid, she lied to him. "Aye, I know."

ON SATURDAY, WHEN IAIN entered the hall for the court of law hearings, he was surprised to find Maggie sitting again at the table next to Artair.

Dozens of people filled the room, the double doors wide open. Another half dozen soldiers were present also, as was customary for the rare instances that an accused might violently disagree with a ruling or judgment by Iain. The crowd stood, chatting amongst themselves, on the far half of the room, as the space directly before the table was reserved for individuals called to answer for charges laid against them.

He strode up onto the platform, waiting for either Maggie or Artair to realize his presence, which neither did immediately as they had their heads together over one of Artair's various ledgers. Only when he moved his chair did they lift their heads.

While Artair displayed his perennial tranquility, Maggie glanced up at him with some agitation, but he thought it had been already present and not caused solely by his appearance.

"Our dear Maggie has kindly agreed to record the proceedings, saving my fingers the task," Artair said by way of explanation.

Maggie seemed to hold her breath, as if she expected he might deny her presence at the proceedings, or her assistance to the steward. While she looked as she always did, so damn bonny, Iain thought she appeared paler than normal, her eyes dull.

One leather-bound sheaf of parchment sat directly before her, opened to a blank page, and in her hand, she held a quill, while she waited for his response.

"That's very kind of you," Iain said and sat down next to Maggie, with Artair on her other side. While he gave no indication, he knew some surprise that she had been taught to write.

The room quieted then, with Iain taking his seat. He glanced up at the crowd, not surprised to see some familiar faces, who appeared with infuriating regularity in this court.

He heard Artair say to Maggie, "Make sure you include today's date, lass, at the top of the page," before consulting his own papers to call out the first name. "Randolph Dowis."

There was a shuffling in the crowd as a man threaded his way to the fore, and then continued until he stood only ten feet before the table, twisting his felt hat in his hands. He looked between Maggie and Artair but would not meet Iain's gaze. He was nearly Iain's age, slight of build with nervous eyes that rarely sat still.

Artair announced the claim, "It is charged, Randolph Dowis, that you have—once again—taken that which was not yours, on this occasion a barrel of herring belonging to Soerlie McEchrine." To Iain, Artair added, "Soerlie states that he hadn't yet salted it so that when it was found, in Randolph's possession, the herring was turned, and of no use to him. He seeks recompense for the entire barrel, two pence."

"This is the third occasion?" Iain asked of his steward, without removing his gaze from Randolph.

"The fourth, I believe," Artair answered.

This drew Maggie's attention, which had been so studious upon her writing, to the man.

Iain could not decipher the accused man's reaction to Maggie giving him consideration. He seemed at once fretful, as he normally was, and then cowed under the weight of her curious gaze, his shoulders and chin seeming to fall with some apology to her, as if the crime were against her personally.

Artair queried the man, "What say you?"

The man only shrugged, giving no defense, that Iain rolled his eyes.

"Randolph, you will pay Soerlie the sum of four pence for the herring, work it off if needs be, and pay to the court the sum of two pence, for the annoyance of seeing your face at each of the last three sessions," Iain announced, and added, "And understand me, Randolph, if I see you here again next month, I will have to consider expulsion from Berriedale, as we dinna tolerate thievery from our own."

The man nodded, but his gaze was on Maggie, who was in the process of recording Iain's judgment that she was not conscious of his scrutiny. So engrossed with his perusal of Maggie, Randolph seemed not at all alarmed at Iain's significant threat to expel him from the territory.

Iain, too, was acutely aware of her proximity, of her very presence at his side. As he sat back in his chair, his forearms on the arms, he was afforded a clear view of her profile as she bent her head over her task. Her hair was held by only a thin ribbon, the length of her red-gold tresses falling in curls and waves down her back. He couldn't recall if he had ever touched her hair, if he knew for sure that it was as soft and silky as it appeared. She smelled deliciously of that sandalwood perfume he'd bought her, and honest to God, he had all he could do not to close the distance between them and press his nose to her neck, giving himself even more to fight against.

Maggie turned and whispered something to Artair, who spoke softly at her side, and then she wrote the word, *annoyance*. Her script was neat and small, but he sensed she was not greatly accustomed to putting words to parchment so that it was rather laborious. When she was done, she glanced up, found Randolph's gaze upon her, and looked to Iain with some question, as if she supposed they were all waiting for her. Her paleness escaped then, just for a moment while her cheeks pinkened.

"I'm sorry."

Iain shook his head, losing his own fixation, and dismissed Randolph with a stern glower that Artair might call the next case.

"Gifford Norrie, come forth."

Iain sighed as a stocky, unkempt man of middle years stepped forward, not at all shocked by the charges read.

Artair read, "Amalie Norrie has charged that you twice have struck her, on two separate occasions, that last of which removed two of her teeth."

This brought Maggie's gaze up sharply to the man, her lips parting while she regarded him, as if she were now directly offended by his alleged crime and at the same time wary of such a man, who would strike a woman.

"What say you?" Prodded Artair.

Gifford Norrie made a face that aptly said to the three at the table that he considered the charges nonsense. "She dinna listen to a thing I say," he defended, "she dinna show no respect for my authority as her husband." Warming to his defense, as none had challenged it thus far, the man began to point an angry finger in the general direction of the table. "And it is not her place to deny my right to relations. But how's a man to perform if she's bawling the whole bluidy time?"

The hall erupted in laughter, while someone called out, "I'd be wailing, too, Giff, if you were on top of me!" More laughter followed this.

Iain's regard was solely for Maggie. She was seething, her fury focused entirely on the unsuspecting Gifford Norrie. Iain did not have to employ any great feats to wonder why this particular crime should have risen Maggie's ire. It had something to do with her marriage to Kenneth Sutherland, he imagined, and the demise of self and power and a voice that might be heard, which likely had been so miserably lost to her husband.

Artair lifted his hands and flapped them up and down, signaling that the congregation should quiet. They did not immediately, not until Archie and Eideard and Duncan stepped forward, Arch's fist cocked in the general direction of the crowd, and his lip curled.

Iain addressed the accused. "I've told you—how many times now?—that we dinna strike women. We bring no harm at all to them—"

"But—" Gifford Norrie began to defend.

"Dinna interrupt, you bleeding arse!" Archie hollered at the man.

Iain continued, "Gifford Norrie, you are hereby sentenced to three days in the cells—"

"Three days?" he repeated with outrage.

Iain continued as if the man had not spoken. "And you will pay your wife, Amalie Norrie, the sum of ten pence for your abuse of her—"

"I'll no' pay her a single farthing," Gifford maintained.

"And you will do this, because I have said that you will and if I hear of—"

The man dared to sputter yet more, "But ye have no' even heard all of my de—"

"There is no defense!" Iain roared, rising to his feet so abruptly as to send his chair onto its back. This effectively stilled and quieted even the faintest murmurings in the hall. He felt many wide-eyed gazes upon him, not least of all Maggie's and Artair's. "If I decree it, then it is so," he shouted at the offender. "And I do. Gifford Norrie, if you strike this woman again, I swear to God I will enjoy tremendously meting out the punishment that will follow—tenfold what you do to her, I myself will bring to you." Archie stood next to Gifford, his heavy hand upon the man's upper arm, ready to either lead him away or reprimand him bodily if he persisted with his outburst. "You'll have no more warnings, only the penalty," Iain promised. He turned and righted his chair, taking his seat once again while Archie dragged the fuming man from the hall.

Iain felt her regard still and turned his face to Maggie.

She was breathing heavily, as if alarmed still by the man's crime, or mayhap Iain's overdone reaction to it. He rarely had cause to employ such rage at these hearings.

At the same time, there was so much faith in her beautiful green gaze just then. Faith in him. For one tiny moment, it was uncomfortable, all that gratefulness. But then this was Maggie Bryce, and he'd sworn to himself she should never be misused again, so that he had essentially already committed himself to be her champion, he supposed.

Without a word, Maggie picked up the quill and when she wrote all this down in Artair's ledger, while the steward watched with an unmistakably satisfied expression, Maggie Bryce wore a wee little smile.

They heard twelve more cases that morning, from charges against Ernst Wiley that he'd shirked his communal duties of plow work to Gavin Ogg, accused of causing damage to the brewers cart while inebriated and joyriding, it was alleged.

There was not one moment, during any of the proceedings, that Iain was not aware of Maggie sitting so close to him. She whispered several times to Artair, asking about the spelling of some words, he thought, and twice he saw her lower one hand beneath the thick wooden table to cover her belly, which drew a curious frown from Iain.

And when all the cases had been attended and the hall had cleared, Iain knew that he wanted more time with her, wanted her to himself for a while. Buoyed by the grateful and steady gaze she'd settled upon him earlier, and provoked further by the smiles she'd given to both Artair, after he'd said something quietly to her, and then to Archie, when he'd approached the table and had advised that she might want to get used to writing many of these names.

"Aye, lass," said Arch, in his usual disgruntled tone, "repeat offenders, that's what we call 'em, and hard pressed I am to no' insist on bashing some heads together rather than doling out the punitive fines."

She'd lifted her gaze and closed the ledger, giving Archie the first cheery smile of the day. Not entirely cheery, Iain thought, noting that her expression was tainted with some stiffness.

He stood abruptly, drawing her regard as well as that of others. "You'll come down to the beach with me, lass?" He invited with about as much finesse as he was sure Gifford Norrie employed when wanting to bed his sorely aggrieved wife.

Iain sensed Archie's frown but did not look his way.

Maggie was surprised by the invitation, he could see, but he gave her no chance to refuse him, standing behind her that he might pull back her chair for her.

Nudging the chair, he silently bid her comply, wanting to be away from the watchful, befuddled gazes of Duncan, Archie, Eideard, and Artair, not entirely sure of the reasons for his own sudden and inexplicable need to have her away with him.

Iain directed her out of the hall and toward the postern gate, not at all oblivious to the fact that she was reticent now, again, her lips pinched when he held the door open for her. He supposed the awkwardness should not have come as a blow. For all intents and purposes, he'd just plucked her out of a fairly pleasant situation, offered her escape she did not need, and had done so with very little elegance. He had to wonder if his private company—no soldiers nearby to offer some outlet if needed, no hall filled with people to keep so much of his attention from her—was the cause of her present aloofness.

Chapter Eighteen

WHEN THEY REACHED THE spot where the embankment declined sharply, he preceded her, jumping down lightly and landing squarely. When he turned to collect her, he saw that she had continued to walk, north along that ridge until she reached a gentler decline, quite a distance from him, and made her way down by herself.

She met him then further down on the beach proper, the bulk of her hair drawn over one shoulder, which she was braiding as she walked. Iain liked the color of her hair, honey and berries, he might have said, kissed by the sun, highlighting all the red and gold.

As he'd done previously, as he'd done a thousand times in his life, he sat in the sand close to the water and shed his boots and left his belt and sword next to them. Facing Maggie, he was surprised that there wasn't need for any cajoling, as she sat as well, removing her hose and shoes, her hands under the skirts of her gown that she bared no skin.

Since he'd taken her directly from the hall, she did not wear her hat. Iain thought she was particularly pale today, but couldn't imagine that owning the hat but one day would have erased what color the sun had given to her in the last few weeks.

"You've been dipping your toes, then?"

Maggie glanced up at him, her eyes as green as the sea, her freckles on greater display in the pallor of her cheeks. "I have, several times now."

She stood, without his help as he'd moved too late toward her, being that he was rather caught up in her indifference. She marched forward, swatting at the sand on the back of her skirts and walked until the water reached just below her knees, her gown and kirtle held up and out of the water.

Iain doffed his tunic at the last moment and followed her to the sea. He went for a quick swim, dunking himself completely to rid himself of the day's grime and dust. The action was nearly as familiar to him as riding or walking that it required no thought, that he was able to consider Maggie' solemnness. While she'd been mostly quiet inside the hall, he'd decided that she had certainly been more animated and engaged than he'd noticed in the past few weeks, excepting their trip to the market.

Resurfacing, Iain stood again, his feet touching the sandy bottom and the water hugging his hips as he remained many feet from her. The sea was not calm today, that he swayed in the water with each wave that rolled past him. Maggie, being closer to the shore, was less impacted by the crashing waves, only once or twice having to lift her skirts higher to keep them dry.

She stood with one hand holding her skirts and one hand holding her belly, staring beyond him at the sea. For the first time, he deduced just the smallest roundness to her stomach, accentuated by her hand pressing the fabric close.

It had not escaped his attention that she looked to him, at him, not once.

"Are you feeling poorly?"

She didn't exactly answer, but asserted, "I'll be fine."

Iain stepped closer to her. "You're not yourself."

"What is me?" She wondered, giving her gown a lift as a wave passed.

"There was a time you found yourself stranded in a cave with seven strangers, any one of them twice your size, carrying swords taller than you...and you—you embraced it, if I recall." And he did recall. He'd forgotten nothing, not one minute of those three days.

"That was a lifetime ago." She met his gaze now, levelly and with more curiosity about this conversation than with any interest in him, it seemed.

"Aye." It was a challenge now, he had to get her to smile, he had to find that light in her gaze. Was he mistaken? Had it been there, even briefly, for others but not him, or had he only imagined it? Was it the pregnancy that had soured her? Had anything changed since their trip to the market? Had his thought to kiss her—a fantastic missed opportunity, he knew—sent them two steps backward?

She was staring at his naked chest. Her mouth formed a small *o* for the sight.

Damn, but he'd rather forgotten about his scars. He was accustomed to them, had carried them for so long, he thought little of them.

But she was shocked. Repulsed? He couldn't know, as she hadn't moved.

"What—how did this happen?" She looked over every inch of his bare torso, seemed to walk toward him without consciousness. There was plenty to keep her gaze busy.

He didn't recall that he'd ever been embarrassed about the legacy of his time as an English captive. Until now. And then more so when she lifted her hand, as if she might touch him, touch all the angry slices and welts and burns. She squeezed her fingers once more, and pulled her hand back, tucked it against her chest.

When she lifted her gaze finally, it was filled with pity. Iain pursed his lips with some scorn—he courted no one's sympathy—and tried to make light of it. "A slight disagreement with a few fine Englishmen some years ago."

Tilting her head, she challenged his dismissiveness.

He returned the challenge. "We all have scars we'd sooner no' make into conversations, aye?"

Her lips parted again. Obviously, she understood his reference and agreed with him, nodding slowly.

Surprisingly, she returned her gaze to his chest and abdomen but he could not say just now that she showed any pity, couldn't say what it was that pinkened her cheeks and had her turning her head away even before she'd removed her eyes completely from him.

"Maggie, have I done something to cause you any upset?"

She lifted her face to him, another frown showing. "No," she lied.

And he knew she lied, same as he had when she'd told him fibs previously. She'd taken her gaze away from him with her answer, gave her regard only to the skirts she held above the water. She'd moved further into the sea that she was forced to hold her skirts up past her knees to avoid the crashing waves. But then she tired, of either the refreshment of the water or of him and the scarce conversation. She turned and headed back to shore. Iain wasn't specifically trying to catch up with her, but his greater size allowed him to stride through the sea with ease that he was at her side fairly quickly, and then fortuitously so. A larger wave, taller and stronger than any thus far rolled over them, sending Maggie teetering precariously to the right. Iain moved swiftly and caught her up with an arm around her waist, lifting her feet off the floor of the sea just before another rogue wave swept past them.

"Whoa!" he said, with a laugh, some far off memory teasing him, of chasing waves such as that when he was a lad. He carried Maggie several more feet before he realized she was pushing against the arm around her waist.

Abruptly, Iain set her down in water that reached only their calves and shins. She backed away from him, her green eyes uneasy.

"Bluidy—Maggie, I'm sorry. Did I hurt you? The babe?" He held his hands out but did not touch her.

She shook her head, but he would swear her eyes were about to well with tears.

She pivoted awkwardly, the water preventing any graceful movements that getting away from him was not so easy.

Lightly, Iain touched her arm, forgetting in his desperation how she abhorred his touch, until she ripped her arm out of his grasp. She marched on, her gaze on the water and her steps. The large waves had undone all her careful attempts to keep her gown dry and it was soaked from the knees down.

"Maggie, Stop. Tell me what—

"Please don't ask me what is wrong," she begged as she trudged on.

Iain raced in front of her, walked backwards as he stated, "I will. I am. Maggie, what has happened?" No small amount of frustration crept into his voice.

"Nothing," she said, "everything is fine. Please, let me pass."

The water only swept their ankles now that she tried darting around him.

"Maggie, what have I done that—"

"You've done nothing."

He persisted. "But I must have or why would you—"

"Because I thought you might kiss me!" she cried, stopping to holler this at him. She stood in the sand, where only the very last breath of any wave might reach and clamped her lips, breathing hotly through her nose.

"I—" he began. But truly, he didn't know what to say. He didn't think there had ever been a time, certainly not after he'd kissed her all those months before, that he had been in any close proximity to her, that it hadn't crossed his mind. At the very least, the memory of it beckoned him often, made incredibly strong after their almost kiss of market day, not lessened at all by the scent of sandalwood that had teased him all this morning.

She composed herself. Speechless, he watched the process: she closed her eyes and breathed deeply through her mouth. She swallowed and opened her eyes to gaze up at him.

"The other day, I thought you'd meant to...." This trailed off, while she gathered her thoughts and words. "Then when you invited me to the beach," she said, her voice level, "I don't know why but I thought you might have done so to...to try to kiss me. And I was terrified—and angry—but then you didn't, or haven't, and—" she stopped, rolled her lips inward, biting back whatever might have come.

He'd get to that, what else might have been revealed, but first: "Terrified? Angry?"

She sighed harshly, which sounded almost like a cry. Her shoulders sagged so greatly that she appeared to deflate in front of him.

"Terrified, because...because I don't want to be kissed." She stopped and breathed quickly again through her mouth, several short breaths, to gather nerve or to get past something, Iain could not say. Her voice was small when she said, "And angry at...him for making me this way."

Jesu, but that was so much information. However, he needed the rest of it to process it entirely and effectively. "But then I didn't kiss you, or hadn't *yet* kissed you and...?"

Maggie closed her eyes, tilted her face to the sun even as her entire person appeared whipped. "And I was—it made me sad."

He supposed he'd not ever been so gape-jawed, so many times, in so few seconds. Bloody hell, but how to proceed?

And then, *Hallelujah*! For all this enlightenment.

"How can you possibly be—what is there to smile about?" She cried, her frustration evident, that he'd forced her to admit what she had, that he could grin now with all this mess between them.

Iain sighed now and stepped closer to her. She backed away, just one step.

But she held his gaze. The incomparable green of her eyes, the tortured expression begged something of him, but he could not know what.

"Give me your hand," he said.

Her chin quivered but otherwise she didn't move.

"Maggie Bryce, I'm only asking for your hand right now."

She didn't move.

Iain was not discouraged. "'Twas only three days in those caves, lass, only a few weeks here at Berriedale, but you ken me. And you ken I'd no' ever harm a hair on your head."

Her gaze just now said only that she wanted to believe this, but that she could not. Nearly imperceptibly, she shook her head back and forth.

Iain lifted his hand, palm up. "Give me your hand, Maggie Bryce."

Maggie lowered her eye to his outstretched hand. Iain waited. When she finally raised her hand and set it into his, the action was accompanied once again by a great and visible stiffening of her body. She only waited, it seemed, for him to reveal a true and nefarious purpose.

Closing his fingers lightly around hers, he held her hand in his palm, traced his thumb over the back of it, along the soft skin. "Maggie Bryce, I recall that kiss in the caves, so long ago. *Jesu*, I've brought it to mind so many times that it seems fairly fresh in my memory."

She folded her fingers but did not pull her hand away.

"I'd like nothing more than to repeat it, if you'll let me."

She moved not at all, not her eyes or her lips or her hand. Indeed, it seemed she stopped breathing. Even the wind seemed to halt, that her heavy skirts were no more flattened against her legs and flapping out toward the east.

Iain stepped closer. She wanted to back away. Holding her hand, he would not let her.

"Look at me, Maggie," he said, waiting until she did. He wasn't sure if that were a small nervousness or outright fear in her pretty green eyes, so still did she hold herself.

"Remember that kiss, lass? The one in the bothy, the one where my lips worshipped you? This one will be the same."

Almost imperceptibly, she nodded, giving consent.

That's my girl.

But for her abject misery—that was what he saw as he lowered his head—and his own heart breaking, he might have laughed. With her eyes slammed shut and face screwed up in a wince, this was exactly the reception she'd given him the first time he kissed her.

Iain touched his mouth oh, so softly to her stiff lips. "I won't ever hurt you. You ken that, lass," was said against her lips as he moved his gently back and forth." He tipped her chin up with a thumb under her jaw. He thought he felt her whimper, applied his lips with some expertise against hers, didn't force her, was content to be patient, thought to remind her of more. "This will be much more enjoyable if you kiss me back, Maggie Bryce." She definitely whimpered now, but Iain thought possibly it was seeped with some delight at these repeated words, certainly imbued with no less than acceptance.

He might have groaned with his own desire and with the joy that came for the chant in his head, *I am kissing Maggie Bryce again*. And when she sighed into him and moved her beautiful lips against his, ever so tentatively, Iain knew such need that he thought surely his soul might scream its joy. Still, he held himself in check, let her navigate this kiss at her leisure. She did so beautifully.

Only their lips and their hands touched. But she leaned into him and answered every bit of desire he showed her, the kiss growing as did her courage, as did his need.

But then she stopped, left him so abruptly he imagined she was pulled away by a force greater than longing.

Until she bent over, her hand holding her middle, a cry escaping that was neither of desire or delight.

"Maggie!"

"Oh, God," she moaned, one hand on Iain's forearm to steady herself.

Iain reacted instantly, only immediately understanding that Maggie was suffering and there was some trouble with the bairn, so he scooped her up in his arms. He grimaced as she cried out again but cradled her securely against his bare chest and made haste to the keep. He was surefooted and furrowed of brow and called out to the guards on the wall when he thought he was close enough that they might hear him.

They had, that the gate was opened for him and he stormed through it, barefoot and half dressed, now shouting for his mother inside the bailey.

Glenna appeared in the doorway of the hall, her hand finding her chest when she saw Iain carrying a visibly distraught Maggie. "Right up to her chambers," she instructed, likewise needing no explanation. Artair and Archie hovered, concern etched on their faces.

Iain took the stairs two at a time, knowing his mother and possibly others followed. He kicked open the door and laid Maggie gently upon the bed. Her face was yet screwed up, her eyes closed with whatever pain gripped her.

But when he tried to straighten, she clung to him and opened her eyes.

"Please don't leave me."

SHE STARED OUT THE window, watching the rain fall. Some of it, made savage by the wind, was pushed inside the chamber. She thought it must be morning, the sky gray not only with the rain but with the dawn. Yet, she couldn't say if it were the next morning, or two days later.

Snippets of conversations returned to her, things said over the past day, maybe two, whispered around her while they thought her insensible. She let the words invade her, thought she should not be allowed the luxury of pushing them away, not after what she'd done.

"She will lose the babe," Glenna had said softly at some point.

"But she will live?" Iain's voice.

"Of course she will."

And later, "The healer says she should have passed the fetus by now." Artair.

"If she does not...?"

"Then there is danger to the lass."

Iain: "You tell that bluidy healer that she'd better fix this, fix this now!"

"Shh," from Glenna. "Go on then, Iain. All that rage will help no one."

"I willna leave her. She begged me no' to leave her."

Artair had suggested, "Then sit with her, but say nothing. Just be there with her, for her."

And so he had. She'd woken several times, had wondered if that healer had given her something that made staying awake so tremendously difficult. But Iain had been there each time, had sat beside her, had held her hand, had brushed her hair away from her face.

And when labor had come, though by her reckoning she couldn't have been more than eighteen weeks along, Iain had stayed with her, reassuring her, holding her as her tiny child was delivered into the world. She'd passed out or had slept again immediately after, had woken now, bathed and cleaned she thought, and without a bairn to hold.

Iain sat in a chair beside the bed with his head and arms on the mattress near her thighs while he slept. Her hand was held by his, trapped under his head, his fingers warm and solid around hers.

After a while, the rain quieted, and Iain roused.

He looked at first to be consumed with guilt that he had slept at all. His features quickly softened though, showing only compassion, and plenty of it, and Maggie protested not at all when he climbed onto the narrow mattress with her. He laid down next to her but did not touch her save to place his hand on her hip. Maggie sighed, rather than wept, and turned onto her side, tugging Iain's hand around her waist as she fit herself against him. She closed her eyes and was swept back in time to those days in the caves when he'd lain so close to her.

Whatever small bit of hope for happiness she'd allowed herself to know since coming to Berriedale, and it was not a regular thing she permitted, might have gone with her babe, she thought sorrowfully.

BY MID-AFTERNOON, MAGGIE had insisted that she might only sleep more, that Iain should leave her, thanking him with a smile though not any words for having stayed with her. She did sleep, fitfully at first, and then soundly with the help of whatever had been introduced to the tea she'd been given around the time of the noon meal.

When next she woke, Artair sat next to her, having moved the lone chair back to its usual spot by the hearth.

Iain's beautiful face, over the last however many hours had shown so much torture and fury, for her pain, for her loss, for things he could not control. Glenna had yet been gentle and kind, but ever pragmatic, telling her that she might continue to bleed for many days, mayhap weeks, but that there would be other bairns.

But Artair, with his soft ways and eyes that could convey so much, brought Maggie to tears, for all the sympathy she found in his gaze. No other emotion colored his gray eyes, just a mournfulness that she was suffering.

He let her cry, gave her no words that would only be trite at this time, would mean nothing to her, just moved to the side of the bed and held her hand while she wept.

After a very long time, and when she'd calmed herself, Maggie said, "I didn't want the babe and now it's gone."

Artair shook his head where it was dropped low against his chest. "You had nothing to do with that, Maggie. There are a million reasons why a bairn won't grow fully to life. That is not your doing. That is God's will."

"But...but what if He took the babe because He knew I wouldn't be able to love it?"

"You are a very intelligent lass, Maggie Bryce, and so you ken very well that is not how He works." She said nothing to this, only bowed her head yet more. Artair persisted, "It wasn't the right time for you or this babe. You can have no guilt at all for knowing this or believing this."

She nodded, comforted to some small degree even as she wasn't quite sure she believed it.

"And lass," Artair continued, "I think I ken you at least well enough that I can say unequivocally that you would not ever withhold love."

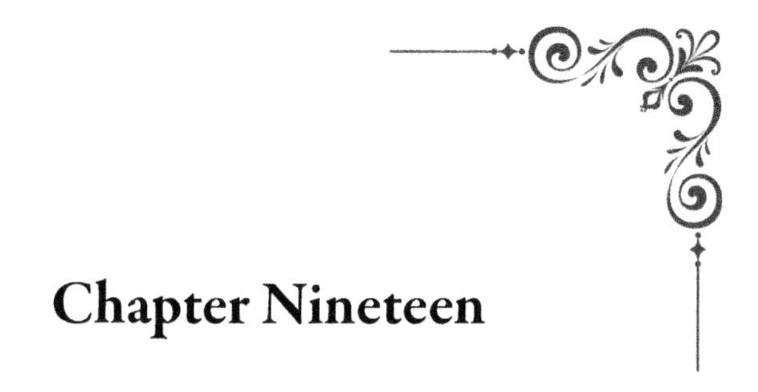

Chapter Nineteen

MAGGIE WOKE AT SOME point to find Iain pressed against her back and his arm around her midsection once again. Night had fallen once more. She did not move immediately, only closed her eyes again and felt him. At some time during the day or evening she'd given a bit of time to thinking this tragedy would have been vastly different if she'd been still at Blackhouse. There would have been none to comfort her, none to share her grief. She might yet have been down in the cells, mayhap would have gone with her babe, having none to see that she lived.

Rekindling this thought now opened her eyes, to her circumstance. She was now, here at Berriedale, surrounded by good people, very dear people.

She slid her hand over Iain's arm. Amazing, she thought, that his touch disturbed her not at all, only brought her peace.

He said something in response to her touch, words whispered into her hair. Maggie looked over her shoulder, about to ask him to repeat it as she'd not understood. His eyes were closed, and his forehead beaded with perspiration. He mumbled more, his tone disgruntled and Maggie understood he was in the midst of another nightmare, the memory of the first one she'd witnessed slamming into her with swift and startling recollection. She'd not thought about that first instance ever again after the event, until just this moment.

"Iain," she called over her shoulder with some sternness, intent on jarring him away from his demons.

This only increased his agitation. He continued to rave in his sleep, his lip curled with a great displeasure, not with fear as it had been during his night terror in the caves.

Maggie swiveled on the mattress, turning completely around toward him.

"Bluidy bollocks," he cursed. "Get up! Get up, Lach!"

"Iain!" Maggie cried. She laid her hand against his cheek. Softly, "Iain."

He growled yet more. With remarkable speed for one who slept, his hand snaked out and enclosed her neck, his thumb on one side and the four fingers on the other. He squeezed, widening Maggie's eyes.

"Iain, stop!" She wasn't frantic, as he wasn't applying great pressure, and ran her hand over his cheek, sliding her fingers into the short hair near his ears. "It's Maggie. Come back to me." She placed her other hand over the one wrapped with such menace around her neck.

He moved his mouth with great anger, shaking his head.

"Yes," she argued against his resistance. "Come back to me."

He went still. All the lines eased upon his forehead.

"Iain, it's Maggie Bryce."

Opening his eyes, he used several seconds to clarify the situation, his dark eyes adjusting to the dim firelight. And when he did, his eyes widened with horror and he mouthed a blush-inducing curse.

Maggie was quick to settle this new distress, her fingers gently peeling his away from her neck. "It's all right."

"*Jesu*, lass..."

"'Twas only a dream."

"Did I hurt you? Ah, bluidy...I'm—"

"You didn't." He was just as fretful as he'd been in the dream, for fear of what he might have done to her. "It's finished. You didn't hurt me."

"If I'd—"

"You would never harm me." She absolutely knew this to be true.

"But when I'm...dreaming, I'm no' in control."

Maggie snuggled against his chest, laid her head just at his shoulder. She wasn't frightened and needed him to be reassured of this. "Do you have these nightmares often?"

He didn't answer for several long seconds. "More often than I'd like to admit. I dinna recall them all, only ken that I wake drenched in sweat quite often."

"You had one in the caves."

He went still. "Did I?"

She nodded against him. Hesitantly, not sure if he wished to speak of it, she asked, "Are these—your nightmares—related to your scars?"

She felt his chin move against the top of her head before he answered.

"Aye."

She didn't press for more, but after a moment he offered in a quiet voice "Back in '98, I was part of a group taken as prisoners by the English." He went very rigid against her. "Seven months. They...they weren't kind."

"Who is Lach?"

"Lachlan Maitland. He was with me."

"Does he...do you think he has night terrors as well?"

"I dinna ken. His...trauma is visible all the time."

"How so?"

"He canna hide his scars. They cover half his face." Quiet, and then, "He has no choice but to deal with it at all times. Least mine, I can hide."

Maggie wondered, "Which do you think is better?"

A short, humorless laugh rumbled against her.

"Aye now, there's a good question."

Maggie moved her arm across his chest and laid her hand against his bare neck.

"I'm sorry, Maggie Bryce."

"That is unnecessary."

"I should go—"

Maggie shook her head against him. "Please don't."

"I dinna want to hurt you."

"You won't."

He was tense yet, unconvinced, afeared still that he might bring harm to her.

"I sleep much better in your arms," she said softly, waiting, watching the rising and falling of his chest.

The arm under and around her tightened. "Aye, Maggie Bryce."

IAIN THOUGHT THAT MAGGIE should stay abed for many days, weeks if needed, to recover from her loss. His mother thought otherwise, said lying about was the last thing Maggie needed. Iain had been surprised when Artair concurred with a softly given, "She is young and healthy now, and her body will heal right quick. Industry will see to the healing of her spirit."

He adopted this strategy for himself as well, as once he'd taken leave of Maggie to depart her chambers after two days, he'd thrown himself into one project after another. Into whatever might help him lose the image of that perfectly formed little human coming into and going out of the world so quickly. The only blessing at the time had been Maggie's incoherency, that certain herbs and medicines had been administered to keep her from becoming too fretful, for witnessing firsthand this tragedy with any clarity that might keep the memory. Yet, her distress, and her absolute solemnness since, was killing him.

But he'd returned to her often and had stayed with her throughout the nights, being mostly wakeful, so afraid he might hurt her if he slept and dreamed again. Few words were exchanged and yet he thought so much had been said.

He was not completely surprised then to find her in the hall on the fourth morning. He'd left her asleep this morn, and she hadn't been in attendance for the morning meal, but she sat now at the family's table, with Artair and those ledgers. Their heads were once again bent together, Artair nodding at whatever she said.

He'd come from the kitchens, having returned from the beach, that he watched them quietly for several minutes, trying to gauge the entire atmosphere around them. However, since he was nearly behind them, at the corner of the room near the corridor, this was impossible. They didn't seem to be working, the quill sat untouched on the table, and yet the hum of their muted chat was constant.

When Artair stood and patted Maggie's shoulder, leaving her, Iain backed into the darkened corridor and waited for his steward. He didn't think he'd ever been able to surprise his steward, or lie to him, as in pretending he was just coming down to the hall himself. So he only waited.

Indeed, Artair was not startled by his presence. He folded his arms into his sleeves as was his way and looked up at his chief.

"What were you talking with Maggie Bryce about?"

Artair raised a brow at his complete lack of subtlety and Iain mumbled something about the scene appearing rather serious.

"Lad, you understand that *other* people sometimes seek my counsel, aye?" A bare hint of mischief shone in his gray eyes.

"Aye," Iain acknowledged with his own grin and with some understanding that Artair's uncommonly lighthearted mood might suggest that Maggie was in good spirits as well. "Just curious." He shrugged then, with some dismissiveness. "None of my affair."

"But of course it is," Artair countered. "You are laird. You said yourself, she's one of our own now."

At this, Iain raised an expectant brow to his steward, who confounded him then by actually smiling and saying, "But I'll keep her confidence, as she begged. If it were not of a personal nature or if it needed your attention, you would be advised."

Iain frowned at this. "But she's...is she...is everything all right? I mean... as right as can be?"

His steward's smile, which Iain could honestly say he saw infrequently, remained. "The lass is well, determined to move on."

This appeased Iain only minimally.

Artair moved around Iain but stopped and turned and said, almost as an afterthought, "You were right about her, by the by."

Iain set his hand onto the hilt of his sword and faced Artair again. "About?"

"Of course you never actually said, *this lass is important*, but I sensed she was. To you. To others." He chuckled, further baffling Iain with this unprecedented show of good humor. "I cannot put my finger on it, exactly, but Maggie Bryce is...a very special person. I'm very proud of you, lad, for what you've done for her."

This put Iain in mind of Maggie's first night at Berriedale, when he'd wanted Artair's approval, thought it was a significant thing to be had.

With one more nod, Artair continued on his way. Iain strode toward the hall, found Maggie where the steward had left her, the quill now in hand as she labored over figures on the pages.

Iain stood before the table.

Maggie lifted her face and smiled at him, her eyes magnificently clear. It was not large, the smile, nor brimming with any true joy, but he thought right now that she was pleased to see him.

"You are...well? Well enough to be away from your chambers?"

Maggie inclined her head. "Iain, your mother and Artair are right. It does me no good to remain abed. I-I need to get back to where I was." When Iain lifted a brow at this statement, she clarified, "Ideally, I'd like to go back further, before I was married, before...everything. I need to find that girl again."

He was taken for a moment by the sound of his name on her lips, by her own admission that she hadn't been that girl in quite a while.

"It's a good plan," he said, "to find her."

With a wee rueful smile, she said, "I hope she wasn't left in those caves. That was the last place I saw her."

"Nae, lass. She's here."

"I am weary of melancholy and tired of sorrow. Artair says there are ways to grieve that should not consume the entire body and mind."

Iain tried a smile on her. "So he gave you the speech?"

Maggie answered in kind, her lips curving again slightly. "I think so. *We must visit and review our sorrows, but they should not control or consume or condemn us.* He's right, though. However would we survive—truly live—if we are burdened with all that cannot be undone?"

"But grieve you must, Maggie Bryce, in your own way, however it makes sense to you."

"I will," she said. Thoughtfully, she added, "He is a very good man. I don't think I've ever met a better soul than Artair."

"And yet here I am," a voice called from behind them.

Maggie lifted her gaze and Iain turned to find Archie striding in through the open door from the yard. His perfectly timed quip was delivered in his usual gruff style that it required several seconds before either Maggie or Iain understood that he was jesting. He stood with his arms spread wide, waiting with some expectancy for them to acknowledge what he perceived as perfect timing.

Iain shook his head. Maggie smiled and set down the quill and closed the ledger.

Archie ambled over to the table. "Aye, lass, it's good to see you up and about."

"Thank you Arch," she said, "and for your visit yesterday."

"But we'll no be leaping head first into too much labor," Archie said, waving dismissively at the papers and ink and quill on the table. "It'll keep."

Iain didn't know what was happening around here. First Artair with his near-constant grinning earlier, and now Archie, of the sour moods, being solicitous and—*Jesu*, was he smiling inside that thick beard?

"So I've come to take you away, lass," Arch said. "The seas are calm and straight, and shining like the sun off my own sword, and I'll be taking you out on the boat."

Her eyes lit up, her lips parted. Iain wished he had thought of it, so delighted was her response, tempered only by her switching her gaze from Archie to him, seeking permission it seemed.

"Aye, lass, you should," he instructed, just as he caught sight of his steward, hovering near the corridor, a missive in his hand, his gaze intent upon Iain.

Archie beckoned her forward. "C'mon now, sun won't wait for us."

She stood, enlivened. "Do I need to—what shall I bring?"

Archie chortled. "Ye bring yerself, lass. Let's go."

"Won't you come?" Maggie asked of Iain.

"Next time, lass," Iain answered. "I'm a wee bit suspicious of a smiling Archie."

Maggie grinned yet again, and Iain watched them leave. His frown came as soon as they were out the door and Iain followed Artair, who had disappeared, likely ducked into his office.

Artair's office was a small square of a room, with so much of the space—walls and floors and furniture—covered with records and journals and papers. A small table served as his desk, and Artair stood from the chair behind it, shaking the note at Iain.

"This has come from the baron Garioch, George Menking," Artair explained. "The man has a web greater than my own. I had reached out for any word on movements from Carlisle, all the comings and goings."

"And?"

"Sutherland has left the city. We can assume that those at Blackhouse must have finally gotten word to him of your taking of Maggie Bryce."

"He may well come here directly," Iain surmised.

Artair frowned. "But how could he? Would he not have to go to Blackhouse, regroup and plan from there?"

"I wouldn't," Iain said, giving this some thought. "If I'd just been informed that a man had stolen my wife, I'd be running straight for him."

"You say this, with Maggie Bryce being the wife in question, and likely you would stop at nothing to recover her, but would he?"

"If not for her, then for pride," Iain guessed. He would do it for her alone, he knew. "But he does have his entire army—or the bulk of it—with him. They've been idle for months in or around Carlisle, essentially ready to go." He paced a bit, not allowed many steps with all the stacks of books and whatnot on the floor. "We ken we dinna want to wait for him to come to us, which makes it imperative that we ken his direction."

"You've got those other units already keeping watch on Blackhouse and elsewhere," Artair reminded him.

"Aye. Mayhap I need to send out several more, not large, just for scouting. I dinna want to leave ourselves vulnerable here. I'll speak with Duncan, put a handful of men on the routes from

Carlisle to Blackhouse and then Carlisle to Berriedale. I want to meet him in the open, not here at Berriedale."

"Aye, lad."

Iain stopped directly in front of Artair. "And you ken what I said about Maggie Bryce? If running up against Sutherland dinna go my way, you and she and my mother get down to Jamie and Ada at Aviemore, or if needs be, by sea, then, to Lach up at Hawkmore."

"Aye."

THE SKY WAS CLOUDLESS, the wind non-existent, and the soft swaying motion of the boat on the water was everything that was peaceful and wonderful.

Maggie did not think the boat was regularly equipped with plaids and blankets, but it was today. She suspected Archie had filched these items with an eye toward her comfort but managed to leave off teasing him about so chivalrous an act as it was simply too sweet to make fun of.

So she laid in the bottom of the boat, upon the soft blankets, and Archie sat on the lone plank that crossed the width of the boat at one end and served as his seat while he rowed, tirelessly and rhythmically, moving them horizontally along the shore, but not taking them out too far into the sea.

The beauty of this exact moment was the complete freedom it offered—freedom from fear, from worry, from conversation even, as Archie seemed as content as she to enjoy each other's company without words right now.

Honestly, she truly did feel more herself today. She mourned still, would no doubt mourn for quite some time, but her earlier chat with Artair had done wonders for her. She could—and she would—mourn all she liked, or all she needed, he'd told her, but she must allow time for everything else as well, the rest of life.

Closing her eyes, Maggie considered that her grief had been shared. With Glenna and Artair and even Archie and Duncan, who'd surprised her by visiting her chambers. Archie had been awkward and shuffling but so very dear for all the things he'd clearly wanted to say but couldn't quite put into words so that Maggie had only nodded, understanding his sorrow was for her. Duncan had sat in the chair, not as close to the bed as Iain had set it, and had talked non-stop, of nothing of any import. And he'd kindly allowed her to respond not at all, had sometimes asked questions and assumed her answer that he kept right on talking. Nervous chatter, Glenna had called it later. "People deal with grief, and the consoling, in different ways," Iain's mother had said, "and not one of them is wrong."

Shared with Iain as well, or mostly, she'd thought, for his coming by with some regularity, for his spending the nights with her. Had he known that the dark and the quiet were the hardest to endure? She'd only thought it just this morning, that because of his attention and attendance, it seemed as if the grief were shared, that someone understood completely. He couldn't, of course, but it pleased her to imagine he did.

How dear they all were.

She was going to be all right, she thought. She needed to understand this.

Yet, allow time for everything else.

"Archie," she said, tipping her head forward on her chest to glance up at him while he continued to row, "did I not once hear that sometimes funeral processions might take this route?"

"Eh?"

"I thought once I had been told a tale of a body, deceased, being laid into a small boat, and sent off to sea. The mourners on the shore would send a flaming arrow out to the boat, burning it, sending the entire pyre to the bottom of the sea. Is that real? Does that happen?"

"Aye, it does. We McEwens dinna do that, but I've heard stories of those that do. No' for me, though. Give me a nice cold crypt in the ground, I'll be fine."

Maggie sat up. "Me as well, but that's what this lovely interlude put me in mind of, with me lying in the bottom of the boat so still, which is rather ghoulish, when I think on it." She sat up and backed up against the solid wood corner of the stern, lifting her arms to ride the side walls.

Archie grinned at her.

"Did Hew like to be out on the sea?" She been thinking about him these last few days as well. "This quietness seems perfectly suited to him, not a soul around to cause him grief."

"He did, actually, but lass, you ken this calm sea is a rare thing."

"I did notice that. What else did Hew like?"

Archie grinned into his chest, then lifted his head and gazed out over the sea while he continued to row. "He liked anything that required order and structure, could no' stand the chaos."

"But then how did he manage to become a soldier? War seems like it would be the ultimate chaos."

"Aye, and so he was happy to be rid of it, would do what he could."

"That makes sense. I wish he were here."

"It's just no' right," Archie said, shaking his head, "the good ones dying young. All that potential and promise wasted. They dinna make 'em like that too often you ken. A shame, that."

"Hew certainly was a standout," Maggie agreed. "Was he always so serious?"

"Aye," Arch said, and was thoughtful for moment. "You could no' rile him. If you did, was only his red cheeks would show it. But he did what was right, always, even when he was ridiculed for it. You could no' ever take him away from that. I dinna ken many—any, mayhap—like that."

"I didn't know him like you," Maggie said, "only but a few days, but his heart was good. You're right, there are too few people like that."

Archie tipped his head down to her. "You've seen some ugly souls, aye, lass?"

Maggie nodded now. "No more than you, I'm sure."

"Aye, but my soul is no' so pretty. I can handle it."

Smiling up at him, she confessed, "You know, Arch, it didn't take me long when first in your company to realize that you only like people to be afraid of you, and that you're naught but a big softy under all that gruffness."

His grin was slow and lazy while he considered her. "Ye got me all figured out."

Lifting her shoulders, Maggie said, "I once heard some sage thing that suggested like attracts like. Your chief is a good man, and so he surrounds himself with good men, wouldn't suffer fools or dastardly types, I imagine."

"Aye, the lad's a good man."

Quiet.

"You're in love with him," Archie said after a moment. Given as a statement, not posed as a question, his arms moving in that circle fashion that the rowing required though his gaze was on Maggie.

Maggie nodded. "I think so. If that's...what this is, that I feel. I haven't anything to compare it. And it's silly, of course, for I know him so little, really."

"Sometimes it just is."

"Maybe it's just gratitude, though, as he has twice now come to my rescue."

Archie chuckled. Maggie liked the sound of it. "As have I and Duncan and Donal."

Maggie made a face. "And dear you all are—but that's what makes me think I might be in love with him, because I sense it's more than gratitude, more than friendship, just...more." She shrugged, not understanding it herself, not quite sure how to explain it. "Have you ever been in love Arch?"

"So long ago, I can scarcely recall."

"Of course, that's not true. If I were removed from Berriedale today, never to see him again, I would...not ever forget him."

Archie stopped rowing, bringing both oars to a halt that he rested his forearms on them, gazing out across the smooth surface of the water.

"Getting on thirty years now, just about," he said after a while. "She was Sorcha. Not the bonniest lass, though she had her charms. Thought we'd wed and have bairns and keep on with the crofting. And then in comes the army near Glasgow." His lips twitched, pursed a bit. "Met a soldier, she did. I begged her choose, him or me."

"She chose him," Maggie guessed sadly.

Archie shook his head. "Nae, but he did her. Dishonored her, not kindly." He bent his head. His lips moved for several seconds before the rest came. "Told her it dinna matter, but she could no' get over it. Hung herself. *Jesu*, from the highest peak in town."

"Archie, I'm so sorry."

"I dinna think even Duncan knows the tale."

"Does it ever work out, then?"

"What's that, lass?"

"Love?"

Archie harrumphed softly.

"I cannot think of one instance where love triumphed. My parents, my own marriage. You and your Sorcha. Duncan and his wife. Can it exist? Survive?"

Archie studied her. "You think no good will come from loving the lad?"

Maggie shrugged. "It's not always easy to believe good things will come."

"Or stay."

"Aye."

"You make of it what you will, lass."

"How so?"

Returned to his usual gruffness, he said, "Means what you do with it will define it. You ignore it because you're afraid, mayhap it'll go away. You find courage and act on it, mayhap it'll stay, grow some."

She gave this some thought, not quite brave enough to ask of Archie if he thought there was any chance Iain McEwen might also be in love with her.

"But then," she said, with a twist of her lips, "I am still wed to another."

Archie shook his head. "That's done, Maggie Bryce, was done the minute we rode through those gates at Blackhouse. You'll never go back to him. The lad kills him, or he kills every single one of us, but ye ain't ever going back." Beginning to row again, he said, "Aye now, that's enough of that. That's more words I spoke than all of this year, right here and now. Close your eyes now, rest. You're a good lass, Maggie Bryce."

She smiled at her friend and did as he commanded. "You're a good man, Arch."

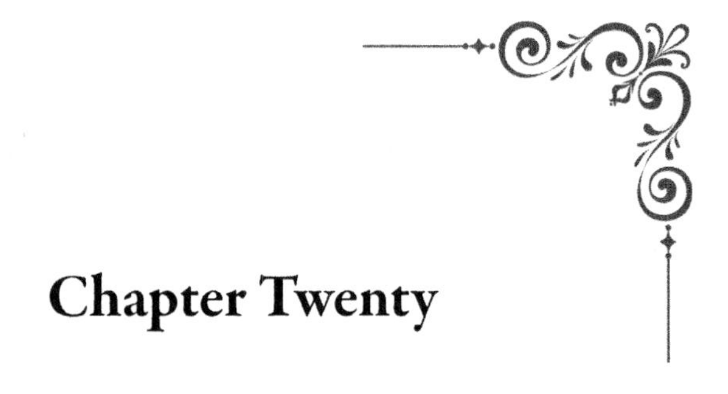

Chapter Twenty

SHE WAS SURPRISED, and then she was not, when Iain entered her chambers late that night, as he had for the last three nights. She'd been prepared to expect him, having changed into her nightclothes some time ago, but then also determined to stave off any disappointment if he didn't show.

Maggie was already abed when the soft knock came, and the door was pushed open.

She was lying on her side facing the door, somewhere between the middle of the bed and the far side. She'd been thinking it had been a good day. She was proud of the strides she'd made.

Iain closed the door and leaned his back against it, eyeing her across the room with only the soft light of a small blaze in the hearth to guide him.

"I dinna ken if...I should come."

"But you have." She'd given this some thought as well, wondering if he came to her tonight, what it might mean. Its sole purpose, she'd thought, had been to comfort her, to make sure she did not cry alone in the night.

"But I dinna need to stay, if you...."

"I'm glad you've come."

She'd been sleeping each time he'd come to her previously, that tonight was the first time she watched his preparations. He nodded at her softly given statement and pushed away from the door. With practiced ease, he removed his belt and sword and propped them against the footboard and then began to unlace his leather breastplate. That stiff piece of gear, which he was rarely without, was set next to the sword. He sat on the bed then, his back to her, to remove his boots.

Maggie lifted her hand, wanted to touch him, to feel his back. She did not, just curled her fingers into her palm and pulled her hand away. But she watched, watched the shadows of firelight play across his back, saw the skin and muscles move here and there under his tunic. She liked it very much, thought there was some primal and raw beauty to all that power he possessed, all contained within the fine linen of his tunic.

Iain pivoted and stretched out on the bed. He did not turn and bend into her as he had previously, as she'd woken each night to the feel of him pressed against her back. He folded his arms under his head and stared at the ceiling, his lips pursed a bit, mayhap with some thoughts.

Maggie waited, thinking he had some conversation to share.

"I dinna ken if I would come tonight," he said, "because it's no' so easy to hold you as I have and no'...want to kiss you, which seemed...offensive—I canna think of another word for it—when you were grieving so."

"Is that why you are so far away from me now?"

The smallest hint of a grin touched his mouth. "Aye."

Maggie reached out her hand once more, touched her fingers to his side, just laid them there over his tunic, her arm and wrist on the mattress. "Not offensive at all," she said, "mayhap untimely." But she understood. She wasn't ready herself, even as she had been so encouraged by how unafraid she'd been by his touch of late. Yet, "There is a splendor in your arms that I've yet to find anywhere else."

Now he laughed outright. "Words like that, Maggie Bryce, will do nothing for my resistance."

"I'll be quiet then."

"Aye."

She wasn't though. She turned over, presented her back to him, thinking this was safe, from kissing at least. "Now will you hold me?"

He'd begun to move before she finished the sentence, his arm sliding around her in time to the word, *me.*

Maggie sighed and closed her eyes while Iain settled himself against her, his face pressed into her hair, his chest and thighs fitted perfectly against her.

The silence that followed was different from that which she'd known with Archie today. This was not friendly and comfortable. This was intimate, tinged with heat and so much more.

"Considering my life as a whole—and not just these last many months—I haven't often been fearful or filled with dread," she said after a while, "but I knew the very first time you touched me, certainly the first time you put your arms around me, that there was safety and security here."

After a moment, he offered, "You could stay here."

"In your arms?" She held her breath.

"Aye."

"How can—what would that mean?"

Long silence until he said, "Canna mean anything until Kenneth Sutherland is dealt with. But then...it could be everything."

Maggie closed her eyes, overwhelmed by the meaning behind words that sounded so very ordinary. *It could be everything.*

Sometimes joy felt like tears, she decided. "I would like that."

IAIN FOUND MAGGIE IN the courtyard a few days later, once again keeping company with Artair. On her hip, she'd wedged a basket, one that showed bits and pieces of linen and other fabrics. Artair, who rarely moved around the keep empty-handed, stood beside her with his ledgers in hand.

They seemed only to be waiting something, their gazes upon the smithy's' shed, or deeper, at the carpenter's area beyond.

Duncan's voice sounded out from within. "It's coming, lass. Never saw Will Carpenter move so quick but for your request."

Maggie laughed and Iain thought the sound the most magnificent he'd ever heard. She called back to Duncan, "We are in no hurry. We can wait." To Artair, she said in a softer voice, "I was only suggesting—I didn't mean for it to be done right today."

Donal came out of the hall, behind Iain, carrying two stacked chairs, which Iain thought might be from Artair's office.

"Where'd you think, Maggie? Sun or shade?"

Maggie turned, noticed Iain's watchful presence and smiled, and then consulted Artair. "I'm for sun on our faces, but what is your preference?"

Artair concurred. "Sun, indeed."

"What's going on?" Iain wondered, approaching the pair while Donal set the chairs toward the rear of the yard, near the bakehouse and away from the comings and goings of the gate.

"Artair and I decided our labors would be so much more enjoyable if they were undertaken out of doors," Maggie told him. "Actually, I decided that, and Artair was kind enough to oblige."

She met his gaze with only hints of shyness, barely that, that Iain found himself smiling at her for reasons that had nothing to do with her want to be outside, or how easily her wishes might be granted by so many eager to please.

Artair explained, "Was only talk, really, until Duncan got hold of it, and insisted Will Carpenter put all else aside this morning." For all the disorder this surely caused, Artair showed not one ounce of regret for what was happening.

"Ask and you shall receive, aye, lass?"

She shrugged, maybe a bit guiltily now, but qualified, "Won't be but a few weeks out of the whole year that we might make use of it, but we will be happy while we do, I think."

Duncan appeared then from the carpenter's shed, walking backwards, carrying one side of a quickly constructed but sturdy looking table. Will Carpenter, a spare man of usually good humor carried the other side, squinting as he stepped into the sunshine.

"Aye, I see," said Duncan as Donal directed him toward the spot where he'd placed the chairs.

Iain was pleased with this circumstance and then more so when Maggie bounced a bit on her toes, her excitement palpable. She threaded her arm through Artair's and bade him follow with her. Iain walked behind, encouraged by her contagious enthusiasm, such as he hadn't seen in some time.

Duncan and Will Carpenter set the table down and Donal held out the chair for Maggie. She slid easily into it, smiling up at Donal. Artair did likewise and set his ledgers and papers on the table, which immediately were mussed by the wind, until Iain stepped forward and thumped his hand on the thick stack.

"Oh, we didn't consider the wind," Maggie said with some disappointment.

"Nothing a good stout stone or chunk of wood won't solve, lass," Duncan said, finding one of the former with some debris near the wall. He tossed this to Iain, who plunked it down where his hand had been.

Her smile reappeared. And the ones on all the faces surrounding the pair at the table stayed as well and Iain thought this was very good indeed.

It became a regular sight then, since that day, to find Artair and Maggie at their table, in the yard, whenever the weather permitted. They spent so much time out of doors, that Maggie's cheeks were given a great bit of color by the sun—as was Artair's balding noggin, which he was teased mercilessly about, though he seemed not to care. They were rarely alone though, often joined by any number of people, most regularly Glenna, Archie, and Duncan, when they weren't about their own work, or had chores that might be undertaken in good company and could be attended there at the table. Sometimes, Archie just sat and whittled beside them. Once, Iain had come upon Duncan having a midday nap right there, his face tipped up to the sun, his hands folded comfortably in his lap, and Maggie and the steward talking in low voices while he slept.

He'd happily joined them himself on occasion, the first time with some self-consciousness, that he'd posed some questions to Artair about the coming jaunt to the village, for answers he already knew, pretending that had been his purpose.

It should not have been an awkward circumstance, considering that he spent his nights in her bed, many nights by then.

He shouldn't, of course, but she hadn't given him any reason to think she did not want him there with her.

It was magnificent, and then torture, to hold her in his arms night after night, and make no move to further what burned and bloomed between them. One night, she'd turned around in his arms to face him. They'd stared at each other for several seconds. Iain had let his gaze fall hungrily to her lips before he demanded that she turn back around, and settle as she normally did, with her back to him. "Dinna face me, Maggie Bryce, until you're ready for what will come."

She'd opened her mouth to argue and he had all he could do to instruct further, "Ready without reservation, without fear."

Her face had fallen, but she had turned her back to him again. "I want to be ready," she'd said softly into the night.

"You will be," he'd whispered against her hair. "I'll be right here when you are."

Today, he sat at their table with them, with genuine purpose, as Artair had brought up the subject of raising rents on the leases of the crofters.

"As you haven't in three years," the steward said pointedly.

"So long as we dinna need to, we won't," Iain maintained.

"If market prices keep as they are, you will need to."

Duncan joined them, likely waiting on Iain to get to the training field. Will Carpenter had since made several more chairs to accommodate the usually crowded table and Duncan sat in one of these, next to Maggie, who was fussing with a spool of thread that had become tangled.

"Hold up your hands, Duncan," she said, and then arranged his hands to her liking when he did, turning them to face each other at chest height, about a foot apart. Artair and Iain exchanged a grin when Maggie began to weave the thread around Duncan's large hands, untangling long sections of it as she did.

But Artair kept up with his argument. "If not this year then most certainly next year. It only needs to be a modest increase, but lad, soldiers and battles don't come cheaply."

"Aye," he said. He wasn't paying attention any more, though, his gaze, all his thoughts given to her.

A thundering of hooves called his attention then, Duncan's as well. Neither man jumped to his feet, not taken up with any great alarm, as there had been no call of a threat from the guards on the wall.

'Twas Archie and Donal and Eideard, returned from checking on the scouting parties. Archie's grim countenance raised Iain's and Duncan's brows. Their silent question was answered quickly enough.

"Longshanks is dead."

A collective silence greeted this news.

While the devil you knew was always better than the one you didn't, Iain had to believe that the son could not ever be so bad for and to the Scots as had been his father, Edward I. But then, that was the thing about devils—unless you were one or surrounded by them you never really understood them.

There was more, though. Archie chewed at his cheek and inclined his head that the rest needed privacy.

"Aye, now, lass," said Duncan, reading Archie's mien as well, laying the looped thread on the table, "Nice knot around the middle'll keep this from tangling again."

Iain spared Maggie only a glance and a soft touch on her shoulder before rising and following Archie and the others into the keep.

Inside at the family table, when all the officers were gathered close, Archie delivered the news in a low voice. "Seems Edward was moving, leading many combined armies north, when he croaked at Burgh by Sands. They sat for a while there, waiting on what, I dinna ken. Some thought waiting on the new king, but some armies kept moving—including the Sutherland force. According to the lads, Sutherland broke off at the Argmore Pass. Spent the night at some little town called Catlowdy near the border and gone the next day. The lads watching ambled into town when they'd gone, chatted up a few of the taproom wenches. They're headed to Stirling, apparently sent by Edward I before he passed, meant to take Doune Castle."

Damn. "I'd rather he came to us, get this thing done," Iain said bitterly. But then, he could not find anything to grouse about with Sutherland being so long gone from Caithness, as all Alpin's activities had ceased in his absence.

"Aye," Duncan agreed, but seemed not as put out as Iain. "What kind of numbers does he have?"

Archie nodded. "Those lads scouting—all three, Eagan, Ned, and Simon—agree on the estimate. Three to four hundred."

"Christ," blasphemed Duncan.

"Likely more than Doune Castle commands," Iain said, his mind whirring. "Artillery?"

"None that they noticed," Archie answered. "They figured a hundred archers, twice that in cavalry, the rest foot soldiers."

"Where the hell did he get those numbers?" Duncan groused.

It didn't matter. "What kind of time frame?"

"Take 'em three days to get there, rate they're moving," Archie said.

"Swordmair's closest," Iain determined. "Would be quicker to send word to Alec MacBriar, get his army to Stirling before we might, straight from here."

"MacBriar's embedded with Robert Bruce," Archie said with a frown.

"Nae, he's north again, Artair just heard."

"Probably wiser not to leave ourselves vulnerable by moving the entire army," Duncan supposed. "I dinna trust that Sutherland."

"Nor I."

To Duncan, "Send forty down to Swordmair, but they gotta ride hard. Tell them to be at Alec's disposal, whatever he needs."

MAGGIE ROUSED WHEN he climbed onto the mattress beside her, well after midnight. Gently, he brushed the hair away from her face, knowing that he needed more of her tonight. She woke softly, a slow smile coming for his presence beside her, a smile he could not resist. There should never be too much time between kisses, he decided.

Cautiously, he touched his lips to hers. She should by now be used to his presence, to any and all simple touches from him.

She did not resist, did not stiffen with any upset, but tipped her bonny face up to him, sleep-shrouded but amenable to this kiss. So much of him wanted to devour her, thought that he'd held himself in check long enough, too long. He wouldn't, of course, reminding himself as he did every day that small strides and an inordinate amount of patience were required.

But then she touched him. Of her own accord, she reached for him, her slim fingers sliding around his neck as she opened to his kiss, met his tongue midway, delighting him beyond hope even. Iain shifted on the mattress, diminishing the space between them. He didn't rise up and over her but drew her nearer that she was above him and could control the kiss.

She did, wonderfully, not embracing the role without hesitation, but with a willingness to experiment. Her hair fell all around them, curtained their faces and their lips and joined tongues. He placed his hand on hers and moved it away from his cheek and down across his neck and to his chest, wishing tonight he'd thought to remove his tunic. He left it there, asked nothing else of her, and was thrilled when she embarked on her own discovery then, splaying out her fingers, sliding her hand slowly across him. He continued to ravish her lips, or she his, and then thought to raise his tunic, get the thing out of the way, wanting to feel her hands on his bare skin. He kept all movements to a leisurely pace, as if he had not this burning need inside. He moved her hand again, lower, just beneath the bottom of the tunic, now just below his pectorals.

Maggie gasped against his lips when her hand touched his ribs. She stilled, but just for a moment, then continued her exploration, even dared to push her hand under the fabric, over the muscles of his chest, over his nipples.

He groaned his delight, enflamed by both her touch and her keenness to explore, all the while raging inside with desire for the knowledge that she wore only a thin nightrail, that so little separated them from bliss. He moved his hand up her arm and over her shoulder, his fingers pulling the loose fabric of the neckline away, down her arm. She stiffened, he felt that. Her lips stilled against his.

Iain paused. "Open your eyes, Maggie Bryce."

She did, so close to his. He laid his head back against the mattress, put distance between them even as his hand held on her nightrail, lowered down her arm, one freckled shoulder shown to his hungry gaze.

Her pupils were large. She blinked twice, her wariness readily apparent.

"It's me, lass, and you ken I would never harm you. You keep your eyes on me, lass."

She rolled her lips inward and nodded, but he sensed she was unconvinced.

Iain removed his hand from the linen and shifted again, sitting up, forcing her away for a moment. He lifted the tunic up and over his head and tossed it aside. When he laid down again, he took her face in his hands and brought her lips to his, touched only her cheeks, did not close his eyes. Her hand settled on his chest once more as she was brought so close.

He kissed her slowly, reverently. Soon, her hand moved again. Her eyes drifted close.

"Ah, lass, I've dreamed of your hands on me," he whispered to her.

And when he moved his hand down, traced a path along the slim column of her neck, over the nightrail and onto her breast, she seemed only to wait. He lifted the weight of her breast in his hand, pushing it upward but not harshly, certainly not in conjunction with the need coursing through him now. Lowering her breast, he let the tips of his fingers slide over her nipple, felt her shudder as the peak hardened.

Her hand upon him stopped moving. Her kiss slowed and her breath quickened.

"Just feel," he said against her hovering lips. He nipped softly at the peak with his fingers through the fabric.

"I feel it further than—not only right there," she said with some amazement.

"Between your legs?" He asked, sliding his mouth across hers, while his fingers continued their play.

She nodded, breathless now. "Aye."

She arched her back ever so slightly, tilted her head. His cock responded. Iain lifted his head and rained kisses along the exposed skin of her neck. "I want you to crave it, Maggie Bryce. I want you to beg me for my touch."

"I think I do," she said shakily. "Crave it."

"Now picture my lips where my fingers are. That's what I want."

She whimpered.

Iain raised himself, turning her onto her back, following, suiting action to word and landing his mouth against her nipple, taut against the linen fabric. He drew her nipple into his mouth, finding the neckline once again with his fingers, lowering it. An inch at a time, until her breast was bared to him. A glorious breast, full and round, the center pink and crested, eager for his touch. He repeated the action, suckled her breast, nothing between them now. He kept on, pulling the nipple between his teeth, using his tongue to elicit a moan from her, that soon she was liquid in his arms, sighing her delight, threading her fingers in his hair.

He skimmed his hand along the outline of her, along her hip and down her thigh. He wanted more, wanted it all, and right now. And while she was, just now, as desirous as he, Iain wasn't entirely sure that her body had healed completely, and this gave him pause. He thought it wise to always move forward, and not ever back. He needed to stop while she was still yearning, still wanting more.

He was hard for her and it nearly broke his heart, but he lifted her nightrail and covered her breast again and brought his lips back to hers, kissing her softly. He raised his head and stared down at her, knowing he would need to address the longing and the question in her gaze.

Before he might have done that, she said, with much hesitation, "I...adore your kiss, Iain. But I...I know I do not like all that follows." Her voice was very small, filled with apology.

This completely broke his heart. He settled himself at her side, thinking whatever conversation followed just now, his intense regard would not help it. Likely, she would open to him if she felt less pressure from him. He laid on his back and rubbed his chest, only touching her where he held her hand, on the mattress between them.

"Do you trust me, Maggie?"

"Yes."

"So, if I tell you something, you will believe me? You'd ken I'd no lie to you?"

"Yes."

"Maggie, I'm no sure of all the particulars of your marriage, but I promise you, lass, whatever happens between you and me, from beginning to end, will be as different from how it was...then, as day is to night." While he had no idea of how it had been for her, her fear of his touch, even up until a few minutes ago, answered any questions he might have had.

She said nothing, but he thought she might have nodded against her pillow.

He would have said more, but there came a firm knock at the door.

Frowning and rolling quickly from the bed, Iain grabbed his sword and pulled open the door. Duncan stood there, fully dressed, his combat helmet held in his hand and lodged against his hip. Iain kept the opening narrow, that Maggie might not see this, that Duncan might not see her.

"Boat just arrived from Hawkmore. Artair's holding the missive that came with it."

"I'll be right down," Iain said without pause. The missive would tell him what he needed to know, but he had a pretty good idea. A note come by water late at night usually gave up bad news. Duncan nodded and Iain closed the door.

"Iain?" Maggie called from the bed.

"I dinna ken what it is," he said, returning his tunic to his person and affixing his belt and sword now. He grabbed his folded plaid as well but only held this in his hand, did not don it.

He knelt at the side of the bed and ran his hand over her cheek with the greatest of devotion, bringing her gaze to him. Taking her hand, he brought it to his lips and pressed a kiss there. This Maggie Bryce, tousled and pink-lipped from his seduction, possibly his favorite yet, was a nice picture to take away with him. He smiled at her. "We have all the rest of our lives to finish this, Maggie Bryce. My longing for you isn't going anywhere."

Propped up on her elbow on her side, Maggie tilted her head onto her shoulder. "Come back to me, Iain McEwen."

"Always, Maggie Bryce."

He pressed a kiss to her forehead and was gone.

Iain found Artair awaiting him in the hall. The sleepy steward did not wait for Iain to reach him, but rushed forward with the note from Lachlan Maitland, which Iain received with a heavy scowl.

"Come by boat?" He asked Artair as he tore through the wax seal.

"Aye, three soldiers," Artair answered. "Those Ramsays have been giving the Maitlands grief for years."

Iain's frown hardened quickly as he read the note. "This is more than grief. Christ—*a wee critical something*." He was very sorry now that he'd sent off that unit of forty to Alec at Swordmair. He passed the plea for help to Artair and chewed the inside of his cheek, his mind tripping over itself. "Artair, I've got to take the whole army."

The steward nodded, recognizing the Maitland steward's handwriting, having no illusions about any hope for the Maitlands if Iain didn't go. "You must, lad. Hundreds of Ramsays pounding at the gates of Hawkmore."

"I'll leave a dozen for you," Iain told him, a twinge of sympathy tinting the grimace that helped deliver these words. "If I'm wrong about Sutherland, if you get even one whiff of Sutherland prowling around, headed this way, you get Maggie and my mother to Aviemore."

Artair nodded. "Godspeed, lad."

Iain inclined his head and left the hall. Duncan had already roused so many that the yard bustled with activity. He spotted his captain and Archie and approached.

"Ramsays are at Hawkmore's gate. We move now and fast." Lachlan would never have used the phrase *a wee critical something* if the situation weren't dire, weren't near impossible. "Leave only a dozen." At Duncan's widened eyes, Iain explained, "Artair has instructions if something goes amiss here."

"I'd almost feel better taking her with us," Archie said.

"As would I," Iain readily concurred. With lightning speed, he ran this possibility through his head. If the situation at Hawkmore were as dire as the missive would lead him to believe, she would be in jeopardy even at his side. "She's safer here. I dinna ken what we're riding into."

"Aye," Archie agreed, soon enough that Iain supposed he'd reached the same conclusion, with similar arguments for and against in his head.

"Let's go then," Duncan said, clapping his hands twice as he moved away toward his waiting steed. He called loudly to all the scurrying soldiers in the yard, "Get to it, lads! We're bound for Hawkmore and a little big war."

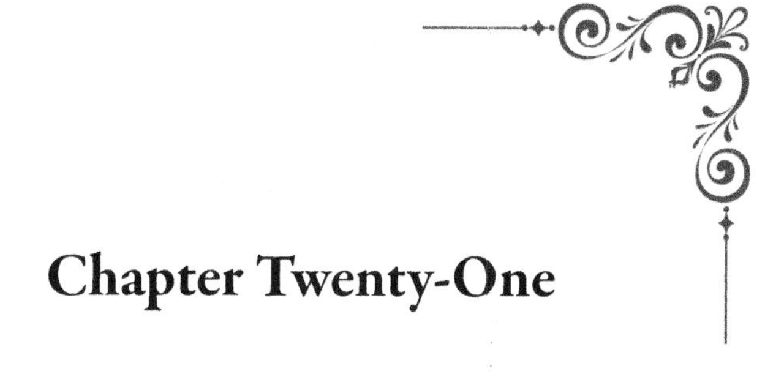

Chapter Twenty-One

MAGGIE WATCHED THE door close and wrestled with a certain sense that something dreadful was happening. She'd recognized Duncan's low voice, had picked out the words, *boat just arrived from Hawkmore.* And Iain had departed fairly quickly. And his regard at his farewell had been bittersweet, intense, and she thought not manifested solely by what they had done only minutes before.

She gave greater thought to his somberness, as if he'd been committing the sight of her to memory. Maggie leapt from the bed, then.

A boat come at night, from his friend Lachlan Maitland, whom he'd only mentioned recently to her. And he'd just looked at her as if he feared he might never see her again.

Good God, Iain was going off to war.

She dressed quickly, thankful that yesterday's kirtle and gown were clean yet. She wasted no time on her hair and dashed out of the chambers and down to the hall. Glenna was crossing from the kitchens to the doorway, with great purpose it seemed, roused early as well, her gait so swift her limp was more pronounced.

"Mistress," Maggie called and met her at the center of the large room.

Glenna was caught off guard and stopped abruptly. She appeared none too pleased to see Maggie about at this ungodly hour. But then she sighed, as if she couldn't avoid the confrontation, and said in her sometimes terse way, "Now, you listen here, Maggie Bryce. They're leaving, the entire army, and you may not raise a fuss."

Her heart dropped. "Was—was he not going to tell me?"

"No, he was not. We agreed you didn't need to know. Of course, you're not daft, and then neither are you still abed—as you should be—so the sight of his entire army gathered quietly in preparation just outside will need the truth now."

She didn't understand. Why would they keep this from her? Why would Iain—

"For this reason," Glenna said sharply, pointing at Maggie's anxious face, "because it would upset you and you in turn will cause unrest in him. And that is not how these things are done."

"But...can I say farewell?"

"Can you do so without causing a scene and in less than a minute? Maggie Bryce, it is a bad omen to send him off poorly. I'll lock you in this keep before I let you curse their mission."

Her eyes widened at Glenna's callousness. But only briefly before she composed herself and nodded. "I will not cause a disturbance."

Glenna nodded and began moving again toward the door. "Do not make me regret this."

The sight that greeted Maggie when Glenna pulled the door open was unlike anything she had ever seen. She'd been in Carlisle for months, where thousands of soldiers daily roamed the streets, visible to one and all. From the Gordon keep, she had witnessed her husband's army gathered *en masse* to move to Carlisle.

But this scene before her now was unnerving for all its quietude, for how the metal and steel of knives and swords and helmets, shone and glinted under the light of a dozen torches inside the bailey. The inky midnight sky, ominous and intent on refusing aid to their departure, only added to the eeriness.

And for the sheer numbers. Maggie had not ever seen all of the McEwen army gathered at once, had seen only smaller units at times. But this, now, there must be hundreds, in the yard, spilling out through the gates. The size of the war horses only added to the magnificence of the scene, shrinking the yard with their size, leaving only small pockets of space where a person might stand or walk.

Maggie found Iain quickly enough, at the side of his own destrier, securing straps and gear about the beast. She did not run to him, determined to cause no commotion, as she'd promised Glenna, who'd marched directly to Duncan, giving him a rolled sheaf of papers and something wrapped in linen. Artair was here as well, Maggie saw, aside the horse of Donal, talking quietly with the handsome twin, as grim as any other man present.

It was Archie, closest to Iain, who alerted the laird of her presence, saying something low over the big black between them. Iain lifted and turned his head toward her, seeming about as pleased as Glenna to see her. His hands continued cinching the straps but blindly, as his gaze was on her. Archie said something more and Iain nodded, releasing the leather bindings and making his way to her.

She stood very still, hiding her clenched hands in her skirts. She didn't bother with any attempt to convey any peacefulness, did not attempt to placate him with any calmness, as she felt this not at all, but she did not become hysterical as her insides screamed that she should.

Maggie descended the steps and Iain met her at the bottom, on the hard ground of the yard. His plaid was now crisscrossed over a shiny steel chest plate, which covered his regular leather breastplate.

Iain tucked his leather gauntlets under his arm and reached between them for her hand.

Only their fingers and eyes touched.

Evenly, she said, "It was wrong of you not to tell me."

"Aye, but you'll forgive me, because you ken I'd no' have ignored it if time were no' already working against us. But you will no' fret, lass."

"I will not...until you are gone." She glanced around at all the faces that watched them.

"We'll be gone but a few days, a week at the most," he promised. "And we'll take care of all that unfinished business between us when I return." His grin then was absolutely devilish and held great promise.

Maggie blushed. "And who do I give all my fretting to, since I will be unable to visit it upon you?"

Iain's lips quirked. "I'm thinking either Artair or my mother would be happy to receive all your concern, lass."

She truly was very angry with him. But then, she wasn't a complete ninny, to send him off badly. His mother's words rang in her head. She shouldn't burden him with too much negative energy. Still, while she tried very hard to be brave and calm for him, tears gathered.

"Do you have anything else to tell me, then?" She asked.

"I'm no' sure, but I'm thinking you will enlighten me. Do I?"

Her shoulders fell. "Well, I've never actually sent anyone off to battle. I thought maybe there was some protocol, of things to be said and promised."

"I promise I'll come back then, lass."

"Very good," she returned primly, "and I promise to love you if you do."

Iain cocked his head, his grin untimely and so very beloved. "You will no' love me if I dinna return?"

Maggie shook her head, her gaze on his plaid, her fingers following, smoothing over the perfect-for-now pleats. "No, that would be impossible. I will be too angry with you."

Iain touched his forefinger to her chin, lifted her gaze to him. In a low voice for her ears alone, he said, "You ken I'm no' a simpleton, aye lass?" When she nodded shakily, he said, "So you ken I'll no' be so ridiculous as to fall while you and everything between us waits here?"

Her nod quickened. "I was hoping you would feel that way," she said, but her words were jumbled with tears and nearly incoherent.

"Good girl," Iain said, his tone patient, "now tell me you love me and let me on my way."

"I love you," she said easily, a reflexive response to his request, no great drama attached to the words she'd spoken for the very first time.

Iain smiled and drew her close, wrapping his free arm around her, his chin at the top of her head, catching sight of their very rapt audience, each and every one of them waiting with great tolerance, his mother teary-eyed herself, Duncan's face screwed up as if to stave off any show of emotion. Iain closed his eyes for just a moment, felt Maggie's arms slide around his waist. Against her hair, he whispered, "I love you, Maggie Bryce."

He pushed her away then, as she did not release him willingly. Clenching her lips to restrain the greater sobs that wanted to come, she nodded quietly at Archie and Duncan and Donal, wishing them Godspeed with a tremulous smile, hoping to convey serenity.

Glenna and Artair gathered near Maggie, away from the huge beasts beginning to move out of the bailey. Glenna threaded her arm through Maggie's.

"You did good, lass."

"I am pudding inside."

"As am I. It never does get easier, seeing them off."

Iain was one of the last to leave the yard. He sent back one last glance to the three near the keep, but Maggie thought his dark and inscrutable gaze was for her alone.

THEY RODE THROUGH THE night. Iain had passed on what little information the missive had detailed, telling Duncan and Archie that they were riding into Lachlan Maitland's war with the Ramsays and their army of possibly six or seven hundred. The news was passed on through the ranks as they traveled, there being no time for a rousing call to arms, no time for an inspiring address from their laird, stirring these men to any battle fever-pitch.

It was unfortunate that the call for help had come so late as the darkness of the moonless night precluded the feverish pace the note suggested was required.

Normally, he was a master at compartmentalizing, was usually able to separate what was left behind from what he moved toward. Tonight was different, of course, the taste of Maggie's lips so fresh on his own. He knew very well that Artair would know that the few soldiers he'd left behind must be on constant guard, that Maggie should not leave the walls of the castle at all, but he still found himself wishing he'd actually said those words to his steward.

They had to stop near dawn, had to rest the horses lest the beasts start dropping beneath them. Iain allowed them only thirty minutes, just enough for the steeds to be watered and rested at the nearby loch. When they moved again, the rising sun allowed them to push harder and faster. And all the while Iain prayed they were not too late.

It was still several hours before Hawkmore came into view. The McEwens erupted from the trees a half mile away from Lachlan's keep. The meadow before them was littered with bodies and tents and strangely, a lone wagon in the middle of the field. Even from this distance, he could see that the gates had been breached, but he hoped and assumed only just, as so many still fought outside to get in.

Iain drew his sword and gave a mighty war cry when all his army was clear of the trees. They raced across the field, the noise of their coming likely subdued by the fighting taking place inside Hawkmore's wall. Some confusion tinted his hard mein as the fighting seemed to stop momentarily, when they were only halfway across the dry, brown grass. It was suspended only briefly though, and only in pockets. Some Maitlands still struggled against the enemy.

Having participated in too many battles to count by now throughout his adult life, he was only mildly stunned by what greeted him as he surveyed the status through the destroyed gate even before he entered. And while it didn't shock him, and he continued to move forward, he knew he was likely to never forget the sight. Directly inside the gate stood a woman, small and frightened, her hair held in the grasp of a ridiculously unsoiled man—the Ramsay, he assumed. Just as his destrier stepped foot inside, just as he understood all within were motionless, waiting it seemed, the woman moved, slicing the neck of the man who held her with a small blade in her hand. Iain's eyes widened but he kept on. Only seconds later, he spotted Lachlan, clawing his way toward the lass.

Whoever she was, she was important to Lachlan.

Iain reached her only seconds after Lach did.

His friend raised his sword and his scarred face to Iain.

"Get her inside," Iain said brusquely to his friend. "We've got this." He did not mistake or underestimate Lachlan's relief at the sight of him.

The yard of Hawkmore erupted again into an all out battle, but Iain thought the numbers were further in Lach's favor now. Iain joined the fray, keeping to his mount, aware of the cowardly Ramsays who turned tail and ran since the McEwens had arrived. Lachlan returned shortly, charging in from the rear yard, his sword raised, his cry vengeful.

The McEwens were the only mounted soldiers inside the yard, giving them great advantage even as it made them larger targets. But it was over quickly, the entire melee inside the Hawkmore yard. The Ramsay leaders were gone, and their army was now only trying to escape. When nary a clang of steel could be heard, when the yard was filled only with the moans and cries of the fallen, Iain spun his mount around, his bloodied sword held aloft. Only Maitlands and McEwens remained standing. He saw Duncan and then Archie, close to him, panting, their weapons likewise still and dripping with enemy blood.

Hearing Lachlan shouting out orders to his men, Iain dismounted finally and made his way to Lach's side, sheathing his sword. "I'll have my men move the Ramsays outside the gate," Iain offered when Lach had just instructed loudly that the first order of business was to get the wounded inside the hall.

Lachlan turned, showing Iain the whole of the right side of his face, the gruesome scar that deformed so much of it. His expression was one of gratefulness and colored with some hint of the near-escape Iain had rushed into not too long ago. Iain struck out his hand to Lachlan, grinning at this belated greeting. Lachlan ignored his proffered hand and wrapped Iain in a tight embrace.

"Little more notice next time would be appreciated," Iain said at his cheek.

"I'll work on that," Lachlan acknowledged with a short and humorless laugh.

Separating, Iain told him, "Go on then, get your lass, wherever you just stashed her. We'll get these bodies out." Already, a wagon had appeared and was being loaded with the Ramsay dead. Likely, Lachlan would give them no proper burial, would possibly ignite one huge pyre far outside the gates to be rid of this rubbish.

"Aye. Iain, I dinna ken how to—"

"Then dinna try," Iain cut him off. "You'd do it for me, I ken."

"Aye." And with a rare humor, almost unheard of from this man, Lachlan said, "Now I have to."

Iain grinned. "We'll catch up when this is cleared."

It was hours later before he met up with Lachlan again, inside the hall, while both the McEwen and Maitland surgeons addressed the needs of the wounded, of which there were plenty. A healer had come as well, an old and bent woman, who was likely to save more lives than the surgeons themselves.

Iain sent his gaze around the hall, but noticed that Lachlan's was stuck on the lass, who'd been returned to safety inside, and tended to Lachlan's captain, Murdoch.

"She have anything to do with this here today, those Ramsays?"

"Aye," Lachlan said, not removing his gaze from her. When he finally did, he showed Iain a grimace. "She was betrothed to the Ramsay son. I may have kidnapped her some time ago, hoping to trade her for peace."

"How'd that work out for you?" Iain asked, lifting his brow.

Lachlan shrugged, but not without some remorse. "It was coming no matter what, the battle with the Ramsays. Been brewing hot for a long time, made worse these last couple years by them taking advantage of my regular absences."

Iain nodded, and sent his gaze to the lass as well.

Honestly, she was almost as bonny as Maggie. Almost.

"C'mon, I'll introduce you," Lachlan offered, and he and Iain walked toward the woman.

Iain supposed he didn't need to ask what might become of her now, or what had transpired since Lachlan had kidnapped her. He thought they should have just worn signs announcing their affection for each other, so blatant was their mutual, heated regard when she turned and found them approaching. It was quite astonishing, to see the oft icy Lach so entranced, hardly able to keep his gaze off the lass, and completely incapable of keeping the emotions from his face.

Jesu, but he had it bad.

"Mari Sinclair, meet Iain McEwen, of the Caithness Mackays."

She dipped a slow and near reverent curtsy, her pretty blue eyes lowered for a moment. When she straightened, she said, "Lachlan Maitland has done a fine job showing what an honorable man looks like, sir, but those Ramsays greatly challenged the concept outside of Hawkmore. I thank you for restoring my faith in humanity."

Iain grinned, appreciative of her comment, but was not of a mind to let Lach off easy. "This your wee critical something?"

Lach answered with an enormous amount of pride, and nary a hint of embarrassment. "The greatest wee critical something."

Iain laughed, happy for his friend. "Good for you, Lach." And he meant it. Lachlan Maitland was an authentic hero, and a genuinely good man, and Iain's best friend.

ALL OF BERRIEDALE WAS agog with curiosity as the alarm horn peeled out across the keep and yard.

As soon as it was heard, Artair had collected Glenna and Maggie and steered them deep within the keep, into tunnels which Maggie hadn't known existed.

"A boat comes to shore," Artair explained, "and we will wait here until the party is identified. If they be hostile, I have instructions to get you both over to Aviemore, if necessary."

Maggie was surprised when Glenna rolled her eyes at this.

"Really, Artair," she said with no small amount of disgruntlement, "I'm expected to abandon my home?"

"Mistress, are you suggesting that if danger comes knocking, we simply greet it with a smile?"

"I'm suggesting no such thing," Glenna answered pertly. "Meet with spears and swords and fire, mayhap, but I'll not waste a smile on evil."

"We—the three of us—will not clash with an enemy, Mistress."

It had already been an impossibly long day, Maggie's nerves on edge with worry for Iain. This then, the half hour they spent hidden in near total darkness underground, did nothing to buoy her spirits. Glenna had not been herself at all today. For all that she'd given Maggie so much grief about not putting her fears onto Iain, the woman had no qualms visiting her own anxieties onto Maggie.

"I will not be made to run, Artair—" Glenna continued, until Maggie cut her off.

"Please stop," Maggie begged, holding her fingers to her temples. They quieted at once, naturally unaccustomed to Maggie lifting her voice above theirs. Staring them down, she wondered, "Shall we not wait and see *who* the boat brings before we engage in this discourse?"

Artair immediately clamped his lips, possibly remorseful for partaking in such a useless argument. Glenna frowned at Maggie and looked for the space of a second as if she would upbraid Maggie for her interference, but Maggie spoke first.

"The alarm has stopped." She could no longer hear the screech of the horn.

"We must wait," Artair insisted yet. "One of the lads will fetch us if the party be friendly."

The party was indeed friendly, having come from Hawkmore where Iain and the army had gone. More anxious people come to Berriedale, the boat carrying Lachlan Maitland's mother, Diana Maitland, and some of her castle staff, including her cook and the castle steward and several kitchen lasses, and two young lads. They stepped into the yard of Berriedale just as Maggie and Glenna and Artair emerged from the keep.

Glenna rushed forward, embracing her old friend, Diana. Artair greeted his counterpart, the steward Oliver, and Maggie smiled encouragingly at the younger folk, inviting them inside the keep while Glenna and Diana had their heads together, exchanging news and worry, it seemed.

Maggie introduced herself by name only, having no actual position or title to add, and learned that the girls were Florie and Edie and the younger lads, possibly not having reached their teen years, were Robert and Rory. The four of them appeared pale and frightened.

"Were you very long in the boat?" Maggie wondered, ushering them inside.

The girl Florie spoke up. "Too long, but it weren't the lads' fault. They rowed as best they could." She ruffled the hair of the boy, Robert.

"Sit here," Maggie said, indicating one of the trestle tables, close to the kitchens. "I'll bring you some vittles, as supper won't be for hours yet."

Not any person from Hawkmore could offer any pertinent information on the battle waging, as they themsevles had been locked away as soon as the enemy came. Only the lad, Rory, who was longest in the yard, shared what he knew.

"There...were so many of them," he said, his eyes staring off into the flames of the nearby hearth.

"And then Mari hopped out of the boat at the last minute," Florie said, looking as if she were about to cry. "And we...we couldn't wait, and she wouldn't listen, and..."

She ducked her head and Edie wrapped her arm around her.

"Who is Mari?" Maggie wondered, assuming she might be another kitchen lass, and questioning why she'd have left the boat.

"She's our friend," Edie said. "She wouldn't leave him."

"Leave who?"

"The chief."

"Oh." Maggie still didn't quite understand who Mari was, but she comprehended this last, that the girl must be in love with Lachlan Maitland, if she refused the chance at escape if he couldn't be with her. "Iain McEwen left here with his entire army, minus those few who remained to guard Berriedale," Maggie told them, "and I promise you, he'll do all that he can to help save Hawkmore."

The remainder of the day was spent in quiet company with those frightened souls from Hawkmore. Indeed, the entire castle was subdued, so many tormented by the agony of not knowing what was happening to their loved ones.

"YOU'LL BE PLEASED TO ken," Iain said to Lachlan early in the evening, "that your missive alone, wax seal unbroken and carried by the sea, would have had me moving right quick from

Berriedale. But Lach, you start tossing around *a wee critical something*, and God's truth, we tore out of there as if the fires of hell were nipping at our backsides."

"Aye, but they were already here," Lachlan said.

They sat atop their mounts, in the middle of the wide field before Hawkmore. Men moved all around them, clearing the meadow of bodies and all the implements and gear abandoned by the dead and fleeing Ramsays.

He'd known Lachlan since they were lads under the tutelage of the fierce Alexander MacBriar. They'd bonded instantly at their first meeting as scrawny twelve-year-olds over an impressive awe and a simultaneous fear of the giant earl, MacBriar. The earl had been fair but exacting, pious and then not adverse to taking a man's life; he'd been sometimes bombastic with a voice that boomed across a room with ease, across a loch without great effort, and over a battlefield with such power a man could certainly mistake it for the voice of God, so resounding and cavernous. Lachlan and Iain had spent two years with the earl at Swordmair, longer than most because of the kinship they'd shared with the earl's son, Alec.

"How'd we first use that?" Lachlan asked.

Iain grinned, though it held no humor. None of his memories of their time in captivity all those years ago did. "Alec started it," he replied, "when he was trying to trap those mice. Thought they'd make for good eating. Remember? Him crouched in that dark corner, hours on end. I kept asking him what he was about. Finally, he turns—he was right pissed for my nagging, but Christ, what else had I to do?—and says, real surly, *I'm working on a wee critical something*."

Lachlan nodded, possibly recalling it as well now. "They were not good eating," he said.

"But they were food."

"Aye."

After, they'd taunted Alec mercilessly, attributing *a wee critical something* to so many things. It was the answer to every question for days, served as the only amusement, such as it was, that helped them stay sane, not give in, or give up. And when the old MacBriar had come to save them, his son Alec had supposed to Iain and Lachlan, *Aye now, we've just survived our own wee critical something.*

"You see him lately? Alec?" Lachlan asked.

"Not since that mess at Methven." Iain let out a large sigh. "He'd gone down to MacGregor at Inesfree then, kept company with them over the winter. I only ken this because Tess wrote my mother. There was some intelligence days ago that the English had moved from Carlisle to Doune Castle, intent on taking it. I sent word down to Swordmair, suppose he went that way. You ken how he loves the battle."

With some conjecture, Lachlan guessed, "He's got more anger yet than I."

"Aye."

"You do well with it," Lachlan said. "Or at least give the appearance that you do."

Iain shrugged, his most recent nightmare brought to mind. "The latter," he acknowledged. Maggie had asked him which might be better, being harangued by physical scars as Lachlan was, or tortured by terror so often in the night. He still didn't know. "It's in the past, Lach. I try to leave it there." He grinned and revealed, "You ken these *wee critical somethings* are powerful tools for pushing all that even further away."

Lachlan sent a thoughtful gaze to Iain, a grin almost forming. "Aye, they are at that."

Passing his gaze once more over the carnage all around, Iain said absently, "Give me the English any day over a traitorous Scot."

Lachlan Maitland turned and gave Iain a wry look, exposing the scarred side of his face to his friend, not that Iain needed the reminder. "You sure about that? The English?"

Iain made a face, half-grimace, half-apology for his thoughts and his poor choice of words. But he teased, as he knew Lachlan would suffer no sympathy. "Not those English, who made you prettier like that, but the other ones—real fighting men, if England ken any such thing."

"Aye," was given with a half grin for Iain's quip. Reflectively, Lachlan said, "We've suffered some attacks in and around Hawkmore last year or so. I thought I'd figured out who might be responsible—but your missive last month had me wondering if I should no' attribute some of those crimes to that Alpin you've named."

"Lach, he's a mean son of a bitch. Violence, mayhem—death for no reason but his own warped pleasure. If you've got something fits that mold, he's the culprit. He dinna leave too many alive. But then, he's also a Sutherland, and bound to the English now. He's the one making war as we speak on Doune castle, by my understanding. He's next on my list, though, soon as he starts heading north."

Nodding in receipt of this news, Lachlan said, "Young Edward is moving now, heading from London to Carlisle."

Iain nodded. "Bruce says let him come. He's no' sure the lad's got the bollocks to keep up his father's fight."

"So, what now?"

"We'll stay a few days, help you get all this settled," Iain said and let a smile come. "But then, I've got to get home to something a wee more critical."

His friend narrowed his eyes upon Iain for a moment. "She have a name?"

Before Falkirk, where they'd been captured by the English, Iain and Lachlan and young Alec MacBriar had spent much time carousing and gaming and sampling the wares of many a bonny lass. But that was then. *Jesu,* to be that young and ignorant again. That was before Falkirk, where their lives had only been spared upon the field of battle by the Maitland signet ring, which had identified Lachlan as higher born than the rank and file soldiers fighting alongside William Wallace and the redoubtable Andrew Murray. Iain and Alec's proximity to Lach at that moment—indeed, Lachlan shouting out that his friends were worth more dead than alive as well—was what allowed Iain to stand here now, alive.

"Aye, Maggie Bryce, she is," Iain answered. "You're welcome to Berriedale, come and meet her."

"We'll come down yet this year, aye?" Turning his horse around, Lachlan called over his shoulder, "Dinna forget to send my mother back to Hawkmore."

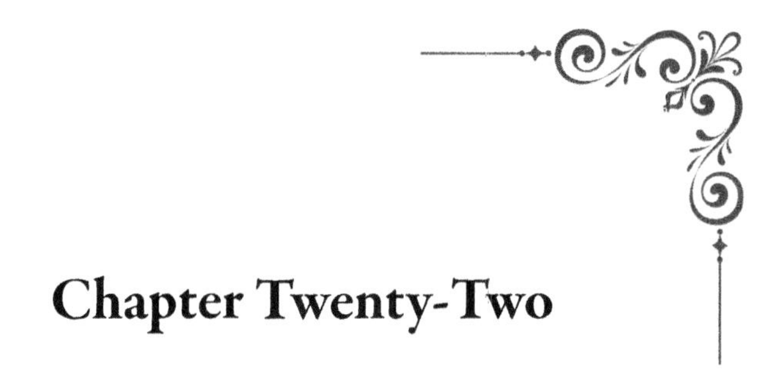

Chapter Twenty-Two

KENNETH SUTHERLAND rode somewhere in the middle of the huge horde of soldiers moving north. His head pounded, the initial ache created by the rage that had come with the news from Blackhouse, and intensified day by day, the longer he thought upon it.

He would string up that bloody steward when he returned to Blackhouse, for allowing his wife to be taken—bloody well snatched from her very own bed!—while in his direct care. Ailith, curse her, might only wish for such benevolence by the time he was done with her.

The missive had come by way of one of the few soldiers he'd left at Blackhouse, which had then allowed him to interrogate the lad, revealing more of the truth behind the sparse and cryptic note from that worthless Oswald. Snatched from the cells below ground, he'd been informed, and not her bed. Because she'd begged Ailith to help her escape, he'd been told. He'd yet to figure out who would receive the greater part of retribution for this—his wayward bride for even daring to think she might ever flee, or that damnable Ailith, who too often overstepped boundaries, thought herself above any penalty.

He recognized that to some degree, his absence, keeping at the court in Carlisle, had allowed these things to happen. Left ungoverned and unmanaged, they thought to take advantage of him. When he did recover his bride and they returned to Blackhouse, he would put everything back to rights, would make sure all persons were reminded of their positions and reminded as well of the consequences when he was made to look a fool.

But the missive was weeks old now, the messenger having first gone to Carlisle, and then marching on to Doune. Of course, Kenneth and the Sutherlands—indeed all the armies that had gone to Doune—had been called away by that simpering fool, the new king. Edward II had essentially abandoned all campaigns save those at the border, *to focus on domestic matters*, was given as the implausible and deplorable excuse. Kenneth seethed over this as well. All that time pandering and groveling before the English and for what? The old man was dead, taking with him all promises of Sutherland glory. And the new king, curse him, seemed already to give no thought or care to Scotland and its noble families.

Upon reflection, recalling the fury he'd known the minute the soldier messenger had finally caught up with him and had revealed what fate Oswald and Ailith had bestowed upon his bride when she'd arrived at Blackhouse, Kenneth could hardly believe the boy lived yet. Perhaps the shock of it, the shock of all of it, had saved the soldier's life. Kenneth had sat, rather slumped into the chair conveniently near, so flabbergasted by the news.

Iain McEwen? Iain McEwen had come for her? The same McEwen who'd allegedly only stumbled upon her in that fierce winter storm months ago?

He could not escape the possibility that he'd been played a fool this past winter. Yet, he'd believed her tale at the time, imagining her too frightened to have lied to him, thinking also that no Mackay would dare to even think of taking what belonged to a Sutherland. This, then, only added to the rage, that he'd been deceived, and so effortlessly.

But what did it mean? Why had McEwen come for her? And, *Jesu,* was this what McEwen had come for months ago when he'd stormed Blackhouse, only days after they'd met on that snowy field in Caithness? When Kenneth had been alerted of this minor siege upon Blackhouse, he'd supposed the identity of Alpin might have been learned, but lost little sleep over this, as he'd been safely ensconced at Carlisle, surrounded by England and English. He feared no one.

But now, he had to consider that McEwen was not after all aware of Alpin's true identity, that he was only sniffing after his wife.

Kenneth frowned, wondering if this were possible.

His wife was bonny, for certain; her breasts alone were magnificent, though she hadn't a clue how to use them, or any parts of herself. However, she had little else to recommend her, was meek and could barely form sentences, seemed ever to be pinch-faced, and Kenneth would never be convinced she hadn't some stick shoved up her backside for how frigid she always was. He considered it abnormal, that she looked as seductive as she did but had no liking and found no joy in coupling. He thought she must be touched in the head, for he knew well that he was pleasing to look upon and that pain and fear only heightened the release.

He spat forth an oath. Of course, he would mourn her not at all if she were truly lost for good, having no relationship with her but for that inside the marital bed, but damn, if a McEwen—a

Mackay!—should be allowed to live, having trespassed so grievously.

Last winter, he'd allowed those few McEwens to live, a choice he now regretted. Of course, it would not have been his preference. But his uncle, William de Moravia, had only days before unleashed a rage on him, having himself just discovered that Kenneth was Alpin. Uncle William had vowed his own retribution if Kenneth did not abandon that other identity, had told him at the time that there was greater glory to be found at the side of the English king, that once they'd proven themselves to Edward I, they would be rewarded with land and titles and coin.

"And you can seek your own depraved pleasures at *that* time," his uncle had raged, "but not before!"

But now, well now everything was changed. Even his uncle could find no fault with this justification for the annihilation of those damn McEwens.

Iain McEwen would pay dearly for this crime.

The softly falling rain did nothing to diminish his musings then or his plans for what abuses he might visit upon the McEwen for his extraordinary encroachment.

Soon, Kenneth felt his headache receding, for the satisfaction his own designs brought to him. He straightened in the saddle, surveying the seemingly endless horizon of green and brown mountains and foothills, thinking they might reach the McEwen's Berriedale by tomorrow morning at the latest.

That pitiful Berriedale would have no warning, Kenneth knew. His army and the Welsh mercenaries cost him plenty of coin each quarter, but damn, if sometimes they weren't worth every penny. Only yesterday his own scouts had run into the McEwen scouts, rather caught them off guard, by his understanding. He smirked, thinking of those bodies left behind and of the others that would fall at his feet come the morrow.

ARTAIR HAD SAID TO Maggie, "We will keep to the schedule. The people have needs that would surely never be met if they were only to be heard around the timetable of war, or any time the laird is called away on other pressing matters."

Maggie agreed, and was happy for the diversion of what Artair referred to informally as the Needs Must Council, where the kinfolk of Berriedale could apply to the laird for wares or items of necessity, or even forbearance in regard to rents or tithes. Artair would sit, as he sometimes did, in the stead of the chief of the McEwens, and Maggie would record the proceedings.

The hall was crowded, perhaps even more so than it had been for any dinner or even the court hearings of weeks ago. The crowd was not so very loud but the torrential rains outside were deafening until the doors had been pulled closed. Even then, the wind and thunder howled through the uncovered windows and stirred the flames of the candles to dance vigorously upon the chandeliers high above.

Glenna sat at the head table with Maggie and the steward, as so often a request would come in for household items that the mistress could quickly say yay or nae, if a spare were available or not. Their guests from Hawkmore, the women and the steward at least, were tucked up in Glenna's solar today, happy to remain close together. Glenna had said they'd spent the morning in the chapel with their prayers, as they had all three days since coming to Berriedale.

This occasion was not so formal as the court hearings, where charges had been filed with Artair and each accused was called forth to answer. Today, Artair only said, "Let us begin," when he'd taken his seat next to Maggie and Glenna.

The crowd shuffled, several people looking at each other, until a woman stepped forward to reveal her need.

Artair prefaced her request with a general announcement. "Please state your name, folks, and an occupation, if warranted, that Maggie Bryce might record the essentials correctly." And to the woman waiting, he instructed, "Proceed."

"Janet Howlk, lass," said the red hair and ruddy cheeked woman. She dipped a quick and sloppy curtsy to the mistress and wrung her hands together while she explained her circumstance. "I'm one of several brewers in the area and it was my cart that the sot, Gavin Ogg, did confiscate some time back." She addressed Maggie specifically, as if it were she who would make any determination. "Aye, he did, and the cart, ye ken, is fine, but his good-time-had did destroy more than half of my jugs. Now, I'm no potter, lass, that I can be replacing these things so easily, and Clara Fraser wants to charge me a farthing for naught but two crocks and I'll tell ye same as I told her—"

A loud crash interrupted the brewer and the proceedings. Another woman screeched for the noise. The doors to the hall had crashed open.

The half dozen soldiers present drew their swords and pressed through the crowd, which moved quickly, away from the ruckus and whoever had come. The throng of people shifted backward, toward the head table even as they faced the opposite end of the hall and the doors.

Maggie jumped to her feet and craned her neck but could not see beyond all the bodies now so close to the table.

Glenna stood as well, grabbing anxiously at Maggie's hand.

"I cannot see," Maggie bemoaned.

In the next second a cheer was raised, and Maggie felt herself breathe again, knew that Glenna expelled a cry of relief as well.

He was home.

Maggie left the table just as the crowd moved and parted, opening a path which showed Iain standing just inside the door.

He was road-weary and dirtied, drenched by the rain even, but generally unharmed that a cry of thankfulness escaped her. For the space of a moment they only stared at each other, across the length of the hall. Though she was peripherally aware that he was followed by others, Duncan and Donal at least, her gaze was for him alone.

His eyes were bright, with the bloodlust that had kept him alive and safely returned or at the sight of her, she couldn't say. She stepped forward, haltingly at first, but then ran to him. She crashed into him and was lifted off the ground by his strong arm surrounding her. She squeezed him and breathed him in and held him close, pinching her eyes tightly closed.

Another loud cheer came, but Maggie heard only him, his heartbeat and his breath against her.

"Oh, thank God," she said, crying into his neck and raining kisses along his cheek.

"Aye, lass." His arm tightened around her waist. "All is well, Maggie Bryce."

People began to move around them that Maggie finally opened her eyes. Iain loosened his hold that she was set back on her feet. She put her palms to each of his cheeks and only wanted to stare at him, be assured he was truly unharmed.

He was home. His eyes were bright and untroubled. All was well, indeed.

Iain kissed her forehead and addressed Glenna, who stood near, was already reaching out to touch her son.

While Iain greeted his jubilant mother, Maggie turned to Duncan and Donal, embracing each of them. Eideard was close and she touched her hand to his forearm. Archie came strolling into the keep and Maggie rushed him, caught only a hint of a grin before she threw herself at him.

"I'm so glad you're safe," she said to him. "I was never going to speak to you again if you were not."

She felt his chuckle rumble against her, felt his hand pat her back. "I figured as much, lass. Thought I'd better get on back."

MANY HOURS LATER, WHEN all the keep was settled for the night, Maggie finally went in search of her own bed. She'd spent the last hour with the party from Hawkmore, who were naturally overjoyed with the glad news of Hawkmore's survival and were eager then to hop into their boat and be gone and be home. It had taken some doing, but Diana Maitland had finally been convinced that leaving first thing in the morning, and with an escort of soldiers, was the better plan. Thus, tonight all of Berriedale and their guests had enjoyed a lively meal, which lasted well into the evening before Glenna and Maggie and the Hawkmore women had left the hall, taking some time to prepare for yet another trip about the sea in the morning.

Pushing open the door to her chambers, Maggie was not entirely surprised to find Iain in her bed. She closed the door quietly and leaned against it, let her gaze fall softly upon him. He slept now, but at some time this evening had given himself up to a bath, his hair damp yet against the downy pillows. He was on his back, one foot on the floor, his hand on his midsection, giving the impression that he'd sat initially, might have waited for her to come, but then had simply collapsed with his surely great exhaustion.

Maggie stepped away from the door and spent a bit of time adjusting the fire, urging the larger log to the rear of the hearth, intending a softer light. Brushing off her hands, she turned and stood near the bed, pulling her hair loose from its ribbon. She'd known for days what she wanted when he returned, but now allowed a wry grin for his sleepiness, which might yet thwart her plans.

Still, she removed the apron she'd worn for more than half the day, and then sat to rid herself of her shoes and hose, dropping all this in the chair near the hearth. Her gown followed, Maggie acknowledging to herself that this was done with much less reticence because he slept yet. Nonetheless, she wasn't brave enough to strip completely and so knelt at the side of the bed in her chemise and moved the hair off his forehead. He stirred not at all.

Folding her arms on the mattress between him and her, she leaned forward and touched her lips to his, feathering a kiss over him, so easy to do as his face was turned toward her. His breathing did not change, as he slept on. Bolder now, she kissed him again, moving one hand up onto his chest, only the linen of his tunic separating her fingers from his warm skin. Closing her eyes, she traced her tongue along his lips, and finally felt him waken.

"Thank you for coming home to me," she whispered. It wasn't her home of course, but she felt as if it were. Certainly when he was here with her.

Drowsily, he said, "I promised I'd come back to you."

"Make sure you always do, please," she instructed and kissed him again.

"I dinna want to scare you, lass, but you keep that up and you're going to find yourself right quick hauled up onto this bed with me."

The boldness did not forsake her. "I was hoping to find myself in such a circumstance."

"Kiss me again," he said, the hint of a smile teasing his beautiful mouth.

Happy to oblige, Maggie leaned forward again, her fingers still on his chest while she applied herself to the kiss. She let it be just a caress at first, moving her mouth back and forth across his. He held himself very still, purposefully so, Maggie thought. Wanting so much more from him, she raised herself a bit on her knees and covered his mouth fully, sliding her tongue between his lips. In no time at all, he growled against her and returned the kiss, his hands lifting to cup her cheeks.

Against her lips, he murmured, "I'll be telling you I love you now, but only because I might be too caught up in you verra soon to be able to utter any words at all."

She felt her insides tickle for the delight these words brought her. "Mayhap I should say as much to you, hoping that likewise, I'll be too dimwitted very shortly to have command of thoughts or speech."

"Aye, you should."

"I do love you, Iain," she said. "So very much."

"Come up here then," he urged, "that I might no' only tell you, but show you as well."

Maggie needed no other prodding and climbed into the bed with him. He moved further across the mattress, which allowed plenty of space next to him that she stretched out along the length of him.

Before she might have kissed him again, he said to her, "You tell me what to do, Maggie Bryce. When to start or stop or—"

Maggie put her finger to his lips to quiet him. She shook her head.

"This is between you and me," she said. "There is no ghost between us. There never was, was only in my mind." She moved her finger.

"I ken you'd figure it out sooner or later," he said, his tone oozing with compassion.

Nodding, she returned, "You were very patient."

He grinned, which raised Maggie's brow.

Gently, he cupped her face. "Sorry, lass. I've waited so long, it seems, for just this—and you say those words, and all I heard was, *have at it*."

Maggie laughed outright, having not expected such absurdity between them at this significant moment. "That is the most unromantic thing I have ever heard."

He smiled that beautiful smile of his, the one that first stole her heart. "But you ken what I meant?"

She was still grinning when she told him, "Actually—sadly—I did."

"Should I?"

"Have at it?"

He nodded, his smile intact as he rose up over her.

"Please do," she begged when she was pivoted onto her back, just before his lips met hers.

This kiss was new, different to them now, its express intent not to taste or know but to please and seduce. When he touched her breast, she reveled in the possessive and confident way he teased her and tempted her, lacking any hesitation as if only waiting for her to recoil. When he doffed his tunic, she eagerly let her hands wander, over the firm muscles and raised scars. And when he lifted her long kirtle, she helped, lifting her hips that it might be gotten out of the way.

His breeches and all other clothing followed the same path, tossed over the side of the bed until they were both naked and entranced. His gaze was reverent upon her breasts, his lips worshipful. She looked her fill as well, the truth before her eyes of his beauty in no way able to compare to what previously she had only imagined.

"It's going to take a long time for me to get used to this, Maggie Bryce," he whispered, his voice low. "You might want to get used to me staring."

She smiled and drew him back to her for another kiss. Never had she ached for a man's caress, until this moment. Never had she wanted to please, to bring pleasure with her touch until now. And he let her, let her slowly and lovingly explore all parts of him, with her hands and her mouth and her tongue—but only for so long.

He reached for her and dragged her up onto him, holding her by the arms very near to his face and kissed her senseless while Maggie instinctively straddled him, needing him with an urgency that was heretofore unknown. Iain assisted, pausing his kiss, meeting her shiny gaze while he slid inside her.

She had no words for the beauty of that motion, for how...perfect it felt. She whimpered, speech beyond her anyway. He lifted his lips and set a tantalizing tempo between them, which Maggie joyfully pursued.

"You're torturing me, lass," he said. "I want to throw you down and bury myself deep inside you."

"Do with me what you might," she said, her tone as languid as all her limbs.

This was Iain; she had no fear.

"The correct response, Maggie Bryce, is what you want, what you desire. Show me."

Never had she so boldly done as she pleased, until now.

She lifted his hands and placed them over her breasts, tilting her head back, reveling in his touch. She kept her hands over his, even as he moved his fingers, pinching her nipples to hardness again. She lifted and lowered herself on him slowly, over and over, until the need increased in her that she craved more and more of him. Reaching back, she set her hands onto his powerful thighs and rode him faster and faster.

Iain sat up and grabbed at her hips, moving her up and down with greater urgency now, his need equaling her own. He laved his tongue against her exposed neck and then abandoned everything but assisting her movements, lifting her higher before bringing her back down on his rigid erection, filling her so marvelously. Maggie moaned as delight crept closer and closer and transferred her hands to his shoulders, attacking him with a fresh kiss, hungry and demanding. And then she gasped, couldn't move, her mouth motionless against his while release crested, showering her with fire, engulfing her in impossible rapture.

He allowed her to feel it, did not push her now that he might finish. He suckled at her nipple, startling a cry from Maggie, for the sensations known just then. He pumped inside her still, slowly, drawing out her release. She thought tears might have fallen, for the sheer splendor of this moment. When she could move again, she kissed him, reminding herself of the joy that all her life, she would kiss only him now.

She began to move on him again, wanting him to know that same ecstasy, but Iain shifted and rolled her onto her back. Every movement was fluid and seamless, was done with every attempt for her comfort, her pleasure.

Maggie widened her legs, and Iain embedded himself deeply within her. She shuddered when he withdrew, nearly all the way again, and then entered her with excruciating slowness. He did this over and over, kissing her further into senselessness, until the heat began to build once again inside her. Astonished, she pushed at his shoulders, meeting his gaze when he pulled back a bit. Without words, but with the movement of her hips and the wonder of her gaze, she let him know she was about to come again.

Iain smiled down at her and began to move smoothly and quickly in and out of her. This time, they found their release together, his fingers sinking into the flesh of her waist to hold her to him when he came.

"*Jesu*, Maggie Bryce," he groaned, his voice nearly unrecognizable. He closed his eyes and dropped his head. "My God, I love you."

She definitely could not move now, but her heart knew joy such as it never had that more tears came with her feverish release.

Many minutes passed before she could breathe normally again. He collapsed against her as she let her head roll listlessly on the pillow. After a while, he moved off to her side. Maggie never wanted to be further than this, not ever be away from him.

She thought she might have dozed for a few minutes but could not be sure. When next she opened her eyes, she saw Iain in profile, so close to her. His eyes were closed. She was immediately put in mind of watching him sleep sometimes when they were stuck in that cave last winter.

Where it all began.

Every day, all my life, I will be with you.

"This is joy, then," she murmured, wondering if she ought to pinch herself, be sure the good fortune was real.

Iain opened his eyes though he did not move, but to say, "When we were held by the English all those years ago, I was verra sure I was bound to die, watched as so many others did over the weeks and months. I kept thinking my mother would be heartbroken, but then I would console myself that I would see my da' again. She would ken it, too, would ken I was with him, mayhap would find some comfort in that. Honestly, it served a purpose, those thoughts." He paused a moment, mayhap taken up by those memories. "I dinna ken if that were giving in, but I accepted that death would come. I had no fear, no regret...no worry." He blew out a slow breath. "But riding into Hawkmore, I was no' ready to die. Those same thoughts did not serve me well this time. I was thinking there was so much more I wanted to show you—not just this, what we've just done," he was quick to assure her. "Just everything." He turned on his side and moved the hair off her shoulder. "I wanted to be around as that girl from the caves returned. I wanted to see her smile at me, for me. I dinna deserve you, I ken, but damn Maggie Bryce, I'm willing to try."

Maggie ran her hand over his cheek and gave him the smile he craved. "You speak so eloquently...truly, it shames me that I can just now only think to say I love you."

He showed her that much-adored grin and asked, "Your brain still squirrelly from the lovemaking, Maggie Bryce?"

Her smile reappeared, larger now. "It might be." But she did think to share with him, "I know that recovering my true self has to come from within me, leastwise that's what Artair had said. And while he's likely correct, I also know that I couldn't have—cannot yet, as I have a way to go, I imagine—done it anywhere but with you. I believe that to be true."

"I dinna want you anywhere but with me."

Maggie sighed and kissed him.

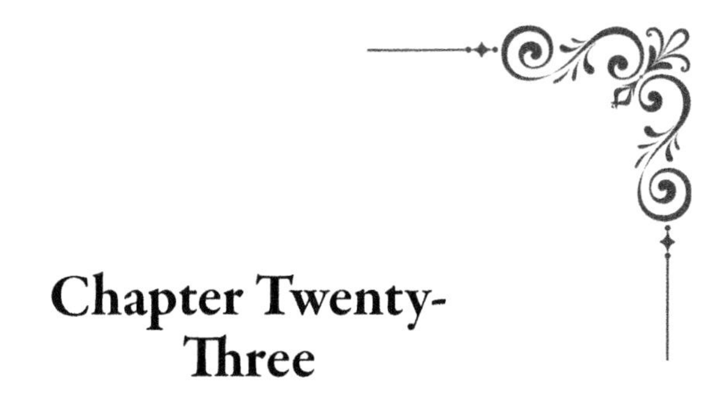

Chapter Twenty-Three

MAGGIE WAS WAKENED the next morning by Iain's hand skimming along her naked hip. She smiled dreamily and opened her eyes to find him up on his elbow, watching her, so much love shining in his gaze. He kissed her fully awake with great tenderness and Maggie wondered how they might possibly stay inside this bed and this room all day.

They managed to eke out almost an hour before the business of the day called them from her chambers and even then, the sun had not been lifted off the east horizon very long. They dressed together, a first for Maggie, and Iain began to teach her how to fold his plaid, how to arrange the pleats and how it was laid over his shoulder and around his waist.

"Takes plenty of practice," he allowed as they worked together with the finishing touches. He kissed her forehead.

"Possibly, I will be more curious to learn how to remove it," Maggie returned with her face tipped up to him.

She was rewarded with a seductive grin and a full kiss before they left the room.

An hour later, they stood side by side on the beach, with Glenna and Duncan and several others, waving farewell to the Hawkmore party as they happily took their leave. The dory had been pushed out to sea only minutes ago, but the soldiers manning the oars had already moved them well away from Berriedale's shores.

"Would it not have been safer for them to go by land?" Maggie wondered, albeit belatedly.

"Seas are calm," Iain replied. "Rhys and William will get them home in time for the midday meal."

"I would think—" Glenna began but was interrupted by the sounds of shouts from the castle wall.

No sooner had they turned to glance up the hill than the alarm sounded, a long wail of a horn. And while Maggie and Glenna were frozen, Iain and Duncan and the other soldiers moved instantly.

Iain addressed his mother and Maggie sharply. "Right up to the keep, inside the hall and you stay there until I say otherwise."

They nodded in unison, and Iain turned and sprinted up the hill, following the others.

Exchanging yet another anxious gleam, Glenna and Maggie followed as well, though not as quickly as the men had.

"That horn is beginning to get on my nerves," Glenna said as they strode arm-in-arm away from the beach.

Maggie completely agreed, letting a wee wobbly grin come for Glenna's grousing. But her mind flew to all the possible reasons the alarm might sound on this glorious day and settled immediately and with a fantastic and horrific surety that Kenneth Sutherland had finally come.

"God help us," she whispered.

IAIN, DUNCAN, ARCHIE, and others gathered at the forefront, high atop the battlements, surveying the scene before them. They were in no immediate danger, but no man staring out at the hundreds of combat-ready Sutherlands lined up well beyond the old chapel thought for one second that they would escape the coming battle wholly unscathed.

"Praise be, ye kept the army near," Duncan remarked, knowing some relief as he watched several units of the McEwen forces, directly below them and on the castle side of the narrow bridge, complete their move inside the gates. Their tents were abandoned, but all weapons, horses, and other gear was brought inside before the drawbridge was raised and secured.

"How's he think he's gonna get four hundred men across a span of a hundred feet, over a bridge wide enough for but two at a time, to mount any kind of offensive?" Archie wanted to know.

"He's coming at us all pissed up," Duncan supposed. "Obviously, dinna do any planning aforehand."

"If he did," Iain said thoughtfully, "they'd be coming from the beach as well."

"They'll be coming from the beach anyway, eventually," Archie said, pointing across to where the Sutherlands gathered, "once he realizes he canna get here from there."

Iain nodded. "Right. Put the focus there, then. They might come, but they'll have a hell of a time charging up that hill and the sand from the beach. There's no reason we canna take out any and every man coming that route. They can try from the river side, but they'll never be able to scale those cliffs."

Duncan agreed and left to address this, intent on setting up the bulk of the archers on the seaside wall for now.

Iain chewed the inside of his cheek and decided, "Arch, send Eideard and Boyd, whoever else you see fit. Tell 'em to come up from underneath, get under that first bridge and take it out."

Archie grinned at this. "I like the way you think, lad." And he spun to leave as well.

"Arch," Iain called. When his lieutenant turned back to him, he reminded him, "Dinna get dead."

Archie harrumphed. Walking backwards, he replied cheerily, "I canna. I saw Rabbie starting on that apple and raisin pudding earlier. You ken that's my favorite."

Iain rounded the entire wall then, checking preparations and provisions, calling out orders as he circled the battlements. The wall was crowded as Iain himself had never seen it, hundreds of McEwen men readying and waiting and praying. He was two thirds the way around when he heard loud shouts at the southwest side again and hurried in that direction. Men were pointing out to where the Sutherlands had gathered that he assumed they'd begun their charge.

He and Duncan, likewise beckoned by the shouting, met at the spot they'd stood at only moments ago. Iain latched on to the stone merlon and leaned out through the embrasure.

"Leaving so soon?"

That was Arch, returned as well, seeing what Iain and Duncan did, the entire Sutherland army turned about face, facing the ridge they'd climbed. They weren't still, but restless, the unit moving with some anxiety but going neither forward nor backward. From the distance, it seemed the Sutherland army shifted in the same manner as the starlings did, gyrating and shifting in changing patterns.

"What the bluidy hell?" Iain wondered.

And then as one, the Sutherland army pivoted again, charging toward Berriedale now. Iain was perplexed by this strange onslaught, and then wholly flummoxed when he spied something rising over the hill beyond the Sutherlands.

"It canna be," Duncan breathed, just as Iain saw it too.

Lifted high into the air upon a long wooden spear and snapping smartly against the wind, a lone banner crested the ridge first. The banner displayed was an unmistakable bright yellow, the center depicting a roaring and fighting red lion.

Archie spat out a laugh and it grew and grew at the sight before him. The Sutherlands still came at them so that Archie drew his sword, but he kept right on laughing as an entire army followed that incomparable banner and chased the Sutherlands toward Berriedale.

Duncan called out to those soldiers who might hear him, "Look lively, lads! Our beloved king is bringing the stampede himself!" And he laughed as well, the very idea so fantastic, that their deliverance should come from so high, from Robert Bruce himself.

"Beyond the gate!" Iain commanded, not about to let his liege lord find any trouble from the Sutherlands on his behalf, even as he supposed that the combined armies of the Bruce and the McEwens probably outnumbered the Sutherlands.

Donning his helm, Iain left the wall as the gate was opened and the drawbridge lowered. In the midst of all the charging McEwens he lifted his sword and bellowed, "To your king! To your king!"

Thankfully, the lads had yet to destroy the small bridge that the planks held as hundreds dashed across it, their war cries constant and deafening. Fortunately as well, the Sutherlands were at a distance yet that the McEwens managed to get across that narrow strip and into the open field beyond, where the first clang of swords sounded out larger and louder than any other noise.

Kenneth Sutherland was distinctive in his bright tartan and ridiculously ornamental helm, judiciously located in the center of his army, yet astride his destrier, neither forward near the McEwens nor at the rear where came Bruce's ragtag band. Iain took on one man and then the next, keeping one eye constantly on Alpin, and working his way toward him.

One known truth about paid mercenaries—such as Kenneth Sutherland had employed—was that when the battle seemed not to be in their favor, they were quick to seek escape rather than fight unto death. The Sutherland numbers thinned quickly then, attacked on two sides, and so many of its hirelings scuttling away from the melee, that Iain reached Kenneth Sutherland fairly quickly. He took note of Kenneth's clean blade and the man's frantic dancing around, all but circling his horse in place while the fighting closed in on him.

Iain was not surprised, had judged him a coward a long time ago. He took advantage of Alpin's prancing and thwacked his sword across him when his back was turned. It was not a death blow—Iain had no intention of granting him a simple demise—but was enough to unseat him.

Kenneth scrambled on the ground, collecting the sword that had been dropped from his hand in the fall and turned anxiously to gauge his situation.

Iain stood calmly, waiting, a dozen feet away. When Kenneth noticed his watching, Iain doffed his helm, tossing it aside, let there be no question who was about to kill him.

Eideard was running at Kenneth from his backside.

"He's mine!" Iain bellowed and Eideard left off, bringing his attack to the nearest Sutherland instead.

In the midst of all the fighting, swords thrusting and bodies falling, limbs detached and blood oozing, Iain and Kenneth faced each other.

With more bravado than conviction, Kenneth seethed, "I'll carry your head on my sword when I collect my wife."

Iain smirked and used his own bloodied sword to point to Kenneth's clean blade. "That sword?"

Kenneth lifted it and set up a pose that Iain supposed was meant to intimidate him. Two hands held the sword aloft to his right side, his fingers flexing repeatedly.

Iain allowed the smirk to remain. "She is no more your wife, will cry with joy when she kens you are dead." He stepped closer, leaving his blade low, his grip upon the hilt firm and sure. "All of Caithness will rejoice, in fact, with the death of Alpin."

He had to know that he was about to die, but Kenneth Sutherland grinned now. "I canna decide which was more entertaining, the abuses heaped upon your precious Caithness or the fun I had with her."

Having been a prisoner of the English, having known pain and torture and unending taunting, Iain was not agitated at all. "She's over it. And your seed dies with you, today, since your son died as well."

This widened Kenneth's eyes, and then curled his lip. He charged, swinging wildly, that Iain easily dodged the wayward blow, listing left but reaching his arm out, slicing his blade across Alpin's thigh as he passed. Facing off again, while blood dripped from Sutherland's leg, Iain let everything clear his mind. He could not let emotion rule this fight, could not afford even one mistake, wrought by cockiness or any superiority.

They parried and danced, moving in time to one another, always the same distance apart until their swords clashed above their heads, Iain deflecting Kenneth's blow. Both their free hands gripped the raised forearm of the other. Iain surged forward, pushing Kenneth back as their sword arms swung 'round, toward the ground with Iain's blade on top. He lifted his hand, drew back his sword and pounded the hilt into Kenneth's cheek. Bone crushed with a sickening cracking noise and Kenneth dropped to one knee. He surprised Iain though by letting no time pass before he swung his blade from right to left. Iain arched his midsection backward to avoid the blade and Kenneth rose and followed, their blades clanging once more. Iain swung at Kenneth's right shoulder, which was easily deflected, but Kenneth did not recover quickly enough as Iain arced his sword in a smooth moulinet, up and over Kenneth's head and down upon his left shoulder, cutting through the chain mail and leather, dipping into flesh, though not deeply. Not yet.

Iain pushed him away, and Kenneth stumbled, now with several injuries, that he fell onto his backside. Fighting continued all around them, but Iain had some sense that it was heavily in the McEwen favor now that several of his men only maintained a perimeter around this exhibition, warding off any who might think to intrude.

Kenneth rose once more. Iain wouldn't have assumed he would, thought he might sit and await the death blow. He did not consider it bravery, though, didn't suppose it was resilience that brought him to his feet, only desperation.

Their blades met once more, first above their heads and then between them, free hands on the other's forearms until Iain's greater strength allowed him to move Kenneth's sword out to the right. Kenneth attempted a lame kick to Iain's groin, which missed that Iain was able to fling him around and away, almost behind him. A counter attack was instant that Iain pivoted and ducked low as Kenneth charged with such poor execution but greater momentum that he impaled himself on Iain's blade.

Immediately, Iain stood, raising the blade as he pushed it further into Kenneth's chest. The man took one last feeble swing at Iain, but this was stalled as Iain grabbed the arm of his sword hand. Iain rose up over him as Kenneth sank to his knees. He rolled both wrists, one turning the blade inside Kenneth, the other forcing him to drop his sword. Kenneth fell onto his back, his knees bent awkwardly. Iain leaned over him, embedding his sword completely.

"For Maggie Bryce," he ground out. "For the monks at Wick. For the souls at Helmsdale, and every other person you've terrorized, slain, or otherwise brought grief to."

He read no emotion in the man's wide-eyed gaze, saw only death. Disgustedly, he yanked his sword from Kenneth's chest. Breathing heavily while Kenneth Sutherland died at his feet, he realized then that all the fighting had stopped. Lifting his gaze, he met that of Duncan and Eideard. His captain inclined his head, sending Iain's attention behind him.

Iain turned and saw Robert Bruce sitting atop his destrier very close to him. The king removed his helm and showed Iain his steady, light brown eyes and his unkempt brown and gray hair.

Iain dropped to one knee and felt all those around him, all the McEwens still standing, do the same. He stayed on the ground for a long moment, his head bowed.

"Rise, my faithful friends," the king called out.

Iain did and stepped closer to his king.

"How did you ken?" Iain had to ask, wondering what had brought Robert the Bruce to his most timely aid.

Robert Bruce chuckled, which was not a regular thing. "Providence, apparently. While Edward II twiddles about, I thought it a fine time to make sense of some of our peskier Scottish nobles. Gregor Kincaid said you'd been down to Stonehaven, that you and others had talked about amassing several armies up here, further north." He shrugged. "Thought I'd come see where you were at with that."

Iain laughed, slowly at first, but it grew quickly. The King of Scotland had just come to his rescue, and shrugged about his blessed involvement, basically admitting he was but out and about and thought he might stop in for a wee spot.

Iain's laugh was contagious, that so much of his army, and all the great warriors on this field began to laugh as well. Iain struck his sword into the air.

"Long live our one true king!" He saluted in a deep and loud voice, his gaze keeping with the Bruce, who was well pleased by Iain's appeal.

The cheer that answered was thunderous.

IAIN BADE DUNCAN ASSUME command outside the keep that he might bring the king within. He then directed Robert Bruce inside the hall.

"Sire, will you allow me a few minutes to recover...the valuables?" His grin was crooked.

The king favored Iain with a wee smirk. "Go on then, bring the fine silver to me. I haven't seen Artair since I was but a lad, nor your dear mother since last we met at Hawkmore."

Bowing briefly, Iain left the king and his few officers in the hall and jogged quickly down to the tunnels, twisting and turning through the corridors and using a nearly unseen door that appeared only to be part of the dark stone wall.

His mother rushed him first, as soon as he came into sight of the seven persons underground. He kissed her cheek and announced to all, "It is done. The Blackhouse Sutherlands are dead or flown." His gaze went further into the tunnels, where Maggie slumped with relief against the cold and possibly damp wall.

A collective and joyous cry sounded. Keeping his gaze on Maggie, he whispered to his mother who waited upstairs. She jerked her cheek away from him and gave him an incredulous look. Iain nodded. "We will join you anon."

Glenna swept past him now with some agitation, a royal guest come to Berriedale and she locked in the tunnels. Others filed passed, Rabbie and the kitchen lads and lasses and then Artair, who touched his gnarled fingers to Iain's forearm and showed him a watery gaze, filled with pride. Iain grabbed Artair by the neck and touched their foreheads together.

And then only he and Maggie remained in the tunnels. She leaned still against the wall, hadn't moved a muscle since his coming. Iain slowly stepped forward.

"Is it truly done?"

Iain nodded.

"Is he...gone or imprisoned?"

"Gone."

"By your hand?"

Another nod.

She wept a bit, lowering her chin to her chest. "I shouldn't feel joy at the death of another."

"Nae, lass," he was quick to counter, closing what little space hung between them, drawing her away from the wall, wrapping his arms around her. "Nae, that's no' joy you feel, Maggie. You're no' made like that. That's relief. Liberation. You are free."

He needn't tell her that his own heart knew joy. He was indeed made like that, happy to rid the world of its most grievous sinners. He rubbed his hands up and down her back and rested his chin on the top of her head, allowing her to compose herself and come to grips with it.

"I had no intention of getting into any boat," she confessed.

"I should have never told you about Mari Sinclair."

"Florie and Edie did first," she informed him, her arms around his waist. She heaved a great big sigh. "I want to be where you are, even if it's not a good place."

He grinned against her hair and squeezed her tenderly. "Here's a good place."

"My favorite place."

"We canna stay, though, love. An army arrived to assist, and I want you to meet their chief."

She nodded against him and pushed herself back. Iain took her bonny face in his hands and kissed her lips. "Always get on the boat though, when I say." He took her hand and led her up and out of the tunnels.

When they returned to the hall, Robert Bruce was towering over Glenna and Artair, listening intently to whatever their conversation was. Iain joined them, drawing Maggie forward, holding one hand, his other at the small of her back.

"Sire, may I present Margaret Sutherland," he said, immediately understanding that his king was not surprised by her identity. Either his mother had spoken quickly to fill him in, or Artair's semi-regular correspondence with the king's camp had preceded this introduction.

As it was, Maggie needed only a second to join the *sire* with the man's majestic bearing and the pride in Iain's voice. Her eyes widened and her lips parted, but she improved quickly, dropping into a graceful curtsy as if she did so daily.

"My king," she said when she rose. She could not keep the amazement from her voice when she asked, "You are the chief come to our rescue?"

"Indeed, and my honor," Robert Bruce answered. "Admittedly, it was rather accidental, if not fortuitous. But we were pleased to assist in the name of justice."

Artair spoke up then. "We've a great debt to you, sire."

Robert Bruce insisted, "The debt is mine." He included Iain and Maggie and Glenna in his gaze. "Would that I could count on more houses of Scotland to extend such honor and justice in the name of our own people, and such loyalty to our crown."

"Aye, sire," Artair agreed.

"But you must excuse us, my king," Glenna said, taking Maggie's hand. "We will insist you take respite at Berriedale and we will want to be sure we do ourselves proud."

Robert Bruce nodded, and the ladies curtsied again before taking their leave. Iain watched them walk away.

The king slapped his hand against Iain's shoulder and gave out a hearty chuckle. "You've all evening then to explain Margaret Sutherland to me."

When Iain sent him a lopsided grin, understanding now that the king had only schooled his features to show no surprise at the presentation of Maggie, Robert Bruce laughed a bit more.

"Here's hoping the clarification also explains your gaze when set upon that magnificent creature."

IT WAS WELL AFTER MIDNIGHT before any dared, or even desired, to leave the hall. Possibly so many long months about the countryside—at times, actually having to hide out in caves—had made the king even more appreciative of the festive celebration, that he was one of the last to leave the hall. Glenna graciously escorted Robert Bruce up to the family quarters, giving him Iain's chambers for the night.

The entire evening had been lovely. True, many persons would likely devote some time tomorrow upon reflection, to how close they'd come to catastrophe. And probably only the merriment of the hall, perceived or connived or real and bolstered by their good fortune, had kept Maggie from becoming too somber.

Still, when she and Iain made their way to her chambers only shortly after the king had departed the hall, they were quiet and contemplative. She went willingly into his arms though, saying a prayer of thanks against his chest while he kissed her hair, that God had decided to throw this man into her path, that He'd guided her steps across the river onto Mackay land that day of the storm.

He loved her tenderly then, showing her more passion and so much pleasure.

Afterward, Maggie was sleepy, her eyes heavy, yet she said with some lingering disbelief, "Our liege lord lies in a bed just beyond this wall and my husband is dead."

Iain scratched his hand over his chest, holding her at his side. "Aye. It's been a day."

"I might be best served by processing this in the morning."

She wasn't sure if she interpreted her own present thinking about this correctly, but some part of her just now asserted that Kenneth Sutherland didn't matter, that he never had.

Only Iain mattered.

"Your husband lies next to you," he said, as if he had now a similar thought.

Maggie tipped her face up to him. "Since when."

"Since whenever Fate decreed it. At birth, five years ago, or last winter during the storm. Dinna matter. You belong to me, and I to you."

"There was a time, not too long ago, I had thought that Fate had no love for me. I have to wonder now if I was wrong."

"About Fate having a hand?"

"Mm."

"I canna believe otherwise," Iain said with some thoughtfulness. "Both of us in places we should not have been when first we met. It makes no sense that I might have fallen in love with you last winter in that cave. It's no' possible, aye? To ken you love someone so soon after meeting them. But, Maggie Bryce, I canna explain how I...nevertheless, I ken it to be true. I came for you at Blackhouse because you'd no' ever been far from my thoughts in all the months we were apart," he said evenly. "Honestly, I used to admonish myself—this lass can no' mean so much to you, no' after so short a time."

"Sometimes it just is," she said, her heart fluttering with joy.

"That's smacks of Artair."

"Archie, actually."

"Impossible."

"But true."

"Please dinna ever bring Archie into this bed again." She sensed a grin in his response.

Maggie let out a sleepy giggle. "But is that not true, that sometimes it just is?"

"Aye, Maggie Bryce."

"I should be thankful then, that you heeded not your own admonishment?"

"I could no' ignore it. No more than I could no' think of you."

Her voice was sad when she admitted, "I am sorry to report that I listened better to the voices in my head trying to purge thoughts of you."

"That's no' good, Maggie Bryce."

She felt the need to explain, to ease the disappointment she detected in his voice. "At first, I closed my eyes and thought only of you whenever...I needed strength. Pretty soon, however, it occurred to me that so many times that I brought your image to mind were during really terrible times, to get me through it. But then that was not fair to you, and I was so afraid I might then begin to associate you with so many...bad things." She finished weakly, sorrowfully. "After a while, it seemed best not to think of you at all, lest our very short time together be forever tainted."

"But you'll think of me now, aye, Maggie Bryce?"

"Always."

"No more a short time together, though. We've all the rest of our lives."

With so much hope inside her, she asked, "It starts now? All the rest of our lives?"

"Aye." He kissed her lips. "As husband and wife proper. Our king has kindly sent for Bishop Belagaumbe. The king himself insists on giving away the bride."

"He does not!" Maggie alleged, suddenly very wakeful.

Iain chuckled. "Aye, he does. Said it would be a great honor to him."

"To him? An honor to *him*? Oh." And then softly, "Oh, my." She sighed with further contentment just as Iain turned and hovered over her.

His gorgeous eyes gleamed. He pressed his lips softly to hers, then placed another gentle kiss upon her cheek.

"Does my husband have any plans to love me again as he just did?"

"He's thinking of little else, truth be told."

"Will he get to it soon, tonight yet?"

A hint of a chuckle shrouded his words. "His wife will have to wait a few more minutes, while he stalls yet to catch his breath."

Maggie slipped her hand beneath the coverlet, skimmed it over his abdomen and moved it lower. "Sadly, his wife has little patience."

Iain smiled down at her, raising his brows when her hand found him. "Nothing to be sad about, Maggie Bryce."

Epilogue

"NO DARLING," SAID MAGGIE, "it needs to be flatter. The round ones don't skip so well."

Another rock was pressed very close to her eye only seconds later. "This one?"

Maggie grinned and backed her face away, which immediately shrunk the size of the stone to normal. Why did children think they needed to place an object only inches from your eye when they wanted you to see? "Oh, that one might do. Show your da', see if he agrees."

She sat on the big plaid, spread wide and flat on the beach, and hoped her husband would pull her to her feet when the time came to return to the keep. She put her hands on the plaid behind her and pointed her bare toes toward the sea.

And sighed.

Everything she loved was before her. The sight would never grow old.

Iain stood in ankle deep water, barefooted and bare-chested, three-year old Gretchen on his shoulders. Archie stood next to him, his tunic tugged by six-year-old Robert, to whom he bent his attention.

Young Hew, who had turned four only yesterday, ran from his mother and went as far as the highest wave, screeching for his father, holding the stone he'd found as high as his little arm would allow. Iain waved him forward. Hew danced all around the smooth rolling waves, trying to find the best place to enter that would see his bare feet wet the least. He never did step into the water until Iain came for him, pulling Gretchen from his shoulders and settling her on his hip, reaching for Hew's hand with his free one. Only then did Hew find his courage. When they'd walked back to where Archie and Robert stood, Iain let go of his son's hand and accepted the rock from him. Hew immediately transferred his hand to his father's leg for security and watched with the greatest of expectation as his da' skipped the rock perfectly across the almost calm sea. Hew jumped up and down, crying out "Seven!" for the number of bounces it made before it dropped to the bottom of the sea.

Maggie closed her eyes, just for a moment.

She was tired. But she was also so very happy. Sometimes she thought she didn't deserve to be so happy; she was no one special, why should she have all this joy? But there was sadness, too. They'd lost Glenna several years ago, and another bairn before Hew, and Duncan had fallen at Bannockburn, which still broke her heart, almost a year later. She missed them all, didn't pass a day without thinking of at least one of them, sometimes all of them.

She opened her eyes when a great force hit the ground next to her. Hew had jumped or stumbled onto the plaid, grinning up at his mother.

"Did the other Hew ken how to skip stones?"

Her son had been fascinated with the story Maggie had told him only recently, how he'd been named in honor of a very special person. She'd relied on Arch and Iain, since the initial telling, to fill in more detail of the very earnest young man she had known so briefly. Her son had many questions.

"He might have," she said. "I'm sure if he'd tried he would have been very good at it."

She looked up to see Iain and Archie and the children walking toward her. Iain set Gretchen onto the sand as soon as it was dry and lifted his gaze to Maggie. When he was close enough he fell to the plaid at her side and kissed her very round belly.

"You have to help me up when it's time," she told him.

Iain grinned and then favored her lips with a quick kiss. With that he laid flat on his back, using the spare linen she'd brought along as a pillow. Gretchen thought nothing of sitting on her father's flat stomach, her tiny bare feet just touching the plaid between Maggie and Iain. She placed her hand on her mam's belly and waited.

Maggie tilted her head with some sympathy to her green-eyed daughter. "She's sleeping, I think." There was no kicking now, not lately.

Pointedly, Archie said, "*He* is sleeping."

Maggie stuck her tongue out at him. "We're already outnumbered. Allow me to dream, will you, Arch?"

Her dear friend hadn't left her side, indeed had not stepped foot outside Berriedale, since a year after Maggie had come to Berriedale. He'd been injured in a riding accident. His leg had never healed quite right that sitting a horse or moving without a limp was nigh impossible. She thought he was content, though, liked to think so anyway, even as his fighting days had ended with that accident. Whatever despair he'd known to have his purpose taken away had disappeared the very moment tiny little Robert had been set into his arms for the very first time. And more of the melancholy left with each passing year, with each new child delivered unto the laird and mistress of Berriedale. Archie was, at varying times, the children's favorite plaything, a strict disciplinarian when needed, and the very one any of her children would seek out to beg boons their mother or father had denied them. But he was, first and foremost, Maggie's most cherished friend, the one who had held her hand during her labor with Gretchen because Iain had been gone to the king's side in Perth at the time.

Several years ago, when Maggie learned how easy it was to amuse her children all in one spot and for hours at a time without fuss, she'd begun regularly bringing them down to the beach. Soon after, she'd employed Will Carpenter for a special project. It hadn't truly needed any great skill, only plenty of brute strength, so that he'd called upon several soldiers to assist and after only a day, they managed to first, cut down and completely strip a wide tree until it was bare. One end had been hacked and hewn to a needle point. Next, the grunts had dug as deep as they could in the sand, just about midway between the water and the bottom of the embankment. The pointed end of the trunk was shoved down into the sand and packed tight; and then the soldiers had pounded away with a huge fat-tipped maul until the stump was secured deep in the sand and only about two feet of it rose above the ground. To that, Will Carpenter had affixed a sturdy and smooth chair seat that had yet to be claimed by the sea.

That was Archie's chair, as he was unable to easily maneuver himself onto the ground and less so able to get himself up, but invariably was with her when she brought the children to the beach. Sometimes, though rarely, Artair would join them as well and Archie would give up his seat to the old man, who moved with far less agility these days than even Archie.

They sat quietly for a time, with Gretchen eventually abandoning her father's belly to chase after her brothers who were higher up on the beach, investigating critters and creatures in and around the dunes and rocks.

Maggie closed her eyes again, listening to the sound of the waves, hearing tiny little voices rise above it with excitement over a *sidewalker*, as they called the crabs they regularly discovered. She wondered how much longer she could hold off the inevitable, what her tightening belly was telling her, and had been telling her since she'd first sat down.

Out of the blue, and to the sky above, Iain said, "We have a good life, aye?"

If Archie were surprised by the reflective query, he gave no indication. He answered, quite readily, "Seems almost criminal, having more highs than lows."

Maggie smiled at this. Iain had never not been demonstrative in his love, but she sometimes thought these casual references to how blessed they were might be her favorite.

Just a man, lying on a beach, surrounded by the beauty of nature and the beauty of love and considering his good fortune.

It pleased her greatly, though she said nothing, was suddenly of a mind that this labor was indeed progressing more quickly than any others.

"Arch," said Iain, "what do you make of my wife's silence? Should I be concerned?"

Archie grinned at Maggie across Iain. "Probably counting the minutes until the bairns can be put to bed and she can find her own. Sleep is a rare commodity."

Maggie pulled her hands in front of her, swiping the wee bit of sand off them.

"There'll be little of that anytime soon," she said and nudged at her husband, whose eyes were closed. "C'mon then, your daughter wants to come now."

Iain's eyes snapped open. In the next second, her husband was on his feet and Archie was laughing and standing as well.

"*Jesu*, Maggie McEwen!" Iain scolded, donning his tunic, affixing his sword and belt to his person with jerky, panicked motions. "Why would you come all the way down here if you ken that the bairn was coming?"

She rolled her eyes and lifted her hands to him. "Obviously, I didn't know until we were already down here."

"Let's go, you three," Arch called to the children. "Your brother's coming now."

Iain pulled her to her feet. His instinct then was to lift her in his arms. Maggie wouldn't have it. "I'll be walking back, helping her out, so to speak."

He wanted to argue. His mouth thinned, but Maggie remained adamant and began the long trek uphill, with Iain anxious at her side.

This was her sixth pregnancy, the fourth she'd carried full term; the labor and work frightened her not at all, but she knew what could happen. She paused while a contraction took hold and said to Iain, "You are in love with me still?"

He held her hand, supporting her, wincing as she made a face for the pain. "I am. You are my world."

"What about those three?" She asked, and then blew out short and quick breaths.

"They're all right, I guess," her husband teased. "But you? You are everything."

It passed and she began walking again. She asked the same question almost every time, whenever he'd been with her for the birthing, knowing of too many women who didn't survive it. She needed to hear it.

And he needed to know. She turned and met his gaze, her gait tedious.

"I am so in love with you. There hasn't been a day, not even one, when I didn't know that or feel that. Not since the moment you opened your eyes to me in that cave."

"I ken that, you have never left me wondering or wanting," he acknowledged. "But Maggie, if you're no' going to move quicker, I *am* going to pick you up."

She knew very well how to have her way. "It hurts less if I walk through it."

This appeased him, but only somewhat. "Aye, but walk faster, Maggie. I'm taking on a lot of years here."

She smiled and lifted her gaze to gauge her position. Even the children, and Archie with his plodding gait, were far ahead of them. Robert was screaming at the top of his lungs, to be heard by the guards on the wall, "My brother is coming!"

The man-door was pushed open, soldiers spilling out onto the ridge above the embankment. Donal scooped up Gretchen and took Hew's hand, his smile wide, ushering them into the yard. Robert waited for Archie, running back to him to take his hand and prod him along.

Another contraction brought Maggie to a halt, and Iain could stand it no more. As soon as it passed, he lifted her into his arms and charged up the rest of the hill.

Maggie rested her head against his chest and thought she was silly to have denied him this. Being in his arms was the very best place to be.

The End

The Highlander Heroes Series

The Touch of Her Hand

The Memory of Her Kiss

The Shadow of Her Smile

The Depths of Her Soul

The Truth of Her Heart

The Love of Her Life

Highlander Heroes Collection, Books 1-3

Highlander Heroes Collection, Books 4-6

Other Books by Rebecca Ruger

Highlander: The Legends

The Beast of Lismore Abbey

The Lion of Blacklaw Tower

The Scoundrel of Beauly Glen

The Wolf of Carnoch Cross

Far From Home: A Scottish Time-Travel Romance

And Be My Love

Eternal Summer

Crazy In Love

Beyond Dreams

Only The Brave

When & Where

Heart of a Highlander Series

Heart of Shadows

Heart of Stone

Heart of Fire
Heart of Iron
Heart of Winter
Heart of Ice

rebeccaruger.com

Printed in Great Britain
by Amazon